RENEGADE LOVE

She lifted one pale hand in the moon-light and pressed it against his face. The contact was jolting for them both. He flinched; the hard line of his mouth quirked down at the corners, and one hand flew up, his fingers wrapping around her fragile wrist, thrusting it away. But only momentarily . . .

The moment he kissed her she knew without qualms—had known since the instant she first saw him—that it would come to this; it could not be otherwise between them. She was as drawn to the forbidden as he was . . .

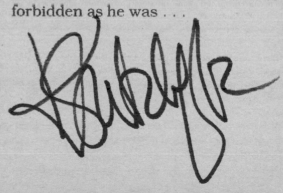

RENEGADE LOVE

KATHERINE SUTCLIFFE

AVON BOOKS · NEW YORK

AVON BOOKS
A division of
The Hearst Corporation
105 Madison Avenue
New York, New York 10016

Copyright © 1988 by Katherine Sutcliffe
Published by arrangement with the author
Library of Congress Catalog Card Number: 87-91620
ISBN: 0-380-75402-9

First Avon Books Printing: January 1988

AVON TRADEMARK REG. U.S. PAT. OFF. AND IN OTHER COUNTRIES, MARCA REGISTRADA, HECHO EN U.S.A.

Printed in the U.S.A.

K-R 10 9 8 7 6 5 4 3

My Thanks to

John Finch, Technical Support genius
who retrieved chapters four and five
from that vast wasteland of missing data.

A special thank-you to those readers
who have written with words of encouragement
and who expressed interest in reading more about
the Bastitas family.
I love you all, and keep those letters coming!

O! Pray for the soldier, you kindhearted stranger.
  He has roamed the prairie for many a year;
He has kept the Comanches away from your ranches—
  And followed them far over the Texas frontier.

Author Unknown

RENEGADE LOVE

Prologue

San Antonio, Texas
August, 1866

He stared at the woman's reflection as she undressed behind him. The image on the glass window was vague and spotted with dirt, reminding him of the sordidness and pretense of the whole affair. He focused again, this time on the scene beyond. A town of squat adobe buildings stretched along the packed earthen street where wagons and horses vied for space and Mexicans peddled everything from women to food.

"There is something wrong, Kid?"

He barely heard her, the woman now pressing her nude, voluptuous body against his shirtless back. His mind was on other things.

"The name is Claudia, if you're interested," she murmured. Claudia ran her tongue lightly along the silent man's spine. She slid her arms around his lean waist, allowed her hands to trace over his heavily muscled chest until her long fingers encountered the crisp hair there and, within it, his hard nipples. She massaged them gently at first, then not so gently. She was growing impatient.

Her hands moved to the waistband of his breeches, along the row of buttons down the front. He tensed. She heard the sharp inhalation and knew by the hard arousal straining within the coarse black cloth that he was not so detached as

1

he chose to appear. Carefully she flicked open the buttons one by one.

"Why do you stare out there when I am here?" she asked. Pressing against his buttocks, she rotated her hips and laughed huskily. Forgetting he hadn't bothered to answer, she said, "God, you're magnificent. Where are you from?"

"Chicago."

It was the first time he'd spoken since they'd entered the room.

"I don't believe you." The waistband yawned, releasing him into her hand. "Men like you aren't bred in Chicago," she told him.

"I never said I was born there."

Scattering kisses along his back and the uneven edges of black hair that spilled well beyond his shoulders, Claudia moved her hand up and down. From his dark skin, the scent of sweat, mingled with the smells of horse and leather, filled her nostrils, making her heady with need.

He closed his eyes, shivering as her teeth nipped at the scar on his back. "Why are you called Kid?" he heard her ask in so breathless a voice she hardly managed it. Small talk. He hated small talk, but it was almost preferable to what would soon follow.

"It's a name as good as any."

"It doesn't suit you." She laughed at the implication and wiggled against him. The woman was growing frustrated, he could tell.

He looked out the window again, the ghosts of memories now vanquished by the reality of the beautiful brunette moving suggestively against him, intimately caressing him with something just short of worship. He should get on with it, he supposed.

He wasn't altogether certain just when he first noticed the girl in the distance. He might not have noticed her at all, had she been dressed like all the other women who moved up and down Soledad Street on that Saturday afternoon. Yards and yards of white material belled around her hips as she walked, parasol on her shoulder, down the boardwalk. Her hair, white as Chicago snow, curled from her milky shoulders to the middle of her narrow back. She stopped before the courthouse and appeared to read the small bronze plaque on the wall. She turned and hesitated a long moment at the edge of the street, but just as she tilted her face in his direction, she swung the parasol around and between them, blocking his view. "Damn," he muttered.

An inexplicable irritation nagged at him as the girl then moved off in the opposite direction. And for the first time since he'd entered the room with the woman behind him, the ache for total sexual gratification washed over him. Before it had only been a way to pass the few hours until six o'clock. There had been so many women in so many towns over the last years that he had ceased to ask names, more likely than not, taking them with his eyes closed, with only as much passion as time and space allowed.

The bells of San Fernando Church pealed into the dense afternoon air, musically at first; then they struck solidly four times. He turned for the woman and slid his hands around her shoulders, down her back, and beneath the smooth mounds of her buttocks. He lifted. She clutched. Moving, he pressed her back against the wall, wrapped her open legs around his hips, and slid inside her.

It was swift and complete for them both. He knew it would be. She'd been tottering on the edge by the time he'd crowned her moist entrance. She cried out at first, more than willing but unprepared for the reality of him. Her mouth fell slack, her head back as her brown eyes widened in pleasure and surprise.

She murmured in her throat, her desire so intense she couldn't speak coherently. Wrapping her arms around his sweat-glistening shoulders, she hung there, feeling the pressure of him inside her as he moved back and forth. He withdrew, then entered her again, each thrust deeper than the first until she was whimpering and writhing and grinding her hips against his, until the first explosive release tore through her. He remained inside her while the moment passed, then began again, drawing and thrusting until she was racked a second and third time, until she was screaming with the pleasurable, intense pain and begging him to stop or she would surely die from the wanton repletion.

He didn't seem to notice. With his hands now braced against the wall, his head down so his night-black hair spilled between their bodies, he was intent only on his release. He drove and drove, the sound of their mating thudding dully against the wall of the hot, stuffy room.

He was close; she could sense it. His body felt like steel against hers; every muscle shone and flexed with power and exertion. His eyes were closed, his mouth pressed and quirked down at the corners. Sweat trickled down his temples. It ran erratically over his brow and puddled momentarily in his lashes before spilling like tears down his cheeks. For a moment she almost believed . . .

He cried out with the final force. Slamming his body against hers, he buried his hands in her hair while, inside her, she felt him throb, and the hot flood of his release drenched her completely.

He relaxed against her, his weight and one slightly bent knee supporting her body against the wall. A weakness assailed him; for a few vulnerable minutes he was drained of life. When he could move again he turned, his hands still holding her up against his hips, then dropped her gently onto the bed. Like a kitten she coiled into the turned-down sheets, her full mouth, yet to be kissed, pouting as she sleepily asked:

"Will you join me?"

Why not? He still had two hours to kill, and this might be the last bed, the last woman he'd enjoy for a very long time— if, indeed, he ever enjoyed either again. Peeling out of his breeches, he dropped them onto the boots he had earlier discarded, then stretched out beside her. Within half an hour he was taking her again. Waking her from a deep sleep, he opened her legs and mounted her. Ill-prepared, she gasped and flinched with pain, calling him an animal and a savage while digging her nails into his back.

"Shut up," he said, and for the first time he kissed her, his mouth taking hers with such strength that she trembled in fear. But soon she was responding, and when they both climaxed again she drifted back to sleep while he lay on his back and stared at the ceiling.

When San Fernando's bells pealed five times, a quiet servant woman called from the door, then entered with a brass tub and hot water. After she filled the tub to the brim and left, he sank languidly into its depths. Steam rose in curling tendrils of gray, prickling the skin of his face and scalp while the ends of his hair, heavy with water, clung to his chest and shoulders. He watched the woman in bed. She lay on her back as he'd left her, her white breasts with their brown nipples rising and falling as she slept.

Attuned by necessity to the slightest sound, he heard doors open and close down the hallway. Glancing toward the chair against the wall, he located the leather belt and holster and the gleaming white butt of his Remington revolver. Normally he would have placed it within easy reach. Without it he felt defenseless. But he remained where he was, rolling a cigar absently between his lips, staring at the stream of smoke that condensed with the steam of his bath against the ceiling like a fog. And he waited.

At ten minutes of six he stood before the washstand. His breeches clung like a second skin to his damp legs, and his shirt, wrinkled and soiled with the dust of several states, hung open to his waist. He gently fingered the bowie knife in his hands, turned the blade this way and that, marveling for a moment at its perfect balance, the fine edge that could smoothly slice off the top of a man's scalp. Then, with great reluctance, he looked into the beveled silvered glass on the wall.

The woman stirred, opened her heavy lids, vaguely aware that sundown was nearing. Pale light filtered through the dirty panes of glass in the window. Sleepily she followed its course to the far side of the room. "My God," she cried. "What are you doing?"

He stood with the knife poised against the side of his head. From within his hard fingers hung what was left of his long, limp black hair. "Cutting my hair," was all he said. The last of the sable mane fell to the floor. When he turned toward her he no longer looked the savage she'd first thought him to be. But the savagery was there still, in his eyes. If anything he was more frightening—and exciting—than before.

The bells of the church announced the hour.

"Will you come back to bed?" she asked him.

"No. Put on your clothes."

"We were very good together, Davis." She smoothed her hand over the sheets. "Come, *hombre*. Claudia will make you smile yet."

He looked toward the door.

"Davis. Come back to bed."

The explosion of the door slamming open jarred the walls. Claudia screamed, throwing herself from the bed and into the corner of the room. A score of men poured across the threshold, all bearing guns pointed threateningly at Davis. He made a quick dive toward the chair but was brought up short as an intruder drove a knee into his ribs. He groaned, doubled, and hit the floor cursing.

Grabbing the sheet and clutching it over her breasts, Claudia wailed, "What the hell is happening here?"

An old man with long gray hair planted his foot in the middle of Davis's back and pointed a gun resembling a small cannon at the base of his head. Lifting a badge in his hands, he responded, "Texas Rangers, ma'am. We have a warrant for Davis's arrest."

"Arrest! For what!"

The Ranger looked up and smiled. "Cold-blooded murder, ma'am."

Chapter 1

Standing in the center of Soledad Street in the heart of San Antonio, Rachel Gregory thought the sun had never felt so hot back in New Orleans. There was only the awful humidity and mosquitoes and the threat of yellow fever every summer . . . and the Yankees; now that the war was over, the Creole city was swarming with carpetbaggers. They were buzzards picking the very life from the dying South.

Lifting her chin, Rachel blinked and tried not to think of the home that her stepmother had been forced to sell for a pittance, a fraction of its former worth. Belle Hélène, named after her mother, had been one of the most profitable cotton plantations around New Orleans. Its stately, stuccoed exterior with its twenty-eight Grecian pillars on all four sides of the house might not have been as grand as Dunleith in Natchez, but it had certainly rivaled Humas House in Burnside.

Fighting back her anger over the injustice of it all, Rachel focused on her surroundings and waited for her stepmother, who had gone about the business of finding them some means of transportation out of this town. The air swirled with dust. It burned her eyes and made breathing next to impossible. Horses and wagons and men dressed in buckskin breeches, with odd-looking half blankets draped over their shoulders, moved up and down the street. Rachel dabbed with her hankie at the moisture on her face and wondered, as she had so often since her arrival in San Antonio two days ago, whether she would ever grow accustomed to the intolerable heat.

7

She'd heard of Texas, of course, and San Antonio. She'd heard of the Alamo and the men who had died there. On Saturday, just after their stage had gotten in, she'd noticed the ruins of the old mission. She'd caught a glimpse of tumbled gray walls where a short, fat Mexican had tried to sell her stepmother what he swore was the very bullet that killed William Travis. She'd paused briefly outside the flat-roofed adobe courthouse and read the plaque honoring San Antonio's own citizen who had died in the awful massacre:

> IN MEMORY OF OUR BRAVE
> WE HONOR SAN ANTONIO'S OWN
> TOMAS EDUARDO DE BASTITAS.
> MAY HIS SACRIFICE LIVE
> IN OUR MINDS AND HEARTS FOREVER.

Rachel had closed her eyes, doing her best to swallow the bitter memories of wars and sacrifices and death. Her own father had died in the Civil War, fighting for what he believed was a just cause. But there were no plaques to honor him.

A sudden racket brought Rachel to her senses with a start. A half dozen men poured through the doors of a nearby cantina. In their midst a couple of wrestling men staggered off the walk and into the street where they fell, rolling and grunting while the crowd around them roared with drunken approval.

"Git off yore ass, Ramon, I got a wad bet on you!"

"What kinda fight do you call this, Estaban? You been eatin' too many of them damn tortillas!"

A woman appeared, running out the mercantile's door, holding her skirts halfway up to her knees as she barreled through the crowd. Her hair was carrot-red and her face was brown with freckles. She was as tall as many of the men she elbowed out of her way, and when she yelled, "I'm gonna tell your ma and pa, you dern fools, if you don't quit actin' like a couple of jackasses!" the entire crowd let out a hoot.

"You tell 'em, Irene!" someone hollered.

"Git on in there with 'em, Irene, and I'll put my money on you!"

The fighters were on their feet now. Rachel stood on her tiptoes, leaning this way and that as she peered over and around the men's shoulders. Her eyes widened as the shorter of the two fighters drew back and hit the other across the jaw. The other careened backward, stumbling through the crowd, his arms flailing at his side as he lost his balance and tumbled toward Rachel's feet, landing flat on his back.

Jumping a little, she bent at the waist and stared into the greenest eyes she'd ever seen on a man. Man? He was no older than her twenty years, on second inspection. "Are you all right?" she asked him.

A slow smile spread across his young face as he responded, "I am now."

Rachel lifted one blond brow questioningly.

"Tell me, *señorita*, are you an angel? If you are then I am dead. In that case I am definitely not all right."

She frowned rather seriously. "Are you flirting with me, sir?"

"I do my best flirting while on my back."

Rachel laughed before catching herself.

The crowd surged around them. The woman with red hair and the young man who had landed the lucky blow stepped forward and offered their hands to the boy on his back. The young men looked very similar, and Rachel realized in that moment that they must be brothers. She also realized that the fight was less than hostile.

"Uncle Alex is gonna have both y'all's butts, Ramon," Irene announced. "You and Estaban done tore up Claude's cantina agin jest for the sake of fightin'. He told you boys last time that if you was gonna beat the hell out of one another, do it somewhere else. He ain't paid off the last damage you done. Are you all right?"

He looked again at Rachel and said, "I think I'm in love."

"Ha!" The woman threw back her head and laughed. "If yore Uncle Alex's boy, yore bound to be in love." Her brown eyes met Rachel's, then widened in what appeared to be surprise. "Well, cousin, at least yore showin' a little good sense for a change."

Ramon took their hands and rolled to his feet. Within a moment he was swallowed by the crowd, which soon disappeared back into the cantina.

Rachel looked up and down the street, feeling conspicuously alone again, and uncomfortable. The hour was near noon. The sun, directly overhead, beat down on her head, making her sweat and itch beneath her corset and layer upon layer of petticoats. There was a tree-shaded plaza in the distance. Rachel gave some thought to waiting there for her stepmother, then reconsidered. No reason to give Audra a cause to get angry. Audra could and would make her life a living hell for no reason at all. Rachel surmised that if she was forced to listen to the woman claim once more that this move was due to her ruining the family reputation, she would scream, or worse. She'd tolerated Audra's pettishness and jealousy for so long only in deference to her father's wishes. Even her tolerant father had come to recognize his second wife for what she was after only a few short years of marriage. But he'd gallantly stood by his vows and indulged Audra as much as he could. Rachel's father was dead now, and Rachel was almost of age. It was only a matter of time before she could strike out on her own. And she would. Somehow she would find a way to support herself until the right man came along and she could marry.

The hot wind billowed her pink silk skirts. They fluttered around her ankles and, despite her vexation over her stepmother's tardiness, she gently smoothed them down with one hand while gripping the handle of her parasol with the other. The parasol had attracted more than its share of attention. Of pink India muslin, it was embroidered with white feather-stitched flowers around its tasseled borders. Its handle was of smooth, white ivory. The frilly ornament had been a gift from her father on her sixteenth birthday, so she cherished it with all her heart.

Rachel shaded her eyes against the sun's glare, again searching the boardwalks for her stepmother. A buckboard rumbled by, stirring up dust that burned her nostrils and settled into every intricate piece of fine lace on her dress.

The door of the nearest building opened then, drawing her attention from the busy street. A bowlegged man stepped out onto the walk, a rifle swinging leisurely at his side. The sun glanced off a badge on his shirt as he turned back toward the door and said, "You is the slowest buncha harebrains I ever seen. Somebody'd think you was aimin' to miss yore own funerals or somethin'. Git a move on. We got to be down yonder at the courthouse in five minutes."

Three men filed out the door. A dirty lot, unshaven and dressed in ragged attire, they shuffled their feet, lagged behind the lawman, and grumbled among themselves that if they could arrange it, someone was going to be *early* to *his* funeral.

"How about a quick stop in the cantina?" the tallest of the men yelled. "There's a pretty little *señorita* there who's just itchin' to see me one more time."

"You done seen yore last *señorita*, Clyde. None of 'em I know is about to cuddle up with a corpse."

"I ain't dead yet," Clyde drawled.

"You will be if'n you don't hurry. I'd jest as soon hang ya right here as to waste all that time draggin' you to Brackettville."

"Wells, I'm gonna take pleasure in killin' you afore this is all over."

"I 'magine yore gonna try, Clyde. I'd be disappointed if you didn't. And it's *Captain* Wells to you, sapsucker."

Chains draped from their wrists to their ankles, a length attaching one man to the next. The one called Clyde had pale gray, lifeless-looking eyes that bugged slightly in his gaunt, beard-stubbled face. Most of his teeth were missing. He looked at Rachel in a way that made her skin crawl as he stepped behind the lawman, onto the street. She turned her face away, trying to ignore him, doing her best to hide the revulsion she felt at his presence. Few times had she ever experienced such an overpowering sense of evil. She was shaken by it.

"Ooowee, would you looka here, boys!" Clyde stopped suddenly, his lips slitting in a smile. "Now ain't that the fanciest piece of skirt you ever seen? Look at all that fine lace. Why, I kin almost smell 'er parfume from here. Well, now, sweet thing," she heard him continue. "Looks to me like you done lost yore daddy. Maybe ole Clyde here can be of assistance." He elbowed the Mexican who had sidled up beside him, then snickered.

She ignored him, or tried to. It wasn't easy to pretend indifference when her face, indeed her entire body, was slowly turning a bright, burning red.

Another man said, "The little lady must have a hearin' problem, Clyde. Either that or she don't like yore looks."

"Must be a hearin' problem," he responded. "The ladies fight over me, or hadn't you heard?"

"Fight ya off, ya mean," Wells stated. He moved up beside Rachel, blocking Clyde's view of her. Rachel closed her eyes briefly, in relief. "Only female I know that'd let you cozy up beside her's got eight legs and hair all over her body," the lawman taunted.

Clyde spat a wad of tobacco on the lawman's boot.

The chains clattered as the men moved on across the street. Rachel stared at her feet and held her breath until she was certain they were gone, waiting for the unease she had felt in their presence to leave her. Yet it didn't leave her. When she looked up again, she understood why.

The throng of rattling buggies, the clip-clop of horses, and the hoots and hollers from the nearby cantina all dwindled to vague nothingness as she focused, with jolting awareness, on the figure in the near distance. The man leaned negligently against the wall near the jailhouse door. Tall, he had broad shoulders and slender hips. His stance, no matter how casual, was arrogant. His clothes were black—shirt, vest, breeches, and boots—all black and somewhat dusty. He appeared oblivious to the heat and commotion that swirled as thickly as the dirt around them.

The bold, open way in which he stared caught her gaze, and no matter how she willed it, she could not look away.

She stared back, unable to blink, unable even to move. His face was dark, darkened even more by a day's growth of beard across his lean features. Though he stood in the shadows she could tell his hair was black, as were the rakishly slanted brows hooding his eyes. Rachel caught herself returning his appraisal with as much intensity, wondering remotely what color those eyes might be.

Demurely lowering her lashes, she allowed her hankie to flutter to the ground.

He shifted and moved toward her.

She looked at her feet, her hands, up the street and down the street, toward the swaybacked mule with its nose in a water trough, and finally back at *him*. With all the lordly grace of a sleek, dark animal he stepped from the walk, the silver spurs on the backs of his boots chinking slightly with each step. Rachel stared at the well-shaped lips that were beginning to curl in a wicked smile — the grooves on either side of his mouth gave his sun-darkened skin a hard, weathered appearance that lent a savage and almost cruel streak to his cool mien. Then, finally, her gaze met his. She was suddenly swimming in the darkest, bluest eyes she had ever seen, their color enhanced by the thickest, longest black lashes she had ever known a man to possess.

A gust of wind tugged at her parasol; she hardly noticed. She was spellbound by his barbaric handsomeness, mesmerized by the long length of his well-muscled legs, and fascinated by his tousled hair, so black that the sun danced in blue shadows amid its thickness.

Gripping her parasol with both hands, Rachel felt her throat tighten uncomfortably and her pulse begin to race. Ignore him, she told herself. A proper young lady would never stand for such a blatant, deliberate appraisal of her body. Yet, after a futile attempt to avert her eyes, they forced themselves back up to his.

Her heart took a plunge to her stomach as he stopped before her. He was a head taller than she, his shoulders broad enough, it seemed, to block out the entire world beyond them. She'd begun to tremble, and an odd fluttering of thrill spread throughout her as he stood towering above her. Breathless and wondering if he'd retrieve her hankie, she ducked her head slightly, and smiled.

From the corner of her eye she noticed another rifle-bearing man exit the sheriff's office. Walking up behind the blue-eyed man, he tapped the barrel of the gun impatiently against the side of his own leg and asked, "You comin' or not, Davis?"

Davis. So that was his name.

Davis held at waist level a black, flat-crowned hat. Rachel's eyes strayed there, absently at first, then froze. Within her, confusion warred with astonishment and disappointment as he raised the hat slowly and placed it on his head, tilting it low over his brow to shade his eyes. There were iron manacles on his wrists.

With mocking slowness he bent, swept up the hankie from the ground, and lifted it nearly to her chin. "Ma'am," came the deep, rough velvet voice that jarred her from her embarrassing state. "You've dropped your hankie."

Staring at the limp square of linen between his brown fingers, she felt her face grow hotter with each eternal second he continued to watch her. "You're one of *them*." She hadn't meant to speak. Realizing she had, she blushed while doing her best to avoid the dark blue eyes boring into hers.

"Disappointed, *chica*?"

"Don't be absurd!" she snapped. She stepped away, ignoring the hankie, and looked again toward the swaybacked mule. Davis continued to watch her; she could feel it. He stood so close that the hem of her skirt brushed his boots. The heat of his body was detectable even through her clothes. Rachel cringed instinctively. She had never encountered such insolence in a man's eyes before! It was as if he were daring her to face him again.

Rachel felt the blush spread all over her body as she became angrily aware that she had actually flirted with this—this malfeasant. The hankie suddenly flapped like a flag in the breeze to remind her. What was worse, he had the unmitigated gall to stand there and smirk about it!

"Do you think it safe to be parading these men among civilized people?" she asked the lawman, who by now seemed to be eyeing the exchange between her and Davis with something akin to amused curiosity. He only shrugged.

"Do you want your hankie?" Davis asked her. Was that amusement she detected in the drawl? Sarcasm? Yes, she decided: sarcasm.

Setting her jaw, Rachel refused to respond.

"I will keep it as a reminder of you, *querida* . . . until we meet again."

"We *won't* meet again," she said, with a lift of her head. She looked at the manacles on his wrists and arched one fine brow, punctuating her remark.

Curling his fingers about the lace-edged linen, he countered softly, "Ah, but I suspect we will."

It was a threat, simple and straightforward, as matter-of-fact as staring at the sky on a clear day and announcing the sun was shining. A threat so direct Rachel was momentarily forced to forget her own recalcitrance and look at him.

He smiled back, not so warmly this time, but with a cold knowingness that shook Rachel to the very ground beneath her satin-slippered feet. His eyes, now a smoky blue, regarded her steadily as he reached with both hands and brushed one tapered finger along her jaw. "We *will* meet again," he repeated. She was genuinely frightened and at the same time nearly dizzy with the sensation the bold stroke caused her. Her skin tingled at his touch.

Slowly tucking the handkerchief into his breeches pocket, he turned then, and with the lawman at his side, he continued in his unhurried swagger to the opposite side of the street. Rachel stared after him, fighting back her disappointment. It occurred to her that she had actually felt something for this total stranger. Not just attraction. No, there was something more. In that momentary encounter, before she'd discovered the manacles on his wrists, a familiarity had passed between them, as if they had met, touched, and more, many times before.

But that was impossible. She had never seen this man before. Even in her wildest imagination she would never have dreamed up a man such as he. Men like Davis did not exist in her sheltered, pampered world in New Orleans.

She was still staring as he looked back over his shoulder. The broad brim of his black hat, low over his brow, obscured his eyes, but she saw the smile, white in his face. With sinking regret she lifted her chin and looked away.

He paused one last time before turning the corner, and looked back. The girl was standing there yet, the wind whipping her frilly white petticoats and pink skirt around her slim ankles. The tassels on her parasol swirled round and round as she spun it on her shoulder. When she peeked again from behind it, her violet eyes widened in dismay.

The courthouse door was open. Sam Wells lounged in a chair against the far wall, his rifle propped on one thigh and his cheek distended with tobacco. Clyde Lindsey, Pedro Gonzales, and Pete Jenkins stood in a row before the judge, who scowled at each one in turn before turning his eyes up to Davis and the lawman as they entered.

The lawman pressed the rifle barrel against Davis's back and gave him a shove. He took his place beside Clyde and looked at the judge.

"Well now, you boys are about the smelliest buncha sidewinders I've seen in a long time," the magistrate said. "Sam, what you brought this buncha no-accounts to me for?"

"These three was caught outside town, Floyd. They're wanted in Brackettville for killin' a Deputy Myers. I need yore permission to transport 'em back there for trial."

"And what about pretty boy here?" He pointed to Davis.

"That's Kid Davis."

Floyd's eyebrows shot up. "Davis! The Davis who shot all them folk in El Paso six months ago?"

"That's him. I finally come across 'im in Austin, but he slipped through my fingers. Followed 'im to town here and found 'im cuddled up with Claudia at the hotel."

The judge let out a whistle. "Marshal Bettinger is gonna be mighty happy to hang him." Looking back at Clyde, he added, "You boys picked the wrong towns to let loose hell in. The court in Brackettville will have you hanged this side of dawn." Sitting a little straighter, he cracked his gavel against the desktop and said, "So be it. You got enough help, Sam?"

"We're travelin' with the wagon train that's headed out the San Antonio–El Paso Road."

"There's safety in numbers, I reckon. All right, I hereby release you buncha no-goods into Captain Wells's custody. And God help yore souls, if you've got 'em."

The judge's eyes came back to Davis. Turning, Davis followed the others out the door.

Clyde fell back from the others. "Kid Davis, is it? Seems I've heard that name before. Was you the one who pulled that bank job out in Austin late last year?"

"Maybe."

"I remember somethin' about Caje's cantina in El Paso bein' tore up last year. Was that really you?"

"Maybe. Maybe not."

"A buncha people was killed as I recall."

Davis looked down the street, searching. The girl was gone.

"You must be pretty damn good with a gun," Clyde went on.

"I get by."

"You mean *got* by. Yore headed for a lynchin', jest like me, Davis. Somewheres you slipped up." Clyde's eyes narrowed as Davis grinned. "Don't see much to grin about. Not much funny about hangin'."

They slogged on, the chains from their ankles stirring up dust that, whipped by the wind, stung their faces and stuck to their sweat-slick skin. They filed again into the jailhouse. The deputy left his chair before the only window in the room and opened the cell door. "I hear the train's leavin' at two," the lawman said to Sam. "They'll be stopping out at Alex Bastitas's place before pushing out in the morning."

The deputy's last comment stopped Davis cold.

"Yep," came the old Ranger's response. "Señora Bastitas

will make certain them travelers are entertained tonight. That's for certain." He looked up as Davis slumped against the bars. "Somethin' wrong with you, boy? Yore lookin' awful white around the gills."

"He just realized he's gittin' his throat stretched purty soon," came a voice from further back in the cell.

Davis met Sam's glance, then closed his eyes. His fingers gripped the cell bars until his knuckles grew white.

Sam turned back to the deputy and continued. "The Bastitases are a fine buncha folks. It's a real shame they've had to endure such heartache through the years. Ya know, Angelique Bastitas won't never git over losin' that boy. She still believes Tomas is alive."

"Tomas Bastitas is dead. Them Comanches don't keep white slaves too long," the deputy said.

Dropping into a chair beside the door, Sam tucked a pinch of tobacco between his cheek and gum and relaxed, his Sharp buffalo rifle planted firmly across his buckskinned knee and his hat shoved back from his face. He stared at Davis a long moment before, uneasily, he shifted and looked away.

"I worked with Alex Bastitas for pert near four years tryin' to find his son," the Texas Ranger said. "You know them Injuns. If the boy wasn't killed outright he was probably sold or traded to some other tribe. After twenty-five years he's probably a savage himself by now."

"If he ain't dead."

Wells spit a stream of tobacco toward the brass spittoon beneath the sheriff's desk. It landed far short of its mark, but Sam ignored it. Scratching his chin through his beard, he rocked his chair back on two legs and shook his head in remembrance. "You was just a lad when them Comanches hit San Antonio. There was a pow-wow down at the Council House at Main Plaza and Market Street. Old Chief Muguara had agreed to meet with Lieutenant Colonel Fisher and discuss treaty affairs. But when time come to discuss the return of captives, things got out of hand. All hell broke out then."

The deputy nodded.

"Buncha good folk was killed then," Wells went on. "A

visitin' judge was killed by an arrow from an Indian child who'd been playin' in the street. Alex Bastitas and his wife was nearly killed themselves. He took an arrow in the chest. Just missed his heart. Angelique took a blow on the head. The councilmen thought at first that they'd captured all the braves, but that weren't the case. One of them sons-of-guns took Tomas Bastitas. Plucked him right from Angelique's arms. They is both still grievin'. Don't matter none that they had other boys. Tomas was their first, and named after Alex's brother, the one who died at the Santa Anna massacre." His eyes strayed back to Davis.

Leaning back against the wall, Davis slid to the floor.

Crouching on his heels, Clyde looked at Davis intently, a smirk quirking one end of his thin lips as Davis struggled to breathe. "Seems to me, Captain," he called to Sam, "that yore prized prisoner here is experiencin' some discomfort."

Sam's chair hit the floor. In two long strides he stood at the door and looked down at Davis. "You ain't dyin' or nothin', are ya?" the old man asked.

Davis shook his head.

"You buncha buzzards move back and give the man some room to breathe." When they did, he said, "Davis, ya look like a ghost." As Davis turned his blue eyes up to Sam's the lawman leaned closer to the bars, blinked as if to clear his mind of the gruesome memories that had earlier occupied his thoughts, then shook his head. He turned back for his chair.

Chapter 2

That afternoon twenty wagons lined the San Antonio–El Paso Road out of San Antonio. Most were great, bulky buckboard crates covered with heavy, dingy white canvas. They looked as if they would suffocate their occupants in the heat and drown them in a downpour. Homer George was their wagonmaster. Over six feet tall, wiry thin with a back as stiff as a ramrod, he stood with his hat in his hand and stared dubiously at the wagon Rachel and Audra had purchased that morning in the city.

"No offense, ladies, but that's about the worst-lookin' prairie schooner I ever saw. You didn't by chance buy it from a snake called Crowbait Jackson, did ya?"

Rachel glanced at her stepmother. Audra's face was expressionless, but her eyes, always hard, glinted like chips of brown glass as she glared at Mr. George.

"What's wrong with it?" Audra snapped.

"Canvas has been patched fer one thing. It's gonna leak like a sieve when it rains. And them wheels is rutted already." He kicked the wheel with his sharp-pointed boot, then shook his head. Throwing open the back flap he looked inside the semidark interior. Squinting, he asked, "Whare's yore supplies, ma'am?"

Snatching up her skirts, Audra moved to the wagonmaster's side and jutted one long finger at the crate at the far end of the wagon, as well as at the few cooking utensils strewn about the floor.

"Is that it?" he asked. "One fryin' pan and a stew pot? Whare's yore coffeepot?"

"I don't drink coffee," she responded.

"Don't drank coffee?" He looked around at Audra as if she'd suddenly grown an extra pair of eyes. "Whare you from, darlin', Chiny? And whare's yore saltpork and spuds?"

"Spuds?"

"Taters." Frowning at the small bag of flour tossed on end by the blue and white speckled tin utensils, he shook his head again and announced, "That won't hardly see ya a spittin' distance out of San Antone. Chihuahua, lady, yore aimin' to starve to death, I reckon."

Her lips thinning, Audra turned and glared at Rachel.

Homer George slapped his hat on his head. "Welp, we ain't got time now fer ya to go back into town and stock up. We'll be stoppin' at the Bastitas ranch in a spell. Alex'll probably have any supplies yore lackin'. And while yore at it ya might think about tradin' in them broncs Crowbait sold ya for mules or oxen. Them horses is as likely to get ya to Brackettville as I am to sprout wings and fly there."

"The horses will have to do," Audra said through her teeth.

Audra waited until Homer had walked on to the next wagon before turning again on Rachel. "This is all your fault," she stated, her voice a high-pitched whang caused by overexcitement. "Had you behaved yourself and not become involved with that white trash—"

"Stop calling Luke white trash! He wasn't trash at all. Just because he's poor—"

"Imagine running off with the likes of him. Whatever did you think you were doing? Thank God your father didn't live to see it. If you turn up pregnant on this journey—"

"Luke never touched me!" Her face burning, Rachel returned her stepmother's glower with as much intensity and added, "You forced Dr. Lisster to give me that horrible, humiliating examination. What more proof do you want that I've not been with a man?"

"Lisster has been a lifelong friend of the family and would lie for you, Rachel, and probably did. Regardless, everyone in New Orleans knew you ran off with that boy. You ruined the family name forever in that city. However could we remain?" Swishing her satin skirt and petticoats aside, Audra walked a distance before turning to face Rachel again. Her brown eyes narrowed slightly as she said, "I'm doing you a big favor, you know. At San Felipe Springs, you'll at least be able to hold your head up with some semblance of pride. My brother owns one of the largest ranches along the Rio Grande. Who knows, if you behave yourself perhaps you'll find a nice husband who'll forgive you your tawdry reputation."

"Beggin' yore pardon, ah, ladies."

Suddenly aware they had company, Rachel forced herself to turn toward the men on horseback. She stared a moment at the old lawman she had encountered earlier in the city, then, beyond him to . . . Davis!

He sat astride his animal with the same casual arrogance he exuded when he walked. The flat-crowned hat still cocked low over his eyes, he leaned slightly forward in his saddle; his wrists, connected by a two-foot-long chain, were crossed and resting on the saddle horn. A flush of embarrassment colored her cheeks as she realized the entire bunch of reprobates had overheard her exchange with Audra. With the exception of Davis, all were smirking. He, however, watched her with something akin to anger darkening his handsome features.

Sam Wells slid from his horse. He wore a gun on his hip now, and his long gray hair hung in braids over each shoulder. Sweeping the hat from his head, he made a slight bow before saying, "I reckon yore Audra Gregory and daughter Rachel?"

"*Step*daughter," Rachel stressed.

"Homer George tole us yore the tail end of this here train. Since it looks like we're gonna be travelin' companions, so to speak, I thought I'd introduce myself. Name's Captain Sam Wells of the Texas Rangers." He bowed slightly again. "Me and my men are escortin' these buncha no-accounts to Brackettville and El Paso."

Audra stepped forward, her agitation growing apparent as she realized that they would be traveling with the scruffy bunch of men on horseback. "But they're criminals!" she announced loudly enough to attract the attention of others who were milling about. "Surely you can't expect to endanger our lives with the likes of *them!*"

"I assure you, ma'am, yore in no danger from these men. My deputies are of the highest—"

"They're animals!"

There came a murmur of agreement from the gathering crowd.

"Isn't it enough that we're forced to contend with the threat of Indians and bandits on this journey?" someone called out. "This lot will probably cut our throats while we're sleeping!"

Wells rubbed the back of his neck before looking around at Davis.

Against her will, Rachel found her eyes continually straying back toward Davis. He was, she decided much to her own chagrin, the most handsome man she had ever met, and she allowed her gaze to linger longer than propriety deemed polite. The brim of his hat shadowed his face; it was a moment before she realized he was returning her look. When he raised both hands and touched the brim of that hat with one upraised finger, she felt the same dizzy sensation somersault in her breast that she'd experienced outside the jailhouse. This time, however, instead of feeling weakened and trembling like a willow in the wind, she felt a flush of hot anger touch her cheeks.

"Rachel!"

Rachel whirled toward her stepmother.

"Get into the wagon," Audra ordered.

As Audra's eyes shifted from her to Davis, Rachel knew that her stepmother's apparent concern over her welfare had nothing at all to do with protecting her from the men's unfavorable attentions. Rachel had seen that look too many times, before and after her father's death, not to recognize it now.

Homer pushed through the crowd and met Sam face to face.

"We've got problems, Homer," Sam said. "Folks here don't cotton to us taggin' along. Whatcha gonna do about it?"

Homer pulled off his hat and slapped it against his leg. "The way I see it, Sam, is this. Headin' toward Brackettville we is gonna be crossin' some of the roughest country between here and Arizona. There's more Comanches and Apaches out there than there are greasers in Mexico, by my reckonin'. If I was the folks in this train, I'd sleep better on my beds at night knowing I had a Texas Ranger and a couple of deputies within shoutin' distance if the need arose."

"But what about them?" A middle-aged woman in calico, thin as a rake handle, pointed a finger toward the prisoners and announced, "I got a daughter to think about." She pulled an equally skinny girl of around fifteen against her. The girl, her face ravaged with blemishes and her lank brown hair spilling around her sunken cheeks, stared with hound-dog eyes toward Davis.

"They ain't gonna cause no harm," Sam explained. "As you can see they're shackled, and you can rest assured that if any one of 'em starts any funny business, I'll blow his head off." He looked around at his charges and smiled broadly.

Opening his arms, Homer ushered the protestors back toward their wagons. "Nothin' to worry about, folks. Now let's get this train movin' or else we is gonna be late fer Rancho de Bejar's fiesta."

Davis's horse moved restlessly beneath him, tossing its head and snorting so he was forced to saw back on the reins to quiet him. Watching Rachel turn back toward the wagon, he thought, *So, the young woman has a past. A lover?* He narrowed his eyes as she looked back one last time and threw him a surreptitious glance from behind her lashes. Possible. But she was too young to have had *many* male friends. If there had been a lover in her life this Luke person must have been special, one of those *first* love affairs that could so easily sweep a young girl off her feet and into the nearest bed.

While watching her that morning from the jailhouse window and from his hotel room two days ago, he'd thought that she was, possibly, the most beautiful woman he'd ever seen.

That opinion hadn't changed. This rugged terrain exaggerated her femininity. She appeared frail, her skin pale, soft, and smooth. Her hair, spilling down her slender back and over her shoulders, was a beautiful array of curls the color of moonlight. He wasn't certain he'd ever seen hair as white as that. And her eyes: violet pools of warm liquid that could wrangle anything she wanted out of a man. But this man?

Never.

"I see you got yore eye on 'er too," came Clyde's low comment from behind him.

Davis closed his eyes. Clyde's tone, sneering and hollow like a well, caused an odd twist of discomfort to sluice through him, and in that instant, he knew that he would be forced to kill the man beside him. It was an instinct that had come from years of sizing up men and their motives, of calculating their speed with a gun and when they would draw it. And as always, when the discomfort settled around his heart like lead and then sank into his stomach, he wondered if *this* would be the time he would miscalculate. It happened to everyone eventually, usually because of age or because their thinking was clouded in that last moment of confrontation. Looking back at Rachel, he was swept with a sense of finality. It sweated his palms and crept like razors up his spine. In response he pressed his knee against the flat leather pouch hidden beneath his saddle, and the fear left him.

"Mou-u-nt up!" came the wagonmaster's order.

Rachel and Audra faced one another, each waiting for the other to climb aboard the formidable contraption. "What do we do now?" Audra asked.

"He told us to mount," Rachel said.

"Well, go ahead."

Rachel looked again at the wagon. Its bed appeared to have been painted green, but that was years ago. The high-arcing canvas sagged a little in the center, like the back of an old mule that had been ridden too long and hard. Swallowing, she said, "You first, I think." Moving aside, she waited for her stepmother to board, aware they were still being watched by the lawmen and prisoners.

"You ladies leavin' with this train or the one next month?" Sam called out.

"Maybe they're plannin' on pushin' it to Brackettville," one of the men jibed.

Frowning, Rachel chanced a quick glance toward Davis, just to make certain the comment had not been his. He returned her look with a curl of his mouth.

Sam approached, his hat in one hand and the reins to his horse in the other. "You ladies got a problem here?"

"No," they answered in unison.

"Who's drivin' this crate?" he asked.

Rachel pointed at Audra.

Audra pointed at her.

He stared at them both. "Seems you do got a problem. Ain't neither of you never driven a vehicle such as this?"

They shook their heads, then Audra stated, "I'm certain it is no different from driving a buggy."

The Ranger harumphed so loudly he spooked his horse; the piebald gave the frayed reins a tug and snorted. Sam then looked each woman over from head to toe. "Maybe it ain't none o' my business, but that wagon seat ain't gonna oblige both o' ya and them petticoats. Ya got enough material there to recanvas half these wagons."

Audra's eyes widened. "How *dare* you, sir! We are *ladies* and—"

"I ain't got no doubts about that," he interrupted, "and mighty fine ladies ya are, too. 'Bout the finest-lookin' two ladies San Antone has seen for a while. But facts is facts. Ya can't drive a team of horses when ya can't see where yore goin'. Ain't ya got nobody what can angle them sapsuckers for ya?"

Rachel lifted one brow and looked at Audra. For a moment her stepmother's features grew livid as she glanced at her, then back at Sam. "This is really all my brother's fault," she suddenly announced.

The old man listened, politely nodding as he studied Audra's flushed, furious face.

"I sent a letter to my brother some two months ago asking

that he meet us in Galveston. He didn't, so I assumed he would be waiting here in San Antonio. He wasn't." Lowering her voice somewhat, she admitted, "My daughter and I don't have the finances to remain here indefinitely. These provisions and this wagon have taken most of what was left us after the War. So you see it's imperative that we reach Brackettville as soon as possible. I just can't imagine why he's chosen to ignore my letter."

"Probably never reached him." It was a matter-of-fact statement. "Mail don't run smooth in Texas since the War, Mrs. Gregory. 'Specially along the Mexico border. Ya see, with the outbreak of the War the troops in forts along the El Paso route were pulled out and sent back east. The border's been without benefit of Federal protection since. Why, anythin' could have happened to the carrier of yore letter. He was probably either skewered by a Comanche or Apache lance, or even snakebit."

Audra turned again to Rachel. "I feel a headache coming on. You'll have to drive while I recline."

Rachel thought her stepmother would no doubt do a great deal of reclining on this journey.

Aware that she was still being regarded by Davis, Rachel did her best to mount the wagon as gracefully as possible. It wasn't an easy feat by any measure. Wells had been right about her petticoats. When, finally, she managed to scale the monstrosity, she flopped down on the wagon seat only to have the voluminous material of her skirts mushroom around her until she was forced to almost lie upon them just so she could reach for the lines the old man lifted to her.

"Thread 'em through yore fingers," he told her. "Where's yore gloves?"

"Gloves?" She looked at her hands. "I have a pair of linen gloves somewhere in my trunk, I suppose."

"A hat?"

"A hat." She bit her lower lip. "In the trunk."

"Maybe yore mother will dig it out for ya whilst she's reclinin'."

"*Step*mother," she stressed again.

"Whatever. Remember, keep them lines up and tight, but not taut. Here's yore brake." He motioned toward the wooden arm jutting up by her left leg. "If ya have any trouble, me or one of my men are jest a whistlin' distance away."

Rachel looked back around the canvas, directly into Davis's blue eyes. Snapping erect, she glared at some point over Sam's head and said, "I'm certain there will be no reason to whistle, Captain Wells."

Stepping back, he replaced his hat on his head and told her, "Remember, Miss Rachel, tight but not taut."

"Thank you. I'll remember."

By now the wagon ahead of theirs had moved a considerable distance up the road. Dust rose like a storm cloud over it. "Wonderful," she grumbled to herself, then slapped the lines against the horses' backs. "Wonderful."

She thought she'd imagined them at first, the ringing of the bells. But there they were again, singing into the afternoon air as clearly as church bells on Sunday. Through the dust Rachel caught a glimpse of white adobe walls—a barricade, by the looks of them—then, seeing the guards who stood casually along the parapets lining the barricade, she realized they were, indeed, approaching some sort of fortress.

There were children everywhere, running with bare feet and laughing faces among the travelers. Behind them came women wearing full, brightly colored skirts and peasant blouses. Many carried jugs in their arms; there were baskets of what appeared to be bread on others' shoulders. Several young men ran up to Rachel's wagon and grabbed the horses' harnesses while throwing her smiles so genuine she almost laughed aloud.

"Don Alejandro Felipe Antonio de Bastitas welcomes you to Rancho de Bejar, *señorita*!" the tallest of the lot yelled.

Rachel heard her stepmother rummaging around in the back before she popped her head through the canvas opening and said in a groggy voice, "What a lot of commotion, and me with this horrible headache."

"Welcome!" the boys greeted. "Don Alejandro asks that you leave your animals and wagons to us and join in the festivities of the evening. There will be food and wine and music before you begin your journey tomorrow."

One of the boys scampered onto the wagon and gently took the lines from Rachel's hands.

It was a very long way to the ground. Rachel perched on the end of the wagon seat and wondered how she would gracefully manage the descent. "May I be of some assistance?" came a low-timbred voice slightly behind her. Without looking, she knew that Davis was there, mocking her with his smoke-blue eyes and taunting her with the slant of his mouth. God, how he could taunt her! He could taunt her without so much as a word or a breath directed her way. His mere presence was an agitation. He'd made a fool of her that morning and he wouldn't let her forget it.

Choosing to ignore him, she looked again at the ground, her mouth twisting slightly in contemplation.

"Miss Gregory?"

The need to acknowledge him was too great, though she told herself it was only because she had never intentionally practiced snobbery. And, of course, she wasn't about to start now. Before lifting her gaze from the ground, she prepared herself for the full force of his eyes. It didn't lessen the impact. Swallowing, she answered, "Sir?"

He looked at her pointedly, his eyes glittering with cynical enjoyment; the slightly upturned corners of his lips had begun to quiver. "Might I help you down from the wagon?"

"You're very obliging for a . . ." Her mouth twisted a little more.

"For a what?" The leather of his saddle creaked as he shifted. "You'd better make up your mind before that gray-haired old coot decides to shoot me in the back for bothering you."

"Well . . ." She glanced again at his manacled wrists, his hands, the long, tanned fingers curling sensually around his reins. "I . . . I don't think so." She stared at her own hands.

"It wouldn't be proper, I think. Not with your being . . . well, you know. One of *them*."

She raised her lashes secretly to see his reaction. His blue eyes clashed with hers; such intensity flickered beneath those half-closed lids that she was left with a sense of unease and astounded by her own awareness of his presence.

How long did she hang there, suspended in time and space, allowing the mere shuttered glance that passed between them to unravel her? She was a lady, after all. No matter what her stepmother chose to believe, her beaux—sparse as they had been through the years of the War—had never garnered more than a passing interest from her. Perhaps they had brushed a kiss onto her cheek, complimented her outrageously, and showered her with flowers and pralines from Celie's on Bourbon Street. But never had they stirred the kind of frightening awareness in her breast that this dangerous, dark man on horseback had.

With a tip of his head and a yank of his reins, Davis guided his horse around and back toward the others. He was angry. She could see it in the set of his wide shoulders, the way the long fingers of one hand tightened into the horse's coarse black mane. For a moment she imagined them twisting into her own hair as violently.

The young man beside her asked, "Is something wrong, *señorita*?"

Closing her eyes, Rachel shook her head.

With the flush of disconcertion staining her cheeks she looked back toward the sprawling hacienda, Rancho de Bejar. Then, doing her best not to further damage her clothes, she climbed from the wagon seat to the ground. Momentarily she was joined by Audra, and both hurried toward the growing crowd outside the barricade's open gateway.

She noticed the man immediately. He stood among the throng, his dark head bent slightly toward a much smaller woman at his side. Rachel watched as he slipped one long arm around his companion's waist and smiled into her eyes.

"Grandpa!" came a child's lyrical cry.

The man looked around as a child of some three or four

years threw herself into his hands. The child soared up and up with a squeal of delight until she balanced atop her grandfather's extended arms, high above his head.

Rachel was so intent on watching the touching scene before her that she was only vaguely aware that she had been joined by someone else. Then the familiar voice said, "So, *señorita*, we meet again."

Surprised, Rachel turned and found the young brawler from the bar back in San Antonio beside her, his green eyes twinkling in amusement, a smile curling one side of his mouth. "I trust you will keep the excitement of our first meeting a secret," he teased her. "Claude hasn't finished tallying up the damage to his cantina so I'm safe, at least until tomorrow." Lifting her hand just short of his lips, he added, "Allow me to introduce myself properly. I am Ramon de Bastitas."

"So this is your home?" She returned his smile.

"It is. The gentleman and lady there are my father and mother. The child on his hip is my niece, daughter of my older brother Estaban. Would you care to meet them?"

Rachel threw a quick look toward the prisoners, now being escorted around the barricades by Sam. Davis lagged behind the others, his interest all too apparently on her still, and on Ramon. Just then, though, Sam raised the barrel of his rifle and poked him in the back.

The troubling thought occurred to her that she found the reality of Davis's being an outlaw much too easy to forget. She cautioned herself to take greater care when he was near. Much greater care. Her compassion and her willingness to believe in a man's basic goodness, despite evidence to the contrary, had gotten her in trouble more than once in her life. The disquieting feeling that Davis *would* be trouble assailed her. Struggling to put him from her mind, Rachel accepted Ramon's offered arm and moved with him through the crowd, aware that her stepmother was close on her heels.

Ramon's mother flashed a brilliant smile full of pride and love at the child now jumping up and down at her husband's side. Her hair was a beautiful auburn, tied at the nape with an emerald satin ribbon that matched her dress. As Ramon called out to her, she turned such startling green eyes on her son that Rachel almost hesitated in her step.

"Mother, I've someone I want you to meet."

The woman looked from Ramon to Rachel. "So I see," came her refined response. Offering her hand, she smiled warmly and said, "I am Angelique Bastitas."

"And I am Rachel Gregory."

Angelique looked again at her son, at the hand wrapped tenderly around Rachel's arm. She then turned and tugged on her husband's coat sleeve.

For the first time since approaching Ramon's parents, Rachel turned her eyes up to the man at Angelique's side. She stared for an embarrassingly long moment into his bluer-than-blue eyes, her heart quivering strangely as she attempted to return his smile.

"How very charming," came his deep-timbred voice. "I am honored, *señorita* . . ."

"Rachel Gregory," Angelique replied, as if sensing Rachel's inability to respond.

Suddenly aware that her stepmother had poked her sharply in the back, Rachel came to her senses as gracefully as possible and stepped away, as she had been trained to do when introducing Audra to company. It was something she did without thinking.

Audra nodded briefly toward Angelique, then turned her full attention on Ramon's father. "You honor us, sir, with this lavish welcome. Let me extend my every thanks and introduce myself, since my daughter was remiss in doing so."

"*Step*daughter," Rachel intruded stubbornly, bringing an unexpected girlish giggle from Angelique Bastitas.

"I am Audra Gregory, sir, and you are?"

"Alejandro de Bastitas, Mrs. Gregory." He shook her hand rather than kissing it. "Have you come far, *señora*?"

"From New Orleans."

"New Orleans!" Angelique's green eyes danced with excitement, and turning again to Rachel, she added, "My dear, we must talk. I'm from New Orleans myself!"

"We're traveling to Brackettville, and then on to San Felipe Springs," Audra continued. Giving every appearance of having dismissed all but Alex Bastitas, she fluttered her black lashes, ran one finger around the edge of her immodestly cut décolletage, and professed, "I hope all gentlemen in Texas are as handsome as you, Mr. Bastitas."

"I'm certain there are men far more handsome than I," he responded, then with an air of cool formality finished, "and *they* are not married. And even if they are they could not be nearly so devoted to their wives as I." He flashed Audra a smile so disarmingly attractive that those who witnessed the polite rebuff appeared to question in their mind that it had ever happened at all.

"You *will* join in our celebration?" It was Angelique who spoke, smiling as pleasantly at Audra as she did at Rachel. In that moment Rachel was awed by the woman's gentility and the poise with which she avoided humiliating Audra further, as she could have so easily done.

Audra wasn't as gracious. She never was when meeting a women more beautiful than herself. "I suppose."

"We could always have food prepared and sent to your wagon," Angelique managed sweetly once again.

Before more words could pass between Audra and Ramon's mother, Rachel grabbed her stepmother's arm. Doing her best to divert the anger rising on her stepparent's high-boned cheeks, she pleaded, "I'm so fatigued, Audra. Shouldn't we rest awhile before the festivities start?"

Audra turned from her hosts and threw Ramon so scathing a glance that he dropped his hand from Rachel's arm. Without further words she marched again into the crowd, tugging Rachel along with her while the Bastitas family looked on in bewilderment.

Rachel's face burned the entire way back to their wagon. How could her stepmother proclaim herself a lady and then insult the Bastitas family so blatantly? She was livid, and humiliated beyond reason.

"Stinking bunch of Mexicans," she heard Audra mutter under her breath. It was that same gutter-edged tone that reminded Rachel of a wharf doxy, the kind who paraded themselves up and down Canal Street back home.

"The Bastitases are Spanish, Audra. They are very genteel people."

"Get in the wagon," Audra ordered. Giving Rachel a shove, she added in a nasty voice, "And don't come out or I swear to God I'll—"

"You'll what?" Setting her chin, she rounded on her stepmother and retaliated, "Will you send me to my room? Have Papa spank me for my obstinance? Well, in case you are unaware, Audra, my father is dead, we have no room for you to send me to, and, furthermore, I'm a grown woman. You cannot continue to treat me like a child!"

Audra's palm cracked against her cheek with enough force to drive Rachel backward. She was too stunned to cry. She wouldn't give Audra that satisfaction. Like those times before, she only stared, her eyes daring the woman to strike her again and knowing that if she did, perhaps, just perhaps, *this* time she would hit her back.

But the moment passed. As always, Rachel retreated. It was her breeding, after all. A lady must never raise her voice or publicly show her discontent. She honored her father and mother and at all times respected their wishes whether they were just or not. And when she married she obliged her husband in every way possible, respected him at all cost, and . . . God, did it never end?

Rachel went to the wagon, and for the next hour sat among the trunks of Audra's clothes, refusing to watch as her stepmother peeled out of one dress and shimmied into another. It was a bright canary yellow on which she had wasted a tidy fortune. Hardly a widow's attire, though. Its plunging décolletage would offer many an interested eye a nearly full view of her more than bountiful breasts. Rachel could still recall how her father had pleaded with Audra not to spend their funds on such outlandish fripperies when the note on the mortgage was begging to be settled. But Audra Gregory had paid him no heed. She had ruined Rachel's father as much as the War had. There were times when Rachel wondered if the bullet that killed him had actually come from a Yankee's gun—or his own.

Chapter 3

Sam Wells stood at the salon window, looking out over the hacienda's formal gardens. He remembered Rancho de Bejar as it once was, nicely manicured but without the splendid array of blooming flowers that, for the last two dozen years, had brightened the walkways to every corner of the barricaded grounds. He wasn't likely to stand and gawk over pansies and petunias and roses, but after spending most of his life surrounded by little more than scrub brush, cactus, and dust, he felt that Angelique's gardens were a welcome sight.

"Whiskey, Captain?"

Sam nodded before turning.

Alex Bastitas poured them each a shot of his best. "I've arranged for a lockup for your prisoners," he said. When Sam didn't respond, he looked up at his old friend. "You seem a little preoccupied tonight, *amigo*."

"I's jest thinkin' . . . You seen that buncha no-accounts yet?"

"I haven't." He handed the glass to Sam, then motioned toward the matching chairs before the marble-fronted fireplace. Once seated he asked, "Is there some reason I should have?"

"Nah, I don't reckon. They're yore normal scurvy lot, but there's one . . ." He tossed back his drink, savored its fine quality as he rolled it around in his mouth, then swallowed. Deciding to change the subject, he accepted one of Alex's cigars and asked, "How's the missus? She was lookin' mighty fine earlier."

"Angel is always at her best."

"Well now, she is at that, I reckon. Ain't no finer lady between here and California. I reckon she's millin' with the travelers now?"

Putting aside his drink, Alex leaned forward, elbows on his knees, looked directly into the old man's weathered face, and said, "I'm certain by now she will have managed to bring up the subject of our son to a few of them."

"She's a mother, Alex. The boy was taken as a child, barely more'n a babe. It's understandable, I reckon, that she still hopes that he'll be found someday."

Alex left his chair, his fingers raking through his black hair as he paced, limping slightly, toward the window and back. "Do you know how I feel when I see her clinging to the fantasy that Tomas is still alive?"

Sam frowned. "Brokenhearted, I reckon."

"Hell yes, I'm brokenhearted. If I'd just done things differently that day, if I hadn't run out in that street like I did—"

"You weren't thinkin', man. It was a natural reaction, and it sure wasn't yore fault that you got hit."

"But if I hadn't been laid up for those weeks with that arrow wound, Sam, I might have found the boy."

"We did our best."

A burst of laughter outside the window silenced the sudden flood of frustration and pain that washed over Alex. He squared his shoulders, stared at the ceiling momentarily, then released his breath painfully slowly. "God help me, but sometimes I almost wish he'd been killed that morning. At least the nightmare would have ended then. I cannot image the hell they must have put him through."

Sam looked toward the window, and for the second time since entering the salon with Alex, he was tempted to bring up the subject of the prisoner in his charge. Kid Davis looked disturbingly like Alex; he'd noted that fact even *before* he'd witnessed Davis's reaction to hearing the Bastitas name in the San Antonio jailhouse. Sam had suffered right along with Alex and Angelique through those terrible years after Tomas's abduction. He had experienced the same hopes of finding him each time news came of sightings of a blue-eyed boy among the Comanches. But those rumors had stopped some fifteen years ago, and so had Alex's dreams of finding his son. Both Alex and Angelique had put their lives back together and dealt with the loss as best they could. Sam decided he would have to be pretty damn certain that the man in that lockup was Tomas Bastitas before he brought up the subject to his friends. He didn't want to put them through that trauma again for no reason.

Just then they were interrupted by a knock at the door. The stranger, dressed in a somber gray suit and black tie, the stiff wing collar of the pristine white shirt cutting into the underside of his chin, entered the salon reluctantly. His hazel eyes on Sam, he said, "I do beg your pardon, but I was told I would find a Captain Wells here?"

"Ya found 'im," Sam replied. Putting his drink and cigar aside, he got to his feet.

"I'm John Hopper," the man said, extending his hand first to Sam, then to Alex. "I'm sorry I'm late, Captain Wells."

"Well now, I didn't realize ya were, sir. Jest who the devil are ya?"

"Why, Hopper, sir, of Allan—" Cutting himself off in mid-sentence, he looked toward Alex.

"Alex is a friend of mine, Mr. Hopper. Say what ya came to say before that damn collar chokes ya to death."

Hopper frowned, blushed, hesitated, then went on slowly. "Hopper, sir . . . from Chicago?" he prompted. "You *did* receive my employer's letter?"

"Well, I figured you for a northerner and all, what with all that fancy git-up—" Realization hit Sam like a thunderclap. "Chicago!" he barked loud enough to make both Alex and Hopper start. "Well, why didn't ya say so, Mr. Hopper? Bastitas, this gentleman is from Allan Pinkerton's agency. He's come all the way from Chicago—"

Hopper interrupted. "Actually I work in Mr. Pinkerton's New York branch." He again shook Alex's hand. "You've a lovely home here, Mr. Bastitas."

Smiling his thanks, Alex said, "I've heard impressive

things about the Pinkerton Detectives. What brings you to Texas?"

"Duty. We've arranged to work with Captain Wells's company on a particularly difficult case."

"Scoundrel robbed a bank and killed some folk up in New York City a while back," Wells added. "Seems he's turned up in Texas after all this time."

"Anyone I know?" Alex asked.

Sam only smiled in response.

Crossing to the window, Hopper drank in the cool, rose-fragrant breeze before asking a little conspiratorially, "Do you have my man in custody, Captain Wells?"

"I do, sir."

"What do you think of him?"

Sam thought a minute. Finally, "I think he's gonna be a tough *hombre* to have to deal with, Mr. Hopper."

John Hopper nodded, smiled, and turning, said, "Yes. He is, isn't he?"

Rachel read quietly from the Bible, something about patience and turning the other cheek. It was getting harder and harder to turn the other cheek these days, at least where her stepmother was concerned.

Tucking the loose and ragged pages into place, Rachel gently closed the book and laid her head back against her pillow, doing her best to block out the delicious aroma of cooking food and ignore the raucous laughter of men and women enjoying themselves. Music filtered to her occasionally. The Spanish guitar hummed such a romantic melody now that she couldn't help but daydream. But even that, in the end, left her frustrated and angry with herself. Imagine fantasizing over that awful blue-eyed brute in chains! The man wouldn't know etiquette if it leaped off the pages of a book and bit him on the nose. He was a criminal, for heaven's sake. An outlaw! The scum of the earth! He was in chains and here she was mentally dressing him in broadcloth and satin cravats with sapphire stickpins to match his outrageous eyes.

"Rachel? Rachel, are you there?"

Rachel sat up.

"Rachel, it's Angelique Bastitas."

Rachel hesitated, recalling the embarrassing scene with her stepmother, then answered softly, "I'm here."

"May I come in?"

"Of course." On her knees Rachel did her best to tidy the clothes Audra had strewn about the wagon bed.

The canvas flap was thrown back and Angelique looked in. "Am I intruding?"

"I was only reading."

With surprising grace Angelique hefted herself up into the wagon. Her red and black satin skirts filled the narrow entrance; a black mantilla flowed in lacy patterns over her gleaming white shoulders. Bent slightly at the waist, as the canvas wasn't nearly tall enough to accommodate her height, she smiled almost apologetically, then stunned Rachel by announcing, "These damnable petticoats are such a nuisance. Do you mind if I sit down?"

"Certainly not." Biting her lip, she pointed to an unstable-looking crate and said, "I fear that's all I have to offer."

"It'll do." Once settled, her skirts mushrooming in a crimson cloud around her knees, Angelique looked curiously around the wagon before bringing her green eyes back to Rachel. "It's a bit stuffy, isn't it? And small. Not at all what you're accustomed to, I imagine."

"Not at all."

The crate creaked as Angelique shifted. Rachel held her breath, frightened it would collapse beneath the woman at any minute. Angelique went on, "I fear this entire ordeal has been most unpleasant for you. There is a vast difference between San Antonio and New Orleans."

"It's really rather . . ." Rachel searched her mind.

"Uncivilized?"

"Oh, well . . ." Smiling, Rachel agreed. "Yes."

Their eyes met again, and Angelique smiled. "I was only eighteen when I came here with my mother. For a young woman accustomed to New Orleans society, I felt alienated from the world. I could hardly imagine a future with any promise awaiting me here. That was, of course, before I met my husband."

Thinking of Angelique's husband, Rachel sighed. "Señor de Bastitas is a very handsome man."

"Yes, he is. Too handsome for his own good, on occasion. If I didn't continually remind him he's mortal, I wouldn't be able to live with him."

They laughed together, then Angelique continued, "He's adept at handling flirtatious women like your stepmother, so please don't worry over her little faux pas. Frankly, I would have been disappointed had she not found him irresistible. Come to think about it, so would he. He might begin thinking again that he's growing old. Such things do such irreparable harm to a man's self-esteem."

"I can't imagine why he should think himself old —"

"My husband is sixty-three."

"I don't believe it!" Rachel protested. "He couldn't possibly be. I thought him no older than forty, and you no more than thirty-five."

"Oh you kind child! I knew I liked you for some reason!"

They laughed again, girlishly, the difference in their ages lessening in importance as the spark of new friendship glowed warmly between them. Elbows on her knees, Angelique said pointedly this time, "I've come here for a reason, you know. My son has become quite morose over your absence."

She had totally forgotten about Ramon. Blushing, Rachel stared at her fingers and said, "He's a very nice young man."

"But?" When Rachel didn't respond Angelique did it for her. "He's *too* young. Am I right?"

"Well." This entire conversation was becoming discomforting, Rachel thought.

"I agree wholeheartedly, Rachel; you needn't bite your lip in two. Ramon is in love with a new girl every week, and though you're much prettier than any he's professed himself to so far, I fear his first real love will eventually win out."

"And she is?"

"Law. He's attending Harvard in a few weeks."

Smiling in relief, Rachel sat back on her bed, her legs crossed comfortably, Indian fashion, as her nanny had called it. The dim light of the kerosene lantern wavered unsteadily as a sudden wind gently rocked the wagon and fluttered the sagging canvas top like sails on a ship. "You must be thrilled," she said.

"A little." The confession brought a smile to Angelique's mouth.

"But Harvard!"

"He's my baby, Rachel. It will be very hard to let him go."

"But you've other children, and a beautiful grand-daughter!"

"Indeed I have. Four sons, to be precise, and two sisters whom I raised from childhood. It's not like my nest will suddenly be empty. Lord knows, I'm fifty years old, I could probably use the rest. It's just . . . I'm so frightened something will happen to him."

"But what could possibly happen at Harvard?"

"There are dangers in the safest places," Angelique reasoned. "San Antonio *appears* to be safe, but its history is far from peaceful. Take the Alamo, for instance."

"But that was war. There was reason behind it."

"What reason was there for the Comanche attack four years later that killed innocent women and children? I'm certain the townships of Victoria, Cuero, and Lavaca all believed they were somewhat safe in their numbers. But by choosing to forget these atrocities we leave ourselves vulnerable for more. I have seen far too much horror and felt too much pain to simply place the memories aside and forget them. My own mother and stepfather were killed at that time, as well as my husband's grandfather. My son was snatched from my very arms, and Alejandro spent four excruciating months recovering from an arrow in his chest."

Her face now frighteningly pale as she stared into the lantern light, Angelique said, "The savage who murdered my own mother is the very one who robbed me of my son."

"Your son was never returned?" Rachel asked softly.

The response was a moment in coming. "No. I have no way of knowing if he . . . I *won't* believe my Tomas is dead. I am his mother; if he were dead I would know it here." She pressed her fist against her heart.

"I assume you've searched for him?"

Angelique nodded. "For four years following the attack my husband and several Rangers followed every lead concerning the sighting of captives. Always, however, by the time they reached the area of the sightings the bands were long gone.

"I can only pray that they spared my son the horrible torture to which they normally subject their captives. He was only a child, barely five years old at the time, and so beautiful . . . so like his father. When I think how they might have hurt him—"

"Please, don't go on!" Rachel took her friend's hand and gripped it tightly in her own while Angelique rocked a moment in her grief.

"The Comanches will sometimes force their captives to live night and day with the scalp of a loved one tied to his person. It is a horrible reminder of what will happen to the captive should he disobey them." Angelique looked steadily into Rachel's eyes and added, "My mother was scalped. Oh, Tomas did so love his grandmother, Rachel. If he was forced . . ." Angelique turned away until she was able to regain her composure. "I'm sorry," she said softly. "I know I'm a fool for continuing to believe my son is alive. My husband believes that if Tomas had survived he would have somehow come home long ago."

"Wouldn't he?"

"It is a known fact that captives fear returning to their families and friends. They fear the curiosity and ridicule. You see, they are taught a certain way of surviving that is totally different from our own. And if, possibly, my son was forced to participate in their ungodly rituals, as many are, could he face us? He may be there, Rachel, wanting to come home, but afraid. If he only knew that we understand, that we love him *still*, perhaps, just perhaps, he would contact us."

On her knees again, her pale hair spilling like a downy white shawl around her shoulders, Rachel forgot her humiliation over Audra's behavior and thought only of how she could comfort the dear, genteel woman before her. Angelique Bastitas's face was a portrait of beauty and heartbreak, of determination and devotion that must transcend all mortal boundaries. Indeed, if Tomas de Bastitas were alive he must know that his mother still prayed for his return. The human spirit, no matter what the diehard fundamentalists of the time chose to believe, was attuned to such things. She truly believed that!

Sensing Rachel's distress, Angelique again apologized for her emotionalism and admitted, "I came only to encourage you to join in our fiesta, and here I've distressed you by pouring out our rather unfortunate life history. Forgive me. Forget the frettings of an old woman and come enjoy yourself."

"My stepmother won't like it."

Angelique arched one fine brow. "You're a grown woman, aren't you?"

Recalling the frequent ugly scenes between herself and Audra, Rachel said, "But she's terribly jealous. Audra expects to be the center of attention wherever she goes. The belle of the ball, so to speak."

"Mrs. Gregory has my deepest sympathies if she is so lacking in self-confidence, but you must not allow her to manipulate your life. I'm speaking from experience, Rachel. Because a woman is older doesn't always mean she's wiser. Had I listened more to my own mother and less to my heart I would never have married Alejandro." Smiling a little slyly, Angelique added, "Oooh, I shudder to think of the limp-wristed young fops she might have married me to had we remained in New Orleans."

"I take it she didn't approve of Señor de Bastitas."

"Oh, my dear, she tried to shoot him once!" When Rachel laughed in disbelief, she added, "He later tried to strangle her, I think."

"And you married him anyway?"

"Can you blame me? Believe me, my dear, when those blue eyes turned on me I was a lost soul!"

Blue eyes. The remembrance of Davis's blue eyes and black hair, coupled with the memory of his finger lightly touching her jaw, left Rachel suddenly breathless.

"Oh dear!" Touching Rachel's cheek with the tips of her fingers, Angelique asked, "Have I shocked you? I fear you've grown quite pale."

Rachel shook her head. "I was only thinking. I met a man today who was very attractive. He had blue eyes and . . ."

"And?"

Rachel did her best to dismiss her attraction for Davis with a flick of her hand. "It was nothing. He was overbearing, arrogant, and as uncouth as a river rat. I hope I never see him again."

Angelique climbed from the wagon. The rising wind teased the curls around her ears and fluttered the lace mantilla around her shoulders. Looking back at Rachel, she said, "Let this be the last order you take from old women with a penchant for running others' lives. Put on your finest party dress and join in our celebration. I would like that very much."

She could hardly refuse. "Where shall I meet you?"

"On the east wing of the house there is a small patio. I'll have Teresa serve us refreshments, then I'll show you around the estate." Dropping the flap back into place, Angelique de Bastitas returned to her fiesta.

Rachel found the patio easily enough. A round-faced Mexican woman with gray hair greeted her with a silver chalice of Madeira and announced that Doña Angelique had been summoned to the family wing of the hacienda on a small crisis. A terrible stomachache had befallen her granddaughter, and no one but *Abuela* could cure it. So Rachel waited comfortably on the willow settee, drank the fruity wine, and allowed the pleasant breeze to relax her.

Yards of lace and ivory silk spread luxuriously over her crinoline petticoats and flowed to the floor in soft, crushed folds. The snug, revealing bodice of her gown was supported by stays; its décolletage, draping from jeweled epaulettes on her shoulders, was of the finest French lace Confederate money could buy. At times she had considered selling it, so desperate had they been for money near the end of the War. After the fall, the gown might have brought a small fortune from many of the Yankee carpetbaggers who would have lavished it on a mistress or bragged to a simpering fiancée that it was simply an extravagant spoil of war.

But she wouldn't give it up. Her father had commissioned the dress from Julian Persac himself after she'd seen its likeness in both *Harper's* and *Godey's*. Audra had been furious, of course, but it hadn't mattered. Rachel had almost died from happiness when her father presented the gift, and few of her stepmother's remarks about the dress being far too mature had bothered her in the least. She felt like a princess when she wore it, though she had worn it only once before the Union occupied New Orleans. Many times she had locked herself in her room, donned the dress, then stood before the mirror and wept, knowing nothing would ever be the same again. Not for her family or for the South.

Refilling her chalice, Rachel rested her head back against the settee and closed her eyes. The soft strum of the guitar was enchanting. A young man's melodious voice sang what would have to be a love song, in Spanish. Rachel wished now that she had taken time to learn the language. It sounded so romantic. Like French, it could roll off the tongue of some admiring young swain and send a girl's heart soaring on a flight of fancy.

Her head came up with a snap. That disturbing image had returned: an image of impudent blue eyes and raven hair. Certainly her mind was becoming depraved. Her nanny had warned her that she'd waited too long to marry. "Pretty soon *anybody'll* start lookin' good!" she'd told Rachel.

Her peers had certainly written her off as an old maid, though many had kindly agreed that the War had certainly spoiled more chances at matrimony than hers. Her own good friend, Lydia Thonars, had lost her fiancé only a week after their betrothal was announced. And there was dear Millicent Chaix, who was widowed a mere two months after her marriage to her beloved Louis. It was all too horrid!

Rachel drained her cup and returned it to the table. The wine made her drowsy, and once again she had to blink away the fantasy image of the dark outlaw in tight breeches. She had always prided herself on being levelheaded over men, refusing to settle for a relationship that went no further than money or position. Her mother and father had married out of love, and it had been a beautiful union for them both. By contrast, her father had wed Audra not out of love, but out of the illusion of love. She had worked her wiles on him, making him feel extraordinarily desirable, posturing as a perfect role model for Rachel when all the while, all Audra had wanted was to be kept—lavishly, of course.

Leaving her chair, Rachel roamed about the enclosure, staring first at her reflection in the round fountain crowded with water lilies; then, sweeping aside the tangle of grapevine draping over the farthest entrance of the patio, she walked down the meandering path until she was lost amid the deep shadows of the willow and pecan trees growing near the house.

The night breeze did much to alleviate the irritation she'd experienced the moment Davis entered her thoughts. Still, why couldn't she get him off her mind? She had never come up against a man who affected her so shockingly. In one moment his smile had swept her from speechless giddiness to appalled fury. She, who was well known in New Orleans society for occasionally surprising admirers with her teasingly flirtatious airs and, more often than not, totally indifferent responses, had been shaken, for the first time in her life, by a man's presence. It was totally unprecedented considering what he was. Absurd and further disturbing was the remembrance of those eyes as they wandered over her person. His perusal had brought about unnerving and inexplicable responses from her body that even now made her blush with shame.

Perhaps she *was* becoming desperate. There was no better

explanation for her behavior. She was so eager to get out from beneath her stepmother's influence that she was ready to throw caution and good sense to the wind and run off with the first man who gave her a second look. Or perhaps she was harboring some perverse sense of spitefulness toward Audra that taunted her into doing everything possible to humiliate the woman, knowing how Audra preened on others' high opinion of her. Rachel realized that she wasn't above such a deliberate show of rebelliousness. She *had* run off with Luke, after all, although it hadn't been a cause to humiliate Audra. After a horrible argument with her stepmother she'd decided in one reckless, thoughtless moment to run away with her childhood friend, although he was but the son of one of her father's sharecroppers, and put the ashes of her ruined family life forever behind her. That little rebellion had been dashed to an embarrassing end when both she and Luke were caught outside Baton Rouge. Luke was thrashed for fooling with a respectable woman of means, and Rachel was forced to submit to Dr. Lisster's humiliating examination of her person. Audra had gotten her revenge, and Rachel would forever be ousted from polite society. Her father had often warned Rachel about her quick temper, saying she was fortunate to have been born a woman. Otherwise she would have long since been shot in a duel and buried behind St. Mary's Cathedral.

Turning her face to the heavens, Rachel gazed at the pulsating pinpoints of light in the velvet sky. Somewhere castanets had picked up the rhythm of the strumming guitarist. In response she began moving gracefully to the tempo, the wine finally having eased her frustration and the anger she'd earlier felt over the outlaw's brazenness. Closing her eyes she pretended she was back at the Comtesse Onvaroff's soirée, when she had worn this very gown for the first time, when her dancing card had been filled with the names of eager young men who argued over whose turn it was to fetch her champagne. Now, as then, she spun until she was lightheaded, until she was forced to lean against the trunk of a willow and regain her equilibrium.

When she opened her eyes again she focused on the men who had materialized from the darkness. They stood some distance away, just off the path, both carrying rifles. The dim light from some nearby source reflected dully from the badges on their shirtfronts.

"This lot is gonna be trouble," came the deep voice. "I don't understand why we've got to take 'em all the way to Brackettville to hang. Any tree in San Antone would have done just as well."

"As long as we're workin' with the Rangers, Tom, we do as we're told."

"Yeah, well, I'm not taking any chances. If this group pulls anything nasty, they'll regret it, I don't care *what* Wells or that Pinkerton man says."

They walked leisurely toward the flat-roofed lockup some distance down the path. Rachel followed, keeping to the shadows, her sense of curiosity compelling her onward.

She came to an abrupt stop as she recognized Davis standing at the window of the lockup. He seemed to be engrossed in watching another two men who stood a short distance away. Rachel recognized the shorter of the two as Estaban, whose lucky punch had landed Ramon at her feet earlier that day.

How closely Davis watched them! His face was emotionless. The set of his shoulders was tense and his hands, propped upon the windowsill, were clenched. The darkness outside the house softened his features; he looked so much younger—more vulnerable—than Rachel imagined possible. It was as if she had caught him sleeping, and though she knew the proper thing to do would be to turn away and allow him this moment of privacy, she could do nothing more than stand in the shadows and continue to stare.

The thought struck her: he was beautiful, in a pagan sort of way. Like a sleek black panther, the kind she'd seen once in a traveling circus. Davis was as wild and dangerous as that animal, and just as compelling. She could not help but compare him to the young men of New Orleans. Here was no doting swain with milk-white skin, whose fondness for her was surpassed by his weakness for frilled shirts and Hessian boots. Davis needed no embellishments to his masculinity. He was, simply, a man, needing no more proof of it than the beard stubble across his squared jaw and the stance that provoked her heart to quiver like the whip-thin limbs of the willow at her back.

But, dear God, he was only a man, and there had been men aplenty in her life. Some for whom she'd felt a slight infatuation. But this man, with his haunted and haunting eyes, she would never forget. Even as she turned and fled into the darkness, back to the house, she knew she would never forget.

Chapter 4

The fiesta was in full swing by the time Rachel returned to the hacienda. Tables laden with exotic-looking foods lined the walks. Servants dressed in festive costumes dodged among the revelers, balancing upon their upturned palms gleaming trays of polished silver that reflected the orange glow of lanterns placed about the trees.

A crowd had gathered about the strolling guitarist. His hands and fingers moved at an incredible rate over the instrument, filling the night air with sounds that made the onlookers clap their hands with the rhythm, then applaud as the red-haired woman Rachel had seen earlier in San Antonio began to tap her heels and sing at the top of her voice.

Backing away from the crowd, Rachel wandered about the gardens, doing her best to put the image of Davis out of her mind.

"Ah! There you are, Miss Gregory. I had almost given up hope of seeing you tonight."

Rachel looked up as Ramon emerged from the crowd. He was such a handsome young man. For a moment she wished he were older. Then perhaps . . .

"Are you enjoying the music?" he asked her.

"It's wonderful, Ramon." She allowed him her brightest smile as he took up her hand and kissed it.

"I suppose my mother spoke with you?"

She nodded.

"Ah. That explains it then."

"Explains what?"

"Your being here, of course. I suppose it was too much to

hope that you had ventured from the dreary seclusion of your wagon to see me?"

She watched as Ramon arched one black brow and looked down at her. He *was* handsome, his olive skin lightly bronzed by the sun and his hair a cloud of black curls that lay loose and lightly wind-tossed over his brow.

"Never mind," he said. "No doubt my mother has spoiled any attempts I might make to seduce you by revealing my plans to attend Harvard in a few weeks. No young lady in her right mind would be swayed by a swain who had every intention of walking out of her life in a few weeks."

"I'm afraid so," she responded.

"Dash it all! And I had such hopes, too." He glanced at her again, his green eyes twinkling with mirth and mischief. "I see I should have a talk with the dear lady before she ruins my reputation completely. I fancy I'll spend the rest of my days in San Antonio in monkish isolation if she continues boasting of my accomplishment."

Rachel laughed. "Oh, I think it's not so bad as that."

"That is easy for you to say. You've not the reputation of a roué to uphold."

"No, I daresay I don't."

"It's my father's fault, you see," he continued. Easily sweeping her around in his arms, he took her right hand in his. Gracefully falling into the easy rhythm of the serenade, he spun her across the ground while she grew dizzier with the effects of wine. "You see, my father was well known among the ladies for his savoir faire. Yes, indeed, he was quite the rascal."

Thinking of Alejandro de Bastitas, Rachel responded, "Oh, I would definitely imagine he was . . . and is!"

"Good Lord, not you too?" He feigned exasperation as she laughed. "What *is* it about that man that the ladies from here to New Orleans find so appealing?"

"He's so tall!"

"*I* am tall."

"He's so handsome!"

"*I* am handsome." A smile quirked his lips. "Shall we continue?"

Thinking harder, Rachel then leaned slightly back in his arms and said, "I know! It's his blue eyes!"

"Ah, there you have me. There must be something about men with blue eyes. I have often cursed the fate that gave me my mother's green eyes as opposed to my father's blue. In fact, all of his sons were born with green or brown eyes— all but my oldest brother, that is. Tomas had blue eyes, I understand. Bluer than my father's, I'm told, though I cannot imagine eyes bluer than his." Tilting his head, he ventured more seriously, "I suppose you've already heard the story of my brother."

Rachel frowned at him. "You don't seem very sympathetic, Señor de Bastitas."

"On the contrary, my dear. We have all been most sympathetic. But there comes a time when one must face reality and go on with life, accept that which cannot be changed—"

"Odd words coming from a future barrister." She felt the pressure of his hand on her hip intensify. But only slightly. The hand gently cradling hers seemed suddenly warmer.

"Rachel!" It was Angelique.

Ramon turned toward his mother, and Rachel smiled as the woman glided toward them, her voluminous red and black taffeta skirts nearly sweeping the ground. Ramon dropped a perfunctory kiss on her cheek as she joined them.

"I trust my niece is better?" he asked her.

"Oh, certainly. Too much pan dulce and chocolate, I think." Catching Rachel's hand, she said, "You look stunning, Rachel. Has my son kept you entertained?"

"Of course he has," Ramon responded for her. "If I have learned anything from my father, it's never to leave the most beautiful woman at the fiesta unattended." Then he said, "He did not, however, teach me what to do with one who was not only beautiful but also exceedingly gifted with . . . brains." Smiling down into Rachel's flushed face, he added, "What a refreshing change."

Within the course of the next hour, Rachel learned that the red-haired woman who'd exited the mercantile store like a banshee was, in fact, Angelique's half sister. There were two of them, it seemed, both with red hair and freckles, who towered a half head over her. Rachel surmised that they were in their late twenties. Neither was married.

She also met Estaban's young wife, the frail, soft-spoken Maria, who doted on her husband and cowered each time Alejandro de Bastitas opened his mouth. Rachel sensed that the man was very close to losing his patience with Maria as she jumped and giggled and blushed her way through the serving of the food and the pouring of the wine.

At one point during the festivities Rachel was taken into the home by Angelique and Ramon. It was clean and airy, with tiled floors and white walls. She was led through the foyer and into a parlor of sorts. In the shadows of the room sat a Negro woman, so old and feeble Rachel thought she must surely be a hundred. She sat in a rocker, a willow twig in her mouth and her white hair pulled into a knot atop her head.

Smiling, Angelique bent low and kissed the woman on her forehead. "Dear Bernice, I have someone I want you to meet."

Bernice's button-black eyes turned up to Rachel's. "Come here, girl, and let me see you." With prompting from Ramon, Rachel did as she was told. "Now ain't you like an angel all in white. Um hm, I tole 'em you was comin' but dey say I is old and silly and should go back to sleep."

"We did no such thing," Angelique responded. "And I'm certain Ramon would never have said you were silly."

"Didn't say it was Ramon. It was yo' husband what called me old and silly! He say I is decrepit and should be put out to pasture wid his old goats. Um hm, he say dat jess dis afternoon when I tole him my dream."

Looking at Rachel slightly askance, Ramon winked and said, "Since the Holy Mary appeared to Bernice in the Room of the Blessed Virgin some years ago she has been gifted with the sight."

The twig in Bernice's mouth bobbed up and down.

Rachel, bending at the waist, propped her palms against her knees and peered into the woman's black, watchful eyes. "Do you have dreams, Bernice?" she asked. "I believe in dreams myself. I dreamed my mother died, and she did. I dreamed my father died, and he did. People laughed at me too, when I told them. What did you dream?"

"Dat Tomas come home."

A heartbeat passed before Rachel could force herself to look back at Angelique, then Ramon. Mother and son touched each other briefly with their eyes. His hand lifted and lightly brushed his mother's arm so compassionately that Rachel felt tears well behind her lids.

Bernice continued to rock, her toes tapping lightly against the slate floor as she stared now into space. "Tomas done arose from the ashes wid de help of an angel in white. I seen it all outside my window. I seen him, I tell you, dis very afternoon."

"I wouldn't," Ramon stated very slowly, "allow my father to hear you talk in such a way."

"Dat man is as stubborn as his grandpappy was! Um hm. I tole him too. I pointed out dat window and tole him what I seen."

"I'm certain he was thrilled," Ramon commented dryly.

"Ach! He looked at me wid them damn blue eyes and tole me to go to blazes. I tole him I was but I was aimin' to take him wid me. He is gittin' old too and is about as likely to drop dead as I is. Come 'ere, girl." She crooked an arthritic finger at Rachel, and Rachel bent close. "Dey think I'm an old fool and maybe I is. But I brought dat child into dis world, in dis very house, and I would know if he be dead."

"Mother, I think you have guests to see to," Ramon interrupted.

"Don't be impudent, Ramon," Angelique admonished. "You sound more like your father every day. When will you both let me alone and stop trying to tiptoe around the issue of Tomas? I am perfectly capable of discussing him without hysterics and have been for some years now."

His handsome lips thinning, Ramon scowled at the ceiling and said, "As long as you continue to listen to such nonsense as this, and to believe it, you will never forget him."

Angelique's head came up, and her green eyes flashed.

Rachel cleared her throat, suspecting that, caught up in their emotions, they had forgotten her presence. Then in the same moment, they all became aware of another presence in the room.

Captain Wells stood in the door, his hat under one arm, his free hand resting lightly on the pearl butt of his revolver. "Beggin' yore pardon," he said with a smile.

Angelique hurried to his side. "You look concerned, Sam. Has something happened?"

"Nah, Miss Angie, but it occurred to me that my friends in the lockup ain't et yet. Would ya be opposed to maybe dishin' out some of that fine braised goat and maybe some of Teresa's pan dulce to the rascals? If they're left starvin' they're likely to turn on one another."

Ramon moved toward the door. "I'll see to it, Mother."

"Certainly not. You'll see to our guests. I'll have Teresa make up a tray and—"

"I'll help." Rachel started for the door, bringing Ramon up short and Angelique around in surprise.

"But that's not necessary," Angelique said. "You're a guest—"

"But I insist." Sweeping by her hosts, Rachel stood in the foyer, the image of Davis standing at that window looming in her mind. After a moment she noticed the captain watching her, his brown eyes intense but his lips, hidden mostly behind a gray thatch of beard, quirked a little in amusement.

"I'll join ya directly," he announced as Rachel, with her hosts, moved down the hall. "Deputies Hale and Rogers will give ya a hand with that food. And much appreciation, Miss Angie!"

Rachel glanced at him again over her shoulder.

Sam smiled back.

Ramon watched one of the sleepy-eyed deputies fumble

with the key of the lockup before turning to face his mother. "Your husband will not be fit to live with when he learns what you've been about. And you," he said to Rachel, "have no business here at all."

"You have your father's manners, Ramon. Now stand aside before I drop this tray of food on your foot. Since the help are serving our guests, we could not spare them even for a moment. So unless you wish to stand here for the rest of the evening you will stop trying to threaten me with Alejandro's reactions to my behavior. He does not frighten me, nor do you. Now out of my way so we can complete this task for Sam and get back to the festivities." Angelique smiled sweetly but firmly at Ramon as he lifted one lazy black brow in response.

Rachel stood in the shadows, listening intently to the boisterous laughter of the men inside the room. The door swung open then, flooding the ground at her feet with hazy yellow light. Shadows moved back and forth across the doorway as the deputies ordered their charges against the farthest wall. The deputies entered first, then Ramon, Angelique, and finally Rachel. The glasses on her tray rattled noticeably. She took a long breath, attempting to soothe her nerves.

"All right, you buncha no-accounts, shape up. You're in the presence of ladies." The wiriest of the two deputies pointed a rifle barrel toward a dark-skinned man in a plaid shirt and said, "Pedro, if you so much as look cross-eyed at these women I'll shoot you."

Ramon stepped aside, but not without reluctance.

Rachel didn't need to look to know Davis was there. He stood in the corner, the chain between his wrists glittering in the half-light. When she did finally force herself to look at him directly she found him staring at Clyde. There was sweat running down his temples and his dark eyes reflected a look of unease.

Deputy Hale placed his rifle by the door, well away from the prisoners, and handed each of the men a tin plate. From Angelique's tray he served Pedro a slab of meat, topped it with chilies, then slapped a tortilla on it. He then moved to the next man.

Rachel glanced back at Davis. He was still watching Clyde. Clyde watched Angelique, his pale eyes shifting from the tray of food back to her face. He leaned casually against the wall, holding his plate up against his filthy shirtfront, the same smile that had repulsed her that morning now coiling one end of his mouth.

From the corner of her eye Rachel saw Davis move. He moved so swiftly there was little time to respond. As Angelique stepped before Clyde, Davis jumped between them, knocking the tray of food to the floor while making what appeared to be a halfhearted grab for Angelique's wrist. It sent her twirling toward the floor. As she stumbled backward, her tray of glasses and water shattered onto the floor, and Rachel cried out. Ramon did his best to shield both her and his mother from the ensuing tussle between Clyde, Davis, and the deputies who were scrambling for control of the suddenly combustible situation.

A gunshot brought a complete halt to the madness. Plaster sprinkled onto heads and shoulders as Sam redirected his rifle from the ceiling toward Davis and Clyde. "Give me a reason," he dared the men in so deadly a tone they all stopped breathing.

Then they all noticed the bloody knife at Davis's feet. The deputy who had been passing out the food kicked it toward Sam.

It was Ramon who moved then. Springing from the floor, he jumped at Davis, who still, oddly, was facing Clyde. Angelique made a grab for her son's arm, but it did little good as he twisted the fingers of both hands into Davis's shirt and spun him around.

"Ramon, no!" Angelique struggled to her knees as her son drove his fist into Davis's ribs, once, then twice.

"Bastard!" he ground between his teeth, then hit him again, bending Davis over double and driving him back into the corner. "Son-of-a-dog, have you no compassion for women? Perhaps I will teach you!"

Frozen in her place, Rachel could only stare and wonder in stunned dismay where the blood was coming from. It was everywhere, but mostly over Ramon. His cuff and the white shirt across his breast were spotted with it, and his hand, the one he continually drove into Davis's ribs, was slickly red.

Angelique's cries for her son to stop brutalizing Davis seemed to come from a great distance. *Everything* seemed unreal to Rachel, as if she were watching a play being enacted before a spellbound, horrified audience. No more than seconds passed before Sam grabbed Ramon's collar and hauled him off Davis, but it seemed an eternity. Each impact on the man's body was crucifyingly loud. The smell of the blood was nauseatingly pungent in the hot, confined quarters.

It was Angelique's sudden exclamation that brought Ramon to his senses and Rachel out of her shock. Her hair tumbling now across her shoulders, *la doña* of Rancho de Bejar was crawling on her knees toward Davis. "Dear God, oh, dear God. Tomas! Sam, it's my son."

Davis was crouching in the corner, his elbows tucked into his ribs as if for protection. Pale and sweating, he stared unemotionally into Angelique's face and said nothing. Nor did he move as she cautiously touched his cheek with her trembling fingers.

"Oh God, don't you know me? Tomas, I'm your mother."

"Davis." His voice was cold. "My name is Davis."

"No! I don't believe you." She turned her pleading eyes up to Ramon. "I would know my own flesh and blood!"

Ramon grabbed his mother and dragged her away from Davis. She fought him. "Stop it! Take your hands off me or I will never forgive you!"

"Mother, please!" Out of desperation Ramon wrapped his long arm around Angelique's waist and hefted her from the floor. He then looked forlornly at Rachel, wanting to help her as well, but unable to.

Frozen in place, Rachel stared at Davis, noting his eyes had not shifted from Angelique's face even for a moment. Dear God, but she *could* see the resemblance herself now:

the eyes, the hair, the stature. Indeed, she could be seeing Alejandro de Bastitas as he might have looked thirty years ago!

Angelique's weeping brought Rachel to her senses. Gathering her frayed wits about her, Rachel climbed to her feet, scattering bits of glass across the floor. Her knees were weak. A lump was swelling in her throat that, no matter how she tried, she could not swallow back. Certainly the notion that this brute could be the offspring of such gentle, refined people as the Bastitases was absurd. After all, *he* had done this. Davis! He was vicious and brutal and . . . He looked at Rachel directly now. She met his insolent eyes with her own and sneered, "Animal. They should have killed you." Spinning around, she followed Ramon de Bastitas and his mother out the door.

Alejandro de Bastitas burst through the bedroom door with the force of a storm. His face dark and his blue eyes snapping like fire, he thundered, "What the hell is going on here? Well?" Ramon was hardly out of his chair before Alex bellowed, "Since when can't you speak, barrister? I have asked you a question!"

Angelique, twisting her hankie in her hands, was against her husband before Ramon could open his mouth. "Our son is in that lockup, Alejandro. It is Tomas! I know it is!"

He looked at Ramon. "What is this all about?"

"I can speak for myself!" Angelique insisted.

Clearing his throat, Ramon said, "There was a little trouble at the lockup—"

"I know that! I want to know why you allowed your mother to go down there!"

"Leave the room, Ramon!" Angelique pointed toward the door. "Just get out!"

"Stay where you are, Ramon!"

"*Dios mio.*" Ramon rolled his eyes.

"Was Miss Gregory injured?"

"No, *mi padre. La señorita* is fine."

"Thank God for that." Pinning Angelique with his eyes, Alex continued, "As for you—"

"Haven't you heard a word I've said, Alejandro?" Grabbing the lapels of his *charro* jacket, she pleaded, "The man in that lockup is—"

"Not our son! Dammit, Angel, we've been through this time and again!"

"But—"

"It's that old woman's fault, filling your head with silly dreams that mean nothing. Nothing!" His fingers digging into her shoulders, he shook her with uncharacteristic roughness. "Tomas is dead, Angelique. They took him and killed him twenty-five years ago!"

They stood in stunned silence until, behind them, the door closed with a quiet click. They were alone.

Her voice, when it came, was a whisper of pain. "You don't believe that."

"I've spoken to the deputies and they say the man in the lockup is a murderer named Davis. They are taking him to El Paso to hang, Angel. Would it not stand to reason that if he *were* our son, he would admit it? That he would do everything in his power to get us to acknowledge him so that he might avoid the noose?"

"Perhaps he doesn't know, he doesn't remember. He was just a child—"

"Exactly. There is no possible way you could now stand before a total stranger and say with total certainty that he is our son."

The tears were coming now, spilling hotly down her cheeks. "Oh God, Alexander, if you would only see him. He is *you*, my husband. Your very likeness. The same man I saw when I walked onto that patio thirty-one years ago, so handsome and tall and dark. His eyes, oh, his eyes, Alexander. His hair, his chin . . . . Please do me this one last favor and—"

"My son would not be a murderer, Angelique!" He spun away, raking his fingers through his black hair.

"Is that what your defiance is about? Your damn stubborn

Bastitas pride will not allow you to believe your sons could be anything but perfect?"

"Enough."

"May I remind you of your own past, my dearest *patron*? Need I remind you that my own father died by *your* hand?"

His body tensed. "Angel . . . don't."

Realizing what she'd said, Angelique stared at her hands. She had promised her husband long ago that the horrible affair with her father was forgiven and forgotten. Alejandro had had every reason to duel Reginald DuHon. DuHon and Alejandro's first wife, Pamela Bastitas, had been caught in bed together. It was no senseless murder, but a duel that had driven Alejandro to pull the trigger that sent Angelique's father to the grave and her mother into a life of bitterness and vengeance. But by all accounts this Davis *was* a murderer, a cold-blooded killer who had killed several innocent men in a cantina brawl.

His voice husky, his back to her, Alejandro said, "Angel, sometimes I feel that you think I don't care a whit for my son. You know I do. I followed every lead, every rumor. I unearthed so many graves and stared at so many corpses over those years that I . . ." He took a breath, or tried to. "We have managed to put the loss from our minds these many years. Let's not open up old wounds again. Let Tomas rest in peace."

"You are asking me to bury his memory."

"I'm not." He turned to face her. "I am asking you not to open old heartaches. I am asking you to finally bury the fantasy that Tomas is alive. I'm not a young man any longer, Angel. I'm not certain I can face the disappointment again. . . ." He closed his eyes, and the tears ran down his face.

"Oh!" Angelique ran to her husband, swept the wetness of his tears away with her fingertips, and tenderly touched the lightly graying hair at his temples. "I'm sorry," she told him, her own voice quivering as she searched his troubled blue eyes. "Of course I know you miss Tomas. I never doubted it for a moment. But I carried his body and soul in my womb for nine months and nourished him from my own breast. He was taken from me long before I was ready to give him up. I have no way of really knowing if he is dead. If I had, then perhaps I could cut this bond that continues to hold me to him. If he is alive—"

"Then wish him happiness." Alex took her small face in his hands and did his best to smile. "Hope that wherever he is he is well and prosperous, that occasionally he vaguely remembers a mother and father who loved him, and love him still."

"I have tried, my husband. But the man in that lockup—"

"I will look in on him, Angel, I promise. But even if the man looks as much like me as you say, we have no proof . . . and we cannot open our home to him unless he accepts us, too. You must try not to jump to conclusions, for the sake of your sons who love you, and your granddaughter and the grandchildren to come. Let us continue to live in peace as we have these last years."

Her heart was breaking, but she responded nevertheless, "I will do my best."

He kissed her gently, his long fingers burying themselves in the red-gold curls that spilled around her youthful face. And as always, the kiss had its desired effect, turning her knees to water and her heart into a drowning thing that left her swimming in desire . . . and surrender.

She swooned against him. He pulled away and teased, "We have guests, don't forget."

His smile was roguish and wicked. He could still make her blush after all these years. "I hope Ramon is seeing to Rachel. I fear her dress was ruined during the fracas."

"So he'll buy her another." He kissed her again while gently tugging the mantilla from her hair.

"She's a very lovely girl."

"Um."

Angelique gasped as he nipped at her ear. "She reminds me of myself at that age."

"Really? I didn't notice she was conceited or pigheaded."

"She could be the daughter I wanted but never had."

"You want a daughter still?" He breathed slightly into her ear, then said, "We can work at it."

"Oh well, I'm a little old to be having . . . babies."

"But not to *work* at it."

"We have guests," she reminded him.

"Forget 'em."

A sharp knock at the door interrupted them. Alex scowled, tweaked Angelique on the nose, and growled, "If it's Ramon again I'll strangle him."

Sam Wells dipped his head apologetically as Alex jerked open the door. The old Ranger smiled and said, "Hope I ain't intrudin'."

"What gives you the idea that just because a man and woman are locked up in their bedroom you might be intruding?"

"Well, at yore age, Bastitas, I guess nothin'." He gave Angelique a perfunctory bow and continued, "I wanted to check on yore well-bein', Miss Angie, and apologize fer things gettin' out of hand. Some sidewinders've got fair to middlin' good sense, but I see this bunch don't. I did want to say that I don't believe Clyde Lindsey was attemptin' to wound ya with that knife, ma'am, but had ever' intention of jumpin' my deputy."

In the process of folding her mantilla, Angelique paused and looked at her old friend in surprise. "It was Mr. Lindsey who made the attack? I thought it was Davis."

"Why, no, ma'am. I know that's how it looked, as if Davis had suddenly got a bee in his breeches and jumped. It was Lindsey what got the knife from somewheres. Davis seen what he was about to do and was attempting to get you out of the way before he done it."

"But the blood—"

"He took the blade himself, Miss Angie. Slid into his side like a knife through hot butter."

Forgotten, the lace floated to Angelique's feet. "He . . . he's all right?"

"Yes'm. Jest a flesh wound. He'll be sore fer a couple of days, but I reckon he's been through worse." Turning his back to Alex, he said, "Sorry fer intrudin'. We'll see ya at dawn, *amigo*?"

Alex nodded, waited as Sam disappeared around the corner, then slowly closed the door and faced his wife. Her smooth face was pale, her green eyes bright with hope. "Don't," he demanded in a tight voice. "Angel, don't."

"Very odd behavior for a cold-blooded killer," she said.

Sagging against the door, Alejandro closed his eyes.

Rachel stared at the bundle in her arms, and though she tried very hard to force back her tears, they gathered in her lashes. Burying her face in the stained, muddied folds of her skirts, she wept as silently as possible, knowing that though she pretended her sorrow was over the spoiled dress, it was more than that. It seemed every time she turned around her life was filled with turmoil: first her stepmother, then the War and the loss of her father and home. Now there was Davis, a man who made her insides feel queer and muddled up her reasoning. A man who could somehow make her forget his notorious past just by turning his blue eyes on her.

"Miss Gregory, are you all right?" came Ramon's voice, full of concern, from outside the wagon.

"I'm fine," she lied. Blinking away the nagging image of Davis, Rachel pressed the heels of her palms into her eyes. Gulping a mouthful of air, she quickly smeared the tears haphazardly over her cheeks, then threw back the canvas flap. Ramon stared at her through the moonlight. "This is really not necessary," she told him as he extended both arms for the dress.

"Certainly it is. My mother will have the dress cleaned and brought to your uncle's."

"You shouldn't. I'll probably never have any reason to wear it again. I don't imagine there will be many soirées on a ranch."

"You never know," he told her. Tucking the dress beneath his arm, he looked back toward the house, his brow lined with worry and his mouth, not yet mature enough to be totally sensual, pressing into a taut, flat line. "I do wish she would give up this foolish notion that the man in that lockup is my brother," he finally said. When Rachel offered no response, he sighed into the darkness and shook his head. "I know losing Tomas as she did was a terrible ordeal for her—"

"Then you must try to understand."

"But twenty-five years is a long time to hold on to the fantasy that my brother is still alive."

Thinking again of Davis's resemblance to Alejandro, Rachel argued, "Perhaps it isn't a fantasy. Perhaps Bernice is right. Perhaps Tomas is still alive. After all, what proof do you have that he is dead? According to your mother there were possible sightings of Tomas by travelers—"

"Oh, for the love of God, not you too. Perhaps it's just as well that you're moving on. With any more encouragement that old woman will have my mother off on horseback searching out the Llano Estacado." Leaning against the wagon, he folded his arms over his chest and stared at the ground. "This isn't the first time this sort of thing has happened—I mean her believing she's found Tomas. It happened with embarrassing regularity during the first ten years after his abduction, I understand. Any child vaguely resembling Tomas was almost snatched from his mother's arms. In this part of the country you can understand how that was happening with humiliating frequency."

"But if he *is* alive—"

"Then let him stay where he is. He'll be happier there." Quirking one brow, he looked down into Rachel's stunned face. "You see, even if he did return he would be a stranger to us. And he would be permanently scarred—if not physically, then emotionally. As tragic as it seems, many returned captives often end up taking their own lives. One would think they would be glad to be free, but once they are, they find themselves outsiders, looked upon as if they were freaks in a sideshow. You see, they become accustomed to heathenish ways of life. Have you ever heard of Cynthia Parker?"

Rachel shook her head no.

"She was abducted when she was a child, only a few years

older than my brother. She was taken by the Quahadis, and later became a wife of Peta Nocona, chief of the Noconi band of Comanches. She bore him children and lived with them for twenty-five years. Back in sixty a group of Rangers came upon a number of the savages. During the melee they discovered Cynthia Parker, and returned her to her family. She could no longer speak English, and answered only to the name Naduah. Though her family took her back and did everything they could for her, she tried to escape and was forced to live under guard. After her daughter died she mutilated her own body, then starved herself to death."

"How very tragic."

"Yes. Now can you understand why my father is so reluctant to continue to search for Tomas? If he is still alive, he is likely a savage by now. The entire affair could only hurt us all." Ramon looked down on Rachel's head. She was staring at her hands. Had she looked up at that moment he might have dropped a kiss on her mouth. She didn't, so with a sigh, he moved up the darkened path, stopping only as her soft voice came hesitantly through the rising night breeze.

"What if . . ."

He turned and stared at her through the shadows.

She lifted her face. Her eyes were wide and troubled. "What if Tomas somehow escaped the Indians and made himself some sort of respectable life? What if he is out there somewhere, wanting to come home but afraid, afraid that you will *think* of him as a savage . . . when he's not. What if . . . the man in that lockup is really your brother?"

There was silence before he replied, "Then, *señorita*, we have all made a grave mistake."

Chapter 5

Alejandro stood by the window, listening as the door closed behind him. He waited, and shortly he watched his wife hurry from the house and down the pebble-paved walk toward the caravan of wagons stretched outside the hacienda's barricades. She might have been a girl again, with her hair tumbling down her back in waves. With the dawn's light filtering through the trees and onto her shoulders, her hair was like a beautiful curtain of fire he ached even now to stroke.

She was still trim, though not nearly so thin as she was when they'd first met. Age and pregnancies had added a subtle roundness to her hips and breasts. The craggy white lines that had shown up on her stomach during her confinement with Rafael, their second son, had been an embarrassment to her. "They add character," he'd teased her. She'd laughed and blushed and wept that she loved him.

Ah, God, but he loved her too.

Closing his eyes, he prayed for the strength to see him through the ordeal of hope, and the inevitable disappointment he knew would follow. Throughout the previous night and the early hours of morning he'd told himself again to leave it alone. The man in that lockup, destined to die by hanging, could not be his son. But he'd promised Angelique, this one last time—and there was that one buried spark of hope in his own chest . . .

Turning from the window, he swept up the jacket from the floor, where he'd discarded it the night before, and shrugged it onto his shoulders. Walking purposefully, he left the room, pleased that the nagging ache that left him limping on occasion was absent that morning. Sometimes he welcomed the pain, mostly when remembering the brother who had died in his place at the Alamo. If it hadn't been for his grandfather's callousness, Alex knew he would have been one of those unfortunate casualties of General Santa Anna. Carlos de Bastitas's loyalty to his beloved dictator had saved one grandson's life and sacrificed another.

He heard his granddaughter cry somewhere down the corridor to his right. Slowing, he listened, heard Estaban laugh and the child suddenly squeal a delighted response. He saw Ramon dash across the foyer and out the front door; he was in a hurry to see the girl, Alejandro supposed. He passed Rafael's room and slowed again. The door was open. Teresa was busily dusting the furniture, smoothing her broad brown hand over the patchwork coverlet on his bed and humming to herself. She looked up, flashed him a white smile, and said:

"Buenos días, Don Alejandro! We will have the room ready when Señor Rafael comes home, *sí?"*

"Sí," he responded, and continued walking. *When* he comes home, he thought, *if* he comes home. His son was somewhere in California, or China, perhaps. On his twenty-first birthday Rafael had announced that he wasn't destined to raise cows. Then he'd kissed his mother goodbye and sauntered out the door. Now Ramon would soon be leaving. And Estaban had talked of buying land in East Texas with hopes of trying his hand at farming.

Alex stopped at the head of the stairs, his eyes scanning the rich but simple decor of his home. What in God's name was he supposed to do with an empty house? What would Angelique do? He had thirty-five thousand acres and a home most people would be proud of, but his sons wanted something of their own. "Times are changing," Ramon had announced in that hoity-toity air of his one morning over breakfast. "I might take up practice in Boston, or perhaps New York City."

"We don't need lawyers in Texas?" Alex had thundered back loud enough to rattle the crystal. Ramon had arched one black brow and rolled his eyes.

"Snob," Alex muttered to himself now.

There was little breeze as Alex stopped outside the house, his hands in his pockets. The air was heavy with fragrance. To his left, stretching at least one hundred and fifty feet, was a bed bursting with bourbon roses: the acidalie with their white blooms tinged with rose, the Baronne Genella's lilac pink, and the flesh white of the Marguerite Bonnet. Beyond that was the brilliant carmine of the Reverend H. Dombrain. He knew them all by name, by heart. Angelique had thrown herself into the task of raising the flowers after Tomas was taken. He'd lounged in the wrought-iron chair beneath the willow and watched as she dug and planted and babied and watered the bushes. Pregnant with Rafael, she'd waddled around and under the flourishing plants, refusing his help, until she'd been forced into her bed for birth. She'd sworn then that she would someday cross two roses and come up with a new variety she could name after Tomas.

He moved automatically down the path, the dread mounting miserably in his chest. For a moment it became so intense that he had to stop and wait for the dull pain beneath his ribs to subside so he could breathe again.

Sam stood by the horses, scratching his head wearily as his deputies walked toward the lockup. "Mornin'," the Ranger greeted him without turning. "I figured you'd be by sooner or later."

Alex stared at the ground and swore softly to himself. Finally, he asked, "What more do you know about Davis?"

"Not much."

Throwing the keys back to Sam, Rogers shoved open the lockup door.

"Where's he from?" Alex asked.

"Drifter's my understandin'."

Pedro was the first out the door. Alex threw him a glance, then looked back at Sam.

"What's this Davis look like?"

Sam shifted his eyes up to Alex's. "He's tall, I reckon. 'Bout like you."

"There are a lot of tall men."

A blond man stepped out of the lockup. He blinked at the sun and followed Pedro to the horses. Alex gave him only a second's notice.

"He's dark," Sam continued. "Like you."

"There are a million people in Texas and Mexico combined who could fit *that* description."

Clyde exited then. He sneered toward Sam and spat a wad of tobacco on the ground.

Sam grumbled and slapped his hat against his knee. Looking back at Alex, he said, "I'll see to the men," and walked off.

The sun, having risen a fraction over the roof of the adobe building, blinded Alex as he looked again toward the door. There stood a figure, black and broad-shouldered. Alex was forced to shield the brilliant white light from his eyes with his hand to better see him.

He did not breathe for a moment. Neither did he blink.

Davis stepped from the door, his face down and obscured by his hat. When he looked up, Alejandro lost his breath.

Their blue eyes met, held. Without realizing he was moving, Alex walked slowly toward him. Face to face with Davis he waited, consciously noting their identical height, the hair, the mouth. The silence was almost tangible about them, as mounting as the heat that beat onto their shoulders, as pulsating as the whirring of insects from the foothills beyond the distant stables. Alex opened his mouth, and nothing came. He clenched his fists and fought the overwhelming urge to take the man's face in his hands and plead for a sign, a hint that the nightmare of the last twenty-five years was over. It was too coincidental that this man so favored him — even more so that his other sons, who each had inherited some of Angelique's features. Yet . . . the man said nothing. Just returned his stare, unblinking, unmoved. Surely Tomas would know him. Surely there would be one tiny spark of memory buried somewhere in his mind of this home and the parents who loved him.

Panic flooded him as Davis turned away. Staring at his back, he called out, "Tomas!"

Davis hesitated.

Alex repeated, "Tomas!" and slowly the man turned. Once again their gazes met.

"The name's Davis," came his unemotional response. "Kid Davis." Then Davis turned back for his horse.

Rachel stared into Angelique's wan face, into the green eyes that were a little dull and red-rimmed for so early in the day. "I don't think I understand," she said. Really she *had* understood, but was certain there had been some error on Captain Wells's part. "You're saying Davis wasn't instigator of that escape attempt, and that he actually refrained Mr. Lindsey from harming us?"

Ramon, standing at his mother's side, shrugged one shoulder. "I suppose I owe the man an apology."

"You certainly do," Angelique said.

Just then, the group of outlaws rounded the corner of the barrier. The busy milling of the travelers died to silence as they waited and watched, uneasy with the men's presence. Clyde came first. Davis was last. They walked directly past Rachel's wagon while she stared at her feet and prayed Davis wouldn't notice her. In light of Angelique's information she felt horribly ashamed of herself. Regardless of a man's position in life, she had been brought up to show utmost respect for his feelings. She had maligned Davis viciously the night before, calling him an animal and wishing him dead.

Angelique also avoided looking his way. She turned her back on him completely, though Rachel sensed it wasn't an easy task. She clung to Ramon's arm, stared at the ground, the sky, the trees. Yet the tears came, spilling down her face. Stepping forward, Rachel grabbed her hands.

"What is he doing?" Angelique asked.

She forced herself to look. "Nothing. Just . . ." He was checking his saddle. "Nothing."

"Ramon, you must find your father. He was going to talk to Mr. Davis—"

"If Father thought the man was Tomas, he would say so."

Rachel frowned. Men! They had no thoughts in their heads about women's emotions.

"Mou-unnt up!" Homer George called out.

Audra poked her head out the rear wagon flap and blinked sleepily at the threesome. "What's all the commotion about?" she asked crossly.

"We're pulling out." Rachel glanced again toward Davis. He moved a little stiffly around his horse, and for the first time she noticed the dark stain on his shirt that extended from his back around to his ribs. A tiny flap of material gaped above his breeches where the knife had cut him.

Forcing her eyes back to Angelique and Ramon, she attempted her brightest smile and said, "I hope you'll write."

"We certainly will," Ramon responded. "When I've settled at Harvard I'll drop you a line and tell you all about it." He then kissed her tenderly on her cheek.

Alex de Bastitas walked out of the hacienda and stood looking for his wife.

Noticing Angelique looked pale and more than a little distraught, Rachel suggested, "Perhaps you'd better see your mother to the house, Ramon. The shock has been too much for her, I think."

Turning her white face up to Ramon, Angelique said, "Perhaps if I speak with Mr. Davis—"

"You'll do no such thing. Father will not allow it. Neither will I." Looking sideways at Rachel, he pleaded, "My apologies?" Taking his mother by the shoulders, he hurried her toward Alejandro, who took long strides across the garden to join them.

*   *   *

Davis mounted his horse, watching the Bastitases gather inside Rancho de Bejar's barricaded gardens. Then Sam rode up.

"Them is mighty fine folk there," Sam said. "Yep, they's good people. Man able to call himself a Bastitas could feel real proud."

"What's your point?" Davis snapped. He focused on the red-haired woman who, by now, was weeping against her husband's shoulder. When Sam didn't respond, he looked around into the old man's face.

"Ain't got no point, boy. Jest statin' my thoughts and feelin' a little poorly for Miss Angie and Alex. They loved that boy of theirs. And that's understandable. He was their firstborn."

Shifting in his saddle, Davis glanced back at Alex.

"Yore lookin' a tad pale, boy," came Sam's voice. "And this ain't the first time you've turned that shade of pea green since we met up. Like yesterday jest after I mentioned the Bastitas fiesta. What neck of the woods did ya say you were from?"

"I didn't." He swallowed.

"Course I reckon you'd know if'n that were yore ma and pa—"

Sweat beaded Davis's brow. Twisting his fingers into his horse's mane, he turned his horse slightly toward Sam, away from the Bastitases, and closed his eyes.

Sam maneuvered his horse closer to Davis. "Yore lookin' a little peaked, boy. I 'spect all the commotion last night and this heat is what done it," Sam speculated kindly.

"Right."

Homer George called out again, "Stretch out!"

Davis took a deep breath, turned his horse toward Clyde, and refused to look back at the Bastitases again.

Clyde smirked and pointed toward Rachel as Davis joined him. "Purty little thing, ain't she?" Clyde chuckled before spitting a long stream of tobacco through his thin lips. "Purty enough fer me, I reckon."

He glanced at Rachel, noting her difficulty in mounting

the wagon. "Why don't you just shut up, Lindsey, and we'll get on a whole helluva lot better."

Leaning slightly over the pommel of his saddle, Clyde hissed to Davis's ears only, "If ya hadn't been so intent on playin' hero last night, we might have been clear to Mexico by now. Friggin' fool, ya must be awful eager to hang."

"Think again, Lindsey. We would never have made it off the ranch, and I'm not about to swing for killing a Ranger. Going to trial for shooting some half-wit who had the bad fortune of getting caught cheating at cards is one thing, but killing a lawman is another."

"Well, seeing as how I already done that, I ain't got much to lose. The way I hear it, neither do you. Them folks in El Paso wasn't the first men ya brung down. I heard that old man Wells talkin'. Yore wanted from California to Kansas fer a whole lot more'n jest murder. With yore reputation I can't believe you'd jest sashay up under some tree and offer yore neck fer stretchin'."

Davis looked away from Clyde's bulging gray eyes and again to Rachel. By now, despite her numerous skirts and petticoats, she had managed to mount the wagon and was in the process of putting on a hat adorned with what looked like huge red bird feathers. "I'm not much for sashaying anywhere," he replied absently. "Especially up to ropes."

"Well, we got about two weeks to do somethin' about it, *amigo*."

"We?" Davis looked back at Clyde and smiled so coldly the man sat upright on his horse. "I'm a loner, Lindsey. Always have been and always will be. When I decide to take a hike, I'll do it alone."

"Then you *are* plannin' somethin'!" He jutted his ugly face up to Davis's and sneered, "I told my boys you was too confident. What ya gonna do, Davis?"

"That's my business."

"Ya can't lose this bunch of Rangers alone. You'll need help."

"All I need is a gun."

"Humph. Ain't no gun good enough to take on two Rangers. Most ain't good enough to take on one."

Cutting his blue eyes back to Clyde, he said, "I'm not most."

The rattling of harnesses and yokes and bawling of oxen and mules filled the air as the drivers whistled and cracked their whips. The lawmen closed in then, their rifles resting across their laps.

"After you, gentlemen," Captain Wells called out. "Fall in behind this last wagon and behave yoreselves. First one what acts stupid is gonna git his butt shot by this here cannon on my hip, and that's a fact, by God!"

"I don't cotton to eatin' dirt, Captain!" Clyde called out. "Maybe I ought to jest ride up front of this wagon with Miss Gregory."

"Or in back!" Pedro joined in.

Wearing nothing but a very sheer chemise, Audra threw open the back flaps and secured them against the wagon. Her brown hair tumbled around her shoulders and over her breasts, which shimmied with each bump in the road.

"*Puta*," Clyde sneered to Davis. "She's got her eye on ya, Davis. For two *centavos* I figure she'd tumble ya quick enough. She might call herself a lady, but I've seen her kind."

"Not interested."

"Nah, I guess ya ain't. Ya got yore eye on the young one, for a fact. But I got news for you, *amigo*, she ain't yore kind. Or rather, you ain't her kind, even if ya wasn't shackled up in them chains."

Davis glanced down at the two-foot length of chain between his wrists.

"She's a lady. Man who crawls in her bed won't smell like a horse. He'll be educated and wealthy. Like that Bastitas *hombre* I seen kissin' her goodbye. Course a man like you, from what I hear, usually takes what he wants from a woman whether they want to give it or not."

An unwilling smile twitched one corner of his mouth. "Is that what you heard, Lindsey?"

"Ain't it so?"

Davis ignored the question and changed the subject. "You don't seem too overly concerned about hanging yourself, Lindscy."

"I ain't gonna hang. These bunch of fools ain't ever gonna get me or my men to Brackettville."

"You sound pretty sure of yourself."

"I got friends, both this side of the border and the other."

"Must be powerful friends."

"I've been loyal. They'll help me out. They have before. Got in a tangle in Matamoros last year, but got the charges dropped."

"Then your ties are government."

"Maybe . . . maybe not."

"The only man I know outside of the Mexican government with such clout is Juan Cortinas. And he hates *gringos*, Lindsey. I would not trust him too much if I were you."

Clyde's slit of a mouth curled under as he snapped, "He won't let me down." Realizing what he'd just confessed, he narrowed his eyes and said, "Think yore clever, don't ya, Davis? Well, I might be in cahoots with Cortinas, but I don't answer to him directly. A.J. Duncan is my boss. He's a powerful man in these parts and he won't let me swing. You'll see."

"I like your confidence, but confidence doesn't count for much when a man has to make a choice between his own reputation or someone else's. What makes your ugly hide so important that he'd sacrifice that to get it back?"

" 'Cause I'm good at what I do, Davis. I'm fast with a gun and I know cows. On a good night I can rustle up two dozen longhorn and have 'em across the border before sunup."

"So you steal cattle for Duncan and he sells them to Cortinas. I've heard about the Mexican's little liaison with Cuba."

"Cortinas is raisin' money for his own revolution against Texas."

Smiling, Davis said, "*You're* a Texan, *amigo*. Don't forget that."

*   *   *

The caravan plodded on, winding through the foothills. Rachel had realized just after the onset of the journey that Homer's prediction the day before had not been wrong. The horses Crowbait Jackson had sold them weren't fit for a team. She wondered if they were fit for anything. They constantly tried to nip and kick each other, attempted to pull in opposite directions, and did their best to buck off their harnesses. At one point they stopped, humped their backs, and kicked the tongue brace so hard that the front wheels of the wagon nearly left the ground. Rachel tumbled backward and Audra let out a scream and a stream of curses that brought Jeromia Peabody, the train's muleskinner, riding back to check on them.

"Shoulda got you some ox!" he called out. "Or some mules. Horses ain't no good fer pullin' wagons. You didn't, by chance, buy this scrappy bunch from a sidewinder named Crowbait Jackson, did you?" He then had the unmitigated audacity to lope alongside and sing:

I'll tell you how it is when
   You first get on the road;
You have an awkward team and
   A very heavy load.
You have to whip and holler, but
   Swear upon the sly.
You're in for it then, darlin'
   Just root hog, or die!

Rachel glared so furiously at him from behind her ruby-colored ostrich feather, he tipped his hat and rode off to the far end of the train.

Within an hour her entire dress was drenched in sweat. Her arms felt as if they were being lurched from her shoulder sockets. Her fingers were frozen around the lines and her hips were aching. Recalling Sam's instructions of "tight but not taut," she had the team constantly stopping and starting as she pulled and released the lines, never certain what, exactly, the difference was between the two.

She soon discovered that Audra was going to be no help at all. She rode in the back of the wagon, half naked, and complained about the heat and the fact that the rocking motion of the wagon was making her ill. So, of course, she was forced to recline awhile longer.

The countryside didn't help Rachel's disposition. The ground was baked dry. The air radiated heat and the horizon stretched forever with only scrubby trees and cacti to break the monotony. She was besieged with grasshoppers. They whirred in the air high above her head as big as hummingbirds, their yellowish-gray bodies reflecting the sunlight like spangles of silver. They floated through the sky in legions, rising, sinking, dilating in immense clouds, sometimes winging onto the wagon seat and, more often than not, on her.

The first time one landed on the back of her neck and gripped her with its pointed little feet, she screamed loud enough to bring Homer George and Captain Wells riding to her rescue, both certain an Indian had somehow sneaked up on her when they weren't looking. She stood on the wagon seat slapping at her shoulders and praying at the top of her voice, "Oh God, oh God, help me; it's chewing on me!" Then Davis rode up and laughed so loudly the grasshopper flew off to destinations unknown.

"There goes the first meat-eating grasshopper in Texas," he said to Sam in his vulgarly sarcastic drawl before turning away. "At least the damn bug's got good taste in women."

"That's a fact, by God," the old Ranger agreed before joining him.

It was noon before they stopped. Homer rode up and down the line calling "Two hours, folks. Git 'em fed and ready to go. Two hours, folks!"

Rachel stared down at the ground and wondered whether, if she closed her eyes and jumped, she might break her neck and end her misery before she was faced with managing the horses again throughout the day. Deciding she would probably break an arm instead, she did her best to climb carefully to the ground, managing to rip her skirts only twice on the way down. Then she slapped the grit from her hands.

Early that morning she had found her gloves after a frenzied search through both her trunks. They hugged her hands and forearms, making her skin itch. The dress she'd decided to wear was little better. It fit tightly through the bodice, flared at the waist, and spilled in multitudinous folds over the three petticoats she'd pulled on in her haste to get ready. And her hat. Its sweeping straw brim would shield her face from the sun, but the bright ruby plume, she was certain, would attract attention. Still, the only alternative was to remove the adornment; that idea was just too ghastly to consider! She had drawn the specifications exactly to her liking and her milliner, Kathleen Guillot de la Malmaison, had searched high and low for a feather just this shade of red, to match the dress she now wore. It made a most fetching ensemble on her carriage rides through the Vieux Carré. She simply would not think of destroying it!

Looking about her surroundings, she noticed Davis still sitting astride his horse some distance away. Separated from the others, his hat cocked low over his brow, he appeared lost in thought—until he moved. Grabbing his side, he winced and attempted to sit a little straighter. The free hand resting on his thigh suddenly clenched in pain.

She bit her lip as she recalled Sam's admission that Davis had not been the instigator of the escape attempt. Seeing Davis experiencing such obvious discomfort exaggerated her feelings of guilt over calling him an animal and wishing him dead. There was only one thing to do to appease her conscience, she told herself: apologize!

Taking a deep breath, she lifted her chin and walked as gracefully as possible toward Davis, which, she discovered quickly, wasn't an easy feat by any means. Twice she stubbed her toe on rocks, and with each gust of wind that barreled over the flat prairie, her skirt belled up around her hips like a huge red mushroom.

Davis was still looking toward Sam and the others when she finally reached him. She waited a moment in silence, then cleared her throat.

Nothing.

She tried it again.

Still nothing.

It wasn't the clearing of her throat that finally caught his attention. As the wind nearly whipped her hat into the air, her cry of "Oh my!" brought his head around. He sat up so suddenly that his horse pranced to one side, nearly unseating him and stepping on her.

"Jesus," she heard him say. "Lady, don't ever walk up behind a horse."

Having successfully dodged the high-stepping animal, Rachel, as casually as possible, smoothed her skirts down again and said quickly, "I'm sorry, Mr. Davis."

Thumbing his hat up a little, he managed something just short of a smile and shrugged. "He's a little skittish."

Realizing he'd misunderstood, she shook her head and forced herself to meet his direct gaze once more. "No, Mr. Davis, I mean I'm sorry about last evening. I understand your thwarting Mr. Lindsey's escape attempt caused you some injury. I hope it's not too terribly discomforting."

"I've had worse," he responded dryly.

"Oh dear, I'm sorry to hear that."

He raised his dark brows.

"What I mean is your act was most noble and I'm . . . sorry for saying those things. I hope you can find it in your heart to forgive me."

All at once his look was challenging. Rachel stepped back, trying hard not to flinch beneath his narrowed blue eyes.

"Let me get this straight," he said skeptically. "You're apologizing to me?"

She nodded and took another step backward. "I do hope you'll accept my apology."

"I'll think about it."

She smiled as graciously as possible and turned back to her wagon. Then his voice came again, slightly lighter this time and not so mocking. It stopped her in her tracks.

"Lose your parasol, Miss Gregory?"

Rachel partially turned.

Looking down from his horse, Davis said, "Tell me something, lady . . ."

She waited, suspended by the eyes that, ice-blue and cold one minute, were thawing with humor as he appraised her hat.

He wagged a finger at the sweeping feather that arched up and over the crown of her hat and bobbed at the tip of her nose. "Just where the hell do you find birds that big?"

"Africa," she responded, somewhat miffed at his tone.

A momentary look of bafflement crossed his features. Shifting in his saddle, he said, "Aha. Is that someplace near here?"

He watched her violet eyes widen in surprise; the gloved hand that had protectively come up to touch the fancy ruby feather paused as she stared into his face. Her pink lips were parted slightly, the corners twitching as she regarded him in wonderment, then disbelief.

He got the distinct impression that he'd said something funny, though he couldn't imagine what. "Something wrong?" he asked, forgetting the ridiculous piece of fluff, concentrating instead on the beautiful sweep of her white throat and the long braid of pale, silken hair hanging over her shoulder.

"You aren't serious, are you?" she asked. "You *do* know where Africa is?"

His stomach tightened up like a fist. "Of course I do," he replied, attempting a grin of total nonchalance. "Africa's someplace east of Atlanta, I think."

She stared again, her eyes wide and the color of royal velvet. He saw the smile begin, then her head fell back and laughter bubbled like clear spring water from her dainty throat. She laughed for an entire minute before she was able to catch her breath enough to say, "Oh, Mr. Davis, what a remarkable sense of humor you possess for one so—so—uncouth. Yes, I suppose it *is* east of Atlanta. *Very* east." She burst out laughing again.

The blood drained from his face. He stopped smiling. He didn't take to being laughed at, and she was laughing *at* him whether she realized it or not. She must have noted the change in his demeanor, for suddenly her laughter died. Her gloved hands twisted into her skirts and she bit her lip.

Sam walked up, looking on in his usual inscrutable way. After spitting a stream of tobacco to the ground, he said, "I reckon you'll be needin' help with them horses, Miss Rachel."

"No doubt," Davis added with as much sarcasm as he could manage.

With that Rachel lifted her chin, turned, and walked back toward her wagon. Watching her go, Sam called out, "I'll have one of my men see to them horses, Miss Rachel!"

They both watched the red bird feather wave in the breeze.

Sam then turned back to Davis. "Yore lookin' a bit puckered, boy. Somethin' eatin' at ya agin?"

Adjusting his hat again over his eyes, he looked down at the Ranger and shrugged. "You ever seen bird feathers that big?"

"A few times."

He looked back at Rachel. "They come from Africa."

"Ya don't say."

"Tell me something, old man. Where is Africa?"

Sam thought a minute, scratching his chin through his beard. "Africa. 'Round the other side of the earth, I think."

Chagrin crept up Davis's cheeks, burning as intensely as the summer sun overhead. "Just east of Atlanta, I guess."

"A spell past Atlanta I'd say. Why you askin'?"

"No reason," he said. Then pulling himself up straight in his saddle, he looked toward the Gregorys' wagon one last time before joining the others.

*　　*　　*

Rachel was massaging her temples and wondering about Davis's mercurial moods when Audra rounded the wagon. "For God's sake, Rachel, why are you just standing there? We've only two hours to prepare our food, and there you are staring into space."

"My head hurts."

"Well, I shan't suffer for that. Had you remained in the wagon last night like I told you, you wouldn't be suffering the consequences now."

Rachel squeezed her eyes shut and counted to ten.

"I beg your pardon." The voice was a stranger's. Squinting the sunlight from her eyes, Rachel turned and, on tiptoe, peeked over the horses' haunches into a man's soft brown eyes. He smiled back. "I noticed you're having a bloody time managing this pair. May I offer you some assistance?"

"You're English," she responded.

"I'm sorry if that offends you."

"It doesn't."

"Jolly good." Smoothing his hands down over his dove-gray lapels, the man doffed his bowler hat and walked around the horses. "You should've purchased oxen, you know. They're slow as Christmas, but not likely to bolt. They're sluggardly creatures and for the most part need nudging to keep them awake. Allow me to introduce myself. I'm Martin. Martin Stillwell, Esquire." He bent over her hand. "And you are Rachel Gregory."

Rachel nodded; the ruby plume bobbed between her eyes.

"I noticed you at the Bastitas fiesta last night. You looked charming." Glancing over her shoulder, he said, "And you must be Mrs. Gregory."

"My stepmother," Rachel responded.

"Indeed." He smiled again at Rachel. "I understand you are without—how would our wagonmaster, Mr. George, say it—menfolk?" At Rachel's affirmative nod, he went on, "This must be a ghastly ordeal for you then. Having to drive a team of these animals is hard enough for a man. God knows I'm thankful I have Jules to help me." He gestured over his shoulder, and for the first time Rachel noticed the slender, silver-haired man standing attentively some distance away.

"You don't drive your team yourself?" she asked Martin.

Slapping his gloved hands together, he replied, "Oh, certainly not, dear lady. But be assured, if you have any need for help, my man is available."

"Your man. Well, how very kind of you." She glanced toward the reed-thin figure of the servant. Dust had settled atop his balding pate; it was streaked with sweat. "But I think we can manage. I'm certain your man has more than he can handle at this time."

He smiled again. "Then I'll let you get to it. Until this evening, ladies?" Sweeping his hat again to his head, Stillwell spun on his heels and headed back up the train.

"Little fool!" Audra hurried toward her, her face flushed with anger. "You should have taken him up on his offer. We've animals to feed and food to prepare."

"We'll do it ourselves."

"Ourselves! What do *you* know of feeding animals and preparing food?"

"You should have thought about that before you got us into this mess, Audra."

"Oh God, I'll kill my brother when I see him. He'll regret the day he was born. Imagine ignoring my letter—"

"Captain Wells thinks he probably never got it."

"Oh, he got it all right. He's just . . ."

Rachel waited, a horrible suspicion growing in her mind. Perhaps Audra's brother wasn't as agreeable to their moving to his ranch as Audra had led her to believe. "He's what, Audra?"

"Nothing. He's just . . . not very . . . reliable, at times. That's all." Mopping her face with a kerchief, she rolled her brown eyes and whined, "God, this heat. I'm miserable and I have this awful headache. I have to lie down. Call me when the food is ready."

Rachel stared after her stepmother. How much longer would she be forced to submit to Audra's harping and shrewishness, and simply turn the other cheek? Surely this awful submission was not what her father had meant by showing respect to one's elders.

"Need some help with those horses, Miss Gregory?"

Damn, she thought. *Him* again.

Closing her eyes, she said, "Mr. Davis, I was under the impression that I said something earlier to distress you."

"Yeah, well, I'm the forgiving sort. Thought I'd just let you know that I don't hold any hard feelings over those viper-tongued little comments you made to me last night."

Her shoulders snapped back. "Well, I'm very glad to hear that. And thank you very much for your consideration concerning my horses. Now, if you will please go away . . ." Only then did she turn to face him fully.

He contemplated her with a half smile. "You seemed pretty eager for my company ten minutes ago."

Rachel recognized the innuendo for what it was. A flush of anger staining her otherwise pale cheeks, she retorted, "You awful, conceited, lopheaded boor! If you think for one minute that I am remotely interested in you, sir, you are sadly mistaken!"

There was a flicker of surprise in his blue eyes, but only for a moment. Narrowing slightly, they perused her with a different sort of interest as he said, "Tut, tut, Miss Gregory, is that any way for a lady to talk?"

"How would you know?" she queried sweetly. "You probably haven't been within ten feet of a *real* lady more than twice in your life."

"I might surprise you."

"I doubt it. I doubt anything that you could do would surprise me."

He stepped closer. She stepped away, or tried to. The horse at her back forbade her escape. "What are you doing?" she demanded. The anger she had felt over her stepmother's behavior, as well as the sorry circumstances in which they found themselves, deserted her like a puff of smoke in a wind as he pinned her with those penetrating blue eyes. She was suddenly all too aware of her reasons for disliking Davis in the first place. "I asked, What are you doing?"

His wide mouth curled in a grin as he slowly reached up, his movements perfectly poised, despite the chain that hung from his wrists. He pulled a silver strand of hair from her cheek and tucked it behind her ear. "Surprising you," he finally responded.

The tip of his gloved finger swept her cheek. It was rough, frayed leather, warmed by the heat of his body and the sun. She stared into his eyes and felt as if she were tumbling into their deepest fathoms; they were searching her face, and she suddenly, inexplicably, felt uncomfortably conscious of how she must look. Her hair, loose of the ribbon she had earlier banded about the blond braid's end, now hung partially unbraided over her shoulders. Her face and throat were covered with grit and sweat, and her dress was blotched with the same.

She felt her face warm as his leisurely perusal moved over her shoulders, hesitated at the form-fitting material of her bodice, then proceeded down, down so slowly to her feet that she thought she might collapse. She might have made good her threat to scream for Captain Wells, but she couldn't find the strength, or the breath, to do it. Instead, she set her chin at a stubborn angle in the hope that her indifference to his immoral behavior and bad manners would prove he couldn't frighten her. Still, she was greatly relieved when Sam walked up behind him.

"By golly, Davis, now ain't you jest as slippery as a rattlesnake? I can see I'm gonna have my hands full with you. Let me jest turn my back for a hair and there ya go tiptoein' off to court the ladies." He tipped his hat at Rachel. "Beggin' yore pardon, Miss Rachel, is this scoundrel pesterin' you?"

Davis stared into her eyes, waiting.

Nervously, she ran her tongue along her lips, horribly aware that—for some reason—she was about to lie for Davis. Good Lord! Two minutes in the man's presence and she was losing her own scruples. "No, he—" She cleared her throat, feeling as if she had swallowed half the dust in Texas. "I don't know how to build a fire, Captain." At least *that* wasn't a lie. "He said he would help me."

Davis frowned, whether in surprise or displeasure, she couldn't tell. "Well?" she prompted. "Didn't you say you would show me how to build a fire, Mr. Davis?"

Davis only grinned in response.

Chapter 6

He showed her around to the back of the wagon while Sam looked on. Walking at Davis's side, Rachel fought the urge to look up and over his broad shoulder, to his face. She'd done it once without thinking, and the sight of his black hair curling slightly over his ear had left her strangely unsettled.

"This is your fuel box," he said in so deep timbred a voice she was certain she felt the ground vibrate below her feet. She stared at his sun-browned and weathered finger as he pointed toward the box.

"The fuel box," she repeated, then looked at the box.

He reached for the lid of the fuel box and, as he did, the chain between his wrists clattered against the side of the wagon. The racket had a sobering effect on Rachel's senses. Focusing on the long box fastened across the back of her wagon, she frowned. It was full of what looked like clumps of dry brown grass, as well as kindling sticks

An unpleasant, pungent smell emanated from the box. Wrinkling her nose, Rachel stepped away.

"It's *bois des vaches*," Sam explained with a chuckle.

"Cow dung," Davis added in explanation. "It makes a good hot fire. If I were you, I'd keep my eye out for any more you might find along the way. Looks like you don't have much here. It won't last you to Brackettville, for certain."

"Cow dung," she snapped. "You expect me to scour the ground and shovel cow dung." It wasn't a question. She stared into the box, appalled. She was appalled even more as Davis reached in with both hands and scooped out as much as he could carry. Wrinkling her nose again, she stated the obvious. "You're—you're touching it with your hands, Mr. Davis."

He stopped, turned, and managed a look of total astonishment. "So I am, Miss Gregory. Maybe if we both try whistling it'll march out here by itself. Go on and try. I'll wait."

Seconds clipped by. Rachel, feeling her face flush uncomfortably, stared at the feather-light particles of digested grass filtering from between his fingers, and said through her teeth, "You could use a scoop, Mr. Davis."

He glanced at Sam, still maintaining the look of mocking astonishment. "Damn, why didn't I think of that? You have a scoop on you, Captain?"

Sam shook his head, apparently enjoying the repartee between her and Davis. "Left it back in San Antone, I guess."

Davis walked over to a clearing on the ground, began gouging out a rut in the dirt with his heel, and then, when finished, dropped the dung into it. "Get some rocks, Miss Gregory, and line them around the fire. They'll retain the heat and help water boil faster."

He squatted on his heels now, his long legs jackknifed under him, straining the black cloth of his breeches almost to the bursting point. She was focusing on the thinly worn material of his inseam when he looked up and caught her staring. "Rocks," he reminded her.

"Oh!" As she whirled away she heard him say, "Maybe she should rattle her head. Any woman who'd strike out on a journey like this without a man's got rocks for brains."

She fumed over the statement as she scoured the ground for rocks big enough to line the puny-looking fire he was fanning. Not because he'd said it, but because he was probably right. The buying and supplying of the wagon had been left up to them and, out of sheer ignorance, they'd bungled the job horribly. They'd purchased a wagon that threatened with each creak and groan of its wheels to fall apart. They didn't know how to do so simple a task as build a fire, and she certainly didn't know how to— Oh dear Lord! She didn't know how to cook!

Davis looked up as Rachel approached. Her face was flushed with heat and shimmered with sweat. "You're feather's drooping," he teased her, grinning. "Looks like you'll have to be going to Africa soon for another one."

She dumped the rocks at his feet, then looked at Sam. "Thank you for your help, Captain."

"If you're asking us to stay and eat—" Davis started.

"I'm not." She cut him off with a sideways glance.

Hunching one shoulder, he looked back down at the fire, gave it a poke or two with a stick, then stood up, slapping the dirt from his hands. He'd never seen anyone so touchy as she was—and all over a silly bird feather. "When you're ready to kill the fire," he told her, "be sure you pour plenty of water over the ashes and kick away the rocks. Stir the ashes up, then pour some more water into them. Grass fires are bad this time of year."

She began tugging off her gloves with short, jerky motions.

Hands on his hips, he added, "You'd better get those horses unharnessed so they can feed and water or they'll be mean as hell in another hour."

Her hands stopped their agitated movements. She looked him squarely in the eye and said, "Thank you."

He stared back. "You're welcome."

She went back to removing her gloves and he asked, "Do you need some help with the horses?"

"Now what gives you that idea, Mr. Davis?"

Her eyes were wide again, and nearly black. As she slapped one glove over her forearm, then the other, he was swept with such an overwhelming desire to plant a kiss on her stubborn little mouth that he almost did just that. God, was he mad? She was everything he'd avoided for the last half of his life. She was a reminder of everything misfortune had denied him. She was part of the very society that had kicked him when he was down, and she had the audacity to stand there with her bird feathers and look desirable enough to make him forget it all, his past and his future, black and uncertain as it was.

He'd known men stupid enough to get themselves killed over women less beautiful than she. She wasn't above using those looks to get what she wanted from a man, and that's what rankled him most. He'd seen her earlier talking to the fancy man with the city clothes, heard the respect in her voice as she addressed him. Yet she stood here before him now like a little bandy rooster with drooping feathers, looked down her nose at him just because he was—what had she called him?—uncouth.

Rachel saw his face darken, noted the eyes that went from sapphire to indigo blue as they moved too slowly over her features. As one corner of his mouth turned up, she backed away. "I'll see to the horses myself," she announced with a little too much bravado to be convincing. As her pulse set up a queer thrumming all the way up in her throat, she turned away.

Wells and Davis watched as she approached the flat-eared animals.

"This ought to be good," she heard one of them say.

Where to start first? There were belts and buckles everywhere. Rubbing her hands down over her skirts, Rachel chewed on her lip, fully aware that her audience had ventured closer. She knew she should admit that she didn't know the first thing about unharnessing the animals, but after Davis's remark about having rocks for brains she would be damned before proving him right.

There was a thick leather strap running over their withers. She decided to start there. Approaching the animals cautiously, she gently stroked the somewhat nervous horse nearest her while searching out the clasp and buckle that would disconnect the bulky-looking harness from the tongue of the wagon. It seemed to be on the animal's belly. Bending slightly, she reached for the formidable contraption, but no sooner had her hesitant fingers touched the strap than, quite suddenly, her hat was snatched from her head.

"Oh!" She whirled around as the horse, with hat in mouth, gave his head a shake and whinnied to the wind. "Oh! You damnable beast! Drop that hat!"

Behind her Davis and Wells burst out laughing.

To little avail she pranced before the animal, doing her best to grab the brim of her hat. As she grabbed it between her fingers, he clamped his teeth so hard upon the delicate crown that he ripped a hole in it as large as his mouth. Rachel flew backward, landing on her backside with a teeth-jarring thud.

With skirt and petticoats hiked to her knees Rachel stared at the remains of her hat, too stunned to cry or even notice, at first, that her ordeal had attracted a great deal of attention. Now all the prisoners, as well as the lawmen, stood in a row laughing, except for Sam, who sauntered bowlegged toward her. And Davis. She threw him a scathing glance and was stunned to find him scowling fiercely at her ankles; Clyde was whispering something in his ear. With no warning Davis spun on his heel and grabbed the weasel-faced man around the throat, and both went tumbling toward the ground in a tangle of arms, legs, and chains.

She heard Sam hiss between his teeth. Suddenly the placid tempered Ranger was drawing his gun, crouching, aiming at the pair and shouting, "That's enough, boys! Let go of his throat, Davis, or I'll blow a hole in ya big enough to drive this wagon through."

Deputy Rogers jumped in then, grabbed Davis at the collar, and hauled him off a beet-faced Clyde, who clutched at his own throat and made horrible choking sounds.

"You—you seen him, Cap'n!" Clyde rasped. "He tried to kill me all because I said I liked what I seen under the lady's petticoats!"

"Well, in that case, Lindsey, maybe I'll kill ya myself. Git up so's I got a better aim. I never did like shootin' vermin whilst they is squirmin' on their bellies in the dirt!"

The others hustled away, leaving the two men lying in the dirt, looking up into Sam's steady, menacing gun barrel.

"Now the way I see it, Davis," Sam began, "I've been fair to middlin' even with ya, lettin' ya roam around as if you was on this side of the badge instead of that one."

Davis's blue eyes narrowed. He spat dust out of one side of his mouth.

Sam went on, "But I can't tolerate this sort of misbehavin'. It does my digestion poorly, here at mealtime. You know what I'm sayin' to ya? As punishment, I'm gonna have Rogers here clamp them ankle lengths to you two fer the next hour or so, so where one of ya hobbles, the other hobbles too. Maybe then you'll git along a little better. Now git on back to our fire and leave Miss Gregory and her hat in peace. Rogers, help Miss Gregory with her horses, seein' how she's taken a tumble and more'n likely's a bit tittery."

Rogers approached and offered her his hand. She ignored him. Climbing to her feet, she watched as he began unharnessing the animals. Then Deputy Hale walked up, fell to one knee, and began clamping manacles onto Davis's leg. Davis slightly clutched his side. His clothes were covered with dust and his black hair spilled nearly into his blue eyes. And the blue eyes were trained on her.

She looked away and did her best to rid her skirt of as much dust as possible. Bully, she thought. Odious, contemptible man. However did she get herself into this incredible predicament? She was stuck on this godforsaken desert with a woman she loathed, forced to tolerate the company of a bunch of villains who behaved little better than children.

"I beg your pardon, *señorita*."

Rachel twirled and was faced by a smiling Mexican woman. Tucking her hat behind her back, she said, "How do you do."

"I am Manuela Alverez. My husband and I drive the wagon before yours."

Rachel glanced toward the reed-thin Mexican hunched slightly over a cooking pan in the distance. He looked her way, tipped his sombrero, and went back to his task of preparing his meal.

"We thought you might care to join us in our meal. It is not much, just beans and tortillas, but there is plenty."

"That's very kind of you, but my stepmother—"

"She is welcome to join us as well."

"I'm afraid she has a headache. Besides, I really should learn to do this myself."

Manuela crossed her arms over her ample breasts and stared toward the men in the distance. "I saw the tall one helpin' you with your fire. I knew that anyone who could not build a fire would know nothin' about cookin'."

Rachel felt her face color.

"You have supplies?" Manuela asked. Her black eyes were twinkling, and curious.

Rachel nodded.

"Flour, lard, and beans?"

"No beans."

"We have plenty of beans to share. Because there is little time to prepare a full meal at the noon break, you will cook them tonight and eat them durin' the day. In the evening you will have more time for meat. We have plenty of tortillas for you now, and plenty of cooked beans. You will take some to your mother, *si*?"

"*Step*mother," Rachel stressed, then gratefully said, "and thank you."

Surprisingly, the meal was a tasty affair, or would have been had Audra not complained during the entire course. "Beans!" she'd shrieked loud enough for the Alverezes to hear, Rachel was certain. "I've waited all these hours to eat and you give me beans cooked by some—"

"Lower your voice," Rachel demanded quietly but firmly. "You should be thankful to get this. You know I know nothing of preparing food."

"You know little of anything," the woman goaded. Lounging back on her bed, she stared at the canvas overhead and said, "You're just like your father, good for little more than decoration and preaching. Well, you see where his 'do unto others' philosophy got him, don't you, dear Rachel? Dead! Well, I'm not dead, I tell you, and I intend to do a little living from now on."

Her appetite gone, Rachel placed her spoon and bowl aside. "Father asked only that we act as befits our social position and that we remember those less fortunate than ourselves."

"Well, you've done a sorry job of that, squandering the family name by running off with Luke that way."

Raising her eyes to Audra's, Rachel said quietly, "Had you allowed me to go you would have been free of me completely. Why did you have me returned, Audra?"

"Why?" Audra laughed, a sharp, harsh sound that grated on Rachel's nerves. "I am your guardian, dear girl, don't you ever forget that."

"But you loathed the responsibility of having a stepdaughter while my father was living. Why the sudden change in attitude?"

Her dark head came up, and propping herself on both elbows, she stated flatly, "Perhaps because now I can pay you back for all the grief you caused me."

"Grief! I never did anything intentionally—"

"Like hell you didn't." Audra sat up straight. Her eyes narrowing, she spat, "Little miss goody twoshoes could do no wrong. 'Rachel will grow to be the most beautiful woman in New Orleans,' your father bragged, until I was ill to death of hearing it."

"Perhaps if you had shared a child—"

"A child?" Audra mocked her. "A child with that old man? Ugh! It was bad enough allowing him his conjugal rights once a month."

Rachel's hands shook as she collected her spoon and bowl and turned toward the back opening of the wagon. The anger was mounting; if she didn't leave now . . .

"Your father was a fool," Audra added venomously.

"You made him a fool," Rachel returned. "He cared for

you, took you in when you were nothing but—" She bit her lip, realizing she had gone too far.

"But what? *What!* Turn around here, girl, and speak to my face!" Audra made a grab for Rachel's arm. "What do you mean by that?"

Flinching, Rachel looked from her stepmother's fingers, into her eyes. "I mean only that you were a widow with little more than a trunk of worn dresses to your name. He married you and gave you everything his money could buy."

"Which was precious little. He was too damn busy fawning over you to barely notice me."

"Had you stayed home more and given him the opportunity . . . Where were you all those nights you said you were visiting sick friends, Stepmama? Seeing Richard Delaney, perhaps?"

"Rich—? How do you know about Richard?"

Audra's face paled and her full mouth twisted in dismay and shock. An odd thrill of vindication swept Rachel at her discomfiture. "I know Delaney was a river rat with a love for gambling." She tugged her arm from her stepmother's fingers. "I know you met him once or twice a week. Luke followed you several times to the docks."

"I see." Relaxing back onto the bed, Audra asked, "And did you tell your father—"

"No! I would never hurt my father in such a way, no matter how much I would have liked to see you banished from our home."

"Well." Her lids were lazy now as she stretched felinelike in her transparent chemise. Her heavy breasts strained at the lace-edged material as she laughed deep in her throat. "Seems you should have told him, Rachel. Your silence has cost you dearly, you see."

"I don't know what you mean."

"Now you're saddled with me as your guardian."

"I'll be twenty-one soon enough."

"Indeed you shall." She laughed again. "Indeed you shall." The noon sun hit Rachel like a blast from a furnace as she climbed down from the wagon. She accidentally spilled the beans from her bowl and scattered the spoons into the dirt. Dropping to her knees, her hands trembling, she did her best to collect the utensils while the entire horrid conversation with Audra ran again through her mind. How could her father have been so blind as to fall in love with that self-centered woman? How would she ever find the patience to tolerate her for the next year?

The commotion behind her made her look back over her shoulder. Deputy Rogers was harnessing the horses back to the wagon. Just beyond him stood Hale, Clyde, and Davis. The ankle chains were thrown over Hale's shoulder. Clyde was shaking his leg and Davis was staring at her.

She met his stare fully this time and without flinching. Perhaps it was her anger that made her do it, the contempt she felt for her stepmother's hypocrisy these last years. She smiled at him with one corner of her mouth and lowered her lashes.

Davis smiled back.

Not in the way the gentlemen in New Orleans smiled back. Not in a gay or solicitous manner. But knowing. Daring. Flagrantly arrogant, as if her smiling at him was the most natural thing in the world. As if a lady would be tempted by his scent of sweat, horse, and leather. As if she found his failure to shave appealing, his way of speaking droll. He was an animal, and any woman in her right senses, any woman with any sort of strict upbringing, would be appalled by his very presence. God only knew what sort of crime he had committed. Yet she could hardly deny the deep sense of strangeness that twisted around her heart whenever he was near, and she suddenly felt the anger she had earlier experienced at Audra ripping away under the impact of this new, frightening sensation.

"Mou-unnt up!" Homer George called up and down the line of wagons.

She was startled by a hot blast of wind; it tore at her hair and whipped it across his face. Her skirts snapped like sails in a gale as did the osnaburg canvases on the wagons. Their sides heaved in and out like a breathing force as she retrieved her spoon. She thrust the utensils through the wagon's back flaps where they clattered to the floor. Her back stiff, she marched up to the horses, smiling her thanks to Rogers, who touched the brim of his hat with the tip of his finger.

It was then that the shadow approached. Narrow at first, and at her feet, it slithered slowly up the side of the wagon, growing broader until it merged with her own: one on one. The hot sun that beat upon her back was suddenly blocked by Davis's shoulders as he stopped behind her. She did not turn; she would not!

"Need a hand up, Miss Gregory?"

The offer came like gentle thunder, summer-warm and slightly threatening. It wouldn't be proper, considering what he was, and she turned to tell him so.

The words wouldn't come. The flurry of reason bloomed and withered beneath his searching, dancing eyes. *All* reason, not just the paltry excuses she'd offered her quivering heart and mind. She stood speechless, absorbed by his presence, flooded with the very essence of his virility.

"A hand," he repeated.

"That's very kind of you, Mr. Davis, but your side . . ."

"To hell with my side."

"Oh well, of course then. If you insist." She smiled suddenly as he gallantly bent over and made a stirrup with his fingers. Lifting her skirts to the top of her ankle, she placed her slippered foot into the handsome cradle. Staring down onto the back of his black head, she was stricken with such an overwhelming ache to touch her fingers to the unruly mop that she almost toppled.

"Careful," he called, then leaned his shoulder into her leg for support.

"You're very gallant," she teased him.

"Yes, I am. Now hurry the hell up."

She was suddenly airborne. Grabbing the wagon seat, she

swung herself onto it. Beating down her petticoats she said, "Thank you very much, Mr. Davis."

He turned away.

She watched the seat of his breeches as he walked slowly back toward Sam, appearing to have dismissed her entirely. Then she closed her eyes.

"Stretch out!" Homer called.

Gloveless, hatless, she picked up the reins and set to the task of doing just that.

Chapter 7

She burned her hand making a fire the next morning. She burned it again when she grabbed the pot handle that had simmered dry of the water she'd been boiling for Audra's tea. She burned the bacon Manuela had given her. She burned the hem of her dress and petticoats as she leaned over to turn the charred bacon. And if that wasn't enough, she suddenly found herself a center of attention. Men and women up and down the line seemed to take great interest in strolling by her wagon. They looked and frowned, then grinned and shook their heads.

Only Martin Stillwell was gracious enough to actually stop and talk. He walked in his dapper manner right up to her wagon and dropped a warm bundle of scones into her hands. "Good morning," he greeted her, making her smile for the first time that day. "Jules is a superb chef so I promise you these will melt in your mouth. May I say you look splendid today!"

She blinked and felt like crying. "You're too kind."

"Such a refreshing change from these rather limp women with their ungainly boots and drab attire."

Rachel looked down, over her robin's-egg-blue silk skirt, at her dainty slippered feet. She looked, then, at him.

Stillwell was such a pleasant, proper gentleman, with a lean rosy face and blond hair, more yellow than her own. His posture was impeccably straight, though he was rather slender-shouldered and narrow-chested. He wore a dark blue jacket with brass buttons that fitted him to perfection, a white silk waistcoat, and tan breeches. It was obvious his knee-high Hessian boots had been polished that morning, or the night before. Back in New Orleans he might have elicited more than a glance or two from her and her friends. But here . . .

"Did you rest well?" he asked her.

Jarred from her confusing comparisons, Rachel nodded absently and lied, "Very well, thank you."

He pursed his lips and, looking over her shoulder, scowled darkly. "A rather unseemly sort, aren't they? I saw the tall one speaking with you yesterday. I hope he's been no nuisance."

She followed the direction of his gaze. The men huddled around their cookfire, noisily scraping food from the bottom of their tin plates and slurping their hot coffee. All except Davis. He sat alone on a rock, cradling the pint-sized enameled cup in his long fingers. His hat was again positioned low over his eyes. He might have been staring into his coffee, by the tilt of his head. She sensed he wasn't. He was watching her, and even as she returned his subtle perusal, she saw one corner of his mouth curl up, taunting her.

"Brute," she muttered.

"I beg your pardon?"

She forced her eyes back to Martin. "I said they're all brutes. Lacking any manners . . ." Her voice trailed off.

"I thoroughly agree. The scourge of humanity. It is a shame you are forced to tolerate their proximity. Would you like me to speak to Mr. George?"

"No! I mean, no, thank you." She looked back at Davis and thought again of a sleek black cat she had seen as a child. His long legs in black trousers and boots were stretched out before him. He seemed lazy and content basking in the morning sun. He wasn't watching her any longer, but was staring out over the unending prairie from which they'd come.

When she turned again to Martin he was staring at her, curious. "Is something wrong?" she asked him.

"You seem bothered by the man."

"Do I?" She blushed. "He doesn't bother me at all. Not at all. Why should he?"

"No reason, I suppose." He looked at the bundle in her hand. "Enjoy your scones."

She'd forgotten them. Their warmth, seeping through the linen napkin, sweated her palms. "I'm certain I will."

By midmorning little had happened to assuage her state of unease. Audra was reclining still and the horses refused to cooperate. She was stiff and sore from the day before, and with each jolt of the wagon or tug from the cantankerous animals she nearly cried out in pain, not to mention frustration.

She broke down and wept once. Sitting there for the entire world to see, had they chosen to look, she finally let the tears come. They were hot and succeeded only in reminding her how sunburned her cheeks had become. With a swipe of her sleeve she rearranged the dirt on her face into muddy little rivulets and stained her dress.

The countryside changed, little by little. It had gone from rolling to flat to rolling again. It dipped and swelled like a sea, stubby grass, an occasional tree, dirt and rock stretching for an eternity around them. And as the landscape changed, Homer George's crew worked the train differently. The distance between them and the travelers grew wider. They appeared and disappeared over the far ridges as they searched for water and game. They swung back and forth, bringing up the rear, then fanning out and around the lead wagon in a manner as regular as clockwork as they kept a sharp lookout for anything or anyone who might endanger the travelers.

She was watching Jeromia Peabody when Davis rode up.

He walked his horse beside her wagon for several minutes before she noticed. When she saw him at last he said, "You're not paying attention."

"I'm not?"

He looked directly at the slack reins in her relaxed fingers. "If the horses bolted now you'd be in trouble."

"Would I?" She blinked and did nothing more. She was half asleep, he could tell.

"Where's your hat?" he asked her.

She thought a moment; her lazy-lidded eyes scanned the horizon beyond him. As they flicked back to him, her little mouth drew up at one end in amusement. "Back in the fuel box by now, I suppose," she finally responded.

He shifted in his saddle. "Bring up your lines," he said.

She did, and sat a little straighter.

"Pay attention. The animals are thirsty. Given a whiff of water they're likely to run for it."

She looked at him again. "So am I. I'd love a bath."

Davis forced his eyes away, concentrating on the countryside and not on her flushed, pretty face. There were too many complications now in his life to let those perfect features distract him. But they *were* distracting him, and every other man on the train.

"Will we stop soon?" came her hopeful voice.

"Maybe," he said. Tipping his head a little, he saw her shoulders slump. The reins went slack. "Bring up the lines, Rachel," he reminded her.

"Go to blazes on a jackass, Davis. I'm tired."

That made him smile. "You can certainly talk salty for a lady."

Rubbing the tip of her nose with the back of one wrist, she replied, "Well, I don't feel much like a lady anymore — or look like one."

"My mother said once that the way a person looks really has nothing at all to do with the kind of person he is." The thought just slipped out; he hadn't intended it.

"You had a mother? I don't believe it!"

For a second, she thought she saw his eyes cloud, nonetheless she went on. Staring at the manacles on his wrist, she said, "She must be very proud of you now, Mr. Davis."

He yanked back on the reins of his horse so abruptly that the animal reared and stopped dead in its tracks. The wagon lumbered on, spilling dust into the air. He continued staring, not really angry — bemused mostly — at her easy way of getting under his skin. He hated her for what she was, and what she wasn't. He hated her for her fripperies, yet they were really no part of her. She was a separate entity from them. Unlike many of the so-called ladies he'd met in Chicago and New York, who—with or without their clothes—could be as cold and untouchable as a tintype, she *was* touchable. So touchable. He ached to touch her. Damn her!

She peeked from around the wagon canvas, her cheeks apple-red and her mouth smiling.

Damn her.

Rachel blinked the dust from her eyes. Davis was gone through the haze, back toward the others who followed at a considerable distance. Funny man, she thought. He speaks of his mother in so gentle a voice, this manacled outlaw accused of harming another. Davis was a hard man; she had no doubts about that. Hard and bitter to his very soul. Yet at times he showed great concern. He was two different men. One forbidding, dangerous, and distant. The other almost vulnerable and lonely—desperately lonely. She could see it at times in his eyes when he sat aside from the others and stared into his coffee cup, or out over the countryside. Perhaps it was remorse over his past that forced up those walls of solitude. Perhaps his soul was salvageable after all.

Whimsy! She sniffed and slipped back into her daydreams.

The path they followed sank between limestone walls that loomed as high as the horses' withers. The light glancing off the white rock blinded Rachel so she was forced to close her eyes: her first mistake. Her second was keeping them closed. Perhaps she dozed. Or perhaps the sun had beaten her senseless. Whatever the reason, the lines slipped from her fingers, down around her feet, and she didn't notice. Her head nodded while the wagons ahead broke free of the rock formations and bumped their way toward the distant riverbed.

Someone yelled behind her. She sat up straight, startled and confused, instinctively throwing her hand up to shield her eyes from the sun. There was a movement there, on the rock nearest her horse, a shadow, long and cylindrical, in the crevice between two boulders. Then it coiled. It rattled, then stretched toward the neck of her horse.

The entire wagon took a great heave, it seemed, and might have tipped onto its side had the wall beside them not been there. As Rachel, realizing her blunder, made a desperate grab for the lines, the horses, screaming in terror, grabbed the bits in their mouths and took their heads. The lines slid like that slithering snake off the foot brace and dangled over the tongue, beyond her reach.

The wagon tipped and swayed like a ship in a hurricane, throwing Rachel from one side of the wagon seat to the other; the sheer will to survive made her at last grip it with both hands before she was flung to the far ends of the earth. Audra's hysterical screams didn't help. The crashing of dishes and the spilling of water barrels didn't either. Every sound sent the animals into further frenzy, until soon they were battling to rip away from the wagon and escape.

She couldn't scream. All the dust in Texas had found its way into her throat and eyes and nostrils. She felt, rather than saw, the wagon sway as far to the left as seemed possible before rocking to the right just as far. They were traveling at an angle from the wagon train; from the corner of her eye she caught glimpses of men riding toward her, but they were so far away. They would never reach her, and by now the horses were running flat out, mindless of the harnesses.

The lines dangled still, there beyond her reach, the ends bouncing freely upon the ground. If she stretched . . .

She went to her knees, cursing the billows of skirts and petticoats that surged up to her armpits. Coiling her legs to her chest, she rolled forward and reached; the right front wheel hit a rock and tossed her. She grabbed the wagon seat. It slid like a live thing back and forth in the palms until, gritting her teeth, she sank her nails into the hard wood.

And then *he* appeared from nowhere, a tall, dark angel sent to rescue her. He came up over the side of the wagon as gracefully as if he were walking into a parlor in New Orleans, his face grim and set to the task, his blacker-than-black hair whipping about his head. She saw his chained hands reach out for her; she was too frightened to move at first, afraid of letting go of the wagon seat and being sucked down into the tangle of harnesses, thundering hooves, and reins dancing on end.

His fingers clamped around her wrist as steadfastly as the glittering manacles around his own. He heaved her up onto the seat, and though she made a desperate grab to hold him, he shoved her away before diving the best he could over the footboard where she'd crouched moments before. He stretched, tottered, and slipped.

As he scrambled for another foothold, she lunged and twisted her hands into the waistband of his breeches. He regained his balance and reached again. His fingers found the lines. With all the strength she possessed she hauled him backward; his full weight landed in her lap, and with little thought she threw her arms around his waist and clutched him to her as he battled the demented animals.

Slowly, they began to stop.

She didn't notice when they came to a final halt. Her face mashed against his back, she gasped through her nose and mouth, swimming in the scent of his sweat and fear. Her head reeled with it. It surged through her senses like a flood until she clutched his hard body to her like a lifeline. She groaned when he moved.

His hands were suddenly around her waist. How he lifted her and somehow carried her to the ground she never knew. Her world was still upside down and careening crazily. All she knew, when she finally managed to open her eyes, was that he was shaking her. His fingers were digging into her shoulders like ten separate vises. The chain between his wrists was dangling in front of her.

"You little fool, what the hell were you doing? Didn't I tell you to keep those lines up? Didn't I? Christ, you were almost killed!"

But for the dark stubble of beard over his cheeks, his face was white, intensifying the blue of his eyes, the heavy blackness of his brows and hair that, dripping with sweat, drooped nearly to the bridge of his nose.

"What were you doing, Rachel? I warned you not two hours ago to keep those lines up, that if the horses smelled water they'd bolt."

She stared at his mouth and thought he had the straightest, whitest teeth of any man she'd ever met.

"Dammit, but you've got no business driving that wagon!"

There was a pulse beating frantically at the base of his throat. Minus a button, his shirt gaped to the middle of his chest. The skin there shone with perspiration and was as dark, if not darker, than his face. Even as she watched, a bead of sweat formed below his ear and ran in a zigzagging course down a vibrating blue vein in his neck. She picked up her hand and touched her finger to it. It beaded on her fingernail.

In some dim corner of her mind she knew he would kiss her. She wanted him to kiss her. She'd dreamed of it constantly the past few nights. Like a child aching for a chance at the forbidden, the thought had filled her mind every waking minute as well. She needed, at that moment, to be touched, held, consoled. And all those needs combined had swept away all pretense and left only herself, her soul, and the realization of her desire.

She was compelled to lift her face to his. She waited a heartbeat before he appeared to acknowledge her offering. *Hurry! Hurry,* her heart and mind beseeched him, *before I remember that I'm a lady and you're an outlaw!*

He shook her again. And this time when her misty eyes turned up, his control shattered. He knew he was going to kiss her and there wasn't a damn thing he could do about it. He'd known for the last two days that it would come to this, since that moment outside the jailhouse, even through the excruciating ordeal at Rancho de Bejar. And he didn't give a damn any longer. He would submit—hell, surrender; it wouldn't be the first time. He'd been driven to his knees before.

But, God. Oh God, not by a woman!

He took her face, small and delicate as china, in his hands. His fingers tunneled through her wild hair and pressed into her scalp. The heels of his palms forced her face up to his. His head dropped, and just before he closed his eyes, he watched her lips open in surprise, or denial; he couldn't tell which. He didn't care. Softly he whispered, "Fool, little fool. Play with passion, Rachel, and you're bound to get burned."

Then he covered her mouth with his own, completely, penetratingly. Harshly. *Clumsy fool!* That thought flashed through his mind. He moved against her until her body had no choice but to sway full length against him. Her hands twisted in his shirt out of desperation. And still he kissed her, forcibly pressing her mouth open with his. She whimpered, and a growl wedged up his throat and hummed between their faces.

"You're . . . hurting . . . me," she managed against his mouth. Her small hands, doubled up like knots, drove into his chest as she attempted to escape him.

A rumble of approaching horses penetrated the tension. Sliding his hands from her head, he backed away.

Her mouth was red and slick and slightly swollen, the skin on either side abraded by his beard. "Beast!" She tenderly touched her mouth. "Don't you ever, *ever* kiss me like that again. Just who do you think I am, some bordello woman you can manhandle as if I had the feelings of a fencepost?" The look of stunned surprise, then anger, on his face filled her with terror. Good Lord, what had she said?

Homer George rode up. He was off his horse in a flash. "Mercy, Miss Gregory, whatever happened here? Are ya all right?"

Backing from the dangerous look in Davis's eyes, she rounded on the concerned wagonmaster and snapped, "No I am not!"

Sam joined them then. Looking from Davis to Rachel he said, "Now that was about the hairiest ride I've seen in some time. Miss Gregory, are ya—"

"No I am not!" She was sounding hysterical.

They all stood with their mouths open, deliberating

whether or not they should say anything else. Then she saw
Audra. Standing some distance away, dressed only in her
chemise and pantaloons, she was dusting herself off and
cursing at the top of her voice. Half the men in the wagon
train were riding rings around her and gawking.

It was all so . . . comical. So why didn't she laugh? She
started shaking and couldn't stop, couldn't control the tears
that puddled in her eyes, and then overflowed them. Homer
and Sam had the good grace to look away, perhaps out of
respect or maybe just because they were uncomfortable
dealing with a woman's emotionalism. She was as alone suddenly as if they had mounted their heaving, sweating animals and ridden back to the train. As alone as she was when
her father died.

She pressed her fingers against her mouth in a futile effort
to hold back the all-too-feminine sound of weeping. Not
here, she thought. Not when the world was composed entirely of men who thought her nothing more than some simpering little ninny with rocks for brains.

Davis closed his hand on her arm. He gently turned her
about. The anger was gone now, though his mouth was set
in a firm line. He took her wrists in his fingers and said,
"Christ, they're bleeding."

She stared through a watery world at her fingertips. The
skin was torn and covered with splinters, yet all she could
think was: *Don't blink or the tears will fall.*

He turned up her palms. There were blisters there, broken
and bleeding as well. "Damn." The word was raw. "Ah,
damn, where are your gloves? And your hat. Look at your
face, lady, you're burned up. Where is your hat?"

"Th-the horse ate it," she only managed.

"The horse ate it," he repeated, exasperated.

She buried her face against his chest, letting the tears fall
silently while she inwardly cursed the chain that pressed between their bodies; it reminded her she had no business
burying her face against his chest. She had no business demanding tenderness from him when he probably had none
to give. She felt him stiffen. She wanted to beat his chest for

no other reason than just *because*. Because he hadn't kissed her adoringly as he had in her fantasies, like some dandy back home might have kissed her. He didn't soothe away her cuts and bruises with words of concern. He didn't do a damn thing but stand there like a board with his hands at his side and let her pour her soul onto his shirtfront.

A horse approached.

"Miss Gregory!"

Martin Stillwell. Rachel rolled her head and peeked at him from the corner of one eye.

Leaping from his horse and wagging a riding crop at Davis, he demanded, "Take your filthy hands off this young woman, sir!"

A chest muscle flexed beneath Rachel's cheek. It was Davis's only response.

"Captain Wells," the Englishman continued, "will you kindly do something about this reprobate? You allow him to wander about this train as if he were royalty, and now he is openly harassing this young woman. I said get your hands off her!"

Before Rachel could fully turn away from Davis, Stillwell took a step between them, jutted his narrow chin at the taller man, and said, "How dare you lay one unworthy finger upon her. You are not fit to wipe her feet, sir."

Davis was seething, she could tell. Yet he did and said nothing. Just stared down into Stillwell's eyes with such glittering coldness that Rachel almost shivered.

"Please, Martin." She thought it best to divert the Englishman's attention before Davis lost his patience. In truth, she was awed by the fact that he had not done so already. "Mr. Davis stopped my wagon. Had it not been for him I would surely have been killed."

Drawing up one blond brow, Martin faced her. A flicker of disapproval showed in his eyes. Whether it was due to the fact that she had actually defended Davis or due to her appearance, she couldn't decide. But in that moment she experienced an instant of empathy with Davis and anger at Stillwell.

Martin caught her arm with surprising possessiveness. "Come away, Rachel. I'll have my man come back for your wagon. We'll work something out—"

She was led only a short distance away before being yanked back so hard her head snapped. She was whirled forcibly about to face Davis. The cold fury in his voice and the mutinous look in his eyes as he glared at Martin brooked no protest—verbal or physical—from either of them.

"Get on the wagon," he said through his teeth, then added, "Miss Gregory."

Speechless, she stared toward Sam. The Ranger moved closer.

"I'll see to the lady's wagon, *English,*" Davis said. "I hardly think your butler can drive them both."

Martin's shoulders snapped back. "He is *not* a butler, Davis. He is my manservant."

Davis slanted a black brow and mocked, "Is that a fact?"

It was time for Sam to move in. "Seems to me Davis is right," he announced to all who stood by, gaping. "Miss Gregory needs help with this wagon."

"For God's sake!" It was Stillwell again. "You cannot be serious, Captain. This—this *criminal,* bound in chains, should not be allowed within a mile of any of us. And certainly not so near an unescorted lady."

"These chains sure didn't keep him from savin' the lady, though I'll be damned if I know how he did it. Anyway, I'll be near enough," Sam explained. He turned back to Rachel and Davis. "He'll be sittin' up there clearly in sight of my men and half this wagon train. If he tries anything, he'll be dead before his carcass hits the ground." Staring up into Davis's eyes, he added, "We *do* understand one another, Kid?"

Davis's only response was, "Get on the wagon, Rachel."

Homer said, "We'll gather up yore stepmother, Miss Gregory, and them barrels ya lost along the way."

She thanked him, noting that Audra was stomping her way to the wagon, rubbing her buttocks with both hands and cursing.

Rachel was still shaking. The weight of what had transpired in those few minutes was, at last, settling on her. She reached for the wagon and was reminded, upon contact, of the sorry state of her hands. Her knees were knocking and all strength seemed suddenly to have evaporated beneath the ungodly sun.

Davis moved up behind her, clamped his hands about her waist, and hoisted. She fell upon the wagon seat. No more than a second later he was stepping over her, sitting beside her, taking the lines in his hands as if it were the most natural thing in the world for him to be there.

Rogers rode up. "Here's your hat, Davis."

He took it and plunked it on Rachel's head. "I told you to wear a hat," he said. "And stop licking your lips. You'll have them cracked and bleeding by day's end." He looked at her hands. "We'll have to do something about that. Jeez, what a mess."

She clutched them to her breast.

"I told you to wear gloves. The horse didn't eat those too, did he?"

Her head slowly turned. She looked into his blue eyes and thought she really should get out of the sun. It was making her feel awfully light-headed. She stared at his mouth.

He stared at her mouth.

Audra climbed in the back of the wagon and ranted something to Rachel.

She recalled the heat of his mouth on hers. She'd been too angry over his harshness and shaken by her ordeal when he'd kissed her to notice more than his lack of tenderness. Now, however, awareness was creeping slowly but surely through her veins and warming her blood to the point of discomfort. His hard arm was pressed against hers. His legs, strong and lean and gray with dust, seemed to take up the wagon seat. She wanted to coil up in a little ball and tuck herself into the large hands that were gripping the lines with uncanny gentleness. Odd to see tenderness from him. There wasn't a tender bone in the man's body.

*   *   *

The others waited and watched from their wagons beside the Arroyo Hondo River as the haggard group rejoined the train. The river snaked between two steep hills and, further west, pooled into a clear lake that offered the weary travelers and animals respite from the grueling heat. But first, they were informed, they must cross the river.

Rachel ignored the curious and sometimes condemning looks from the other women — or tried to. They continually looked from Rachel to Davis and back again to Rachel as he went about preparing her wagon for the crossing.

The sturdiest two wagons in the train were singled out by Homer. Davis, as well as the other prisoners, was then enlisted to help unload the heavy freighters. It was a comical sight. Scattered about the grounds were beds, mattresses full of cornshucks that the children took delight in jumping on, brushbrooms, trunks made of leather stretched taut over wooden frames, and a sizing mannequin studded with pins and paper patterns that flapped like birds' wings off the shoulders of the shapely form. Jeromia took hold of the wasp-waisted contraption and pretended to dance the "Chicken in the Bread Tray" with it. Everyone laughed, and the tension eased.

The two empty wagon beds were hauled by the prisoners to the river. Four empty water barrels were lashed inside each, then the beds were inverted and shoved into the river where they were attached to a rope Homer had tied to a tree stump on the opposite bank. Rachel watched it all with interest. But mostly she watched Davis. He went about the efforts as knowledgeably as the train hands. And while Clyde, Pete, and Pedro dragged their feet throughout the ordeal, causing Sam to swear and threaten them with his Sharp, Davis worked as hard if not harder than Homer himself. And she was glad, deep down, that he was driving her wagon.

The inverted wagons made a rudimentary floating ferry, eight or nine feet square, but big enough to handle the wagons the travelers carefully maneuvered onto them. Then they were each tugged across the deep, fast-flowing river. It was a slow process, and since Rachel's wagon was last on the train, she took the time to lounge in the shade of a live oak and decide whether or not she liked Kid Davis. Looking curiously into a bird's nest that was tucked within the thorns of a prickly pear cactus, she decided she did like Davis, a lot. Regardless of what he was. She then turned her attentions to her hands.

They hurt horribly. But calling attention to them would only remind everyone of the awful inconvenience she'd caused them from the onset of this trip. Her fellow travelers weren't happy she was along. After all, no other women were without some sort of male escort. Single women were a threat in themselves, at least to married ladies. Well, she would have to show them that she was just as tough and brave as the rest of them. Nothing as menial as—she looked at her ravaged palms—*hands* were going to keep her from doing her share of the work. Not if she could help it.

The crossing went smoothly. In all, the entire effort took little more than two hours. When Rachel's wagon was rolled onto the muddy riverbank, Homer informed them all they would yoke up and continue on their journey, as there would be enough sunlight to see them another four or five miles down the road. Having refreshed themselves and their animals in the river these past two hours, they were eager to get on with it.

The travelers hurried to regroup, reload, reyoke, and harness. Homer called out, "Stretch out!" and as Davis, having climbed aboard the wagon beside Rachel, let out an ear-piercing whistle to the animals, the wagon gave a shudder, a wobbly, uneven lunge . . . and broke.

Chapter 8

She'd have to be blind, as well as dumb, not to realize that the entire wagon train full of people had begun talking about her relationship with the outlaw.

"Ouch!" Rachel closed her eyes and gritted her teeth as Manuela poked with a needle at the splinter in her finger. The sliver slid easily from her skin and she watched as the woman dabbed with a piece of cotton material at the tiny blossom of blood that oozed atop her fingertip. Rachel looked around her then. "They're staring at me, Manuela."

"Nonsense. Now hold steady."

"They are staring, I tell you. For heaven's sake the man is only driving my wagon. You would think we were courting the way they look and whisper."

"People will talk." She poked again.

"Ouch! But there is nothing to talk about! Ouch!"

"Perhaps they talk of other things."

"Such as?"

Frowning, Manuela shifted Rachel's hand into better light and said, "Your clothes, perhaps."

"My clothes! What is wrong with my clothes?"

"They are very nice for New Orleans, I imagine, but not here."

"Oh well, forgive me. If you'll just excuse me I'll step inside my wagon and slip into a towsack. Ouch!" Rachel's lips tightened as she stared toward the group of children kicking about a great ball of tightly wound quilt scraps in the distance.

"They are very expensive," Manuela explained. "Much more expensive than these people can afford."

"I'm not asking them to buy them."

"They are not very practical."

She couldn't argue with that one. Her shoulders slumping, she winced again and said, "I don't have anything else."

"Then pay no attention to what the others think." Wrapping Rachel's hand in gauze, she said, "Keep them bound until they've healed a bit."

"But how will I cook? Build a fire? Drive the wagon?" She waved her arms for emphasis. "My stepmother will swoon with the vapors if she believes I shan't be able to cater to her every whim, Manuela. I will hear again that I'm pampered and spoiled and care not a whit for anyone but myself."

Manuela gathered up her first aid supplies—gauze, salves, thread, and needles—and motioned toward the group of men in the distance. "It seems you have plenty of help, Senorita Rachel. No need to worry that your stepmother will starve."

That, she thought, as she peered toward the sweating, cursing, laboring men, was little consolation.

Davis positioned his knees against the side of the wagon, crouched slightly, and, setting his back straight, heaved, along with Lindsey, Gonzales, and Jenkins, lifting the wagon bed high enough so Homer and Jeromia Peabody could wiggle the wheel on and off the axle. The muscles in his arms, thighs, and shoulders burned. His temple throbbed with the strain.

"That's what I figured," he heard Homer say. "Damn wood shrinkage. We'll have to soak that son-of-a-gun in the river." Scratching the back of his head, the wagonmaster said, "Put it down, boys, if you can. Ain't nothin' we can do till tomorrow mornin'."

A groan sounded from the onlooking travelers.

Someone said, "I take exception, Mr. George, to the fact that you allowed them women to travel unescorted on this train."

"Is that a fact?" Homer said.

"It is, sir. They've been nothin' but trouble since the onset of this journey. Why, just look at them. They don't even know how to handle the horses. Now that prisoner has been brung up among us to do it for her, endangering all our lives."

"Well, I declare. I didn't hear nobody else volunteerin' to do it."

Another voice spoke up. "You should never have allowed them to travel with us in such an ill-equipped wagon. It simply is not fit to make the journey."

"Wheel shrinkage is to be expected. It'll probably happen to all of you."

Several travelers called out, "We've lost a half day of travel!"

"It won't be the last," he reasoned. "Just be thankful it's by a crik and not out in the middle of nowhares. Enjoy it whilst you can, folks, because it'll be another several days afore we camp 'side another."

The group grumbled as they turned away, several looking back over their shoulders and shaking their heads.

Peabody and several of the other train employees hurried to prop up the wagon with a rudimentary-looking brace. The wagon bed had barely been shifted onto it before Clyde, Pete, and Pedro peeled to one side, leaving Davis alone to manage the sudden weight. The brace shifted, and before he could jump away, the wagon gave a lurch and toppled directly onto him. He went down beneath its cumbersome bulk, his leg within inches of being crushed beneath its weight.

"Oh my!" It was Rachel's voice. He looked backward through the dust, watching as she barreled through the gawking onlookers, her silk skirts swirling around her ankles, her silver-blond hair a mass of tangles, and her bound hands waving frantically about her. "Someone help him!" she cried out.

"Git that wagon off that man!" Sam ordered the smirking prisoners. Lifting his Sharp, he pointed directly at Clyde and said, "Now!"

Rachel fell to her knees beside him. "Oh dear, Mr. Davis, I fear this is my fault. Is there a great deal of pain?"

"Yes," he lied, doing his best to feign agony.

Placing a comforting hand upon his chest, she said, "I'll do what I can to help you. I did some volunteer work during the War, you know. You may hold my hand if you wish. At least until they remove the wagon from your leg."

He wrapped his fingers gently around her bandaged hand. The soft halo of hair around her face made her flawless features look like those of an angel. He wondered briefly if the fall beneath the wagon hadn't killed him after all.

"Oh my," she said again with her soft, red mouth, "I fear you've gone quite pale, Mr. Davis."

Had he? Suddenly flinging her hand away he said, "Leave me alone. I'm in no pain."

"But you—"

"I said there's no pain!" His head and shoulders left the ground for emphasis; then, propping up on his elbows, he slid his legs from beneath the wagon. He watched her eyes go black.

"Oh! Oh, well." She snatched her hand into the folds of her dusty skirt. "I might have known you would take advantage of the situation."

"Why not? It's not every day a beautiful woman throws herself at my feet."

"I don't doubt that for a minute." Standing, she glared so hotly at him he almost regretted his little prank. *Almost.* "Isn't it enough that you have the entire train questioning my reputation?" she demanded with a tilt of her fine-boned little chin. There was a smudge of dirt across it that made her all the more appealing.

Moving to his feet, he slapped the dust from his breeches and looked directly at the curious men and women who had reluctantly begun returning to their wagons. "Next time I'll let your wagon go off the damn cliff, Miss Gregory," he said in a lower voice. "I wonder if you would be so concerned over your reputation had Martin Stillwell plucked you from death's door."

"Well, he didn't." She crossed her arms and set her chin in a decisive way.

Jabbing a finger at the end of her nose, he retorted, "Exactly, sweet cheeks! *I* did, and don't forget it."

They glared at one another a long minute before he turned back to the wagon. Joining the others, the prisoners lifted and tried once again to balance the front right corner of the wagon on the brace. This time it stayed.

Sam sauntered up. Cradling his rifle like a baby in his arms, he nodded pleasantly to Rachel and said, "'Spect we'll camp here seein's how that wheel's got to soak overnight in the river. Should be some fair huntin' possibilities along this creek bank, and I was wonderin', Miss Rachel. Seein's how ya brung so little in the way of grub, maybe I can help ya out with vittles. Me and my men here've got enough on our hands tryin' to keep these renegades under control, so I propose that we supply you with meat if'n ya cook fer us."

"Cook?" She swallowed back her panic. "Me?"

"Nothin' special. Stew, dumplin's, bread."

"Bread?"

"Course in turn we'll see to yore animals, harnessin' and unharnessin', and keep ya stocked up with kindlin' for yore fires. Mr. Davis there will continue drivin' them animals as long as ya need 'im—and as long as he behaves 'imself, o' course."

"But—"

He lifted one hand, callused palm up, to hush her. "Now, no need to fear that we'll be makin' a nuisance of ourselves. No, ma'am, we don't plan on doin' that. We'll jest keep our distance as always and when them vittles is done my deputies'll pick 'em up and haul 'em back. I wouldn't impose these men's proximities on yore fine character." He pointed to the prisoners, shifted his wad of tobacco from one cheek to the other, and smiled before adding, "I know it's tough enough havin' to deal with Davis there."

She opened her mouth to protest, then thought again of the beans they'd eaten the last two days.

It was Davis who spoke next.

"Maybe the lady doesn't know how to cook, Sam."

Rachel narrowed her eyes and shot him a glance. His gaze was friendly, his smile a little too taunting, however, not to agitate her pride.

"Go on, Davis," Sam said. "All women know how to cook. It's like motherin'. Jest comes natural."

Looking down at her feet, then back at the Ranger, she pressed her gauzed hands together and sighed. "Well. I—I suppose—"

"Fine! Fine! We're much obliged, Miss Rachel. Now you jest get that stew pot ready 'cause one of my men seen some jackrabbits earlier." Tipping his hat, he spun on his heel and, waving his rifle barrel at Clyde, joined the deputies who were preparing to make camp some distance away.

She might have protested again had Sam not immediately become involved in conversation with Deputy Hale. So she looked back at Davis. He had turned away again and was testing the wagon, making certain its weight was steady on the brace. Her eyes traveled down the long expanse of his back, over his slim hips, and down his long, well-muscled legs. Up again they went to his shoulders. The back of his shirt was dusty; it clung to his skin, and blotches of sweat spotted it here and there. His black hair curled slightly over the collar and gently, almost boyishly, around his ears.

As a wave of heat suffused her cheeks she looked away. This wasn't the sort of interest a lady of her upbringing should be experiencing, yet she was experiencing it a great deal these days. Even more often since the kiss that morning.

The quilt ball came from nowhere and thumped against the back of Davis's right boot. It ricocheted under the wagon.

Davis turned as a towheaded youth with a face full of freckles made a dive practically between his legs. Making a grab for the seat of his breeches, Davis hauled the boy from under the unsteady wagon, plunked him on his feet, and said, "Here now, boy, you looking to get squashed?"

"Shoot no, mister, I'm aiming to git my ball back."

"Looked to me like you were aiming to get squashed."

"Nah." The child shook his head full of tawny curls.

Davis grinned, went down on one knee, and fished the huge ball of scraps from just behind the wagon brace. When he turned again the child was sucking on his thumb. "Sucking thumb'll make you bucktoothed," he told him.

"Aw, I ain't suckin' thumb."

Davis stared intently as the boy jerked his slimy-wet thumb out of his mouth and hid it behind his back. He then looked up at Rachel, who had watched the scene with nothing short of fascination. It brought to her mind the memory of Alejandro de Bastitas with his grandchild, and that made her recall Davis's staggering resemblance to the handsome older man.

Just as staggering was the change that had suddenly come over Davis. She'd never seen *anyone* go through such a transformation as he had the moment the child came up. The sight made her feel all weak and fluttery inside, like a cloud of butterflies had all taken wing in her stomach.

"What do you think, Miss Gregory?" came that mellow deep voice that made her not only fluttery but dizzy as well. "I think he was sucking thumb."

"I wasn't! Five-year-olds don't suck thumb! A bee stung me is all. See!" Up went his thumb again, nearly into Davis's eye.

Davis squinted at the swelling on the tip of the child's finger.

Rachel joined them then, knowing even as she went to her knees in a cloud of blue silk and white eyelet lace that her reason for doing so wasn't strictly because of the boy. "Why, Mr. Davis, I think he's right. And look there, I do believe the stinger's in there still." She reached for the child's hand, only to be reminded that her own were little better. There was little she could do with them bound as they were.

Davis took the child's hand, his long dark fingers making hers and the boy's look as small as a doll's. She stared at the black hair sparsely covering the back of his hand and wrist before forcing her gaze back to the child's face.

Davis studied the thumb a minute. Very carefully then, he lifted it to his mouth, slid the tip of his tongue ever so lightly over the swelling before pressing his teeth against it. The boy flinched. His eyes flew wide, and for an instant Rachel thought he might cry. Davis came away with the stinger on the tip of his tongue. He spat it away.

Rachel quickly unwrapped a portion of the gauze around her hand. Nipping it with her teeth, she tore off enough to string around the child's thumb. "There now, is that better?" she asked him.

"Ricky! Ricky, what in God's name are you doing over here?"

Rachel, Davis, and Ricky looked around as Ricky's mother came swooping at them like a hen with her feathers ruffled. Her eyes very nearly popping from her head, she grabbed up her son and turned her horrified and vicious glower on Davis.

"How dare you sully my son by touching him! How dare you!" Smothering Ricky's face in kisses then, she asked him, "Did he hurt you, pet? There, there, did the mean man hurt my boy in any way?"

Rachel leaped to her feet. Her heel caught the hem of her petticoat and ripped it, but she hardly noticed. Her face was burning all the way to her ears. "What an unkind thing to say," she told the woman. "This man did nothing but save the boy from getting hurt beneath this wagon!"

"He fixed my thumb, too." Ricky held up his padded thumb for his mother to see.

His mother ignored him. "You people shouldn't even be on this train. You're a menace to us all!" Tucking the boy's head against her then, she turned and marched away. Ricky, his eyes filled with tears, peered back over her shoulder, lifted his hand with its bandaged thumb, and waved.

Rachel watched them go, her anger mounting. "Such cruel insensitivity is unforgivable," she said. "I—" She turned back to Davis.

He had left her and joined the others.

That night she couldn't sleep. The bedroll stretched out beside her wagon offered little or no comfort, and there was always the fear a snake would take advantage of her body warmth and curl up in the blankets with her. Rolling from her pallet, Rachel sat for a long while, staring out over the moon-drenched countryside. The breeze was cool, but offered little relief from the discomforting heat upon her cheeks, heat put there by her shameless dreams of Davis.

The kiss that morning had affected her intensely. She could hardly think of anything else. While eating the rabbit stew Manuela had shown her how to make, she'd tried to imagine again the way his hands had felt against her sun-blistered face. They'd been sturdy, for certain, and rough.

She'd attended a square dance put on by the wagon hands after the evening meal. And though Jeromia Peabody had adroitly played his fiddle, and Martin Stillwell had danced with her through every bouncing tune, she'd found herself throughout the evening comparing his suave manners and dapper dress to Davis—only to realize that there could be no comparison. Not in manners, appearance . . . or kissing.

Yes, she'd allowed Martin to kiss her at evening's end. She'd closed her eyes and turned her face up to his, hoping the same flood of response would leave her just as unsettled as she had been that morning by Davis. It hadn't happened. Closing his gentle fingers about her shoulders, Martin had pressed his dry mouth against hers, and her response had been . . . revulsion?

Attempting to stem such thoughts, Rachel pulled her shawl up around her shoulders and, careful not to wake Audra, walked quietly from the wagon to the shadowed outcropping of rocks some distance away. Outside the circle of wagons, where the wind gusted more briskly, molding her white nightgown against her body, she climbed the flat plateau of rock and stared out over the river, a long, twisting ribbon of onyx and sapphire. On the far bank and atop the low-rising hill of silver-tipped grass rode the night guards, their black silhouettes on the horizon reassuring her, even in these hostile surroundings.

After pulling her gown up to her knees, she sat down upon the rock's ledge and dangled her feet in the water. The gentle waves, ruffled by the wind, lapped at her legs but felt warm on her ankles. Her feet, she mused, could use the respite. Stillwell had done an abominable job on her toes throughout the evening. Gentleman he might be, but he certainly couldn't dance.

"Nice night."

She jumped and twisted around, grabbing her shawl about her shoulders like armor. "Mr. Davis! Whatever are you doing out here?"

"Enjoying the scenery, Miss Gregory. What about you?"

"I couldn't sleep," she said, squinting to better see him in the shadows.

He stepped onto the rock, his hands tucked into his breeches pockets, and looked for a very long time out over the river. "Me either," he finally said. "Did you enjoy yourself at the dance this evening?"

The moon glanced off his nose and cheek and chin. It reflected like stars in his hair. Clearing her throat, she responded, "Yes, I had a very nice time, thank you."

She splashed the water with her toes and tried to concentrate on the night watchman in the distance. Impossible. The night was filled with Davis. Every star, every shadow. The very breeze had warmed upon her face and the silent air crackled with his slightest movement.

Gripping her shawl more tightly about her shoulders, anxious to put the heavy silence between them to an end, she said, "I fear, in all the commotion with the wagon wheel falling off, I forgot to thank you for your somewhat heroic deed."

He looked down over his shoulder.

"Thank you, Mr. Davis."

He smiled, then realized that he was doing that with frightening regularity the last few days—every time he was near Rachel. He was going soft, and that bothered him. He'd worked damn hard to develop his character. He'd had no choice if he wanted to survive in his world—a world that had nothing to do with satin frocks and ruffled petticoats. Not that he had ever regretted the life he'd chosen to live. "What you never had, you never miss," Barnard Davis had once told him, just before his patrol had ridden out of Fort Bliss and been massacred at Antelope Creek by Chipota of the Lipan Apache.

He frowned with that memory. It was a wound, like so many others in his life, that would never fully heal. He'd cared for Barney Davis as much as he'd cared for anyone.

Barnard Davis had been a strict disciplinarian—all army from the top of his regulation hat to the tip of his regulation boots. He'd devoted his life to righting the injustices inflicted on the settlers *and* Indians throughout Texas and New Mexico. He'd taught a kid who was dead inside how to live again, how to deal with his failures and triumphs and how *not* to look back at occurrences that he couldn't change. On the day the scout patrol returned the captain's body, that kid, unable to voice his thanks for the generosity the cavalryman had shown him over the previous four years, took the name Davis as his own, walked out through the fort gates, and never looked back.

Yet he found himself wondering now how his life might have been different if he'd stayed. Had he enlisted in the army, as Barnard had hoped he would do, he might have worked his way up in rank, perhaps to captain. A woman like Rachel Gregory might find a man with stripes respectable enough for . . . For what?

He looked down on her head. Her hair, bathed in moonlight, swam in the breeze around her ghostly white shawl and nightgown. She could be an image conjured up in a sleeping man's dreams, an earthbound angel with her halo slightly askew. Askew? He smiled to himself. Given a good hard nudge it would tumble right off. Beneath that unpretentious innocence was a woman, full-fledged. She just hadn't realized it yet. Or maybe she had. There *had* been Luke . . .

Rachel looked around as Davis squatted beside her. There was something different about him that she noticed immediately. A wave of pleasure and approval swept over her as she noted that he'd shaved and bathed and changed shirts.

And there was something else she couldn't quite put her finger on.

He caught her staring. "I shaved," he said.

"So I noticed." She was bothered by it, but didn't know why. Then allowing herself to look more intensely at his features she suddenly *did* know why. Extraordinary. That word came to her mind. Clean-shaven, the man was exceptionally handsome. Even more than she had ever imagined. She bowed her head, refusing to look at him again, yet despite her best intentions she found her eyes drawn back to his.

In that pulsebeat of a moment he realized that he was going to do something stupid like kiss her again if he wasn't careful, so looking back up the river he asked, "How is our Mr. Stillwell tonight?"

"Clumsy on my toes, I'm afraid to say. I shan't be able to walk for the next day or so."

"What a shame. Don't you rich folk take dancing lessons or something?"

"Ordinarily. He must have missed his."

His head swiveled slowly about until he was facing her once again. "And how does he kiss, Miss Gregory?" He looked at her mouth.

Her mouth dropped open. His heavy-lidded eyes revealed only polite interest, but the firm set of his lips hinted otherwise. "Why, Mr. Davis, that is none of your business. What were you doing? Spying on me?"

"Not much spying to it, Miss Gregory. Half the wagon train saw you."

Her eyes widened.

"Does he kiss any better than Luke?"

"Oh! I don't think I care to discuss it." She made a move to stand. The soft white gown slid to the top of her thighs as she pulled her feet from the water.

"Sit down," he said sternly.

Rachel colored angrily. "I did not venture out on this night to be maligned by the likes of you, Mr. Davis. Good night!"

"I said . . . sit . . . down." He slammed one large sun-browned hand on her shoulder and shoved her back down on the rock.

She yielded reluctantly, throwing him a scathing glance that said far more than any words could have. A faint frown appeared between Davis's eyes as his gaze met hers, and for a moment, silence descended between them.

"You're certainly sensitive about this Luke person," he finally said.

"I simply do not wish to discuss him," she told him. "My friendship with Luke has been a very dear gift to me throughout my life, and I refuse to be reprimanded over it again."

"Did his parents work for your father?"

"Yes." She stared at the water.

"Sharecropper?"

"Yes," she answered, "although his mother worked in the house. Luke and I were born within days of one another. We both lost our mothers during the yellow fever outbreak of fifty-three."

He had to ask. "Were you in love with him?"

Rachel's head came around again and those astonishingly soulful eyes were suddenly upon him, bringing to mind the kiss they'd shared earlier in the day. He was becoming more and more displeased at the thought that other men had sampled her sweetness. He'd stood in the shadows only that evening and watched Stillwell kiss her. Fortunately, he'd been linked up with Pedro at the time; otherwise, the possessiveness he'd experienced at seeing the man's mouth on hers might have driven him to . . .

"I loved him, Mr. Davis. But I was not *in* love with him. There is a vast difference between the two."

"But he loved you."

"Why, no—"

"I don't believe a man would give up what little respect and position he had to go off to God-knows-where with a woman outside his social class, unless he was in love."

Her face stung, the words having distressed her far more than Davis could know. Hadn't she suspected once that Luke loved her, though when she'd confronted him with the idea he had thoroughly convinced her that the idea was preposterous, that their flight together was only a matter of practicality.

Annoyed, she retaliated. "Love! You talk like an expert, Mr. Davis. What could *you* possibly know about such an emotion?"

"Nothing more than that it is a general waste of time. It muddles up a man's thinking and more likely than not ends up getting him killed."

"How very cynical. How very sad." She splashed her feet in the water, then, curious over Davis's silence, she looked at him from the corner of her eyes. One knee braced upon the rock, he stared into the water as the wind whipped his dark hair over his brow. His light chambray shirt contrasted with his shadowed features. He'd changed boots as well. The fringe on the knee-high moccasins swung back and forth in the breeze.

"Have you never had the desire to marry, Mr. Davis?" What prompted her to ask such an asinine question she could not guess, but it was there on her tongue before she could check it. And she found, in the space of the eternally long seconds before he replied, that she was quite anxious over the response.

Without returning her look, he finally said, "I have."

"You have?"

"I have . . . married."

"Oh!" Her heart did a queer little lurch that prompted her to sway in surprise. Staring again at the river, she repeated, "Oh."

A whippoorwill sang out in the darkness; cicadas hummed from the nearby rushes. Rachel hardly noticed. Her mind was too busy asking, *Why? How? Who was she? And where is she now? Is* she *the reason you've become so hard and bitter and violent?* Suddenly, she wanted desperately to blame his lack of decency on someone other than him.

"Well? Where is she now?" she blurted, unable to contain her curiosity a moment longer.

"I don't know. It was a very long time ago and—"

"Did you love her?"

How quickly the shoe had been shifted to the other foot. Frowning, he said, "I don't remember."

"You don't remember?"

"That's what I said." He stared at her ankles, white above the inky blackness of the water. His eyes then traveled up the shapely form of her calf to her knee and hesitated along the frilly hem of her nightdress.

"Are you still married?"

He wet his lips. The breeze, finding its way under her dress, billowed it softly over her thighs. "No," he said. "No, Miss Gregory, I am no longer married."

"Well, is she living?"

"I have no way of knowing, nor do I care. I would not have cared if Cochise had ridden into our bedroom and spirited her away on our wedding night. It would have saved me from having to hunt her down myself."

She stared at him, waiting.

With the moonlight reflecting from her face she was as white as china, as frail and translucent. He found himself wondering, not for the first time, how she would look spread out on a bed of white sheets and counterpanes and—

"How very odd," she stated, mystified.

"There was little odd about it. I was nineteen years old and thought I knew something about the world. Obviously I didn't. I met a whore in a saloon; she took me upstairs and turned me inside out. At that age love and lust are one and the same. They look the same, taste the same, and smell the same."

He stood up, angry now with the remembrance. "She convinced me that life's injustices had brought her to ruin, and since I was no stranger to those injustices myself it was easy to believe her. She assured me that should the right man come along, she would leave the passions of the bordello behind her forever and settle down to making tea cakes, raising babies, and adoring her husband. At the time I was in the mood to be . . . adored."

"You married a—a prostitute?"

"Who else would have me, Miss Gregory? I had nothing but a few hundred dollars bequeathed to me by a friend, a gun on my hip, and a growing reputation for trouble. I grabbed what looked like a lifeline and found, instead, a snake in the grass."

Rachel scrambled to her feet. Placing her hand lightly on his hard arm, she said, "Who else would have you? But that's ridiculous talk! Other people's opinions of you shouldn't mean more than your opinion of yourself. If you don't believe in yourself, who *can* believe in you? You must try harder to like yourself, Mr. Davis."

He faced Rachel again. The wind, behind him now, teased at the sleeves of his shirt, its cuffs rolled halfway up his forearms. It whipped sporadically at his smoke-black hair and unsettled his stance so he tottered slightly closer to her.

She did not retreat, and the throbbing anger of his own foolishness dissipated with the sight of her small, upturned face and the seriousness in her wide, tilted eyes.

"I assume you divorced?" she asked cautiously.

When he responded, his tone was mild and tinged with a self-deprecating bitterness. "The morning after we were married I woke up to find she was gone, and so was my money. Every cent I owned. It took me months to find her, but I *did* find her."

There was something unnerving in the cold way in which he answered. Shivering, Rachel clutched her shawl more tightly about her and asked, "*Then* you were divorced?"

"It wasn't necessary. The marriage was about as legal as the fake justice of the peace who performed the ceremony. It seems she and the fellow were in league together. They'd pulled the same stunt on fifteen or twenty men before me."

"What did you do?"

His eyes narrowed. "Don't ask, Miss Gregory. The answer may offend you. Just suffice it to say the young woman's reputation as a *femme fatale* came to a rather unfortunate, painful end that day."

"She's—she's not—"

"Dead? No, *querida*, I have never killed a woman, although I'm certain that, by the time I finished with her, she might have wished she was dead."

Looking up into Davis's face, Rachel saw the implication of his words in the hard, glittering depths of his eyes, and it seemed, suddenly, that her heart had forgotten how to beat.

She felt anger—not at him, but at the foolish woman who had bartered his attempt at love for a pocketful of useless money. And for a moment, as his hard-edged appraisal swept over her features, she caught a glimpse of that lost and reckless youth who had ached so for home and love that he had married the first woman who would have him.

She lifted one pale hand in the moonlight and pressed it against his face. The contact was jolting for them both. He flinched; the hard line of his mouth quirked down at the corners and one hand flew up, his fingers wrapping around her fragile wrist, thrusting it away. But only momentarily. For no sooner had she recovered from the abrupt dismissal than his arm came out for her again, wrapping firmly about her waist, impelling her slender body against his. Her attempt to struggle free was fruitless, for he merely bound her more tightly to him, her body having little choice but to arch against the length of his, the intimacy of the shameless embrace filling her scattered senses with a desire she had grown tired of denying.

The moment he kissed her she knew without qualms—had known since the instant she first saw him—that it would come to this; it could not be otherwise between them. She was as drawn to the forbidden as he was. And though she trembled in that instant, it was not due to fear but to the languorous delight singing like music in her blood.

It was wrenching, the kiss, impassioned but withheld, a force contained inside him, fraying the very edges of his willpower to the brink of pain. He moved his mouth gently over hers, remembering the look of anger and irritation on her face that morning, letting his tongue ever so lightly slide over her mouth until, timidly, it opened. And still he withdrew from the invitation for deeper intimacy, dragging his lips from hers and burying his face in her shoulder, her temple, her nape.

"Rachel," he whispered into her ear, disturbing the fine, silken hair at her temples. "God, I want you."

She moaned in response. Her eyelids fluttered and opened as he kissed the soft underside of her chin. She stared at the stars overhead and wondered what madness had consumed her that she should stand beneath the moon and allow this man's sweet, crooning love words to sway her virtue. For indeed, her virtue was coming to an embarrassing end as his hands swept up her spine and around her ribs and crept slowly, slowly, slowly to the swelling undersides of her breasts. And as his large palm opened and then spread over her breast, she swayed against him, drained of all strength and thought, all reason.

He fumbled with the tiny pearl buttons down the yoke of her muslin shift, then impatiently shoved it open with his fingers, driving urgently beneath the material until the cool flesh of her breast quivered against his sweating palm and trembling fingers, until her soft inhalation of breath filled the night sky like a sough of the breeze. And, in a moment of hesitation when she might have backed away, he pinned her ever closer to him until the hot, hard rise of his desire could be detected through his clothes, as well as hers.

"See what you do to me," he said through his teeth. "*Feel* what you do to me."

His thumb and forefinger circled her nipple and squeezed, plucked, until he filled his palm with the firm-soft fullness of her and kneaded with growing urgency. Shifting, he shoved his knee between her legs until she was forced to lean against his thigh, the hard muscle pressing against that mound of femininity that burned him, even through the coarse brown material of his breeches.

This was new, so new, the kiss, the forbidden touch of his hands on her breasts. His mouth came back to hers, all pretense of gentleness gone now beneath the hunger of his kiss, and suddenly she could no longer breathe; the hold on her waist was almost crushing. Wedging her arms between them, she attempted to shove him away. She needed a breath, that's all. This was all getting too far out of hand . . . Only a breath, a moment's respite . . .

"Please!"

He kissed her eyes, her nose, her chin. "Relax," he whispered. "Just relax."

"Mr. Davis—please!"

"You want me, Rachel, I know it. Don't deny it, sweetheart." He would have kissed her again, but she twisted her face away. "Rachel! Dammit, look at me."

"Please! You're hurting me!"

"Then stop fighting. I won't hurt you if you'll stop fighting."

"This isn't the way"—she shoved at him again—"to treat a woman!"

His chest heaving in frustration, he released her and snapped, "You show me a *woman* and I might act accordingly."

She looked stricken. Rubbing her wrists, she cried, "What do you mean by that?"

"Exactly that. Grow up, Rachel. You don't know the first thing about men and women, so why pretend? You're a little girl playing at grown-up games. You're a tease."

"Oh! Oh, you awful, rutting *heathen*!"

"And you kiss like a frigging corpse."

"Oooh!"

"Ice princess. You're as cold and stiff as a damn icicle. Well, let me tell you something, princess, I've held women far less fancy-talking, and beautiful, and rich, who were ten times the woman you are. They weren't opposed to being handled a little rough. In fact, they enjoyed it. A lot. *They* knew how to make a man happy and *they* didn't kiss like a corpse!"

She stumbled backward, her lips parting in mortification.

Regret seized him about the throat as Rachel spun and ran back through the darkness to her wagon. She couldn't help being what she was any more than he could.

Tenderness wasn't in his nature, and he was too old to

change. Even for her. But he had to admit she was almost worth the effort. He'd discovered that night just how much he wanted Rachel Gregory. He wanted her with an urgency that was tormenting.

God, oh God. What was he going to do?

Chapter 9

She tossed and turned on her pallet until just before dawn, the memory of Davis's accusation nagging her cruelly. Ice princess, he had called her. He didn't understand. But neither did she. Her body, indeed, her reasoning was a stranger to her. She should be appalled by his very presence, but his presence played havoc with her better judgment. She had never known a man so physically compelling.

She twisted in her blankets, her mind drifting in and out of sleep. Her hand brushed her breast, conjuring up the image and feel of his forbidden touch within her clothes. Her body's response had frightened her as much as the demands he'd asked of it. She twisted again.

Forget him, whispered her dream shadows.

I'm trying!

He's no good.

But—

No telling what sort of crimes he's to be judged for.

I'm certain they cannot be too serious.

Ask him!

I can't! I'm too afraid!

He's no good.

But he saved my life!

He's dangerous!

But so . . . handsome. He makes me feel so . . . strange.

It's not right.

No. No, it isn't.

Something wasn't right tonight.

He was different. He'd bathed and shaved and changed his clothes.

Something wasn't right tonight!

Her eyes flying open, Rachel sat up with a start. Something certainly wasn't right tonight.

He was not wearing his chains!

Rachel awoke with a pounding head and voices buzzing like angry bees in her ears. Somewhere among it all a woman was crying, a long wailing sound like mourning. Rolling over, she nudged the white hair from her eyes and looked at Audra. Her stepmother was dressed and sitting on a crate, her pale chin resting in the palm of one hand, her elbow propped on her knee.

"What's happening?" she managed groggily. Then struggling to sit up, she looked around, squinting against the morning sun, and asked, "Why didn't you wake me? Why hasn't Homer begun working on the wagon?" Again, the crying. Rachel came to her knees. "Audra, what is happening!"

"It seems that mousy little girl whose mother was so opposed to the Rangers joining the train back in San Antonio has met with misfortune," she said. Then, "She's dead."

"Dead." It wasn't a question.

"Yes. It seems she wandered off in the dark sometime during the night and got herself raped and strangled. She was found just after dawn by the river. Over there." She pointed in the direction Rachel had ventured the previous night. "By that outcropping of rocks, I think."

Oh, no! she thought. *No!*

The crowd in the distance began moving toward the rear of the train. Scrambling to her feet, she lifted the hem of her gown and joined them, her senses attuned to the pain and anger roiling in and around the men's and women's twisted faces as they approached the lawmen who were readying their rifles in anticipation of the mob's reactions.

Shoving her way through the crowd, Rachel stopped dead

at the sight of Davis lounging relaxed beneath a tree, his wrists again manacled. He sat up when he saw her.

She shook with outrage. And fear. She shook in disbelief. She could not—she *would not*—believe it of him.

The dead girl's father stopped before Sam. "Out of my way, Captain Wells! One of them animals killed my baby! I demand justice!"

The crowd roared. "Here! Here! Justice!"

The girl's mother wept then, "We warned you! We all warned you that this *trash* would bring us no end of grief! Now they have taken my little girl and, oh . . ."

She collapsed in her husband's arms, her face blanched and contorted in utter grief. "My baby," she moaned. "My darling baby girl."

Sam cradled his rifle while shifting his eyes among the staring, angry faces of the people. "Yore mistaken," he said in a calm voice. "Couldn'ta been any of these men, sir. As you can see, they's under guard here. Besides, I seen them tracks about the river and yore daughter's body. Them's soft-soled shoes. More'n likely moccasins. It were an Indian, sir, what killed the girl."

"Indian!" The word rifled through the onlookers.

"We ain't seen no Indians in these parts yet!" someone hollered.

Sam leaned to his right and spat a stream of tobacco to the ground. Squinting one eye then, he said, "Ya will. And shortly, I reckon."

"If it were an Indian, Captain, we'd have seen some inklin' of it. No! I say it was one of these heathens who done it!"

The crowd roared again.

"Do you deny they is all being taken to Brackettville and El Paso to hang for murder?" The girl's father shook his fist toward Clyde.

"They is all goin' to stand trial for their crimes, sir. But that don't change matters none here. The fact is, I was on guard duty myself last night, and I vow to ya that none of these men ever left my sight. At all times they was cuffed and chained and in their bedrolls. The villain here is some

Comanche or Apache scout who managed to work his way through the night patrol and come across yore daughter by the river. By now he's probably returned to his party and informed 'em of our whereabouts. If I's you I'd keep a sharp eye out fer trouble 'cause I can feel it brewin' like a storm; I'd stake my reputation as a Texas Ranger on it. If'n you'll take my advice, you'll git the girl buried and Miss Gregory's wagon fixed as soon as possible so we can move out and put as much distance between them and us as possible!"

The angry throbbing din of the crowd dwindled to a low murmur. One by one, they turned back to their wagons.

Rachel, however, stood her ground, unable to avert her eyes from Davis. They were lying—dear God, Davis, the Ranger—they were lying, and looking at her. And she knew within that space of a moment that they were waiting to see if she'd speak up.

Then Davis moved. Slowly he came to her, his dark brown hands adjusting his hat lower over his eyes as he left the shade of the scrubby mesquite tree. He no longer wore the moccasins he'd had on the night before, and his hands were manacled again.

She looked frail in the sunlight, and oh so small. Her hair, thick and wild as a lion's mane, spilled over her shoulders and fluttered in the breeze about her waist. Her face looked as pale as death. "Miss Gregory," he said softly.

She backed away,

"Rachel." He tried again, smiling this time. "Rachel, please . . . go back to the wagon and put on some clothes."

"Don't—touch me."

"Go back—"

"It was you. *You* killed that girl!"

He stopped, drew himself up, and said, "You don't believe that."

"But he lied!" She glanced at Sam. "He lied to protect you, Mr. Davis."

"Keep your voice down, dammit!"

"I want to know why!"

"It's none of your business."

Fists clenched, she threatened, "I'm going to Homer right now and tell him."

"Go ahead, but before the rope snaps my neck in two your precious reputation will be as dead as that girl."

She slapped his face with all the force she could muster. "How dare you think that is all that is important to me!"

"Isn't it?" he snarled. His eyes as cold and emotionless as a reptile's, he hissed, "Isn't that what this is all about? You're not angry at what happened to that girl, you're still angry at me for last night. I brought you down a notch off that ivory tower and you don't like it."

She looked again at Sam. He looked away.

Davis went on with savagery in his voice, and bitterness, knowing his next words would cut her to the bone, but in that moment not caring. Her believing he'd actually killed the girl had wounded him deeply. "You know I didn't kill that girl. And I didn't rape her. If I needed a woman that badly, I'd've had you."

She turned and ran. Blindly, clumsily, choking and breathless, she stumbled to her wagon, dropped to her knees, and retched.

Rounding the wagon, Audra looked on and asked blandly, "What on earth is wrong with you? Oh God, it's not morning sickness, is it? You're not pregnant, are you?"

"Go away." Her stomach heaved again. "For God's sake, just go away and leave me alone."

The men slowly lowered the girl's blanket-wrapped body into the grave, while around the grieving parents the onlookers shook their heads and thanked God that it hadn't been one of them who'd been so horribly killed.

"Let us pray," came Homer's voice over the low weeping. Standing at the head of the shallow grave, he wrung his hat in his hands and began, "Dear God . . ."

"I'm tellin' ya," someone whispered, "it weren't no Indian what killed that girl. You think he would have stopped with one, if'n it was an Indian?"

"No," came the husky reply.

"Hell ño," came another.

"Well, I don't know about you boys, but I'm keepin' my eyes wide open, else it's liable to be our wives and daughters next."

They mumbled in agreement.

The wind kicked up sand about the grave and filtered it over the mourners' feet. Rachel closed her eyes as the girl's mother bent over the yawning earth and sprinkled dirt over the body.

"Ashes to ashes, dust to dust," came Homer's voice. "Amen."

Rachel turned away from the grave with the others, leaving the parents of the girl alone with their grief.

Homer was the first back to her wagon. She saw him shucking his "fancy-dress" buckskin jacket as he prepared to repair her wheel. A fire was already burning nearby. Davis was standing to one side of it, his back to her. He was shirtless, and the heat from the fire as well as the searing sun overhead flushed his skin until it shone like slick, damp copper.

Despite her anger at Davis, her step slowed as she noticed the deep crescent-shaped scar on his back. It wrapped from below his right ribs, up between his shoulder blades. Ignoring the pang of sympathy that shot through her breast at the sight and the jolting, almost frightening realization of how close he must have come to dying, she lifted her chin and walked directly by the lot of them, ignoring Sam's good-natured greeting as she joined Audra in the shade of a live-oak tree.

"You'll never believe what that oaf of a wagonmaster intends to charge us for repairing that blasted wheel," her stepmother whined. "Two dollars! And five dollars to replace broken spokes. It's robbery, I tell you."

Spreading her pink taffeta skirts out over the crate on which she'd sat, Rachel stated, "The least you could have done was to attend the funeral, Audra."

"Funerals are depressing."

"Is that why you opened bottles of champagne after burying my father? You needed cheering up?"

Audra looked at her askance, and smiled.

"Git that fire hot!" Homer called out. "You got that iron tire ready, Jeromia?"

"I do!" Jeromia called back.

Homer said, "Captain Wells, if'n you'll ask yore boys there to git ready—"

"I will, sir," Sam responded. Lifting his rifle at the prisoners, he said, "All right, boys, it's time to work fer yore fare on this train. Put some muscle to it and git that wagon up when we tell ya to!"

Jeromia, having rolled the wheel up from the river, placed it beside the fire and waited as Homer reached into the flames with a long black hook and yanked the red-hot iron out of the ashes. Then, with surprising dexterity, he and Jeromia centered the smoldering metal rim over the wheel and, with a mallet, deftly drove it into place. As soon as that was done, they snatched the wheel up off the ground, lifted, and aimed for the greased axle while Davis and the others heaved the wagon off its brace for the mounting. The wheel slid on like a snug glove.

"Git them buckets of water, now, quick!" Homer called. He and Jeromia whirled and each grabbed the first two buckets of many they had lined up beside the wagon. Immediately they began drenching the radiating tire with bucket after bucket of the water that hissed and crackled and filled the already heavy air with billows of suffocating steam.

Finally Homer stepped back. "That ought to do it, boys. You kin step back now and take a breather."

They emerged from the smoke and steam, their faces and bare torsos redder and damper than before. Davis was wet to his knees. His hair plastered to his forehead, he looked Rachel's way just as Martin Stillwell walked up and said, "Rachel, my dear, there you are. I see they've repaired your wagon. What a relief. I'll be glad to put this terrible place behind us."

He took her hand gently in his and helped her to stand.

"I didn't see you at the funeral, Martin."

"Oh dear, no. No, my sinuses were bothering me dreadfully throughout the night." Holding his head back, he pinched the bridge of his nose and sniffed deeply. "It gives me these dreadful headaches."

"I see." Wrinkling her nose, she looked away.

"I've come to ask if you would join me at midday meal. I'll have Jules cook up something special. More scones, perhaps, with honey?"

Her eyes lit up. "Honey?"

"All the way from Skipton, Yorkshire. It's heather honey, the sweetest on earth." He dabbed at his red-tipped nose with a hankie and said, "Come join me."

She almost agreed, then thought of her obligation to Sam. "But I promised the captain I'd prepare their meals. I really shouldn't."

"Oh, let the bloody buggers starve. They deserve little better."

Rachel gave him a sharp glance. "Thank you, Martin, but after last night I think it not the best idea to be seen too much together."

He dropped his hand slightly. "Indeed."

"People are beginning to talk, you see."

"I do?" He lifted one brow quizzically and peered at her down his narrow, pointed nose. Then, grinning a little too snidely for her liking, he remarked, "Why should we care what this bunch of ruffians think? I daresay *their* reputations were tarnished the moment they were born to their mothers." Her eyes widened and, realizing his blunder, he excused himself by saying, "That was unkind of me, wasn't it? I apologize. It's just these blasted cavities in my face. They are draining like mad and driving me crazy." Waving his kerchief in the air for emphasis he added, "And this annoying heat, the flies, and the stench of those damnable oxen is putting me out of sorts."

"I'm terribly sorry, Martin. I didn't realize the ordeal was having such an effect on you." She patted his hand in concern. "Perhaps you should have Jules prepare you some tea before we pull out."

Blinking his red-rimmed eyes, he sniffed again and exclaimed, "What an excellent idea, Miss Gregory! You *will* join me, of course?" When she hesitated again, he lifted one of her hands to his lips, kissed her fingers adoringly, and in a huskier voice, teased, "After last night I thought you might be more inclined to see me again."

"Last night?" Visions of Davis and his insinuations scuttled across her mind's eye. Chewing her lip, she looked questioningly at her curious companion. "Last night?"

He tweaked her nose with his clammy fingers. "You let me kiss you, my dear. Do you not remember?"

"Oh! Oh, that." Her mouth twisted with the remembrance.

"If we were back in England I might be expected to marry you for such an offense."

Her attention perked up with that one. Frowning as he bent his blond head over her fingers again, she stared at the part in his hair and said emphatically, "Fear not, Mr. Stillwell, we are *not* in England. Far from it. Over here a chaste kiss in the dark with a *friend* is no cause to hustle out the wedding bells."

"Chaste?" He looked up over her knuckles, revealing his sly smile. "I would not call the kiss chaste exactly."

Compared to Davis's it had been downright demure she wanted to say. But she didn't.

"Excuse me?" came Davis's deep voice then, and she thought, *Speak of the devil.* Both she and Martin looked his way.

Still shirtless and leaning against her wagon, one naked arm propped up to support his weight and the other planted on his hip, Davis flashed her a broad startlingly white smile and asked, "Are we having fun, you two?"

Stillwell's back snapped erect as he faced Davis.

"Why, you cad. How dare you eavesdrop on gentlefolk's conversation? If you weren't wrapped up in those chains, I'd call you out."

Davis only laughed. "Maybe if you sweet-talk Wells like

you were Miss Gregory when I walked up, you might convince him to remove the chains long enough for me to kill you, Martin. Go ahead. I'll wait while you do."

Martin's body vibrated with outrage. His once pallid cheeks blazed with hot color. Tugging his coat down around his hips as far as it could go, he stated flatly, "I will see our wagonmaster about you, Davis. You are a menace to this young woman, indeed, to this entire train."

Davis's eyes narrowed.

Sliding his finger into his starched shirt collar, Martin tugged it away from his sweating throat as he turned to Rachel and said, "I will see you later, my dear. You know where I am if you need me. Rachel?"

Forcing her eyes from the black thatch of curling hair on Davis's chest, she asked mistily, "What?"

"I said—"

"Of course. Yes, yes, I'll see you later. Thank you for your invitation to dine, Martin. I shall certainly consider it."

Throwing Davis one last scathing glance, Martin spun on his heels and strode back toward his wagon.

"Mou-unnt up!" Homer called in that instant.

Davis was still grinning as Rachel turned back to the wagon. Without looking at him directly she addressed him as aloofly as possible. As she did, she realized she'd never before stood this close, much less spoken, to a man so nearly naked. "How dare you approach me in that—that *offensive* manner," she reproached him.

"You should see how I sleep," he drawled.

"No thank you. I find the idea almost as appalling as I find you." She swept past him and stopped by the wagon, waiting. Looking back over her shoulder, she said, "Well? Do y'all intend to stand there all day, or will you help me mount?"

"Y'all want *me* to help *y'all* mount?" He moved toward her, his swagger exaggerated for her benefit. "Why, certainly, Miss Gregory. I'm real good at mounting . . . almost anything."

Whirling to face him, she stared furiously into his amused

blue eyes. "You filthy-minded cur! I'm going to Sam right this minute and demand that he take you off my wagon!"

"Go ahead. But by the looks of those hands you're still going to need help driving this wagon. Maybe Clyde will volunteer."

Giving in to her frustration and the overall helplessness she felt at her circumstances, Rachel buried her fists into the folds of her pink skirts and hissed through her teeth, "Oh! I—I hate you! You awful, smelling, uneducated moron of a man!"

His eyebrows went up.

"You were absolutely right marrying that whore. No decent woman with any common sense would want you within a mile of her!"

Realization of what she'd said struck her as his face turned dark as a thundercloud. Good Lord, what foolishness had provoked her to say such a cruel thing? She waited, expecting that at any moment he would wrap that length of chain around her throat and squeeze the very life from her body.

"Are you finished?" came his deadly calm voice.

Her lips pinched, she nodded.

"Good." He approached her, watching as she lifted her white chin in defiance and backed away. When finally she was pressed as far against the wagon as she could go, he thrust his dark face up to her pale one and said through his teeth, "Good. Then *y'all* can heft *y'all's* sassy little butt up on that wagon yourself, *princess*."

Davis spun on his heel, snatched up his shirt from the ground and walked away.

She was chagrined, stupefied, mortified at her inexcusable bout of ill manners. What was becoming of her? She'd never spoken to another human being as she had to Davis. But then no human being had ever prompted her to it . . . except Audra, perhaps. But somehow she'd almost always managed to hold her tongue where her stepmother was concerned. Oh, the woman continually chafed her tolerance, there was no denying that. And many a time she'd become frightfully angry over Audra's treatment of her father, but the woman's *existence* had never unsettled her like Davis's did.

Spinning the parasol on her shoulder, she looked out across the monotonous countryside and scowled in contemplation.

"I think you should get in the back of the wagon," came Davis's voice in her left ear. "It's too hot out here and besides, you keep jabbing me with that damn frilly contraption."

She spun a little harder.

"And while you're at it, peel out of some of those petticoats. You must have half the cotton in Louisiana and Mississippi under those skirts. Three-quarters of the rattlesnakes in Texas could find their way in there and get lost for the next year."

"Crinoline," she responded. Tipping her face slightly toward his and smiling a smug little smile, she taunted, "They are crinoline, Mr. Davis. And for your unenlightened mind I will tell you that crinoline is a fabric of linen and horsehair."

"Oh well, hell, that's different then. What rattlesnake in his right mind would want to curl up in horsehair?"

How, she wondered, did he always manage to make her feel like the fool?

They plodded on in silence.

After an hour he said, "How're your hands?"

"Attached to my wrists," she quipped.

He grinned despite himself, no longer angry over being called a moron. He looked down at her perfect little profile and noted, for the first time, that her brows and lashes were a wheat-colored gold, not nearly as white as her hair. Her upper lip, shaped like a heart, was soft and red despite the drying effect the sun was having on her skin, and she had the smallest, daintiest ears he'd ever seen on a woman.

Something inside him gave just a fraction. It was a weakening, debilitating sagging in his gut as if he had spun around too quickly in one place. Just a flash of dizziness, then it was gone. But it left him tired and feeling as if he didn't want to fight with her anymore. She had an uncanny way of making him feel guilty when they fought. And he felt guilty enough for the sins in his life without her adding to it.

Shifting on the hard bench seat, he offered, "If you'll put that . . . parasol away I'll show you a little something about driving this wagon." She twirled a little harder on the handle of her contraption, forcing him to duck to avoid the many sharp-pronged little ribs jutting out around the thing.

"Why would I want to do that?" she asked him.

"To get rid of me."

"Oh well, then by all means." Rachel snapped the parasol shut, then tossed it back through the canvas flap. Bandaged hands propped primly on her knees, she said, "Then let the lessons begin, Mr. Davis."

Their eyes clashed.

He shifted closer to her.

She shifted away.

He rolled his eyes and up went her chin.

"Do you want to drive the wagon or not, lady?"

"Must I allow you to sit in my lap to do so?"

"Take the damn reins."

"Must you always use such offensive language?"

"Take the reins. Please."

"Very well." Holding out her hand, bandaged palm up, she waited for him to lay them gently across her fingers.

Back went the horses' ears, and Davis thought, *Damn smart fellow.*

Hunching his shoulders and propping his elbows on his knees, he explained, "The horse on your left up there is the nigh animal. He leads the other. A long, steady pull on the lines will make him turn to the left. Go ahead and try it."

She did so. Gradually the animal began to veer to the left. Rachel sat up a little straighter.

Davis grinned to himself. "Now, a series of short, sharp jerks will cause him to throw his head up and to the right to avoid the pain of the bit. As he does that he will swing to his right, and the animal to his right will respond in the same manner. Go on and try it."

"It works!" Laughing aloud, she wiggled in her petticoats, licked her lips, and tried again.

"Very nice, but I would caution you not to get carried away. That's a special bit, and too much tugging will make the animal's mouth sore." He allowed her to drive the animals awhile longer before taking the reins from her hands. "That's enough for today," he said. Then, noticing the slight frown between her eyes, he teased, "You didn't think I was about to let you off the hook that easily, did you, sweet cheeks? It'll be a few more days before your hands have healed enough to manage the lines."

They rode on, this time in a companionable silence.

It was Rachel who spoke next.

"I don't really think you killed that girl, Mr. Davis." He looked at her, his surprise obvious in the upward tilt of one heavy, black brow. She chanced a quick look at his lips, then glanced as quickly away. "What baffles me, however, is why Captain Wells would lie to protect you."

"Ever think it wasn't me he was protecting?" he responded.

Her head snapped around so quickly a pain shot up the back of her neck. "Mr. Davis, are you saying he knew we were together last night?"

"Maybe."

"And he allowed it?" She huffed a little in disbelief. "I find that even more curious, Mr. Davis. And come to think about it, why were you roaming around in the dark without those hideous chains?"

She stared at him hard now.

His head tilted back slightly. The brim of his hat nearly touching the bridge of his nose, he seemed half asleep as he watched the horses' heads bob rhythmically up and down. Finally he said, "I was stretching my legs, Miss Gregory."

"You might have escaped."

"Ma'am, no one escapes a Texas Ranger, and even if they did they'd eventually live to regret it. That old man back there is one of the best. He was hired and trained by Jack Hays. He's ridden with Sam Walker, Ben McCulloch, and Big Foot

Wallace. He's fought more battles than Sam Houston, Andrew Jackson, and George Washington combined."

"You sound as if you actually respect the captain, Mr. Davis."

"I respect the gun on his hip, Miss Gregory. It doesn't miss." Sitting a little straighter, he thumbed his hat to the back of his head and said, "Besides, even if I had decided to take a hike to Mexico, I couldn't have done it without a horse, or a gun of my own. I'd rather take my chances with a jury than half the Comanche or Apache nation . . . or that one old man."

The opportunity had just laid itself at her feet, and though sensing she would regret it, Rachel took a deep breath, stared at the tufts of hair between the nigh horse's alert ears, and asked, "What crime will you be judged for, Mr. Davis?" The ensuing silence made her uneasy. She always talked too much when she became uneasy. "I'm certain it couldn't have been too serious. You're not like those other men. Not really. Not at all like Clyde. He's dirty and vile and . . ." Why didn't he respond? "Well?"

Slowly, she turned her face up to his. His hat was cocked jauntily on his head. His black hair was mussed, and several long strands had escaped over his brow and were fluttering slightly in the breeze. He looked like a boy. He looked innocent and lost and . . . frightened, suddenly. But only briefly. As she watched, that wall of anger and defiance crept slowly over his features, turning his profile into stone once again. All of a sudden she didn't want to know.

Twisting her sore fingers together until she flinched with pain, she blurted, "Never mind! Forget that I asked. It doesn't matter. I don't know what got into me. I'm certain everything will be straightened out during your trial. It's probably some terrible misunderstanding, or simply a case of mistaken identity."

She watched his long-lashed eyes blink sleepily, then he said in a low voice that offered only minimal explanation:

"Maybe."

Chapter 10

She awoke gradually to deep, flowing laughter; she had dreamed of diving head first into calm blue water. Warm on the surface, it welcomed her at first, but deep beneath that beckoning exterior it turned bitterly cold and frighteningly black; she found herself battling for her life as she attempted to reach the surface.

How long had she slept? She couldn't be certain. All she knew was that it was stiflingly hot in the back of the wagon and that she felt empty inside and slightly nauseated. As the wagon swayed from side to side she could understand now why Audra stayed ill with a queasy stomach. Audra. Glancing toward her stepmother's discarded blankets, Rachel frowned. Where was Audra?

"She was always frightfully frail, the poor little thing. My dear deceased husband pampered her outrageously because of it, I'm afraid. Needless to say, she became so spoiled and accustomed to getting her way that she soon became unmanageable. You have no idea, Mr. Davis, how difficult it's been for me, having to deal with her little tantrums as well as that awful war. I only hope that my brother can help settle her down. After that terrible fiasco with Luke, however, I'm not certain we'll ever find a man willing to forgive her lack of virtue."

"Is this move to Brackettville for her benefit?" Davis asked.

"But of course! Her reputation was ruined in New Orleans. The girl would never have found a husband among what little of our society was left. Had she chosen to fall from grace with an equal, then perhaps things might have been different. But that awful land tiller! What man would want to touch her now? Besides, I understand that Brackett-ville is a military outpost. The place should be swarming with soldiers in desperate need of women."

"Yes, ma'am, Brackettville *was* once a military outpost. But Fort Clark was deserted back in sixty-two, as were most of the outposts along the San Antone–El Paso Road, though I understand there's been talk of reestablishing the entire area with Federal troops now that the War is over. I'm certain, when that's accomplished, there'll be plenty of lonely young soldiers who would find Miss Gregory exactly what they need to make this solitary existence a bit more tolerable."

Rachel, aghast, sank back down on her bed.

"Maybe you'll be looking for a husband yourself, Mrs. Gregory," Davis continued. "Woman as pretty as you should have no trouble at all landing yourself a captain or two."

Two dozen, Rachel thought. *And landing wasn't exactly what Audra would do with them.*

"Why, Mr. Davis, what a kind thing to say. It's been a very long time since a man has complimented me so."

"Now, I can't believe that."

"It's been a very long time since I've shared a man's company at all . . . "

"Why, that's a real shame. A *real* shame. Men in New Orleans must be blind or fools to let something as fine as you slip through their fingers."

"Mr. Davis, you are turning my head, sir. If you slide over here a little more, Mr. Davis, you might share my parasol. That sun is so dreadfully hot. I fear I'm becoming quite uncomfortable."

"Would you like me to stop and get you some water, Mrs. Gregory?" His voice sounded huskier.

"Why, how kind of you, Mr. Davis, but no. I wouldn't think of holding us up. And please, call me Audra."

"All right, Audra. Um, I like that perfume. That smells real nice."

"Perfume is my weakness. I love drenching my entire body in it."

"A beautiful woman like you probably smells just as good without it."

"Would you mind if *I* drove for a while, Mr. Davis?"

"By all means. Careful now. Those hands are much too pretty to roughen up. Hold them just this way."

"*Show* me, Mr. Davis. This way?"

"Wrap your fingers around it just like this. Gently, sweetheart. Take it easy. Give it a little jerk every now and again. Would you like to wear my hat? Your nose is getting a little red. Course I'd hate to cover up all that pretty brown hair. I was always partial to brunettes myself. You know, it's a pleasure spending time with a real lady for a change. Yes, ma'am. A real pleasure."

Squeezing her eyes shut, Rachel drifted back to sleep.

"Now this is a pleasure. Yes, sir, a real pleasure. Miss Rachel, you have outdone yoreself. What'd I tell you, Davis? Didn't I say that cookin' comes natural to a woman?"

Rachel glanced casually Davis's way, silently thanking Manuela for once again helping her with the preparation of the food. Her eyes widened at the sight of her hankie—the one she'd dropped at his feet in San Antonio—sticking slightly out of his shirt pocket. She looked quickly back at Sam.

The Ranger smiled, revealing large, tobacco-stained teeth that took nothing at all away from the pleasantness of the smile. "Why looka there, boys. She done fixed ash cake! Why, it's been two months of Sundays since I et ash cake. And looka there. She's took them rock squirrels Hale shot and made a fine stew with dumplin's." Shaking his grizzled old head, he said, "I declare, Miss Rachel, but yore gonna make some young man a mighty fine wife and mother to his young'uns. Yes, indeed. If'n I was thirty years younger I'd do my goldarnedest to court ya myself. Not that you would consider a sidewinder such as me as fittin' to court ya, but that wouldn't keep me from throwin' my hat in the ring. No,

I suspect you'll be lookin' to some tall, handsome son-of-a-gun such as, say . . ."

Her eyes wide, Rachel stared at Sam and held her breath.

"Stillwell!" Sam exclaimed, "By golly, don't ya look as if yore dressed up fer Easter Sunday. I'm feelin' as if I ought to go back to San Antone and fetch my Sunday-go-to-meetin' duds."

Helping Rachel into her chair, Martin inclined his head toward her ear and said softly, "My dear, you failed to inform me that we would be joined by guests."

She tilted her face a fraction to his and asked innocently, "Did I?" Smiling at Sam then, she confessed, "I thought it was the least I could do to thank Sam *and* Mr. Davis, of course, for helping Audra and me with our wagon. They have provided us with such splendid fare the last two evenings I thought they might enjoy a chance to eat more comfortably . . . with us."

"What you mean," Davis countered, "is a chance to eat more civilized."

She met his narrowed blue eyes with her own. "Very well, Mr. Davis. If that is what you care to think. Actually I was growing tired of crates for chairs and eating off tin plates. When I asked Martin to join us for our stew, it was Jules who thought to provide the china, linens, and table."

They all looked at Jules.

"Remind me to thank you, my good man," said Martin, dryly. Taking a chair between Rachel and Audra, he spread his delicate lace napkin across his lap. "I can't remember when I've supped with such gracious companions."

Tucking his napkin into his shirt collar, Sam said, "Aw, go on, Stillwell, you've probably et with all sorts of fine folk back in England. Tell me somethin'. Did you ever meet Victoria?"

"Victoria?"

"You know, Victoria the Queen."

Martin sat back in his chair. "My good man, one does not refer to Her Majesty as Victoria. And no, I have never had the honor of meeting Her Majesty. She does not sit upon some street corner like a beggarwoman and shake hands with every clod who happens by."

"Well, now, I wouldn't call ya a clod," Sam said, smiling, "exactly."

They all waited in silence as Jules lit one of the twin tapers in the center of the table, then the other.

Sam's mouth dropped open, then his parchmented face broke out in a smile. "Why, this is like dinner on the ground, ain't it? That's what we, as young'uns, used to call a covered dish meal our mammies supplied after an all-day preachin'. We used to spread blankets out under a tree, eat, and swat flies. And speakin' of flies, that one there is gonna be a real pain, I can see. He's got his eyes on that ash cake, fer sure. Want me to get a switch, Miss Rachel? Why, I was once so loose-wristed with a switch I could snap them sapsuckers right out of the air."

Martin coughed into his napkin.

Rachel only smiled. "Why, thank you, Sam, but that won't be necessary. We have a fly catcher on the table."

"A what?"

She pointed to the potbellied frosted glass in the center of the table. "Watch very carefully. See the fly—"

"By God, Davis, look at that son-of-a-gun go right to that sapsucker!"

Rachel looked again at Davis. His eyes narrowed further, he joined Sam as he leaned over the table to watch the fly crawl around the feet of the tiny, ornamented glass flume.

Smiling again, she explained, "As you can see, the fly has crawled under the glass and will now fly up into the cavity. That's because we've laced the inside with honey. The silly creatures haven't the sense to find their way out again, so they simply remain there and die. The glass is frosted that way so the ladies needn't see the insects collect."

Sam shook his head. "Well, now, I suspect the man who invented that's made himself a tidy little fortune." His face lighting up then, he exclaimed, "A man could use that contraption for catchin' fish bait!"

Martin groaned.

Rachel laughed. "Yes, Sam, I suppose he could." Her eyes drawn back to Davis, she said, "Jules, would you be a dear and serve us our stew?"

Davis sat back in his chair, taking in the scene before him. The china reflected the yellow candlelight, as did the heavily ornate silver on each side of his plate. There was delicate crystal stemware that refracted the glow of the flames into tiny stars of white and red and green; still, he thought as Rachel raised her violet gaze to his, neither the stars on the crystal, nor those in heaven could compare with the dancing light in her eyes.

He liked the way her hair, swept off her neck, had been plaited in coils around the back of her head. Her throat was long and white and graceful; her bared shoulders were smooth and the color of cream. What he *didn't* like was the daring plunge of her décolletage. It left far too much of her breasts displayed. He noted Stillwell's eyes drifting there time and again. And time and again he refrained from leaving his chair and—

"Mr. Davis?"

Frowning, he blinked and looked remotely at Audra.

Assessing him with heavy-lidded eyes, she said, "I was just saying to Mr. Wells, you don't really think we are in danger from Indians, do you?"

"Yes, ma'am. It was an Indian who killed the girl." He sat a little straighter in the high-backed chair.

"Oh my, you sound terribly certain."

He looked at Rachel. "I am."

Staring through the steam rising from his squirrel stew, Martin demanded, "Then why haven't we seen them, Davis? Why haven't they attacked?"

"Because they know we're anticipating an attack. They'll wait until we're most vulnerable; dawn is usually a good time. The guards won't have had much sleep and their responses will be sluggish. That is, if they're Apaches. Comanches will wait until the moon is at its brightest before attacking. Usually in the dead of night." Picking up his knife,

Davis turned it over and over in his fingers before saying, "I hope, Mr. Stillwell, that you know how to use a gun."

"Of course I do. Back in York pheasant hunting was quite the sport on holidays."

His blue eyes came up again, to Stillwell's face. The knife in his fingers went still. "Pheasant?"

"They're somethin' like big fancy turkeys," Sam joined in.

Davis again sat back in his chair as Jules placed the bowl of bubbling brown stew on his plate. "There is a big difference between shooting a bird and shooting a man, Stillwell."

"No doubt, sir. And I'm certain you are quite the expert."

Rachel closed her eyes, regretting having thought up this ridiculous scheme to get even with Davis for flirting with Audra. Martin had been annoyingly complimentary over her appearance the night before, but now he was absorbed in trading insults with the blue-eyed savage across the table and was totally ignoring her.

"Perhaps," Davis said. His long lashes lowered thoughtfully as he once again regarded the silver utensil in his fingers. "I know the first time you kill a man a little of *your* soul will die with him, Mr. Stillwell. Then after a while it ceases to matter—the guilt, I mean. You tell yourself that you did what you had to do. It was his choice to die, not yours. *He* pulled the gun or knife. You can tell yourself that all you want, but when you start avoiding sleep at night because you keep seeing their faces as they were when they took their last breath, you start wishing the other man's gun had been a little faster. Sometimes you start inviting trouble because you're so damn tired of the dreams and the guilt you just want to end it all."

"Then why not just put the gun to your own head?" Stillwell sneered.

A pall fell over the group, as thick as fog and as heavy as the encroaching darkness outside the camp.

"Well?" the Englishman demanded, causing everyone but Davis to start.

Slowly those blue eyes came back to Rachel's and Davis said, "Because you can't help thinking that somewhere out there, there may be something or someone who can help you forget."

Martin laughed sharply. "Only God can help you, Davis."

"Perhaps," Davis responded. "Or an angel."

Leaning slightly over Sam's shoulder, Jules swept back the linen napkins from the bread and said, "Your ash cake, sir."

"By golly, if'n it ain't! Miss Rachel, this looks jest like the ash cake my poor ole mammy used to make, God rest her soul."

With great effort Rachel forced her eyes from Davis. Her skin was burning, and she wondered if she hadn't laced her corset too tightly. Her lungs refused to cooperate.

"I—I followed your recipe, Sam. I bought cornmeal from Manuela, molded the dough, and wrapped it in clean cloth, just as you said. Then I covered it all with hot ashes, then hot coals, and allowed it to bake."

She buried her hands in her lap, unable to find the strength to lift her spoon from the table and eat. Sam, his head down so his long gray braids swung back and forth over his bowl, ate voraciously while Martin jabbed at his squirrel and Audra, steaming because she had not yet managed to catch Davis's attention, chewed on the bread as if it were Rachel's throat.

Rachel had dressed for Davis, cooked for Davis, secretly borrowed Audra's perfume in hopes that Davis would notice. All because she couldn't stand the thought of his desiring another woman. Silly ninny! The man was on his way to jail to be tried for some heinous crime—murder, no doubt, judging from his earlier discourse—and she was attempting to seduce him!

Good Lord, what had come over her? She felt horribly disgusted with herself and the entire affair; she had to get away now, before she made a spectacle of herself!

She leaped from her chair, crashing against the table with her leg, sending crystal and china dancing and stew slopping onto Martin's white linen tablecloth. As four stunned faces turned up to hers, she covered her mouth with her hand and wept, "Oh! I'm so clumsy. It's just—" There was stew dripping off Martin's chin. "I'm just feeling a trifle hot and not so well. Forgive me, please forgive me!"

As she whirled away she caught a glimpse of a man jumping from his chair. Davis? No, it couldn't be. He was no doubt slouched like a panther at a kill, licking his lips in satisfaction that, without a word this time, he had managed to unsettle her. Oh, it was getting so much easier, she thought, in the tiny portion of her mind that was still rational enough for thinking, so much easier for him to tear her down to *his* level. That's what he wanted. He hated her because she had morals and conscience and values. He wanted to strip her of those sacred ideals to assuage his own guilt for being a failure.

Running to the far side of the wagon, away from curious eyes and into the dark, she turned her face up to the sky and wondered what crime she had committed to make her deserve Kid Davis.

"Miss Rachel?" Sam stood at the end of the wagon, the campfire lighting only half his features. "Are ya all right?"

Staring at her hands, she shook her head. The tears spilled onto her fingers.

Tugging his napkin from his shirt collar, he sauntered up beside her. "Well now. I reckon this is as good a time as any to be havin' ourselves a chat." He caught her chin with his finger and tipped up her face. "Here now, what's this?"

"Stupidity."

"Is *that* what stupidity looks like? I always figured it looked like my cousin Ezekiel. He come into this world lookin' like the south end of a northbound mule and had about as much sense as a dirt dabber."

She laughed. She couldn't help it.

Sam's whiskered face softened in a smile. "Been a rough trip, ain't it, darlin'? Havin' to drive that damn wagon yoreself the first coupla days, then gittin' them purty little hands all tore up. And if my eyes and ears ain't givin' me fits, I suspect yore stepmama and you don't exactly see eye to eye. Ain't ya got no family at all besides her?"

Wiping her tears away with the back of her hand, Rachel shook her head.

"That's a shame. And you no bigger than a minute and still a child. What ya need is a man to take care of ya. Someone who is needin' to settle down and make a good home for a wife and a buncha young'uns. Somebody like old Stillwell there."

"Stillwell!"

He pursed his lips, contemplating her distressed face. "On second thought, that Britisher wouldn't know what to do with a plow horse. He'd probably try to ride it after one of them fancy-tailed foxes or somethin'. No, ya need a man, a real man, to complement yore femininity. Ya need somebody like—"

Rachel felt the hot, unreasonable tears start to flow again. Ashamed, she covered her face with her hands and beseeched him, "Don't! Oh, please don't. It just isn't fair, Sam. It isn't right. Something must be wrong with me to even think it. He's coarse and crude and rude and—"

"Don't forgit stubborn."

"And stubborn and so damnably arrogant I could spit!" Catching her breath, she sniffed and said less emotionally, "He is an outlaw. Any man who would purposely harm another human being must be twisted in his mind."

"I reckon. Life plays tricks on people though. Things happen we can't help, and we survive the best way we can. Sometimes we ain't got no choices, Miss Rachel. It's that instinct for survival that links us to animals, I think. None of us wants to die."

Looking up into the old man's face, she said, "You cannot be excusing him!"

"That ain't fer me to do. All I know is, ya can't be too hard on yoreself fer what yore feelin'. Feelin's of the heart shouldn't ought to have anythin' to do with what a man is or ain't. Shouldn't ought to have anythin' to do with what he can or can't give ya in the way of money or riches. Ain't it what's inside that counts the most? What he *wants* to give ya or do fer you?"

"But Davis has nothing inside. The man is heartless."

"Aw, I don't know. Would a man with nothin' inside take a knife in the back fer somebody else? Would he risk his life runnin' down a runaway wagon? I didn't exactly hold a gun to him and say go haul up that wagon. Fact is, my deputy called him back twice as he took off after yore team. I had to cut Hale off or he might have plugged Davis in the back. He could have easily kept on ridin', could have taken advantage of all the commotion to make a gitaway. But he didn't."

Attempting to see the Ranger better in the darkness, Rachel squinted hard into his face and whispered, "Sam, what is it you're trying to tell me?"

"Tell ya?" Tucking his napkin back into his shirt, he shook his head and responded, "Nothin'. I'll jest tell ya what my mammy used to tell me: 'Judge not lest ye be judged.' Now then, there's a dumplin' with my name on it somewheres in the middle of that table and I'm aimin' to chase it down. Might I escort ya, m'lady, back to yores afore it goes cold?"

Touched by Sam's compassion, she tucked her hand through the crook of his elbow. "Sam," she said, smiling, "you've a kind heart. I haven't had anyone show me such understanding and compassion since my father died. In fact, you remind me a great deal of my father. Might I thank you as I would have thanked him?" His eyes widened as, on tiptoe, she pressed a kiss onto his whiskered cheek.

Clearing his throat, he ducked his head and mumbled, "Aw, it ain't nothin'. Jest never did like seein' nothin' good come to hurt, is all."

"Is that why you lied about Davis this morning? Do you feel that beneath that rather abrasive exterior of his there hides a heart of gold?"

He thought a moment while staring at his boots. "Welp, ain't that what this is all about? Ya wouldn't be feelin' what yore feelin' if'n he was anythin' like Clyde."

"I'm asking you about *your* feelings, Sam."

"Don't, Miss Rachel, 'cause I can't tell ya. I don't know what to think about the boy. Fact is, since leaving San Antone he's gotten under my skin in a fashion that's caused me a few sleepless nights lately."

Surprised, Rachel searched her friend's face. "Are you referring to Angelique's belief that Davis is really her son?"

He didn't respond.

"Sam, do you think Kid Davis is really Tomas de Bastitas?" She felt his body go rigid. "Sam?"

"I got no way of knowin' that, Miss Rachel. That secret's locked up in the Kid's head and I figure if he wants to own up to it, he'll own up to it."

"But perhaps he doesn't remember!"

"The outcome of that fracas won't never be forgit by Texas or the Comanches, darlin'. I'm certain the Comanches who took him wouldn't *let* him forget it. Besides that, the man out there's got a mind as sharp as a razor and as crafty as a coyote; he'd remember if he was Tomas de Bastitas. I don't believe anybody could ever forget seein' his own grandmother scalped before his eyes, or his ma and pa struck down in the streets and left for dead. Yes ma'am, the thought has crossed my mind that Davis is Alex's boy, mainly 'cause I got no doubts that he's somehow been linked with them damn savages—"

"How do you know, Sam?"

"'Cause he's the closest thing to a Comanche I've seen since I had a run-in with Little Buffalo out by Clear Fork back in late sixty-four. He's got that shifty way of lookin' and listenin' to things, and no normal man can ride an animal like he does, 'cept maybe a Ranger; and he ain't no Ranger, Miss Rachel. He rarely eats and he don't sleep more'n a catnap now and agin, same as a Comanche. And a Comanche's got a way of lookin' at a white man, a superior way like he thinks we is vermin that needs squashin' under his foot. Sometimes Davis gits that look."

"You're saying, if he *was* Tomas de Bastitas, they took him and changed him into one of them? But how could he allow it? How could a boy born into a gentle, aristocratic family become a savage?"

Looking directly into Rachel's eyes for the first time, he

said, "Fear, darlin'. Livin' day and night in fear fer yore life, in fear of pain and torture. It can do things to a man's mind, Miss Rachel."

"Is that why you are excusing the crime he's committed?"

"Crime?" He looked confused.

"He *is* going to El Paso to stand trial?"

"Oh! Right. Yep. I mean, nope, I ain't excusin' nothin'. That's the jury's job. Now, didn't I mention somethin' about a dumplin'?"

At that moment Deputy Hale came around the wagon. "Cap'n!" He gasped an uneven breath before explaining in a thin voice. "We've got trouble. Homer just come back. Jeromia rode in and—"

Alert now, Sam dropped Rachel's arm and demanded, "Well, speak up, man. Have we got ourselves an Injun fight on our hands or not?"

"Comanches, sir."

Before Rachel could take another breath, Sam grabbed her arm and propelled her around the wagon. They came face to face with Davis. Suddenly Rachel found herself between the two, the men's eyes locked in silent communication.

Finally Sam said, "Seems I'm gonna be a mite busy, Davis. Can I trust ya to keep an eye on things at this end?"

"I'll do my best with what I have available."

"Rachel!" It was Martin. Taking her arm, he forced her toward Audra, who paced, wringing her hands and looking frantically about the enclosure of wagons. Martin continued, "This is maddening. Maddening! I was told at the onset of this journey that those heathens were not so inclined to attack white men any longer." Running his napkin over his face, he groaned. "Good God, but those people actually cut off the tops of men's heads."

Audra grabbed her coiffured curls and whimpered.

The entire camp burst into sudden activity. A wagon was temporarily removed from the circle, allowing horses and cattle to be driven into the confined space.

Martin's mouth dropped open as a huge steer pointed his outspread horns and charged their way. He yelped something about his china and dodged toward the table just before the animal crashed into it, sending crystal, silver, and china into a shattered heap across the ground.

Grabbing Rachel and Audra, Davis ordered, "Get under your wagon and don't come out for any reason."

"But what about you?" Rachel stared into his eyes, aware that her voice sounded worried, and that she was clutching his arm now in desperation.

"I won't be far, Miss Gregory. I assure you you'll be safe if—"

"I'm quite certain of that, Mr. Davis; I have asked about you. You have no gun! How will you protect yourself?"

He watched as Audra ducked beneath their wagon, then, pulling Rachel to one side, he bent his dark head to her ear and asked, "Do I detect some real concern on my behalf, Miss Gregory?"

His warm breath on her cheek made her go liquid inside. The sound of shouting voices and bawling cows faded as she turned her head slightly, pressing her cheek against his. "Yes."

He was quite still, his breathing heavy against her temple.

Finally he said, "Get under the wagon, Miss Gregory, and don't trouble yourself overly much on my account. I'm not worth it."

Stepping away without looking at her again, he joined Sam at the far side of the encampment.

Chapter 11

The night dragged on, endless. Rachel and Audra crouched beneath their wagon, knees pulled tightly into their chests and their arms locked like vises about their shins. Occasionally they would peek from behind their barricade of crates and boxes, but all they could detect in the shadowed distance were warped images of scrubby trees and the more fearsome silhouettes of cacti, whose sprawling branches resembled arms and legs with flowers that, reflecting the moonlight, might have passed as feathered headdresses.

The prisoners—Clyde, Pete, and Pedro—were shackled to the freight wagon. Throughout the wait Clyde took great pleasure in taunting the listeners with tales so horrible that women and children could be heard crying throughout the camp.

"Hell's a holiday compared to what them Injuns are gonna do to ya when they gitcha!" Clyde cupped his hands around his mouth and called out, "They stake ya to the ground and cut off yore eyelids so the sun bakes yore eyeballs out of their sockets! They's each gonna have their way with yore womenfolk . . . and there's prob'ly two hundred of 'em!"

Sam materialized from the darkness and kicked Clyde in the ribs.

The hour was midnight before Davis rejoined Rachel and Audra. Walking casually around the idle cattle, he crawled into the confined space beneath their wagon, lay down between them, then gave a shove to one of the crates offering them protection, allowing a draft of cool air to eddy into the crude, stifling hospice.

"You can relax, ladies," he told them.

Rachel stole a look at him from under her lashes. He was without his shirt. His skin, reflecting the dim glow of a distant campfire, was slick and moist. It was becoming easier to understand why her body was betraying her. The smooth brown skin, copper in the firelight and defined by perfect muscles, hinted of a dangerous strength that made her feel frail and weak in comparison. There was no denying Kid Davis was physically magnificent.

She suddenly noticed that the heavy manacles were abrading his skin, leaving angry red burns above his wrists. Without a second thought she reached for her petticoats, tore two long strips from the hem and, offering them with slightly trembling fingers, stated, "It may help, Mr. Davis." When he made no move to accept her offer, she reached for his wrists and gently tucked the ribbons of material between his skin and the irons.

He studied her fingers resting lightly on his arm. They trailed slowly away, reluctantly burying themselves in the folds of her dress. Then Audra broke the spell by asking, "When will those damnable Indians attack, Davis? I'm not certain I can tolerate another hour of this suspense."

"With any luck, there won't be an attack," he responded. "Homer and Sam are out parleying with them now."

"You mean we're safe?"

Rachel and Davis stared down at the long-fingered white hand Audra had maneuvered to the middle of his chest. Rachel felt her face go hot. Davis only grinned.

"Oh, I think we're safe enough," he said in a rougher voice. "It's only a small scouting party; they know they're no match for us. But there's enough men to make themselves a nuisance if they decide to stay around awhile."

"But what about the girl they killed?" Rachel asked, still staring at Audra's hand.

"They deny it, of course."

"But what shall we do?" Leaning slightly closer to his face, Audra feigned a slight disconcerted pout. "Whatever do those painted creatures want from us, Mr. Davis?"

"Whiskey, more'n likely. Some tobacco. There's plenty in the freighter. We'll give them what they want and go on our way."

"It's as easy as that?" Audra's full lips turned up in so sultry a way Rachel almost choked.

"Maybe. Maybe not. Depends on how far away from home they are. It might take them days to get back to the tribe. If that's the case, we're safe enough . . . for now."

He looked back at Rachel. The corners of her mouth were drooping. Her eyes, like dark oval buttons in her pale face, seemed vacant somehow as she stared at Audra's hand. Audra's hand. There was no misinterpreting Mrs. Gregory's attentions. That was no coy brush of her fingers upon his chest. The lady wanted him as much as he wanted . . .

Without excusing himself, he rolled out from under the wagon and made for the freighter. Deputy Hale, his Sharp resting across his knee, eyed him speculatively from his perch beside the wagon.

Dropping to the ground, Davis leaned against the wagon wheel and stared back at Rachel's wagon. Clyde, grown weary of harassing the travelers, joined him and asked, "Been entertainin' the ladies, have ya? Seems to me that old man Wells lets ya git away with a helluva lot."

Davis grinned.

"Seems to me ya could use that to yore advantage," Clyde went on. "Seems to me we could use this whole affair to our advantage. We could make a gitaway while ever'body's got their minds on them Injuns."

"Nope."

"We'll be makin' D'Hanis in a day or so." Stretching out beside Davis, and leaning on one elbow, he said, "Yore up to somethin', Davis, and I want in on it."

"Don't know what you mean, Lindsey."

"The hell you don't. I seen the way you been pussyfootin' around that old man, kissin' up to him and playin' like a wet-nosed schoolboy who would piss 'imself if somebody pointed a gun at 'im. From what I hear, there ain't nobody in three states what could outdraw you, Ranger or not. So me and the others are figurin' yore jest playin' at gittin' in that old man's good books so's ya can catch 'im unawares."

Davis laughed at that one.

Clyde's features clouded as, jutting his face nearer Davis's ear, he hissed, "If yore lookin' to jump, I'm jumpin' with ya."

Waiting a long moment before responding, he finally asked, "And what do I get out of it?"

"Four guns are better'n one."

"And one horse leaves less trail for that old man to follow."

"Then we kill 'im. We can kill 'em all."

Davis looked at Clyde and said, "No one dies." He fingered the tattered material about his wrists before looking back toward Rachel's wagon. "So what happened to your friends, Lindsey? Where are Cortinas and Duncan now when you need them?"

"They'll come through."

"They haven't so far."

"You expect 'em to jest sashay in here and say, 'Let 'em go, purty please'? They'll be there for me if I can get to 'em. They'll set me up in Mexico; I'll work awhile for Cortinas, maybe run guns or cattle to the gulf."

"Sounds like some impressive operation."

"It is. Duncan's been easy with his money. Believes in rewarding his men for a job well done. But he only takes on the best." Closer, he said, "Help me git out of the mess, Davis, and I'll talk to A.J. and Cortinas. You could work for them in Mexico until things cool off round here. Man with yore reputation could demand good money, and they'd pay it."

Sliding so he lay flat on the ground, Davis pillowed his head with his hands and stared at the stars. "I'll think about it," he said.

The attack never came, and by dawn, though the travelers were weary from lack of sleep, the train pushed forward, anxious to put as much distance between them and the strangely complaisant Indians as possible. Homer informed them that with luck and no more breakdowns they would make D'Hanis by dark. Though it was only a tiny settlement, there was a trading post, fresh water wells, and a saloon.

Rachel slept in the back of the wagon until the midday break; she awoke to the luscious aroma of frying bacon and Sam's good-natured singing:

> Bacon in the Pan
> Coffee in the Pot
> Git up and git it
> Git it while it's hot!

Dressing quickly and quietly, so as not to disturb Audra, Rachel joined Sam, soon discovering that Davis was eating with the others beneath a distant chaparral tree. Noting her surprise and apparent disappointment, Sam thrust a plate of bacon and skillet-baked biscuits in her hands, and said, "The Kid woke up a bit on the testy side this mornin', darlin', and declined my invitation to eat."

Without responding, she plopped down on a crate and began nibbling at the fluffy hot bread.

"We got some of Mr. Stillwell's honey," he said.

"No, thank you."

Pursing his lips, Sam poured a stream of the sweet syrup over his biscuits. He'd just popped a fairly good chunk of bread in his mouth when she turned her dark eyes on him and asked:

"Will he hang in El Paso?"

He hunched his shoulders and tried to swallow.

"Did he murder someone in cold blood, Sam? He *did*, didn't he? And those weren't the only crimes he's committed, are they? He told me himself that by the time he was nineteen he had a growing reputation with a gun. He hates himself for it, Sam. I know he does. If he was only given another chance I honestly believe he would do things differently. If he only had someone to show a little faith in him, you know, believe in his worth, then he might believe in himself. Did you know he married a prostitute because he thought no one else would have him?"

Honey dripped from the corner of Sam's mouth into his beard as he frowned.

Wagging a piece of bacon in the old man's face, Rachel said, "His circumstances remind me of Luke's, Sam. Society looked down on Luke simply because he was deprived by being born to poor parents. He was a dear boy, and a good friend to me, though I must admit he was somewhat of a troublemaker to others. But he had little choice. He had to survive in his world, didn't he? But because I treated him with kindness and sympathized with his plight, he became a dear and trusted friend. I believe Davis—if Davis is his real name—secretly yearns to better himself. He's just too stubborn to admit it. He's proud, despite it all. Too proud for his own good, I imagine. And I've been thinking . . ."

Sam stared at his plate and swallowed down his biscuit.

"I've asked myself, if Davis is Tomas de Bastitas, why wouldn't he say something—if, as you say, he does have some recollection of who he is. I think it's true what Ramon and Angelique said. People are crass enough to judge others on their past, even in the case of survivors of Indian captivity. But I'm not certain only that would cause Davis to deny his heritage. No. I think seeing his brothers, perhaps, might have had something to do with it. They are all well educated—Ramon is going to Harvard—and Estaban is respectably married with a child. I think comparing himself to his brothers might be one of the reasons for his feelings of worthlessness. I think he would like nothing better than to admit who he is, but he's afraid. There must be some way to get him to confess that he is a Bastitas. What do you think, Sam?"

"I'm thinkin' you been doin' more considerin' than sleepin', Miss Rachel."

"Yes, I was awake until dawn. But the man is an enigma, Sam. On the surface he pretends to be this big, bad outlaw. But is he? If he is a cold-blooded killer, why should he seem so different from Clyde? Clyde is a snake; I wouldn't be surprised to see him slither out of his skin any minute. Clyde is a killer. Not Davis. If Davis killed a man, there must have been a reason for it."

Forgetting his biscuits, Sam placed his plate on the ground between his boots and wiped his mouth on his shirtsleeve. Looking at the pale blue sky, he ruminated, "I have a friend who lives up north a ways. Name's Hickok. James Butler Hickok. He's a young man, 'bout like Davis there, and jest as handy with a gun. Saw 'im last year and we was speakin' on the state of things. He says to me, 'Sam, whenever you git into a row, be sure not to shoot too quick. Take time. I've known many a feller to slip up for shootin' in a hurry.' Appears to me Davis's been shootin' too quick fer too long. He slipped up. Now he's payin' fer it."

"But he could change, Sam. I know it! If that jury would only give him a chance! Perhaps they would if . . ."

He eyed her suspiciously.

". . . if *you* would testify for his character."

"Me?"

Bestowing on Sam a blindingly bright smile, she asked, "Why not? You're a Texas Ranger, the epitome of law and order—justice!" She punctuated her words with a shake of her fist.

Sam shook his head. "Lord have mercy, gal, you need to go back to bed so's ya can wake up from whatever dream's been rattlin' around in that purty head of yores. You got no way of knowing if he *is* Alex's son—"

"But you yourself said—"

"I know what I said, darlin', and I'm kickin' myself for plantin' that idea in yore brain more'n it already was. There ain't never gonna be no way to know for certain if he's Tomas unless he confesses and he jest ain't gonna do it. Why should he? If'n he's got one speck of heart in him he won't put the Bastitases through that kind of heartache, 'cause Tomas or not, he is what he is. No good. Now ya got to git yore mind off that rascal completely. Ya think a man like Davis is always sweet as cream as he's been behavin'? Darlin', Kid Davis is a livin', breathin' example of a man-killer. We Rangers learn early on what to look for in them sapsuckers, 'cause the most dangerous ones is all alike. They's quiet in demeanor, sober, and as lost in thought as a monk. They always dress like they is perpetually ready for a spur-of-the-moment funeral. They can drink ever'one else under the table but seldom be affected by the spirits themselves. They'd put their last coin on a gamblin' table knowin' the dealer's dealin' from under the deck, and when he calls 'im about it he ain't got no plans on quarrelin'; he jest lets the cheater make his move so's there's witnesses all over the room to testify who drew first. He's quiet—fatally quiet—and seventy-five percent of the time a killer's eyes are as blue as a spring sky at noon. We in the law profession call 'em *shootists*. Bein' a shootist is their profession, and they do it with cold-blooded nerve."

Shocked, Rachel stared at her friend and said, "Why, Sam, only last night you were excusing him and practically inviting me to befriend him."

"Ash cake and dumplin's make me sentimental. So do weepin' women."

She looked hurt, Rachel supposed, since no sooner had Sam responded than he was nudging the rim of his tin plate with the toe of his boot and apologizing.

"I'm sorry. We're on edge after that Injun affair last evenin'. We're nearly a third of the way to Brackettville and I don't mind tellin' ya I'll be thankful to git there. I don't trust Clyde and his boys no further than I could throw them. They've had their heads together too much, and since last night Davis has seemed to join 'em. Now, Clyde ain't got the good sense to fight his way out of an old towsack, but Davis is another matter. The truth is, Miss Rachel, I'd certainly hate to be put in the position of havin' to shoot the boy, but if he tries my hand I'll have no choice."

"You don't think they'll try to escape?" Her voice quivered with panic.

"Men like that don't jest saunter into a courthouse and trust a jury to take pity on 'em, Miss Rachel."

Setting her chin, she said stubbornly, "I don't believe it. I *won't* believe he is beyond redemption, and I will not give

up the notion that he is Angelique's son until he convinces
me otherwise."

Sam scratched his chin through his beard and contemplated her face. Finally he said, "Maybe I ought to take him
off'n yore wagon."

"You can't!" She jumped to her feet, spilling biscuits and
bacon over the ground. "My hands are still sore, Sam. I can't
drive!"

"Then I'll get Deputy Hale—"

"I refuse." She crossed her arms in defiance.

Sweeping his hat from a crate, Sam slapped it on his head
and ambled back toward his charges, mumbling something
about mule-headed women.

Much to Rachel's discomfiture, she soon discovered that
Sam was right. Davis, withdrawn and surly, had little to say
throughout the next few hours. And the longer he perched
beside her, stony and apparently blind to everything but the
monotonous countryside, the more nervous she became.
And the more nervous she became, the more she talked.

"Haven't you noticed something *different* about me, Mr.
Davis?" She studied his profile and waited, wondering, after
a moment of continuing silence, if he had even heard her.

Giving the lines a flick that brought up the nigh horse's
ears, Davis eventually shook his head.

"I'm without my petticoats!" she explained.

His head came around only slightly. The corners of his
mouth might have twitched, but she couldn't be certain.

"Yep," he said.

"You were absolutely right, you know. A wagon train is
no place to be wearing such attire. I must have looked a sight
to the others. I'm so much cooler, too. Are you listening to
me, Mr. Davis?"

He nodded.

"Do you like my hat?" She brushed the tiny brim of her
bonnet with her fingertips. "I had forgotten I brought it
along. Is there something wrong, Mr. Davis?"

Again, he only shook his head.

Sighing, she stared out over the countryside, wondering what he found so enthralling about the horizon. The terrain, with gray-green tufts of spiky grass and jagged fragments of limestone, appeared no different than it had the last two days. In the distance were the usual orchardlike clumps of mesquite trees, their pale olive-green leaves shimmering beneath the intense sun. Prickly pear cactus lined the road, and beyond that, the brushy greasewood and the gray ceniza covered the ground as thickly as a forest.

Since breaking camp she had formulated a plan for getting Davis to open up about his past. She would have to approach the subject very carefully. If he *was* Tomas de Bastitas, opening such wounds could be very painful for him. Still, he must know what a wonderful family the Bastitases were. He must know that they still hoped for his return. If she was right in her earlier discussion with Sam, perhaps he was simply afraid of returning to his family due to feelings of inadequacy, or because he was ashamed of his past. He simply must be convinced that Alejandro and Angelique would stand by him no matter what!

Clearing her throat, she forced herself to ask, "Were you born here in Texas, Mr. Davis?"

He shifted on the wagon seat.

"Sam and I were discussing family earlier," she said a little shakily. After a slight hesitation she added, "The Bastitas family, actually."

The arm brushing hers tensed. Her heart leaped.

"I think it would be wonderful to have such a large loving, caring family. As an only child I always wished for brothers or sisters. Angelique's and Alejandro's sons all seem very close. I can imagine they were very helpful to one another while growing up, and helpful to their parents too. I'm certain Alejandro and Angelique spent many years of heartache after losing Tomas."

Watching a roadrunner dart from under one of the many towering Spanish dagger plants to the dense foliage of the ceniza, Rachel closed her eyes and listened to the jingle of harnesses and the rumble of wagon wheels. Why didn't he say something?

With her fingers twisting into her skirts, Rachel lifted her chin, focused on a distant tree, and said, "I think Alejandro de Bastitas is one of the most handsome men I have ever met. So are his sons, for that matter. I can certainly understand why Angelique fell so hopelessly in love with him."

Davis stared at her now. And she didn't have to look to know it. She could feel it.

"Of course Alejandro is desperately in love with Angelique as well. You can see it in his eyes when he looks at her. Imagine a man looking at you with such love after thirty-one years of marriage. Well, I've decided *I* shall marry a man as handsome, as arrogant, as exciting . . ." Turning her face toward his, she looked up into his blazing blue eyes and finished softly, "Someone like Alejandro de Bastitas."

His face darkening further, he snapped, "You should've hung around the Bastitas ranch awhile longer. Looked to me like that fancy-talking Bastitas fellow was willing enough to court you."

Stunned by the realization that he had even noticed Ramon's interest in her, Rachel opened and closed her mouth before she could find the strength to speak again. "Ramon?" she responded thoughtfully, acknowledging with a slightly dizzy head the escalation of her heartbeat. Had she actually witnessed some jealousy there? Dear God, she thought, he was jealous of his own brother! This was not what she had intended at all!

"Ramon is dreadfully young," she explained. "I like older men, you see."

"How much older?" he demanded.

"Well, old enough to have learned a little something about the world. A more *experienced* man."

"Educated?"

"Not necessarily. My father had no formal education beyond what was taught to him by a tutor, but he was the smartest man I ever knew. He knew everything there was to know about running a plantation and raising cotton. Everyone excels at something." She looked at him squarely. "Even you, Mr. Davis."

"Oh yeah?" His dark brows flared over his eyes as, suddenly angry, he mocked, "Yeah, I guess I do. I'm real good with a gun, Miss Gregory. As you can see it's brought me much success."

She threw up her hands in exasperation. "Well, pardon me for attempting to bolster your sadly lacking self-confidence. I have never known anyone who so enjoyed immersing himself in self-pity."

"Self-pity!" He boomed it so loudly Sam rode up closer to the wagon to take a look.

"Exactly! You've done nothing but brood over your circumstances all morning!"

"I'm not brooding, lady. I'm just fed up listening to your idle feminine chitchat and your attempts to reform me!"

"And I, sir, am growing tired of your hateful acerbities!"

"Ass what?!"

Nose to nose, she glared into his piercing eyes and spat, "Acerbities, Mr. Davis. If you don't know the meaning of the word, I suggest you look it up in a dictionary. You *do* know what a dictionary is . . ."

He let out a derisive snort and stared at the horses' ears.

"Well? Do you?"

"I know what a dictionary is."

"What is it?"

"It's a book with meanings in it."

"Obviously. Any moron could put two and two together on that one."

Up went his eyebrow again, and he made a nasty little sound with his mouth that might have been meant for the horses—or for her.

Jeromia rode by then. "D'Hanis dead ahead!" he announced.

"It's about time," she heard Davis grumble.

They camped outside of town, not far from St. Dominic's Catholic Church and a farmhouse owned by a pleasant Mex-

ican couple who were more than eager to sell the travelers
fresh milk and butter and a foul-smelling balm that supposedly did wonders for red bug and wood tick bites. Rachel
purchased a jar of milk, disappointed to find it was thin and
tasted like wild garlic and onions. The butter, she learned,
was nothing more than congealed animal fat.

Homer ordered a cow to be slaughtered. For the remainder of the afternoon and early into the night it roasted over
the fire while the travelers mended their wagons, tended their
few head of stock, and soaked their water casks in the creek.
The evening meal was a feast, with beef, catfish caught from
the creek, deep-fried cornbread cakes, and potatoes roasted
in the ashes of the fire. Then Jeromia played his fiddle and,
after much deliberation, Homer broke out his crate of whiskey. Eventually most of the men and a few women, including Audra, walked into town to the saloon. Their raucous
laughter could be heard occasionally above the tinny piano
that played the same tune over and over:

> *Buffalo gals, won't you come out tonight?*
> *Come out tonight!*
> *Buffalo gals, won't you come out tonight,*
> *And dance by the light of the moon!*

Rachel secretly wished she could join them, but Martin
had deemed her his responsibility throughout the evening and
reminded her that a lady such as herself would never frequent a saloon.

Martin, Rachel decided, was beginning to get on her
nerves.

"There is something I wish to discuss with you, Rachel,"
he said after escorting her back to her wagon.

She wasn't inclined to listen at the moment. Once again
he'd punished her toes abominably while dancing, and the
hour was growing late. But she paused out of politeness.

"As you've probably guessed, I've grown quite fond of you
these last days," he continued, staring at some point above
her head.

Rachel frowned, growing uncomfortable with the tone of this approach.

Clasping his hands behind his back, he rocked slightly forward and back on his balls of his feet and said, "I think it would behoove us to marry."

She was stunned. "I—I beg your pardon?"

"I have asked you to marry me."

He looked down his nose at her, and Rachel laughed. "You aren't serious, Martin? We hardly know one another. And we certainly don't—"

"Love one another?" He dismissed the idea with a flip of his hand. "Love is a mundane notion, my dear. It is nothing more than a severe case of bubbles in the stomach. You get the same effect with indigestion. Fondness is more realistic, and I am quite fond of you.

"I have deliberated over this all day, my dear. I have money and a tract of land outside San Diego where I plan to build my home. Naturally it would be convenient if I had a companion. You, on the other hand, are saddled with your stepmother and, thanks to the War, you have little money and no prospects of marriage, except perhaps to some uneducated clod who smells like a cow. It would be a terrible waste of your beauty and breeding to settle for such a man. Well, what do you think?"

She stared at him a full minute before realizing that her mouth was open. Snapping it shut, she stuttered, "I—I—oh well—"

"You're speechless."

She nodded.

"I don't expect an answer right away, of course. You needn't make the decision until we reach Brackettville. But know that until you say yea or nay I plan to devote my spare time to courting you in hopes you will see my view of the situation. Now, however, I will bid you good-night." Stepping against her, he slid his arm around her waist and tipped her face up to his. She stood there like a limp rag doll as he pressed his dry mouth against hers. And though she closed her eyes and waited for the same swirling sensation in her stomach that Davis had aroused, it never came.

He left her without another word, but with a smile that said he had little doubt she would come around to his way of thinking. Standing in the darkness, Rachel leaned against the wagon, weak with the horrible realization that he was probably right.

"So, are you going to marry him or not?"

Whirling around, Rachel glared into the shadows at Davis's blacker-than-black silhouette and very nearly shouted, "How dare you sneak up on me that way!"

"I didn't sneak. If you and Stillwell hadn't been so sucked up together, you might have heard me."

"You're disgusting, Davis." His smile infuriated her further. She was amazed at how easily he could do that—infuriate her—without saying a word. Plunking her hands on her hips, she said, "You know, you could learn a few manners from Martin."

She sensed that he smiled again, but she couldn't be certain. He'd moved deeper into the shadows.

"All right. Next time I drink coffee, I'll stick my little finger out," he responded.

"What do you want?" she demanded.

"Now *that*, Miss Gregory, is a loaded question."

Feeling her face heat up, Rachel attempted to move around him to the back of her wagon, but he stopped her dead by grabbing her arm and pulling her up beside him.

"You've been drinking, Mr. Davis. I smell it on your breath!" Their eyes met, and that queer thrill of excitement grabbed her stomach as she attempted to struggle from his grasp. Then her eyes widened further as she discovered, "No chains! Sam's released you again, Mr. Davis, and I demand to know why!"

"Nosy little thing, aren't you, sweetheart. Curiosity's going to get you in trouble someday."

"Then I'll ask him myself!" She wiggled furiously as his grip tightened.

"All right, all right," he drawled. "If you must know, Miss

Gregory, I'm a good guy here to bamboozle the bad guys and—"

"Ha!" With a toss of her head, she declared, "Now *that* is the best one yet. Did you go to school to learn how to lie, Mr. Davis?"

"Nah, it comes natural, darlin'." Looking off in the distance, he abruptly changed the subject. "Where's Audra?"

"Audra! Is that why you're here? To attempt a rendezvous with my stepmother? Oooh, I should have known!"

"Jealous, love?" He smiled again.

Her head snapped back at this insinuation. Staring into his dark eyes and feeling as if she'd just attempted a somersault and landed upside down, she tried to laugh again, wondering why it wasn't so easy this time.

"Jealous!" She choked it. "Why is it men are so drawn to women like Audra? She has that widower up the train rolling over and begging for her attentions—"

"Trail's long, and a man gets lonely. Sometimes he needs a warm, obliging woman to ease the strain."

"Well, she certainly is obliging. Given six months she will have obliged every man in West Texas." She wiggled again. His grip tightened.

"Nothing wrong with that. In case you haven't woke up to the fact, Miss Gregory, women have needs too. You must have them or you wouldn't be dallying in the dark with ole Stillwell." Looking at her again, he asked quietly, and with an inflection in his voice that wasn't quite teasing, "Is he a better kisser than me?"

She stopped wiggling. Her eyes just sort of naturally flew up to his mouth, and her heart danced to her throat.

"Well?" his lips asked.

Swallowing, she managed, "You're . . . too rough."

"That's called passion. Most women like a little passion."

"I can't imagine why."

"It's also called desire; you might like it too, if you gave it a chance."

She laughed harshly. Clearing her throat, she demanded,

"Release me." He obliged so abruptly that she stumbled. "Now, if you'll excuse me, I plan on retiring."

He watched her rub her arm and turn back to the wagon. He wasn't ready to let her go. Leaning against the bulging underside of the osnaburg wagon canvas, he said, "Are you going to cuddle up under the covers with that Bible of yours and ask God to forgive you for lying to yourself and to me, Miss Gregory?"

That stopped her. She turned back and scowled. "How do you know I read the Bible at night, and what do you mean by that?"

"I hear you reading. Sometimes I stand out here and listen. You read real nice. In fact, that's why I came by . . . just to hear you read." He *was* a pretty good liar, come to think about it, he thought.

Appearing to forget her anger, she perked up like a schoolmarm who'd just discovered a delinquent student with his ear pressed against the schoolhouse door. "Do you enjoy books, Mr. Davis?"

He stared at her smiling red mouth and clutched at an idea. "Sure I like books. I read all the time when I was a boy."

"Why, that's wonderful! What works did you enjoy?"

"The Bible. Just the Bible. My ma wouldn't have anything else in the house."

"The Bible." Rachel crossed her arms over her breasts. "How very commendable of her. I can imagine your entire family gathered before the fire while your father recited homilies."

Frowning, he shook his head and said, "No, he only read the verses."

She smiled a little wider. "Would you like to join me in reading the Bible tonight? We could sit here on the rear of the wagon and read verses."

"On the rear of the wagon?"

She nodded and her hair rippled like moonlight on water. Pushing away from the wagon, he answered, "All right."

With a swirl of her skirt, Rachel turned for the wagon. The rear door was down flat, suspended by chains on each side. With little effort, Davis hoisted her onto it. She fumbled in the darkness for a candle, and having lit it, found the tattered Bible she had placed inside a trunk. She returned to the rear of the wagon, then plunked onto the shelf, letting her feet dangle halfway to the ground. Her ankles were showing. Davis stared at them for a moment before backing to the door and hefting himself up beside her.

Swinging his feet, he grinned while staring down on the top of her head. She rifled through the book for several moments before looking up at him. He took note that, although his arm was pressed up against hers, she didn't move. He also noted that her pale throat was becoming blotched with color. So was her face. And her mouth was beginning to pinch at one end. Forcing his eyes from her face, he leaned to the right, peering around the wagon canvas to see if anyone was coming. The coast was clear, so he straightened and looked back down at the book as she jabbed it in his belly.

"What's that for?" he asked her.

"To read."

"But I thought *you* were going to read it."

"Later. I'd like you to read first. You have a wonderfully mellow voice that I should enjoy hearing, I think. Go ahead, Mr. Davis. Don't be shy. I await this with rapt anticipation."

He looked at the book again, then back to her face. "All right." He slowly took the Bible, turned it this way and that, opened the cover, and flipped through the tissue-thin, ragged pages before leafing back to the first page. He cleared his throat.

Leaning slightly against him, she peered over his hands at the black and white page and smiled. "What are you going to read me, Davis?"

"Genesis."

"Genesis. What chapter?"

"One. It's my favorite."

"Then by all means, do read it."

Dragging his eyes back to the book, he lifted it almost to the end of his nose, squinted in the dim light, and began clumsily In the beginning . . . ah . . . God created the heaven : d the earth."

"Very od, Mr. Davis." Her hair brushed the back of his thigh as ...e attempted to peer over his shoulder. "Go on."

"And the earth was without form, and void; and darkness was upon the face of the deep. . . . And the spirit of God moved upon the face of the waters. . . ."

"Go on, go on!"

"And Go i said, Let there be light: and there was light."

"Fascina ng!"

"And God called the light Day, and the darkness he called Night. And the evening and the morning were the first day." He snapped the book shut and thrust it into Rachel's hands. "Now it's your turn. I was never much for reading aloud."

"But you do it so well."

He stared at the dusty toes of his boots, somehow discomfited by her intense scrutiny. He had never known a woman who could make him squirm the way she could.

"In fact," she continued, "I would call that recital just short of miraculous, Davis, seeing how chapter one of Genesis is tucked somewhere near the back of the book." She flipped open the cover of the Bible and stared down at the page he'd supposedly read. "You see, this is a very old Bible, and some time ago the first few pages were torn out. To keep from losing them I—"

"All right, dammit." Grabbing the book from her hands, he glared into her wide, twinkling eyes and snapped, "So I can't read. So what. Is there some crime in that?"

"No." More softly, she said, "No crime, Mr. Davis, and no reason to lie out of shame. In fact, you did a beautiful job of reciting the passage. Where did you learn it?"

He looked off into the darkness. "Fort Bliss. Barney Davis read it aloud every night before bed."

"Was Barney Davis your father?" She watched his profile, her heart thumping against her ribs as she anticipated his reply.

He didn't respond but twisted and threw the book back into the wagon before wrapping his fingers insistently around

Rachel's arm. Taken aback, she frowned and demanded, "What are you doing?"

"We both know why I came here, Rachel, and it wasn't to read the Bible. And it wasn't to see Audra. Get in the wagon."

She tugged on her arm. "Don't be absurd!"

"I said get in the wagon. Please." He pulled gently on her arm. "I just want to share your company for a while, and I swear upon my honor that I won't do anything you don't want me to do."

"You *have* no honor, Mr. Davis!"

"I might surprise you."

"No!"

He swore beneath his breath before catching her chin in his fingers. Before she could recover from her shock, he moved his mouth on hers with a fierceness that left her struggling weakly against him. Pulling away, he whispered near her ear, "You don't struggle this much with Stillwell, sweetheart."

"He doesn't make me feel this way." She tried to turn her face from his, but he caught it again and looked into her eyes.

"And how do you feel, Rachel?"

"Angry. And—and . . . confused, and . . . Oh please, Davis, just let me go and stop making me feel this way. I don't like it." His breath beat fast and warm on her face as he moved his mouth slowly over her cheek, back to her lips. Yet, much to her own shame, she found herself lifting her face to his. Unlike Martin's, Davis's kiss was wet and warm, and she felt her resistance melt away under the tidal rush of excitement that surged inside her.

"That's it, love, just relax. It's not so bad if you'll just stop fighting it. Come on, Rachel, just blow out the candle and come sit beside me."

The words were luring, hypnotizing. She followed him obediently, wondering what madness had besieged her, what spell he had cast upon her that she would throw caution and good sense to the night breeze and follow him into her wagon. She watched him, as through a long, black tunnel, snuff the candle out with the palm of his hand.

Chapter 12

I'm going mad, she thought as she lay down beside him.

His hands came at her through the darkness, both cupping her face, urging her closer until she was lying half across his body and her lips were suspended just above his.

"Someone may come, Davis, I—"

His mouth hushed her, warm and sweet like the whiskey he'd been drinking. And the swirling started, deep, deep in the pit of her stomach, tugging at her insides so violently she wondered if it would kill her. She heard him groan and wondered if he experienced the same thing, this consuming, pulsing heat that sluiced to every point throughout her body. Then the tip of his tongue touched her mouth, and she gasped.

"That hurts," she whispered.

Davis pulled away. Her face and hair looked ghostly in the shadows. "What hurts, love. The kiss?"

She shook her head. "No. Here." Rolling slightly, she placed her flattened hand on her stomach.

"You'll like it when you get used to it." His fingers moved feather-light across the back of her hand. He felt himself smile as he asked, "Didn't Luke ever make you hurt there?"

She shook her head.

"What about Stillwell?" His fingers stilled.

"No," came her firm assurance, making him believe it, all of it: the trembling, the shyness, the hesitation. "It makes no sense why it should only happen with you, Davis."

He touched her cheek with his fingers, marveling at its texture, thinking that if he was honest with himself he'd ad-

185

mit that there were a few strange things happening inside him as well. He was falling for a girl with the face of an angel, a girl who had known neither passion nor desire, a girl who came willingly into his arms though she was aware, for the most part, of his past. The kind of girl he'd always dreamed of finding, but had given up hopes of finding long ago.

He buried his hands in her hair until the silver skeins of silk poured over and through his fingers and spilled in white, soft puddles in the middle of his chest. He kissed her again, this time acknowledging a new, more violent flame around his heart. It took his breath away.

In that moment he felt the solid walls of his resistance begin to crumble. Here and there fragments of blinding white light, hinting of hope, penetrated his darkness. For the first time in ages something was real and warm in his life; feelings were surfacing that left him as confused—and, yes, as frightened—as she. She was the kind of woman who drove men beyond reason; the kind of woman a man could die for.

He thought, *I would gladly die if only . . .*

Davis clutched her to him, dragging her resisting body against the hungry, hard length of his. This time when he kissed her he drew her mouth into his, forced open her lips with his tongue—gently at first, then more urgently until he could slip inside her, until he could plunge inside to explore her mouth intimately. Rachel's heart skipped, then hammered in a frantic race that sent a jolt of wild sensations through her body. She trembled and clung, feeling as if she were slipping down some beckoning but bottomless abyss.

Dragging his mouth from hers, he whispered, "Ah, Rachel. Rachel, what am I going to do with you?" Then laughing huskily in her ear, he said, "I know what I'd like to do with you, but I'd hate myself in the morning."

She blinked, wishing he'd quit grinning and talking and kiss her again. When he laid his head back on the floor of the wagon and stared at the canopy overhead she thought she would die if he did not kiss her again.

She reached with her hand and touched his lips. When his head came up, she said, "Again, please."

"Again what?"

"Kiss me. Like you did before." She smiled a little with one corner of her mouth and admitted, "I liked it."

"You admit it, do you?"

Rachel felt herself blush. Perhaps young ladies didn't admit to such things, even in Texas. They certainly didn't in New Orleans.

With a groan he wrapped his arms around her and rolled so his entire length was stretched upon her. A whole new flurry of sensations burst inside her. Like an eddy they whirled through her arms and legs and heart and stomach, and funneled into her nether regions. "Oh my." She breathed it. Then looking up into his dark face with its dark eyes and the smile, not quite happy and not quite sad, she closed her eyes and thought, *Oh my.*

He did kiss her again: her cheek, her eyelids, the tip of her nose. He nuzzled the underside of her chin with his face, and her breath became fast, a rapid, feverish sound that was as foreign to her as the growing need inside her.

She clamped her arms around his back. How broad and hard it was. How hot. His shirt was hot, too, and moist against her palms. Braver now as his mouth slid up and down her throat, she timidly stroked his hair. Her fingers trailed lightly along his ear and wrapped loosely around the back of his neck where the thick, slightly coarse black hair curled gently around her knuckles.

Why, why, why did this all seem so right, so . . . sinless?

She welcomed his kiss, even opened her mouth for the tormenting plunge of his tongue, returning the touch with her own until he appeared to lose control of what he was doing, of where he was and who he was doing it with. His hands were everywhere, in her hair, on her face, her throat, seeking and finding the soft swells of her breasts. The buttons down the front of her blouse gave way easily to the pressure of his fingers, and before she could deny him, his hand was sliding beneath her chemise, cupping over the high, hard points of her breasts that were curiously sensitive to the touch.

Her head rolled back and forth. Her hands made ineffectual motions that meant nothing. Closing her eyes, she concentrated on how warm and wet and soft his mouth was moving over the hollow of her throat, her chest and down . . . down. She gasped and jumped as his lips slid over her ripe, sweetly swollen nipple. Her hands flew to his head, buried themselves again in his hair . . . and did nothing.

"No," she sighed. "Oh no."

"Beautiful," she heard him murmur. "Sweet God, you taste good."

Without leaving her breast, he lifted her skirt. She barely noticed until his fingers suddenly tugged at the strings of her drawers, and with an expertise she would never have believed possible, pulled them halfway down her hips. Her shoulders rolled off the floor; her hands grabbed his shoulders. "No! Oh no, Davis, you promised! You mustn't! We can't! It's not . . . "

His finger slid inside her.

His head came up and their eyes locked. Her mouth dropped open and she felt as if her body and senses were being torn in two. No, she thought, people don't do this, touch this way and enjoy it. Involuntarily she shivered, mesmerized by the rhythm of his hand and what it was doing to her. She grew uncomfortably warm there. Embarrassingly wet. She wanted to press her legs together so he'd stop, but she didn't. She couldn't. And to her own horror she found herself opening her legs further, lifting her body against his hand, meeting his rhythm with her own until her hips were writhing and the sweet, awful pain there, buried around his finger, grew so unbearable she began to fight it, to thrash against him and whimper for a relief she knew must be there, but couldn't quite grasp.

She pleaded, she didn't know what for. Pressing his big body against hers, he kissed her, rotated his hips against her leg in the same rhythm as his hand. But oddly enough she couldn't kiss him back. Her body was frozen, every vibrating, humming sensation now centered between her legs. It grew and throbbed and grew until—

"Don't fight it," he said in her ear. "Ah, love, just let it happen!"

It did. The release came like an eruption, sailing her high, shattering her outward. Her shoulders left the floor. Her hands flailed. A cry tore at her throat, but she kept it there, where it rasped and burned for the escape her lower body felt. And still his hand moved, wringing from her stranger's body every last ember that burned her until she collapsed beneath him, numb, limp, and more complete than she'd ever felt in her life.

She opened her eyes to the sight of him gazing down at her, his mouth smiling in the pale canvas-filtered light of the moon. Stunned, Rachel remained motionless, staring up into his eyes, bewildered over what had just taken place within her own body, and embarrassed, too. She could hardly deny that she'd enjoyed this sort of lovemaking, and judging by his smile he was very aware of that fact. It had a sobering effect on her mood.

She turned her burning face from his and said, "You promised, Davis."

He laughed. "I said I wouldn't do anything you didn't want me to do." He pulled his hand from her drawers and gently tugged down her skirt. "I could have done more, love."

"I wouldn't have let you!"

"No?"

Frowning at the humor in his voice, she glanced his way and said, "You're shameless. You know that, don't you?"

"So I've been told." Raising up on one elbow, he looked at her intently as she rebuttoned her blouse. "Rachel?"

There was an urgency in his voice that gave her pause.

"Don't marry Stillwell."

A heartbeat passed as she stared at his features. His mouth was again stubborn, his eyes hard. A thrill of excitement flickered in her heart. "Marriage to Martin would certainly solve my problems. Why shouldn't I marry him?"

"I don't like him."

"You don't like him? Well, *you* shan't be living with him."

"Well, you will, and that's the problem. I wouldn't like it much."

This was a Davis she hadn't seen before. It unnerved her, though often, while sitting upon that splintery wagon seat, she'd fantasized about him charming her with words and gentle caresses. Then she remembered: he'd been drinking.

"Are you inebriated?" she asked him.

"I must be. I sure as hell wouldn't be saying this if I was sober."

Leaning closer to him, she said, "What *are* you trying to say, Davis?"

Damned if he knew. But the thought of Stillwell doing to Rachel what he'd just done unsettled him. Angered him. Frustrated him beyond words because there really wasn't a damn thing he could do about it. And who was to say she'd really *want* him to do anything about it? She was a virgin who'd just experienced her first taste of passion. For all she cared, she might have experienced it at Martin's hands.

Didn't she, after all, deserve someone like Stillwell? Someone with clean hands and a spotless reputation? Someone who could hold her in his arms at night and sleep peaceably without the tormenting nightmares of his past sending him thrashing from his rest?

His anger grew as those thoughts tumbled through his mind. She was out of his league. She deserved someone better than he was. Sam's liquor had numbed his better judgment and she hadn't really submitted to his advances. He'd coerced her into the wagon and seduced her. Stillwell wouldn't have done such a thing . . . not to a lady such as she.

"Davis?" Rachel touched his arm.

He rolled to his knees, stumbled toward the rear of the wagon where he jumped to the ground. Raking his hands through his hair, he walked off into the darkness where he could think without the scent of her intoxicating him to the point of madness.

Rachel watched him go, and said nothing.

* * *

She gradually awoke, watching dust that floated, weightless, in the suffocating, sweltering heat inside the rocking wagon. She lay that way a long while, recalling the events of the previous evening, closing her eyes and imagining Davis in the dark, touching her, kissing her, asking her not to marry Martin.

Throwing her wrist over her eyes, she contemplated his future. He'd made a mistake—albeit a big one—but men made mistakes. She was certain he was remorseful over it, whatever *it* was. He could change. He was changing already. The trick was to convince him to admit his true identity, then to convince the jury that he would walk the straight and narrow. They might be convinced to forgo a hanging, considering the sad circumstances of his past, but what about prison? He might spend years in prison. . . .

Looking across the narrow confines of the wagon, she noticed Audra was missing.

Crawling on her knees to the front opening of the canvas, Rachel yanked back the flap—and stared at Deputy Hale's back.

Tipping his hat, Hale peered back over his shoulder into her stunned face, and greeted her. "Mornin', Miss Gregory. Or should I say afternoon."

"Where is Audra? And where is Davis?"

"Mrs. Gregory's up front of the train with the widower Taylor, and Davis is back with the others."

"Why?"

"Ma'am?"

She licked her dry lips. "Why is Davis not driving my wagon?"

Hale shrugged. "Don't rightly know. Captain Wells just come to me this mornin' and ask that I take Davis's place. Said he wouldn't be drivin' you no more."

Backing away, she tied up the opening and sank back on her bedroll. She sat that way until she heard Homer call out, "Pull 'em up, boys!" Then she hurried to dress in the only muslin gown she owned before dropping the back gate of the wagon and jumping to the ground.

There was a heaviness to the air that was stifling. She saw Davis and Sam as they dismounted their horses some distance away, and the annoying heat and breathlessness seemed to mushroom inside her. It made her ribs ache, not to mention her heart.

Was Davis ignoring her? He'd seen her, for certain, so why was he acting as if she were nothing more than another clump of that ungodly cactus lining the road? She watched in distraught silence as he followed the old Ranger over to the others—Clyde, Pedro, and Pete. When he squatted in the shade of a live oak, his back was to her.

Jeromia rode up then and informed her that Homer had requested all travelers meet at the head wagon. Joining Manuela and her husband, Rachel hurried toward the others.

Homer was pointing to a bank of threatening black clouds on the northern horizon when Rachel and the Alverezes arrived. "It looks bad, folks," he said, "and it's movin' this way. That's a toad choker if'n I ever seen one, so I have to warn ya—if ya choose to begin crossin' the Sabinal now, there's a chance we won't all make it afore the storm. There's a chance the storm'll hit us while we're crossin', and it won't be pleasant. The rivers north of here have been swollen by the rain, and ya can be sure this creek here is gonna suffer."

"Then the simplest thing to do is to wait!" someone called out.

A chorus of agreement followed.

Removing his hat, Homer scratched his balding head and stared at his feet before replying. "In most cases that's true, but this river has a bad reputation when she's swollen." He pointed to the washed-out rock sinking just beyond them. "As ya can see fer yoreself she gits purty wicked, and I'm meanin' deep and rapid. Crossin' when she's high'll mean turnin' back and headin' south for six maybe seven days afore we kin reach a place narrow enough to attempt it."

"Seven days!" a man shouted. "Then another seven days to

get back this far? That's two weeks lost! I say cross now while we can and take our chances!"

"Here, here! Cross now while we can!" most agreed.

Others didn't. Manuela and her husband were among them. "That is easy for you to say," he argued, "because you are in the front of the train with your wagons. But what about us who are in the rear? What happens to us should the waters come before we cross? Then we are left with few numbers and must make the detour alone. I say no!"

Homer said, "We'll take a vote, and only one vote per wagon. Those votin' to push on now? Those votin' to wait it out and move south? Movin' on now gits it. Folks, git yore belongin's strapped down best ya can. Ya know the rules. Do yore best not to cross directly behind the wagon afront ya 'cause the river bottom'll be too mushed up to support ya proper. We'll work together as a team and pray to the good Lord we beat the rise."

Thunder rumbled in the distance and a hot blast of wind whipped the women's skirts as they hurried back to their wagons. Rachel, intent on finding Audra, ran up the line until she located her stepmother at the widower Taylor's wagon.

"What are you doing here, Rachel? Why aren't you preparing our belongings for the crossover?"

"Certainly you don't intend that I should do this alone? How dare you leave this responsibility to me! And what if you make it across and I don't? What then?"

Grinning smugly, Audra purred, "Then a fond fare-thee-well until I see you again, dear daughter."

Swallowing back her disgust, Rachel whirled back down the train, stopping again at Martin's wagon. He stood staring into the wagon bed while Jules worked frantically rearranging the numerous crates packed to the canvas ceiling. A raindrop plopped on the middle of Martin's forehead as he turned to face her. Blotting it with his kerchief, he said, "Ah, my dear, there you are. Are you prepared to cross?"

She shook her head.

"Is something wrong?"

"I . . . I'm just worried; what if Audra makes it across and I don't?"

"Then you'll have a wonderful reprieve from her company, won't you?" Frowning at his manservant, he snapped, "Good heavens, Jules, take care, man, before you shatter that crate of china. Isn't it enough that I had five place settings brutalized by those clumsy bovines?"

Backing away, Rachel said quietly, "But I've never been on my own before. What shall I do? She's liable to leave me, you know. Then what would I do?"

"Jules, perhaps that trunk of crystal and linens should be stacked there, just in case the water does rise. . . ."

Rachel turned back to her wagon. All down the line the people talked.

"Might've knowed it'd rain. There were a ring around the moon three night ago."

"I noticed the birds gatherin' and flyin' low. I coulda sworn I seen a buncha bats night afore last."

"I noticed the smoke from the campfires last night stayed close to the ground."

"The bullfrogs were croakin' to beat Sunday at the last creek we crossed."

Another half hour passed before the first wagon began crossing the Sabinal's riverbed. The slow-moving team of mules stalled halfway across, allowing the wagon to sink slightly in the mud. The water, already more rapid than it had been on their arrival, churned around the lower third of the wagon's wheels, making dozens of tiny eddies that sucked at Homer and Jeromia's shins as they waded in to help. By the time the stubborn animals were coerced into moving, the sky had grown dismally dark and the rain had begun to fall steadily.

The prisoners were taken over river early and deposited on the opposite bank where they were watched by deputies Rogers and Hale. But as usual Davis was never far from Sam's side; the Ranger ultimately removed his manacles so he could assist at the crossing. With Manuela's help, Rachel busied herself arranging then rearranging hers and Audra's belongings, telling herself that all this commotion was for nothing. This was only one of those freak summer storms that blew themselves out in a matter of minutes. They would cross safely and laugh as they had over the Indians, come morning. But as thunder shook the ground and the sky turned dark as night, her fear returned.

The water continued rising. By the time the sixth wagon rolled into the creek bed the current was surging nearly to the axles. Rachel sat bravely just inside her wagon, peering out into the rain, hoping against hope that Deputy Hale would return in time to drive her wagon across the creek. She listened as rain poured through the repaired seams of the canvas and into the tin pail they'd been using as a chamber pot. After emptying the vessel twice in ten minutes, she finally ignored it.

Lightning spooked her horses, so she had little choice but to climb up on the wagon seat and take hold of the lines. From the distance she heard the bawling of cattle, the whoops and hollers of the train employees as they did their best to maneuver the animals and wagons over the swelling river.

She thought she saw Jeromia a few wagons up. Then a bolt of electricity split the air and the man on horseback became . . . nothing. Wiping the rain from her eyes, she stared, blinked in disbelief, then noticed Jeromia's body thrown against a nearby tree, his horse lying some distance away.

She buried her fists against her eyes, curled her torso toward her knees, and let the raindrops pound her back. Faster and faster they fell, becoming harder and harder, turning into ice that pummelled her and the horses unmercifully. The animals, too terrified even to move, ducked their heads between their front legs and braced for the worse.

The black clouds boiled above them. The continuous roar of thunder vibrated the ground while lightning ripped the sky like flashes of daylight. And with it all came the wind, tearing at the wagon's canvas, rocking the thing like a cradle until Rachel thought for certain the vehicle would overturn and crush her beneath its weight.

Then, as he had the day he'd climbed aboard her runaway wagon, Davis appeared, coming at her through the downpour, closing his hands about her arms as he prepared to lift her off the seat and force her back into the wagon. She cried out in relief.

Davis grabbed the lines from her hands and yelled, "Get in back! I'm taking you over!"

There were still several wagons in front of hers. The Alverezes hadn't moved. "But you can't! It wouldn't be right, Manuela and—"

Shaking the rain from his eyes, he shoved her back through the opening. "We'll come back for the goddamn others. I said I'm taking you over!"

She heard Sam yelling, encouraging her horses to move, despite the flashes of lightning and the continual crack of thunder. She dropped to her hands and knees on the floor of the wagon, into the water that had leaked through the canvas overhead. She clutched her sodden bed blanket to her breast, closed her eyes, and prayed that God would forgive her for this selfishness. She prayed Sam and Davis wouldn't be hit by lightning like poor Jeromia, and she prayed for Jeromia.

She knew the minute they hit the water. The wagon shuddered and slowed to a snail's crawl. Throwing open the back canvas, she stared at the water only inches below the wagon bed. Limbs of trees raced past her, swept away by the current. Something struck the wagon, and the entire bed creaked and groaned as if it would break apart at any moment.

Terrified that the unstable wagon would fall apart and be swept downstream, Rachel stumbled back up to the front of the wagon, lunged through the opening, and wrapped her arms about Davis's waist for protection. He called something back to her, over his shoulder, but the roar of wind and water and the pounding of hail drowned him out. Then, sooner than she had thought possible, she felt the wagon jerk and realized they'd reached the opposite shore.

She was out the rear of the wagon before Davis could jump from his perch. Shielding her eyes against the rain, she watched the other travelers as they attempted to cross the creek. By now several wagons had become stuck in the mire. Their owners, having given up any chance of saving their precious cargo, were doing their best to unharness their animals before the poor mules and oxen drowned in the rising water. Then she noticed the Alverezes just urging their animals into the swirling water.

Manuela, having left the safety of her wagon seat, fought her way through the waist-deep torrent and was pulling on the mules' lines. The woman slipped. Only a quick grab at a harness saved her from being sucked into the rushing current. The animals heaved forward, but the wagon wouldn't budge. Jose Alverez left the wagon, and both he and Manuela attempted to push the wagon wheel from its muddy rut. An inch . . . then two . . . three . . .

Her heart pounding frantically, Rachel watched the dear couple who had befriended her on this awful journey struggle to save everything they owned in the world. "Someone help them!" she cried out. But no one came. She moved haltingly toward the water, fear choking the words in her throat as she screamed again for help.

Manuela slipped again. Only a desperate grab from her husband saved her.

Without thinking of the danger to herself, knowing only that the couple needed help and there appeared to be no one at that moment to give it, Rachel kicked off her shoes and ran into the river.

"Rachel! Rachel, no!" came Davis's frantic cry behind her. But she plodded on, fighting the slimy muck that sucked up around her ankles and the rushing, peaking water that slashed at her thighs. It took every ounce of strength she had to battle her way to the Alverezes' wagon. Falling against the wheel, she gripped it with both hands while trying to regain her breath. Then leaning against the wheel, she began to shove.

The roar was barely audible at first, due to the pounding rain and rolling thunder. Then the very earth beneath her feet began to tremble. The water suddenly swelled up to her armpits.

Davis came at her through the silver sheets of rain, a rope tied around his waist to prevent his being swept away in the current. The water whirled around his chest and threatened to drag him down. She reached for him, feeling the water rush against her shoulders, her throat—oh God, she was going to drown! But he wrapped his arms around her and lifted her up against his chest. Then over his shoulder she saw it.

The wall of water, black and brown and churning yellow, roiled onto them, driving Davis against her, and her back against the wagon. Then her world was nothing but blackness, cold and cloying and vicious as the water sweeping over their heads, lifting them from their feet, pinning them against the wagon, which trembled with the force.

Her lungs were bursting. Then, when she thought she could go no longer without a breath, the force seemed to ease about them; the hope gave her the strength to hold out seconds longer. She felt Davis lift her. She fought him, frantic, attempting to break free so she might claw her way to the surface. The surface. God, where *was* the surface? She strained toward a tiny pinpoint of light above her head, thrashing aside the swirling mud while batting away his arms. His hands dug into her ribs and brought back the cold reality of their surroundings. She clung to him as they broke the surface of the water.

They drifted along in the current before the rope about Davis's waist snapped taut. Someone was hauling them in. Rachel closed her eyes and drifted, allowing the low cadence of his voice to soothe her. When she realized he was cursing her, she turned her face up to the now gentle rain and laughed.

Sam and Homer and Deputy Hale were there when Davis lifted her in his arms and stumbled onto the riverbank. They fell in the mud, he on top of her so his shoulders covered her face from the rain. She heard his heart thud like a fast-beating drum against her ear, and she turned her mouth into the crisp thatch of hair on his chest, where his shirt, shorn of its buttons, gaped open, and kissed him. She didn't care who saw her do it.

The fear that only moments before had given him super-human strength now dissolved in relief as he lay face down in the mud. But with that relief came the awful realization that the thought of living without the half-drowned girl beneath him had frightened him more than all the floods and all the Indians in Texas ever had.

Angrily he rolled away, yanking at the rope around his waist. Her hands came for him and he batted them back. "Get the hell away from me," he demanded. "Get away!"

"Please, please don't leave me! Don't ever leave me!" Rolling against him, her face drained of all color and spotted with mud, she wept.

He tried to muffle her mouth with his hand, leaving streaks of mud from his fingertips across her lips. People were beginning to gather, and though her voice was hoarse and strained to a whisper he wasn't about to take the chance that something she said in her irrational state might be overheard by anyone else.

"Stop it!" He shook her until her head fell limply toward her chest and her shoulders heaved. He said as quietly as possible, "Ah, God, stop it, Rachel. You're a fool, sweet-heart, and if this thing between us doesn't stop now you're gonna get hurt. I'm no good, and nothing you can do or say to me is going to change that. Just leave it be, Rachel. Just leave it!"

He rolled away, stumbled to his feet, and marched up the riverbank. He spied Martin Stillwell, apparently more concerned over his wagonload of china than he was over Rachel, and his control left him.

In three strides he went up against the Englishman, twisted his filthy hands in the man's wet but pristine shirtfront, and threw him against the wagon. "You son-of-a-bitch, why didn't you help her? I'll kill you, Stillwell, if you hurt her. I swear to God I'll come after you if I have to do it from the grave!" He found his hands around the man's throat, but he couldn't stop. "Why didn't you help her? You coward, you sniveling coward!"

There were cries behind him of "Stop him," and he was vaguely aware of Sam's voice yelling, "Yore killin' 'im, boy! Let 'im go, Davis!" Then the hard surface of Sam's rifle stock met the back of his head, pain ricocheted through his brain like the lightning that had earlier ripped the sky. It drove him forward into the gasping Englishman, and suddenly his world tipped and swayed and collided with blackness. He felt himself falling, and somewhere in the shadows Rachel's voice came to him:

"Oh God, don't hurt him. Please, please don't hurt him!"

Chapter 13

Jeromia was gone. Deputy Rogers had been killed when trying to rescue a child who'd fallen into the current. Only that morning the Alverezes' bodies had been found some four miles downriver. And still the rain continued, falling gently on the survivors' shoulders as they buried the couple. Among the travelers there was little spirit left to carry on, but they had no choice. After a two-day layover they would begin their trek at dawn.

Davis, hunched and miserable beneath a makeshift tent, watched the mourners plod their way through the mud from the Alverezes' graveside. Deputy Hale, his felt hat pulled down low over his brow, dozed as water ran in a silver rivulet over the brim and pattered on the front of his brown slicker. Davis watched as the barrel of the lawman's rifle dropped toward the ground, then he looked toward Sam.

Clyde shifted closer and whispered, "We could do it now, ya know. That deputy's wore out from watchin' us all night. By dawn we could be across the border."

Davis closed his eyes. The image of Rachel's face, wet with rain and tears and streaked with mud, came back to haunt him. He hadn't spoken to her since he'd fished her out of the river. He wouldn't let himself get that close to her again. She'd already weakened him, put futile thoughts in his head of how life would be if he settled down with her right this minute—just forgot his reasons for being here, turned his back on it all and walked away. But then he'd be running again. And it was the running he was tired of. He wanted all the mistakes behind him so he could start new.

Maybe take what little money he'd saved and buy some land, some cows. But there were those damnable obligations hanging over his head as dreary and black as the godforsaken rain clouds overhead.

The iron cuffs were making his wrists bleed; his head hurt, thanks to Sam's slamming his rifle-butt into him. Seeing Rachel escorted back to her wagon by Stillwell didn't help matters. Maybe Clyde was right. Maybe it was time to move on . . . before Rachel made it impossible for him to continue.

By dusk the rain had stopped. Unlike the others Rachel didn't bother to scour the ground for dry firewood. She sat in her wagon, her knees inches from a candle, and read Genesis, chapter one, verses one through five, over and over in her head. Several times she closed her eyes and tried to memorize the verses, but the words didn't come, not in any order at least. They kept getting confused with images of Davis lying face down in the mud, blood oozing from the back of his head, and Sam standing over him, blinking up into the rain. "God forgive me, Alex," she'd heard him say.

So Sam too believed Davis was Tomas de Bastitas. Perhaps that's why he'd taken such an interest in Davis's welfare. It wasn't really because he believed Davis was redeemable. Sam cared very deeply for Alejandro and Angelique Bastitas, and out of respect for that friendship he'd treated Davis more fairly than he might have another prisoner. Like her, he *wanted* to believe Davis could turn around. Davis's brazen assault on Martin the afternoon of the flood had proven them all wrong, though. Now he was chained like an animal to a tree.

She had a decision to make. Martin had approached her again about marriage. After speaking with Homer, he'd discovered the wagonmaster could perform the ceremony, if they so desired. But did she desire?

Why not? She had no ties, other than her stepmother. Audra's disappointment over Rachel's surviving her near-catastrophe had been obvious even to the others. Rachel had realized long ago that her stepmother hated her, but to wish her dead . . .

Shivering, Rachel tugged her shawl more closely about her shoulders and stared into the candle flame. She'd once visited a gypsy woman who'd predicted her future by looking into a candle flame. Now, staring very, very hard, she tried to visualize what that woman had seen. But all she saw was Davis, smirking, taunting, laughing, cursing. She closed her eyes.

Should she marry Martin?

Yes. No. Yes. No more Audra. *No more Davis!*

Some time just after midnight, as Rachel slept, Audra came aboard. Smelling of whiskey and a man's cheap perfume, she trod on Rachel's feet as she stumbled into her bed. She slurred insults at Rachel for no reason, as she had back in New Orleans when she'd imbibed too much dinner wine or soirée champagne. Finally, when she could take no more of the woman's incoherent babblings, Rachel fumbled in the dark for her dress and her slippers and left the wagon.

She marched directly to Martin's tent.

Taking a deep breath, she whispered loudly, "Martin!" She heard him grunt and shuffle as he came to his senses. "Martin, it's Rachel. I must speak with you."

She looked away as he staggered through the opening, his white nightshirt making his thin shins look as appealing as a bandy rooster's. Recalling Davis's admission of sleeping in nothing, she swallowed back her strange sense of disappointment over Martin's attire and said, "I should like to talk with you privately. Might we take a short walk?"

"Must be after midnight." Covering a yawn with the back of his hand, he asked, "Can't this wait until morning?"

She shook her head. "It's now or never, I think. If I don't speak with you immediately, I fear I will surely change my mind."

Grumbling, he ducked back inside his tent, emerging again in trousers supported by suspenders and his nightshirt tucked into it all. Hopping up and down on one foot, he pulled on one boot, then the other, before trailing behind her like an obedient pup.

She proceeded beyond the circle of wagons, just where the dark was heaviest. As she paused to wait for Martin, however, angry voices brought her attention around to the upthrust of rock near the riverbed, where Sam and Deputy Hale were camped with their prisoners.

Running to catch up, Martin demanded, "What's this about, Rachel, and where are you going?"

"Shhh!" Throwing him a telling glance, she shook her head and tiptoed toward the river.

The glowing embers of the campfire cast elongated shadows across the ground and nearby trees. Within the dancing shadows she could see saddled horses: Sam's, Hale's, the prisoners', and Homer's. Leaning against a ledge of white, jagged rock, Rachel attempted to distinguish among the moving figures in the distance. Someone was crouched in the foliage of a bush, his hands and feet bound. Someone else—Sam, she suddenly realized—lay flat on the ground, face up, and over him, pointing the long barrel of a gun in his whiskered face was . . . Davis!

Then with no warning sound a hand came from nowhere, wrapping around Rachel's mouth, lifting her from her feet and up against a sweating, heaving chest. Shoving a gun into her ribs, Clyde sneered in her ear, "One peep out of ya, darlin', and the top of yore sweetheart's head'll be found somewhere's over river there."

Straining around, she stared with wide eyes at the gun Pedro was pointing at Martin's head. Then Clyde, dragging her into the camp, called out quietly, "Davis, we got company."

Davis froze at the sight of Rachel struggling in Clyde's arms. Looking down again at Sam, he spat, "Dammit!"

Sam said, "I reckon this is gonna complicate matters a mite. You might wanta reconsider . . ."

"Too late now, old man, I've come too far. It's now or never and we both know it."

"But the girl—"

"—is comin' with us," Clyde intruded.

Rachel stared at Davis as if he had sprouted two horns and a pointed tail. Her look, no longer surprised or even frightened, was resigned and angry. He could almost read her thoughts—he always could: She was feeling like a fool because she'd trusted him, because she'd allowed herself to be convinced that there was something worth salvaging in that shell of a heart of his. Still, she paled and drew back as he rose to face her, and the vulnerability on her face—the very same vulnerability that had attracted him to her in the first place—kicked out at his conscience so forcefully he felt winded.

Walking slowly to her, his gun at his side, he asked, "What the hell are you doing out here with him?" He flicked the barrel of his pistol toward Stillwell as he stopped before her.

She didn't respond, just glared at him with those violet eyes full of loathing and regret.

He looked then at Stillwell and felt his blood rise. "Now just what the hell am I going to do with you, Martin?"

"I say we take 'im, too," Clyde said. "Two hostages are better'n one."

"No!" It was Martin. His face as white as his nightshirt, he stumbled toward Davis, went down on his knees, and pleaded, "For the love of God, Davis, don't do this. I'm a young man! I'll give you money if you'll just let me go. You don't need me, you have her!"

The silence seemed almost palpable about them. Rachel, her head jammed against Clyde's chest, managed a furious gasp behind the outlaw's fingers.

Looking back at Martin, Davis asked, "How much is your freedom worth?"

"I have two thousand in my wagon."

"*Where* in your wagon?"

Closing his eyes, he said, "Beneath the china is a false floor. It's hidden there."

Pete, who was crouching by a tied and gagged Homer, disappeared into the darkness, toward the train.

Lifting the long barrel of his gun and shoving it against

one of Martin's nostrils, Davis said, "Do you know what I like about you, Stillwell? Nothing. Absolutely nothing. Now, I want to see you crawl on your knees over to that clump of bushes where the good deputy is resting. Then you're going to spread-eagle face down and pray I don't kill you for selling out Miss Gregory. Now, crawl!"

When he had done so, Davis turned back to Clyde. "Let her go."

"The hell you say, Davis! This one's mine, by God. I've had my eye on 'er since the beginnin'. Besides, that old man's posse'll think twice before pepperin' us with bullets if she's along."

"She'll slow us down, Lindsey."

"I'll handle 'er."

Davis looked again at Rachel. Her pale throat was arched, her head, with its thick, tangled white hair, was thrown back as she stared up at him, her eyes unblinking. The look of desire that had warmed her features the days and nights before now burned with fury. Damn little fool. He'd warned her once that her curiosity was going to get her in trouble.

Pete reappeared, waving the satchel of money in the air.

Sam, up on one elbow, looked beyond Davis to Clyde. "Boy, takin' that girl ain't gonna benefit you one iota. If'n I want to shoot ya I'll do it whether she's around or not."

"And you, old codger, will have to shoot her down afore me," Clyde snapped, " 'cause she's stayin' right where she is until we reach Mexico. Then, when I'm finished with 'er, *maybe* you'll git 'er back."

"Yore just addin' fuel to the fire, Lindsey. You go kidnappin' and rapin' a woman and the jury in Brackettville won't even bother paradin' ya through the courthouse. They'll string ya up in the street and take target practice on yore corpse."

"She's goin' with me!" He gave Rachel's head a twist into his chest, just to punctuate his intentions. "Now, I don't know about the rest of ya, but I'm fer gittin' outa here afore somebody else comes along."

Pete and Pedro moved for their horses. Davis remained

where he was, his gun at his hip, his eyes on Lindsey, then Rachel. Her breathing was coming rapidly now, her chest rising and falling raggedly, then jerking as Clyde tauntingly slid his gun up over her breast.

Spinning on his heel, Davis looked down at Sam. "All right, old man, I owe you one. Face to the ground and I'll try making this as painless as possible."

"I'm gonna be behind ya ever' step of the way . . . Davis. You can count on it." Sam rolled to his stomach.

Going to one knee, Davis tipped up the handle of the pistol and brought it down on the Ranger's head.

After eight hours of traveling, Rachel, too exhausted even to notice when Clyde had pulled up his horse, barely managed to lift her head and look out over the endless expanse of Texas badlands before her. Forced to ride with Clyde the entire time, she had expended her strength in fighting off his pawing hands the first grueling hours of their journey. Now she rested limply against his sweating, stinking body and tried to ignore his crude assaults on her person. Still, it wasn't easy. As he ran his hand again into her blouse and squeezed her breast, she closed her eyes and shuddered with revulsion.

"You want a drink or not?" came Davis's voice.

Rolling her head against Clyde's shoulder, she stared into Davis's set face and cold eyes. "I would rather die than drink after you," she told him. "In fact, doing so would probably kill me. You're poison." She stiffened as Clyde chuckled behind her.

"Seems to me she's changed 'er mind about ya, Davis."

"So it seems." Taking his eyes from Rachel, Davis lifted the canteen to his lips and drank deeply, allowing the clear, cool water to run out the corners of his mouth.

Wiping his chin and mouth with the back of his hand, Davis stared out over the flat badlands toward Mexico. Concentrating on that, and not on the hand Clyde was running in and out of Rachel's blouse, kept him from blowing the man off his horse, for the time being.

"We should make Fort Clark by nightfall," he said. Positioning his hat lower over his eyes, he shifted in his saddle. "We'll rest over a few hours before pushing on."

"You're crazy!" Clyde, his eyes bulging, stared at Davis. "Brackettville is waitin' to hang us, Kid."

"I'm not asking you to go parading through Brackettville, but that old fort outside of town will give us some shelter from that." He pointed to the dark clouds building again to the north. "If we're lucky the rain will wipe out our tracks; besides, that old man sure as hell wouldn't expect us to be sleeping just outside the town that wants to hang you, would he?"

"Fine," Clyde came back grudgingly. "That'll give me enough time to do what I've been itchin' to do since San Antone."

Shrinking from Clyde's implication, Rachel looked desperately toward Davis. Dear God, was he so inhuman that he would allow the animal behind her to continue his depravities? Apparently so, she realized despondently. He had done nothing so far to stop Clyde's mistreatment. The idea that she had, at one time, believed that Davis felt something for her made her even more miserable. She thought again of pleading for Davis's mercy, but the idea appalled her. He would no doubt smirk and drawl out some sarcasm that would further humiliate her.

Her breasts were sore, the back of her neck and the sides of her face were abraded by Clyde's beard stubble. But that discomfort paled in comparison to the terror that welled up inside her each time he taunted her with threats of what was to come. Still, she didn't show it. No matter that her heart was pounding out of control and she'd grown nauseated with dread: she wouldn't show it. She wouldn't give Davis that satisfaction!

Rachel tried to moisten her lips with a tongue that was dry and swollen from thirst. It wasn't possible. How Davis must be laughing at her, she thought. How damnably gullible she had been. How childish to harbor such infantile fantasies that a man such as Davis could be anything other than what he was. Yet not a moment passed when she wasn't aware of his presence, like all those days on the train—the way he sat his horse, wore his hat, shifted his eyes, or smiled. Except he wasn't smiling now. A grimness, a coldness had set his face like stone, and the wit that had once brought a spark to those fathomless blue eyes had vanished.

To her horror she realized she felt a new fascination for him. She'd been aware of his masculinity before, but now there was something more, a savagery and a control that left her weak and wretchedly helpless against his appeal.

He caught her watching him once. Twisting suddenly in his saddle, he turned his dark face toward her and their eyes clashed: blue-violet and blue, fury and mockery. They burned into her as his mouth, dry and cracked from the sun, quirked down at the corners, and she thought, though she couldn't be certain, that he whispered her name. Then Clyde began kneading her breast again and, for a heartstopping moment, Davis's hand went to the gun on his thigh.

The hour was near noon before they stopped. In utter exhaustion, Rachel slid limply from Clyde's arms to the ground, collapsing as the impact sent shards of pain skittering up her legs. Clyde followed. Before she could bring her pounding head up, he'd wrapped his bony fingers around her arm and hauled her to her feet.

"I reckon this is as good a time as any to take what I want from ya, darlin' "

She was so tired she scarcely understood his words. But the feral glint in his eyes as he yanked her head back with a handful of her hair jerked her from her half-dazed state. She threw herself backward, breaking his hold on her arm, then fell to her hands and knees as Pedro and Pete and Clyde burst out laughing behind her.

"She's got spunk," Clyde howled. "Come on, cotton-top, show us how hard ya can fight!" Planting his foot on her backside, he gave her a shove. She landed on her raw and sun-seared face and slid across the baked earth. "Don't much look like a lady now, do she, boys?"

Rachel closed her eyes, her abused and battered body

throbbing with heat and pain. She gritted her teeth, wishing in that moment that they would kill her and be done with it. She'd rather face death than one more minute of Clyde's assault. And the others? Dear God, would they take her too? The idea filled her with new terror, and she nearly wept aloud.

"Wonder if that fancy dandy from England would want ya now, darlin'. Reckon he'll want ya when ya get home? Me and the boys'll do our best to educate ya so's ya can teach him a thing or two. He looks like he prob'ly don't know too much."

"He prob'ly has that butler feller do it fer him!" guffawed Pete.

"Well, then, by all means, boys, let's get to it!" Clyde made a grab for Rachel's skirt, not anticipating her response. With her last vestige of strength she surged upward, driving her shoulder into his stomach and knocking him flat on his back.

Incensed, Clyde was back on his feet before Rachel could stumble away. As she whirled to escape, he grabbed a handful of her hair and yanked her off her feet. Still she fought him like a hellcat, clawing at his face and hands and doing her best to kick at the turgid erection in his breeches. It wasn't until he had forced her to her back and lifted his fist to hit her that a cold voice stopped him dead.

"That's enough, Lindsey. Let the girl go."

His fist frozen in midair, Clyde looked back over his shoulder.

Davis stood casually to one side, not far from his horse, his back to the sun. "I said let her go."

Rachel closed her eyes and prayed.

"You got to be jokin', Kid. She deserves a good lickin' after what she done."

Davis shifted his weight from one leg to the other. His right hand dropped toward his gun. "Get off her."

"Bullsh—"

"You've had all the fun with her you're going to have, so back off."

"Maybe I don't wanna."

"Then maybe you'll die."

Clyde's short, sharp laughter was incredulous. Backing off Rachel and standing up straight, he said, "Ya might be good, Kid, but ya ain't no match fer me. I'm the best in Texas, or ain't ya heard?"

"I *ain't*," he mocked him. "You know what they say, Lindsey. There's always someone out there better."

"And you figure yore it."

"One more move toward Miss Gregory and you're liable to find out."

Rachel looked from Clyde to Davis. Davis neither moved nor blinked. His hand rested slightly relaxed near the butt of his pearl-handled gun. An odd silence surrounded them. Even the earlier whirring of insects and the distant *tweeah, tweeah, tweesy* of the golden-cheeked warbler could no longer be heard. The entire world appeared to be holding its breath in anticipation of Davis's and Clyde's next moves.

"Is she worth getting yourself killed over, Clyde?" Davis asked.

Pete and Pedro shuffled backward toward the horses.

"I might ask you the same, Kid," came the response. Then faster than Rachel could blink, Clyde's hand swept down toward his gun, but before Clyde could clear leather, Davis had drawn, aimed, and was poised, knees slightly bent in preparation for firing.

"*Dios!*" Pedro squeezed his eyes closed in disbelief.

"I will ask you again, Lindsey." The cold fury in Davis's voice and the dangerous, threatening look in his eyes cut the heavy air like a double-edged knife. "Is she worth dying over?"

Clyde's Adam's apple bobbed in his scrawny throat as he dropped his hands and shuffled his feet. "Nah, Kid . . . ya didn't really take me serious, did ya? Gawd, who'd want somebody that puny anyhow? She ain't got enough tit to int'rest a hungry babe. Go on. You take her if ya want. No skin off my nose."

Rachel, dazed beyond rational thought, wondering whether this entire occurrence could be anything but a nightmare, watched in disbelief as Davis approached her with that catlike walk she'd come to recognize. His close-fitting black pants and knee-high black boots were dusty. The leather belt and the holster tied snugly against his right thigh exaggerated the slimness of his hips. His chambray shirt was wet through with sweat, and his unshaven jaw was as dark as the hair tumbling over his brow to his ice-blue eyes.

"Get up, Rachel."

His voice held a warning note that made her grow cold with fear. He was so different from the man she'd grown fond of since leaving San Antonio. How could she ever have believed that there was any semblance of goodness in him?

Frustration and despair growing inside her, she met his frigid gaze and demanded, "What are you going to do to me?"

He didn't respond, just offered her an insolent smile and repeated, "Get up."

She did so with as much dignity as possible. She tried to smooth back the mass of matted white hair over her shoulder while following him reluctantly to his mount.

Upon reaching his horse, he lifted his canteen of water from where it hung from his saddle horn. He then turned toward Rachel so suddenly she gasped. His left hand came at her, and before she could stumble away he grabbed her face in his fingers and snapped her head back so she had no choice but to meet his eyes. "Just so there's no misunderstandings between us, sweet cheeks—you're no safer with me than you are with them."

He kissed her—brutally, ravaging her blistered mouth so forcefully Rachel feared she might faint. His mouth was hungry, his tongue hot and hard and urgent. Her knees grew weak. Her heart set up a pounding that deafened her to her own whimper of pain. She longed to claw his face. She thought she might try if given the opportunity. But he thrust her away so suddenly she could think of nothing more than regaining her balance before she fell to the ground at his feet.

Clyde and Pedro's guffawing fanned the desperate anger she felt toward Davis in that moment. Throwing her head back defiantly, she hissed through her teeth, "Bastard! You filthy, stinking—"

The savage look in his eyes stopped her cold. His mouth twisted in a way that dared her to continue.

"You were saying?" he taunted.

Wisely she kept her mouth shut. Davis stepped toward her again, and though she anticipated some sort of retaliation for her remark, he only caught her chin less brutally in his fingers and lifted the canteen to her lips.

"Drink," he commanded softly.

She refused at first, allowing the water to run out the corners of her mouth. But as the scent of the liquid filled her nostrils she grabbed the canteen and turned it up, gulping a great mouthful that left her choking and gasping for air. Davis snatched the vessel from her hands before she could drink again.

"Steady! You'll kill yourself if you're not careful."

"So what!" The words were thick with contempt. "It'll save you the bother of doing it yourself."

His face hardened. His eyes narrowed. A slight twitch played at one corner of his mouth as he ever so gently released her chin and replaced the lid on his canteen. Without speaking again Davis turned for his horse and mounted. Looking down from his lofty perch, he held out his hand and offered the stirrup for her support. In relief she mounted behind him. At least she would not be subjected to Clyde's disgusting mauling of her person any longer, she thought. But as Davis forced her to wrap her arms about his waist, Rachel reconsidered. Davis's presence was as unsettling as Clyde's, she discovered, though for very different reasons.

The group rode for hours in silence, toward the hazy blue hills in the distance, forced by necessity—since the countryside was thick with mesquite, cactus and ceniza—to plod along slowly, to zigzag back and forth through the brush so as to avoid leaving a definable trail for Sam Wells to follow. When Rachel, mumbling to herself, mentioned she could hardly believe *anyone* could follow a trail through such dense terrain, Davis said, "That old man could eventually pick up a trail blindfolded."

The rain hit long before dusk. Unlike the storm that had come close to destroying the wagon train, this downpour was steady but gentle, washing the sweat and grime from Rachel's face as she pressed her cheek against Davis's spine.

"Why were you out there with Stillwell?" came Davis's quiet voice over his shoulder.

She thought of lying, then reconsidered. "I was planning to accept his marriage proposal."

He went a long moment before responding. Then, "Seems you don't have very good judgment in men."

"Obviously," she countered. His shoulders came back slightly; he'd taken her point.

They rode on, hour after endless hour. The others traveled beside them; at no time did Davis allow them to ride at his back. Dusk was only minutes old when they finally reached Fort Clark. The black shapes of the deserted officers' quarters and enlisted men's barracks suddenly loomed at them from the growing darkness. The barred windows of the old stone commissary looked bleak and hostile in the dreary half-light. The rusty hinges of the winch above the sagging double doors, just at the top of the muddy unloading ramp, creaked; the wind, cooler from the north, whipped the ash trees in the distance so their leaves rattled, sounding like gentle rain on a tin roof.

Clyde, Pete, and Pedro rode their horses into the gaping rear door of the commissary. Clyde hesitated, looked back at Davis, and grinned that same fiendish smirk that caused Rachel's skin to crawl. "Enjoy yoreself, Davis," he said.

Davis rode on, just up the hill, to what Rachel surmised must have been the living quarters for the married soldiers. She stared at the crude *hackal,* whose vertical timbers jutting from the ground supported a slanted roof of questionable reliability. Its glassless windows were boarded. The porch sagged. With the air having been washed fresh by the rain and with the lights from the distant town of Brackettville twinkling in the encroaching darkness, the scene might have been serene, but the turmoil inside her made Rachel weak with trepidation.

Shoving back the lush green madeira vines cascading from the porch roof to the ground, Davis nudged Rachel through the open front door. She stood inside the room, which smelled of damp earth and rot, and thought of home. Never had she missed Belle Hélène as much as she did at that moment.

Davis walked by her, deeper into the shadowed interior, leaving Rachel free to move about as she wanted. Turning toward the door, she stood half in and half out of the house and stared at the blurred image of waist-high weeds, shrubs, and cactus as far as she could see toward the horizon. The horizon: how beautiful it looked, despite the ugliness of her surroundings. Beneath the dark, low-lying clouds, against the glow of red and orange and gold heat, lightning streaked over the earth, and for a moment she almost imagined that she was a soldier's wife, at home and waiting for the return of her beloved. Odd that her thoughts always came back to the same things: security and love and . . . Davis. Despite it all. *Fool. Silly, stupid little fool!*

With a scratch of a match, Davis set the twigs of mesquite inside the hearth on fire. Drawn closer to the warmth, Rachel left the door, fully aware that Davis watched her. She stood in a box-shaped house, its one room divided in two by the fireplace. Beneath the single window stood a dilapidated table. In the farthest, darkest corner were the remnants of a bed. Above it, dripping cobwebs that fluttered in the draft through the window, was a tiny net hammock, once used as a cradle.

They stood in silence, he across the room, she shivering before a fire; somehow its heat could not find its way inside her skin to warm her. She had decided long ago that whatever he did to her she would deal with it bravely, as she had dealt with her father's death, the loss of her home, and the ten years with Audra. At least, she thought, there was no more Audra.

She refused to watch as he crossed the room to the door,

but eventually, compelled by his silence, she glanced his way. He stood with the light from the fire playing in red and gold hues across his broad, damp shoulders. Was that weariness in his stance? Where was that arrogant set of his jaw? His fist opened and closed as he propped his arm up against the doorframe. It was as if he'd forgotten her presence. Was there any way at all to escape?

He turned. Stepping back into the house, he slammed the door.

Rachel backed toward the fire.

Davis tugged at the leather holster tie around his thigh. It slipped away. He unbuckled his gun belt so it swung free of his hips and drooped from his hand.

Refusing to acknowledge his calculated movements, Rachel lifted her chin and met the brilliant hardness of his eyes with her own. He was only trying to frighten her, to punish her for stumbling into this idiotic affair. He wouldn't hurt her. She couldn't be *that* wrong about his character!

Placing the gun belt on the table, he walked toward her. "Can you scream?" he asked softly. He watched her chin go up another notch, and something in the way she stared at him, her eyes like a doe's, wide and watchful and frightened, made him almost hesitate in carrying out his plan. "I asked you a question, lady. Can you scream?"

"I—I won't," she managed in a voice thick with fear. "Kill me if you must, but I will never give you the satisfaction—"

"I like women who scream," he said through his teeth, cutting her off. She was so close to cracking . . .

Without taking his eyes from her bloodless face, he kicked out at the table, sending it crashing against the wall.

Her tiny hands clutched together at her chest, and her body shook.

"Women always scream when I rape them."

Rachel backed away, farther and farther into the room where the fire was dimmest and the coldness of the night and the rain seeped through the roof and gusted through the disintegrating mud of the walls. Something slithered across her foot, and she collapsed against the wall.

"Would you like to know how many women I've raped, sweetheart?"

"I—I don't believe you."

He smiled. "You should've joined a convent, love. You have the faith of a damn nun."

Turning her face away, she repeated, "I don't believe you."

That faith. That damnable faith! He wanted to wrap his fingers around her beautiful throat and shake some reality into her innocent head. Stopping, he stood above her, watching as, little by little, she shrank to the floor.

And he hated himself. Hated what he was, what he was doing and why. Going down on his knee, he moved to touch her face . . . and she broke.

Springing at his eyes, her fingers like claws, she threw herself onto him, her voice ragged and full of tears, screaming, "You bastard! I trusted you! I had faith in you, you filthy, lying, murdering animal! You savage! I hope Sam finds you and you hang in El Paso. Bastard snake! I hate you!"

He tumbled to the floor on his back, catching her flailing hands, attempting to divert them before they could do more damage to his face. She sprawled atop him, her hair like a cloud raining down on his face and shoulders and chest.

Throwing her head back, she glared through the wild curls and hissed, "I cared! I truly cared for you, despite the fact that you are a stinking dog!"

Wild-eyed and spitting contempt, she wrestled until he managed to force her to her back. Pinned by his weight, her breasts heaving, she met his burning eyes with her own and sneered, "You will have to rape me, Davis, for I'd rather die than submit to you willingly."

"That's not how you felt four nights ago," he countered. "I could have taken you then—"

"I thought you had a heart then, and a soul. You have neither. You're an animal!"

His hands closing more tightly about her wrists, Davis

narrowed his eyes. "Don't call me that. Don't ever call me that."

She thrashed again.

"Stop fighting me, Rachel. I won't hurt you if you'll just stop fighting and listen to me."

"Liar! I won't scream! I won't give you that satisfaction . . . animal!"

He felt the hot, stifling anger rise like bile in his throat. Suddenly she was just like all the other women who had taunted him and accused him of being an animal, when it was his very savagery that filled them with desire. Grabbing her chin with one hand, he growled, "I thought you were different, but you're not. You're a tease who thought it'd be fun flirting with a man like me. Did it give you some sort of thrill? Did it? Did you laugh behind my back every night when you curled up in bed with your Bible?" He shook her. "Did you? And all the while I was lying out on that goddamn ground staring at the sky and thinking maybe, just maybe, you were different from the others, hoping . . . wanting you so bad I was sick!"

He struck out at the ground, thudding the dirt floor by her face with his fist. Her body trembled. Her mouth, cracked from the sun, fell open slightly as the words began to take shape in her terrorized consciousness. Like a trapped animal she watched him cautiously from the corner of her eyes.

Closer, so his warm breath beat like a fast pulse on her cheek, he said more coldly, "I'm not an animal. I did what I had to do to survive. Do you know what it's like to have to submit until you can't stomach yourself any longer? Do you know what it's like living every day of your life trying to appease a conscience that won't let you sleep at night, or eat because it burns the food up in your gut so you want to vomit? Do you?" Fingers digging into her face, he shouted, "Answer me, dammit!"

"N-no!"

"No, you don't know the kind of fear that makes a boy plead on his hands and knees for mercy; you're a *lady,* after all, always tucked up safe and sound in your warm, comfortable bed at night. . . ."

His tortured eyes burned with the flame of memories and Rachel knew without a doubt in that instant that the man spilling his heart and soul to her *was* Tomas de Bastitas. The certainty of it made her weep.

"Have you ever been hungry? I mean, really hungry. When you haven't been fed in so long you start eating anything that can't outcrawl you?"

She shook her head, beginning to understand. Still pinned to the earth floor, her arms outstretched above her mass of tangled hair, she longed to reach out and console him, to soothe the anguish and anger from his bitter features.

His voice husky, his breath more rapid, he asked, "Have you ever wept for compassion, Miss Gregory? Have you ever ached so badly for a kind word or touch that when it finally comes your way you fumble with it like an idiot because you're not quite sure what to do with it? Or wanted it so badly you'd believe a prostitute really meant it when she said she loved you?"

The tears came, rolling from her eyes and down her temples.

"Of course not," he said in a voice sounding almost drugged. "You have your Stillwells and Lukes and a hundred others. How many fools like me, who dared to hope, or dream, did you leave back in New Orleans, Rachel? How many?"

He rolled away and sat up. His back to her, he faced the door, his shoulders rising and falling unevenly while he struggled with his emotions.

Unsteadily, Rachel pushed herself up, understanding completely now why the giving of tenderness, the sharing of love didn't come easily to this man. How could he share that which had never been shared with him?

Cautiously she lifted her trembling hand and placed it lightly on his back. He flinched as if the butterfly touch had been a dagger she'd driven through his hot flesh. Shifting closer to him, she carefully pressed her cheek against his spine and said very softly, "I care."

He didn't move.

"I care," she repeated more loudly.

He turned slowly to face her. Backing away, uncertain of his motives, she looked into his burning blue eyes and held her breath.

"You care," he sneered. "Seems I heard those words before. They sound more believable coming from a whore's mouth than they do from yours."

Rachel swallowed and repeated, "I care."

That telltale smile curled his lips and before Rachel could react he had caught her jaw bruisingly in his fingers. "All right, sweetheart, maybe you want to show me just how much you care. Go on. Show me, lady, how and why a woman like you could ever give a damn about a man like me."

Despite the excruciating grip on her jaw, she lifted her hands and pressed them gently on each side of his face. His eyes narrowed. His jaw flexed beneath her palm. Slowly, very slowly, she leaned forward and kissed his mouth.

His fingers, cruel and gripping one minute, trembled as he drew them from her face. She continued to kiss him, though his lips remained rigid under hers. She stroked her fingers through his hair, down his throat, and trailed her hands over his tense shoulders and around his neck. She thought she felt some spark of response, and sliding her mouth around to his ear, she whispered, "I care."

"Ah, damn," he said, sounding raw and broken.

He turned his face to hers and kissed her, the hunger of it driving the breath from her lungs. Easily he forced her backward, pressing her into the cool, earthen floor as he stretched out against her. He covered her face with clumsy kisses before murmuring in her ear, "You'll be sorry . . ."

She lifted her face to his in silent assent.

She felt the quickened thud of his heart against her breast as he kissed her. And the fire started. The forbidden burning that took flame in the very depths of her soul when he touched her was there, turning her insides into an inferno of desire. She wanted him—dear God, how she wanted him! How could she ever convince him that she *needed* him as desperately as he needed her?

Rachel closed her eyes as his hands ran slowly up the inside of her thigh beneath her skirt. She shivered at the feel of his callused fingers against her sensitive skin, quivered with the memory of the magic they had performed on her before. His hand fumbled with her underwear, drawing the garment down her hips to her knees and ankles. As he sat back on his knees and began releasing the buttons on his breeches she met his still suspicious gaze with her own, and opened her legs. Wordlessly she lifted her arms in invitation.

He moved against her, the reflection of the fire painting his face and hands and jutting maleness in burning crimson. The velvet-smooth hardness of his desire poised against her, throbbing with passion's blood that made the world red and dizzy and breathless between them. Their eyes met: hers wide and searching, his cautious, still, and disbelieving.

He eased her thighs open further, and pressed the hot shaft of his being into her.

The pain was immediate and intense, catching her off guard. She cried aloud, "No! Oh God, please . . ." and she writhed beneath him.

"Too late," he hissed in her ear, and in that awful moment Rachel realized that he had misconstrued her reasons for crying.

His fingers digging into the damp earth on either side of her head, he began moving on her, imbedding himself deep, deep inside her with each impassioned thrust he took. Each plunge was fierce, grinding, and deliberate. Squeezing her eyes shut, she prayed the discomfort would subside before she screamed.

And it did.

As the initial shock and pain of his body entering hers faded, a new sensation took hold, a feeling so intense that she almost wept again. Not from the pain—there was little of that now—but for the joy of becoming one with this man.

For no matter how the rest of the world saw him, she *knew* him. Knew what he ached for: understanding . . . love. Oh, she had so much love to give him, if he would only let her.

Rachel closed her eyes. Somewhere in the center of her being a warm spiraling bliss grew, spread throughout her heart and mind and body so she found herself responding by lifting her hips to meet his.

She heard the swift inward rush of his breath as he noted the response. The low groan that wedged up his throat stirred a startling arousal in her. She moved again, feeling her body expand to accommodate him even more. Rapture, vivid and wonderful, unfurled inside her, and she moaned, clutched him to her, suddenly startlingly aware that she was unfulfilled by his body inside her. She wanted his soul.

"More," she whispered, a ragged, husky sound that was strange to her own ear. Twisting her fingers into his shirt, she closed her eyes and said, "Please."

His breath of wonder fanned her cheek. His body responded, moving more urgently, powerfully, until she was clutching his shoulders, matching each turbulent thrust of his hips with her own.

Yet she could feel the resistance building inside Davis with each breath he took, and she understood. He would not accept an offered love easily. He would not trust such a love because he did not think himself worthy of it. She did the only thing she could do to stop the maelstrom inside him. Lifting her arms, she wrapped them about his shoulders.

He froze, then sank against her, buried his face in her hair, and groaned. Then, as if all strength and will and anger had drained from him, his body relaxed.

Still she held him, wrapped her legs over the backs of his thighs, stroked the coarse hair on the back of his head. Her hands moved over his back, beneath his shirt, discovering how beautiful his body felt, how wonderfully the bone merged with hard muscle beneath satin skin. She counted his heartbeats that slowed to beat in rhythm with hers, against her own. Finally he said in a voice so shallow she barely heard him:

"Forgive me."

Gripping him more tightly to her, she swallowed, waiting until the force of emotions inside her could subside, then responded steadily. "There is nothing to forgive. I was cruel and vicious to have called you such names after everything you've done for me." Smiling, she nuzzled the nape of his neck, trailed her fingers over the hard planes of his back and along the scar across his ribs. "You saved my life twice . . . three times. You might have turned me over to Clyde, you know."

"He might have treated you better," he mumbled into the dirt.

"I don't think so." She smiled again. "Look at me."

He didn't.

Taking a deep breath, she admitted again, "I care."

He didn't move for a long moment. Then his head came up slowly. He looked down into her eyes. A flush of heat touched his cheeks, his eyes, making them breathtaking and brilliant. Lifting her fingers to his face, she lightly traced his mouth, his chin, his brow, holding him with her adoring gaze, letting her eyes, her smile, and the touch of her hands convey the truth of her words.

He closed his eyes, absorbing the gentleness of her touch, drinking it in slowly, as if he were afraid to take in too much too quickly. Then, without speaking, he rolled to his side, to his knees, and stood, turning his back to her while he fumbled with the buttons on his breeches. He left the *hackal*, quietly closing the door behind him.

Rachel stared at the ceiling, listening to the distant rumble of thunder and the timid patter of rain that had begun to fall. Stiffly she got to her feet. She walked to the window and looked out on the fort's dark grounds.

A flash of lightning in the night sky illuminated Davis's form. He stood in the rain, his face tilted up to the heavens.

Turning, Rachel went back to the fire and stretched out on the floor where she and Davis had lain before. The pain was there yet, between her legs; she'd be sore tomorrow. But there was another ache somewhere deeper that intensified when she thought of how intimate his body had felt buried in hers, moving inside hers. Such a forbidden fire, it brought hot color to her face and warmed her skin far more than the measly embers of dying ash in the hearth.

What seemed like hours later, Davis returned. Roused from her exhausted sleep, Rachel lifted her head and blinked sleepily at his tall, dark form in the doorway. She waited.

He said nothing, just walked over to her, gently tucked his saddle blanket about her shivering body, then lay down beside her. Hesitantly his arms came out to hold her, and she didn't resist.

Chapter 14

He dreamed of a red-haired woman, the most beautiful woman in the world, holding him in her arms, pressing his face against her breast and kissing the top of his head. She always smelled of violets, sweet and clean. And she always smiled. Always laughed. She loved him. Oh—God, she loved him.

Coming awake slowly, Davis shifted in the chair he'd moved to some time during the night and blinked blearily at the windowsill at his shoulder. A pair of scorpions, their light brown bodies scaled and their needle-pointed tails arched high over their backs, danced back and forth at each other: a mating dance.

"Good morning."

Davis sat upright with a start. There, within dawn's pale gray shadows, was Rachel on the floor, leaning back against the wall of the *hackal*, holding his gun in her hands. Looking down the nickel-plated barrel, he said softly, "Good morning."

"I was wondering, Davis . . ." He saw her head tilt. The white-blond hair spilled, wild and tangled, over her shoulders. "How many women *have* you raped?"

"I was only trying to frighten you."

"So I'd scream?"

He looked back at the scorpions. Their outthrust pincers were locked in silent combat.

"You *enjoy* women who scream?" she asked.

He shook his head no. Then, closing his eyes, he said, "I wanted the others to think that I'd raped you." Looking back

225

at the gun, Davis released his breath. "Are you all right, Rachel?"

"Is it normal to bleed after the first time?"

His insides turning cold, he sat forward in his chair, straining to see her face better in the dim light. "How much?"

"Some. It's stopped now, but I'm sore."

"It's to be expected."

He heard her laugh to herself. "It seems he is the expert on virgins, as well as guns. Have you had many virgins, Mr. Davis?" The gun went up a little more. "The truth now."

"Some."

"Willing or unwilling?"

"For God's sake, Rachel —"

"The truth."

"Both."

"And when was the last time you took an unwilling woman, Mr. Davis?"

Raking one hand through his hair, he responded sharply, "I don't remember. Fourteen, fifteen years ago, I suppose."

"My, my. You must have been a delinquent young man. Would you care to tell me more about your troubled childhood?"

"No!"

"Perhaps I can help. It always helps to talk about what's troubling you."

He looked at the gun again, then back at her face. What the devil was she getting at? "No one can help," he replied, leaving his chair.

She studied him for several long, silent minutes. Then she said softly, thoughtfully, cautiously, "I think you could begin by admitting who you really are."

He backed away. "I don't know what you're talking about."

Rachel's voice was breathless when it finally came. The gun barrel began to shake. "You — you're really Tomas de Bastitas, aren't you? You were taken from your parents in that uprising in San Antonio many years ago."

"No."

"Liar."

A slow burn started in his stomach, crept up his chest and into his face. He repeated, "No."

"It was the Indians, wasn't it? They forced you to do those things against your will. Either you did what they told you to do, or you died. You wanted to survive. It's only natural."

He swung away from her and began pacing. Rachel swallowed back her fear and told herself that she was doing the right thing. She'd thought about it the better part of the night. There was so much he was holding inside him. So much he needed to let out if he was ever going to regard himself as an acceptable human being. She could help him. But she had to know everything. . . .

"You are Tomas de Bastitas," she said more forcefully.

Picking up a plank of wood, Davis slammed it against the windowsill, crushing the mating scorpions. "Shut up," he demanded. "You don't know what the hell you're talking about."

"Angelique and your brother told me about the ostracism Indian captives face when returning home. Is that what you're afraid of? That your family won't accept you? That you won't fit in with society?"

"I said shut up!" He turned on her. The wood shaking in his hand, he glared at Rachel and shouted, "Just who the hell do you think you are anyway, trying to pick a man's brains apart? What do you know about what civilized society would say about Tomas de Bastitas?"

His voice going hoarse with emotion, he sneered, "Can you imagine what it would mean to an aristocratic family like that to suddenly have a savage among them? Why, he might do something to embarrass them, like dribble food down the front of his shirt when he eats, or use improper English. And God forbid that he might be walking down some street in San Antonio and come face to face with someone he'd hurt in his past. The good people of the city would have the entire frigging Bastitas family run out of Texas."

He paced again, swinging the wood angrily. "I've seen it all, Rachel. While living at Fort Bliss I saw the captives the soldiers rescued from the Indians. I saw the letters that went out informing families of the rescue. And I also saw the letters that were returned, *begging* the army's pardon. But they really didn't think the woman or child would be happy in surroundings such as they could offer. It would be too stifling for their character."

"The Bastitas family isn't like that. They love Tomas very much."

He whirled on her, his chest heaving. "Tomas de Bastitas is dead. Do you hear me? He's dead!"

"How do you know?"

"If he's not, then they should just leave him alone, because he's probably wishing that he were and their meddling is only going to make matters worse."

"I'm certain he would find that Angelique and Alejandro would stand by him no matter what, should he decide to go home. That they would continue to love him and be proud of him, no matter what."

Christ! Why wouldn't she shut up? He stared in her face as the first streaks of morning sun wedged between the boards on the window, spilling over her eyes, which were dark, red-rimmed, and concerned.

Blinking slowly, she smiled a little absently and said, "I think I could almost envy Tomas, having such a large family who loved him so. I only had my father, as my mother died when I was very young. He was always so busy with the farm I rarely saw him. My nanny raised me until Audra came. Then what little family happiness we had fell apart." Shifting the gun in her hands, she frowned, looked him directly in the eye, and said, "You know, Mr. Davis, we're alike in a way. We're both orphans, aren't we? But where I daydream of the future, of finding someone who loves me, settling down and raising a dozen children, you dwell on the past, horrible as it is. You've let it destroy the man you could be. And you have such potential!" She beamed him a smile.

The sudden burst of anger he'd felt evaporated at the sight of her angelic face, haggard but beautiful, smiling up at him. She always had that effect on him, he realized. She made him forget everything but the new emotions she'd put inside him. He liked those feelings. They dulled the raw ache of memories, made him feel cleansed somehow of all the pain and anger.

Lowering the gun, Rachel said rather seriously, "I think, Mr. Davis, that you should really try harder to like yourself."

"I'll try," he responded. He began to smile, and pointing to the gun asked teasingly, "Are you going to shoot me with my own gun?"

She contemplated the idea for a long moment, then, grinning, she lowered the gun to her lap. "I don't think so," she responded. Then she lifted the weapon again, propped it against her uplifted knees, and ran her finger lightly over the barrel. "I find this most interesting," she said. She tipped her face up, read the confusion in his eyes and explained, "You took this gun from Sam, but it doesn't strike me as the kind he would wear. It doesn't suit him. Despite what he is, a Ranger, he's a small man. Wiry. This gun is big, suited more to a man *your* size, Mr. Davis. And something else . . . he mentioned once that he'd rarely been outside of Texas since he joined the Rangers. Yet right here on the barrel of this gun is an engraving. I must say, I'm most impressed, and I can't imagine *why* he never mentioned such an important event in his life. It's engraved on this side:

PATENTED FEB. 21, 1861
E. REMINGTON & SONS, ILION
NEW YORK, USA, NEW MODEL

"But the *most* impressive engraving is this one plated on the stock:

IN COMMEMORATION FOR HEROISM
IN GRATITUDE
A. LINCOLN, PRES. OF UNION

"Now I ask you, *what* might he have done to deserve such a tribute?"

Davis stood before her, barely hearing her idle chatter about the gun. His mind had drifted back to last evening. He was at a loss over what to say or do about the clumsy affair.

He wasn't even certain he should bring up those intimate moments they'd shared together. He'd convinced himself as she lay sleeping in his arms that he'd taken advantage of her sympathy, certain she'd feel different this morning. She would no doubt be full of regrets and recriminations toward herself and him. He hadn't exactly been an ideal lover. She deserved something special, and much to his own chagrin, he realized for the first time that he just didn't know how to show such tenderness. He'd never bothered before. He'd heard the term "making love," but had never, until now, understood what it meant. Since he'd taken his first girl at thirteen it had been nothing but a physical release . . . or an act of violence.

But last night . . . last night he'd fought the feelings, tried to ignore them. True enough, for a while he'd wanted to hurt her because she'd actually made him feel vulnerable and human for the first time. Now he wanted those moments back so he could make it as special for her as it had been for him. He'd taken her virginity, ruined her for other men. She deserved better.

If he was Martin Stillwell he'd go on one knee right now and propose to make up for his stupidity. If he was Martin Stillwell, she'd accept. But he wasn't. Perhaps he should tell her the truth, admit *what* he was and *why* he was doing what he was doing. Maybe then she would have him. And maybe not. He wouldn't want her to want him that way. No matter what title was stamped on his forehead now, he was the same man who'd treated her so shabbily last night. He *was* that man. Deep, deep inside he would always be that man. She could never love a man like that.

Clyde kicked the door open then.

In one sweep Davis snatched up the gun from Rachel's hand, turned it on Clyde, and cocked the trigger. "Knock next time, Lindsey."

"Reckon I'd better." He sauntered into the room. "Enjoy yoreself, did ya? Me and the boys've been thinkin', maybe it's our turn now."

"Forget it."

"Keepin' 'er all to yoreself? Come on, now, Kid. That ain't right neighborly."

"No."

Clyde thought about it a minute, looking every few seconds from Rachel back to the gun pointed steadily his way. Spitting a stream of tobacco to the floor, he then turned and left the house.

Davis stared out the door as Rachel got to her feet. Clyde's sudden intrusion into the room had been a disgusting reminder of his and Rachel's circumstances, and of the role he would be forced to play out.

"Let's go," he ordered tersely. Glancing down into her sunblistered face, he noted the look of distress, then disappointment that settled in her eyes and on her mouth. He followed Clyde out of the house.

In dawn's light, the countryside was almost pretty. The crisp air soothed the lacerations on Rachel's sunburned face, but it did nothing for the soreness between her legs. She wasn't looking forward to straddling Davis's horse.

She was given a few moments of privacy. Walking a short distance from the others, she noticed a small graveyard just beyond the commissary. She wandered there. Standing alone at the edge of a weed-infested cemetery, Rachel looked down on the grave at her feet, and the wooden cross crudely inscribed:

APRIL 28, 1856
J.J. HAMMER

She wondered what had killed him. Indians? Bandits? Disease? Loneliness? Looking about her, she thought a person could die of loneliness out here.

She rejoined the others, washing her face and arms in the Las Moras spring as Davis filled his canteen with the icy, clear water. About the oasis grew mulberry, pecan, and oak trees. Within a shallow arc in the surrounding rock grew water lilies and lush green grass that might have made a fine bed on which to sleep. Rachel eyed it wistfully until a rattler slithered out from under the bedrock and disappeared in the knee-high grass. A serpent in paradise.

She looked at Davis.

"I'm hungry," she told him, feeling it for the first time since leaving the train.

"We'll eat later."

Remembering what Sam had said about Davis's never eating or sleeping, Rachel frowned. She remembered how heavily he'd smelled of whiskey that night in the back of her wagon, and Sam's description of a shootist. Recalling last night, and his confessions this morning, she felt despair press down on her shoulders. He was everything he appeared to be. And worse. So why was all that mattering less and less these days? What was happening to her sense of decency?

She thought that one over during the next hour. Clinging to Davis's back and wincing each time he broke the horse into a trot, she finally realized why she kept glancing back over her shoulder. Sam. He was back there, somewhere. And he would kill Davis when he found him. He'd promised as much.

A noon sun beat the countryside mercilessly when they finally stopped for respite. Having flushed rabbits out of the bushes, Pedro set about skinning, gutting, and skewering them over an open fire. Fat from the meat dripped into the flames, sending pungent black smoke into the air. It made Rachel ill to her stomach. She was hot, tired, and miserably dirty. She longed for a bath. The pool between the rocks where the horses watered would do just fine.

Pete and Clyde and Davis had their heads together, arguing about where they were going and who they were going to see. Several times she tried to eavesdrop, but they shut up tight as clams when she ventured near. So she remained in the shadow of a rock and eyed the pool with growing desperation. Just a quick splash on her face and legs would do the trick.

Davis, his hands on his hips, glared into Clyde's narrow

face and said, "I'm going no further than San Carlos until you can assure me that Cortinas is willing to cooperate. And I want to see this A.J. Duncan as well. I'd like to know who I'm working for before I make my decision. And I'll want some money up front. If I'm running cattle over the border, I want to know who the hell I'm stealing it for."

Clyde slapped his hat against his thigh as Pete turned away to join Pedro. "I can't promise ya nothin' like that, Davis. And besides, A.J., he don't like crossin' the border much. He lets us do all that for 'im."

Taking Clyde's shirtfront in his fists, Davis gave the skinny man his most threatening smile. "If you're trying to put something over on me, Lindsey—"

"I ain't, Kid! A.J.'s a fair man. I swear to ya, he'll see yore set up. We jest might have to go to *his* place, is all."

"And where's that exactly?"

"He's got a spread out by San Felipe Springs. Owns some fifty or sixty thousand acres up and down the big river. Raises sheep."

"Sheep! I thought it was cattle."

Clyde shook his head. "Nah . . . he only steals the cattle."

"And where the hell did he get so much money to buy that much land and sheep?"

Clyde shrugged.

Narrowing his eyes, Davis asked, "How do I know he's got the money to pay me what I deserve? I charge a lot to steal cows and kill people."

"He's got it, I tell ya. I seen it in his vault. Piles of it." Clyde's eyes shifted nervously to some point beyond Davis's shoulder. Davis spun.

Where was Rachel?

Where was Pete!

He struck out in a run, hurdling the clumps of cactus and brush in his way. He heard it then: a muffled cry beyond the rocks. Rounding the ledge of limestone, he stumbled to a stop. For an instant the world turned red, like hot, hot fire; he could do nothing—move, speak, reach for his gun.

"Jenkins!" His voice, raw with fury, cracked in his throat.

Pete's head came off Rachel's breast. One hand slowly removed the knife from against her throat while the other slid off her mouth. He rolled from atop her, very slowly, where she lay half in and half out of the water. Lifting his hands in the air, Pete laughed nervously and called out, "Ain't no harm in a man havin' a little fun now, is there, Davis?"

"Get away from her, Jenkins," he grated. "I'm going to kill you."

The smirk on Pete's face faded as Davis moved his back to the rock. Wading back into the water, he lifted his hands slightly, dropping his knife, and said, "Look. I ain't got my pants down. I didn't do nothin'—"

"And now you never will." Davis moved slowly toward the water.

Pete swallowed. "I won't touch her agin, Davis."

"I warned you. I warned you all. If one of you laid a hand on her—"

"I was just funnin', for God's sake! She was out here bathin' like the Queen of Sheba. Hell, Kid, what would *you* have done seein' a woman who looks like her, with her dress half open and her skirts to her knees—"

"Shut up and move."

He did. Slowly, clumsily, Pete made a desperate grab for his gun.

Davis responded, the explosion of his gun ricocheting against the distant hills like thunder. Pete spun, the force of the impact and pain in his arm sending him back into the water.

Wading up to his thighs in the pool, Davis grabbed the choking, groaning man and shoved him onto the muddied bank. "Get on your horse and ride," he told him. "If I ever see you again, I'll kill you."

Coughing and clutching his bloody arm to his breast, Pete scrambled to his feet and ran for his horse. Dragging himself into his saddle, he looked back at Davis and sneered, "Self-righteous son-of-a-bitch, ain't ya? Tryin' to make up for what *you* did to 'er last night. You ain't so different from the rest of us, Davis, no matter what you'd like to think."

Rachel, her hands crossed over her breasts, stared stupefied at the swirling, bloodied water lapping at her feet. In a foggy corner of her mind she heard Pete's horse trot off, then she turned her eyes up to Davis. His look was fearsome, standing above her as he was, the gun still in his hand and his clothing drenched in sweat. His jaw, covered with a week's growth of beard, worked in anger as he apparently decided whether or not to use the gun on her for wandering out of his sight.

Sliding her knees up to her chin, she clasped her arms about her shins and offered in a tiny voice, "I only wanted a bath."

"A bath," he returned. "A bath! The lady wanted a bath! She's out in the middle of no-man's-land with three wanted criminals and the woman wants a frigging bath!"

Lifting her chin a little, she glanced at him cautiously. "You don't have to yell."

"Yell!"

"And it's *four*. There are *four* wanted criminals. Or there were. Now that Pete's gone, however, there are three." She bit her lip and stared out at the water. Finally he turned and walked back to camp.

The old Davis was back: snappish, surly, and sarcastic. One minute Rachel wished Sam Wells and every Ranger in Texas would ride up over the hill, the next minute she didn't. He was punishing her for an error in judgment. What was so wrong about bathing her throat and arms and legs? He should have been paying more attention, after all. Had he been keeping his eyes on the rangy bunch of cutthroats, the entire affair never would have happened!

Rachel felt confident that Davis had no intention of turning her over to Clyde and Pedro. Or she did until they camped for the evening. Then Clyde, in his usual taunting manner, began to sneer insinuations and insults at her with every other breath. Davis said nothing. When Clyde went hunting and returned with two dead rattlers for their meal,

Davis remained silent when the man threw them at Rachel's feet and ordered her to cook them.

She screamed at first, thinking them alive. She screamed again when Clyde began kicking them around her feet and laughingly lied, "If their poison gits on yore skin, you'll die as quick as if they'd bit ya!" And still Davis said nothing. Clyde and the others made fun of her manners, her breeding, her family. They insulted the color of her hair, calling her cotton-top and snow-head. When they began ruminating on women's anatomies, Rachel decided she'd had enough. Hot, exhausted, and wishing that she'd never been born, she took her anger out on the only one she felt safe enough to take it out on—Davis. When, relaxing against a rock ledge, he ordered her to bring him more meat, she obliged. It smacked across his cheek, sizzling hot.

Clyde and Pedro whooped as Davis came to his feet, clawing at the greasy meat as it slithered off his face and down his shirt. "Why, you little—"

She threw more, hitting him between the eyes. "You're *all* disgusting!" she yelled. "You make me sick, you and your filthy mouths and manners, and I don't intend to tolerate it a moment longer. You want more meat, you stinking bastard, you get it yourself, because I've had it with the lot of you!"

Twirling, she blinked twice at the intimidating countryside from which they'd come, then started on her deliberate way, tattered skirt lifted to her ankles and her head thrown back so her tangled hair brushed the small of her waist. She walked and walked, it seemed, though no more than seconds had clipped by. And all the time she listened for the click of their guns, certain they would shoot her in the back at any minute.

"Rachel!"

It was Davis.

Rachel speeded up, keeping her head back and her eyes pointed straight ahead.

"Get back here!"

"Ha!" she responded.

"Get back here!"

"You'll just have to shoot me, Mr. Davis; I don't intend to tolerate your brutality any longer! I'm going home!"

Clyde and Pedro burst out laughing. It echoed all the way over the hill.

"Rachel, dammit, get back here!"

"No!" She marched on.

"Rachel . . . there are Indians out there!"

Onward.

"Whole tribes of them!"

I'll hide, she thought.

"You can't hide from them, Rachel!"

Her mouth twisting, she plodded around a cactus patch studded with thorns and pear-shaped purple protuberances.

"Rachel . . . there are spiders out there as big as my fist! Tarantulas! Black and hairy with teeth like a dog's! They'll take your foot off before you know you're even on them!"

Her eyes searched the ground around every rock, bush, and cactus before her.

"Snakes, Rachel! There are rattlesnakes out there as long as I am tall! They're as big around as your waist!"

Her pace slowed.

"Rachel." The threat was there now, in his voice. "Rachel, I'll shoot you if you don't turn around."

Her ears hummed in the ensuing silence. Her body drew in on itself as she continued, more slowly, to walk.

Davis looked down the barrel of his gun, at the back of Rachel's blond head and gritted his teeth in frustration. Flipping the barrel up a little, he released the hammer ever so gently while Clyde and Pedro snickered behind him. "Rachel!" he barked. "I'm going to shoot you, I swear to God! I'll give you one more chance to—"

"Go to hell, Davis!" came her small voice in the distance.

Clyde poked Pedro in the ribs and said, "Don't sound much like a lady these days, do she? What's wrong, Davis, seems ya can't handle women near so good as a gun. If I's you, I'd teach her a lesson, Kid."

Davis started walking, slowly at first, then faster. She was almost over the rise, just a point of whipping blond hair that looked strawberry-yellow in the dusk. Then she was gone.

Breaking into a run, he jumped cactus and rock, sending lizards scurrying and a covey of birds exploding from a crop of thistled shrubs. He was up and over the hill before she had time to reach the bottom of the opposite side. Running up behind her, he caught her arm and spun her around. Her eyes, purple within her wind- and sun-abraded face, stared like those of a startled, defiant child's up into his.

"What the hell are you trying to do?" he demanded, aware his own frustration and anger over their circumstances were getting the better of him. "Don't you give a damn that I might have shot you in the back? Don't you care that you could have walked over this hill and been grabbed by a Comanche or an Apache or bit by a snake? Well? Answer me, dammit!" He shook her with his one free hand.

The tear came: one silver dewdrop reflecting the gold and vermilion sky overhead. It trickled down her cheek, hesitated at one corner of her lips, then wiggled to her chin. "I . . . I want to go home," she finally responded.

The quiet plea drained the anger, indeed, the very life from his soul. A sense of defeat weighing him down, he stood stiff as rock as the tear spilled off her chin. He asked, "To your uncle's?"

"Oh no." Shaking her head, she dashed away a second tear. "No, not my uncle's."

"New Orleans."

She sniffed. "No. There's nothing for me there."

"Where, then?"

Her lip quivering, she looked at him, unblinking, and asked, "Will you take me there if I tell you?"

Ah, damn, he thought. *Damn.* "Rachel, you don't understand."

"I understand that you're nothing like those awful men back there. What I *don't* understand is why you continue to stay with them."

Shifting, the gun growing heavier in his hand, he shook

his head. "How can you say I'm not anything like them after the way I treated you last night?"

"We were both angry, and hurting." Laying her hand on his chest, she said more softly, "I think if you allowed yourself to forget those terrible times with women in the past, you might find that making love with someone who truly cares for you is not so bad." Smiling a little, she added, "You might even enjoy it."

He stared at her fingers, long and white, spotted with grease and dirt. Her clothes were torn and ringed with sweat. "Did I hurt you?" he asked in a dry voice.

"Only for a moment. Will it always hurt?"

Groaning in his throat, he shook his head and tried to concentrate on the tiny crimson flowers beginning to open on the slender fingers of a low-growing cactus near his feet.

"Davis?" She moved closer.

He moved away so abruptly he almost stumbled. Then waving the gun in the direction of camp, he ordered, "Let's go."

Will it always hurt? For God's sake, he hadn't even stopped to realize that he must have caused her unbearable pain the night before. He disgusted himself.

Davis wouldn't allow himself to relax, even to move from the light of the campfire until he knew for certain Clyde and Pete were sufficiently unconscious. The pair, with legs and arms sprawled to their sides, lay on their backs, their mouths open and snoring, the heavy effect of whiskey diluting their blood. Davis had found two bottles of liquor, one half empty, in Homer's saddlebags before leaving the train.

Restlessly Davis walked about the camp, fumbling with the cigarette he'd been attempting to roll for the last half hour. Flinging it to the ground, he stared toward the rocks where Rachel was sleeping.

Away from the fire the night air was cooler. He stood in the shadows, focusing on the empty saddle blanket for a long moment before realizing she wasn't there. Panic sluiced through him, but then he saw her slim silhouette in the distance. What the devil . . .

Pirouetting on her toes, Rachel spun round and round, her arms out to her sides, her head thrown back so her hair rippled like moon clouds around her shoulders. Dancing in and out of the shallow water at her feet she bowed and swayed, turning her face to the moon, letting it drench her in soft white. Cautiously he approached her, this mystical, ethereal beauty who found music where none existed.

"Do you hear it?" she asked him, showing no sign of anger or surprise at his sudden intrusion.

Frowning, he looked out across the gently rolling terrain.

Taking his arm, she turned her smiling face up to his.

Placing his fingers gently on her forehead, he asked, "Do you have a fever?"

"Oh, silly goose. Of course not."

Silly goose? Dropping his hand, he frowned again. She smelled sweet and clean, having bathed and washed her hair. He'd made certain Clyde and Pedro minded their own business while she carried out her ablutions after dark.

Rachel watched a look of uncertainty cross his features as he stood so tall and dark and solemn above her. She longed to smooth away the furrows between his eyebrows, to ease away the tenseness of his jaw. Taking a deep breath, she said, "You're thinking I've cracked."

His head tipped forward, shadowing his face from the moon over his shoulder.

Dancing backward a few feet, she ordered him. "Close your eyes."

He didn't.

"Go on. I shan't explain until you close your eyes. Very good. Now listen. Keep your eyes closed! What do you hear?"

"A coyote."

"Did you hear it before?"

Opening his eyes, he stared at his feet. "No."

"Close them again . . . forget the coyote. What do you hear?"

Motionless, he stood in the moonlight, his hair shining like wet, black ink, his shoulders rising and falling silently with each breath. Swallowing, or attempting to, he looked at her again and said, "Music."

They both listened together. The wind, barreling over the north plateau, hummed low as it swept through the dips in the plain, then sang in a medley like a soprano choir over the crests of the hills, far, far away.

"It's a game, you see," came her voice. "When I was a child, and something at night frightened me, I would pretend that all the noises were *good* things that made me happy: the whirring of crickets was violins . . . do you understand?"

His head came up. Looking into her white, expectant face, he stated, "You were frightened tonight."

"Yes." She lowered her eyes, feeling foolish, and desperate and insecure and alone. "Yes. I was afraid because they were drinking. And because you've been so angry. I was afraid of the darkness and the sounds."

His hand came up in a tentative gesture. His finger—just one—brushed her cheek. "Come here," he whispered.

She did so.

His hand slid beneath her hair, curled possessively yet gently around the nape of her neck. She was forced to lean against him, because her knees had grown ridiculously, embarrassingly weak. Pressing her ear against his chest, she listened to the beat of his heart and thought it more wonderful, more melodious than all the desert songs in all the deserts throughout the world. She almost sighed.

"I won't . . . I don't want to hurt you again, Rachel," he said above her. "I never wanted to."

"I know that." She backed away again, removing herself from the shameless need to touch and be touched by him. It was wrong. All so wrong, yet it was there, the need. As big as the yawning countryside, as expanding as the star-filled universe.

Separated, they continued to watch one another as the wind whipped the sand in eddies about their feet and sighed in a mournful aria, a lover's lament, over the land.

Finally he said, "I'll see that you get home."

"You'll take me."

"No. I have something to finish."

"With Clyde?" When he nodded, she lifted her chin and announced stalwartly, "I won't go without you."

"You're pretty anxious to see me hang, aren't you?"

"You won't hang. I'll—I'll go to El Paso and testify on your behalf. So will Sam. We'll convince the court to give you a second chance."

"You would do that for me?" His voice was incredulous.

I would do anything for you, she thought.

He released his breath sharply. "God," she heard him say to the night wind. His head back, he stared at the stars.

What moved her, she couldn't guess. That need again, she supposed. Her eyes trained on the dark vee of skin where his shirt was open, she approached him, wondering what she would do if he stopped her, if he turned her away and told her to go back to her blanket and leave him alone.

He didn't move as she stepped against him, as her hands slid up his side, around his ribs, and scaled his back to his shoulders. But she felt him tense, heard the breath catch in his lungs and the low, painful groan that seemed to start deep in his chest and shudder upward.

Pressing her face against his chest where the last fastened button on his shirt strained for release, she opened her mouth and inhaled, filling her senses with his scent of musk and his taste of salt. Unbuttoning the shirt with her trembling fingers then, she gently nudged it off his shoulders. It fell to the ground. The crisp, slick hair on his chest cushioned her lips as she kissed him, curled about the tip of her tongue as she tasted him. Her arms entwined around the back of his neck, and she melted against him.

He felt his knees give, just a fraction. And though he tried his damnedest not to respond, he felt his arms come stiffly up from his sides and enfold her, wrap about her trembling shoulders so her body heat could flow through his clothes and skin and melt his resistance. Then his hands found their way to her hair, buried along her scalp while he reminded himself over and over again of the promise he'd made to himself: he wouldn't use her that way again.

"Rachel." He grated her name between his teeth as she nuzzled his chest with her face. Such an innocent, childlike move but it unraveled him. Slowly, reluctantly, his hands fell to her shoulders, down her back, around and up to her breasts. Several minutes ticked by while he held them gently in his palms, neither moving nor breathing, it seemed, while he waited for her response. When she backed away he fully expected her to shame him with her eyes, to flee in fright. She didn't, but there in the moonlight began to undress, allowing her skirt to puddle about her ankles, and then her blouse. She wore nothing underneath.

She turned her face up to his.

He swept her up in his arms, carried her to the blanket and fell to his knees, easing her gently to the ground and lying atop her. Her mouth opened beneath his, timidly at first, then boldly, meeting the thrust of his tongue with her own until each, consumed by the growing need inside them, broke apart, gasping for air in the suddenly airless night.

His face buried in her hair, he whispered, "I don't want to hurt you."

"Then don't hurt me," she said in his ear.

"I'm too rough."

"Then be gentle."

She heard him laugh. "Ah, God, but I want you so badly it hurts."

"*Where* does it hurt?"

Rolling away, he caught her hand and pressed it against his breeches. "There. It hurts there so damn bad . . ." Shifting her hand to his heart, he finished, And there. It hurts there, too."

He stared at the heavens.

She stared at him.

"Ah, to hell with it," he finally said. Rolling, he kissed her eyes, her nose, her cheeks in a tender, fierce assault that made her catch her breath. His hands stroked her breasts; his mouth kissed them. His thumbs circled her nipples until they peaked and strained and ached when the wind touched them, then his mouth . . . ah, his mouth. His tongue laved the excited points until they burned and throbbed, until she whimpered from the wonderful swelling pain and buried her fingers in his hair, twisting the dark, coarse strands into her palms.

This was passion. She knew it now. This was desire. She felt it now, surging through her body as surely as the wind whipping the earth, vibrating through the night sky in song. It smelled of heavy, heady musk and sweat and leather. Of him. It tasted of salt and tobacco and whiskey. Of him. It was abrasive and hard and demanding. It was the man and the night and the song. It was Davis. From the first moment she'd met him, it had been Davis. In her dreams, her fantasies, her nightmares: Davis. With his ice and fire eyes, his callused hands, and his taunting smile . . . always Davis.

He touched her in places that made her body quiver in surprise and desire. His mouth trailed kisses over her breasts, her stomach, down, down to the insides of her thighs. His hands moved over every inch of her until she was groaning and clutching him to her, until she was weeping his name softly and urgently. This was so very new for him, she realized: this tenderness, this *giving*. It made the exquisite pleasure of his touch all the more precious and desirable.

His body moved over hers, shadowing her face from the moon, and though she closed her eyes in anticipation she knew the movements: his fumbling with his breeches, cursing under his breath at the stubborn buttons, then the groan of satisfaction when he'd successfully flicked the last one open. Then his weight was against her and, shamelessly, she opened her legs as he poised above her, his turgid manhood pressed against her until that softening place between her legs wept like tears on the dirt beneath her thighs. *God, oh God, it's so awful to want him like this.*

"Please," she said through her teeth. "Oh, please."

He slid inside her slowly, all throbbing, sleek skin. Slowly, stretching the glove-tight enclosure ever so carefully until she was driven to wrap her legs around his buttocks and press him to her, until their bodies were sealed, loin to loin, with heat and sand and sweat.

The movement began, the rocking, working of his buttocks as he slid in and out, thrusting harder and deeper each time until she was forced to cling to his shoulders and match the rhythm that was wild and painful and searching. She responded with abandon, letting her body fly, allowing this new desire to swirl through her while his mouth moved passionately, almost savagely on hers. The surface of her skin burned, and the effort to breathe, as he arched his back and buried his face against her throat, was made fevered by her hoarse, ragged gasps for air.

It burst upon her abruptly, the same wondrous ecstasy that had shattered her in the wagon, a tumult of the senses, a bliss so intense and near pain that she screamed aloud to the sky; a joy that verged, for one brief, despairing moment, on desperation. With a strangled cry she went still, even as he continued to plunge inside her, pressing her down, until the renting spasms left her weak and as close to death as she'd ever felt. When he stopped she opened her eyes.

He smiled and she was awed by the beauty of him. She became aware, then, of his body, hard and still inside her, of the faint mantling of perspiration from his exertions that gave a gilded sheen to his shoulders in the moonlight. Unconsciously, she reached out to touch him, traced her fingers over the planes of his face, through the dark hair that tumbled in a slight wave over his brow. He kissed the tips of her fingers as she lightly touched his lips.

There was an awakening inside him, throughout his body and mind as she smiled timidly at his tenderness. The depth of longing he felt for this woman was amazing; he had not known that he could love, truly love. And he did. God help him. He loved her.

He imagined himself saying it: *Rachel, I love you.* And imagined her response. While her attraction for him was undeniable, it was physical. And while she cared for him, those feelings were no more than she had offered Luke. Showing kindness for another was an important part of her, one of the many virtues that had attracted him to her in the first place. If he admitted such a thing, would she not withdraw? Of course, he would *never* admit to such a thing; he was a fool for even thinking it. It could—would—destroy him in the end.

He closed his eyes as she pushed her fingers through the hair at his temple, through the curling hair that grew low on the nape of his neck. She raked his shoulders with her nails, lightly, so lightly, sending shivers up his spine and vibrations through the very heart of him buried deep inside her. He could hear the singing race of his blood in his head as her body moved invitingly against his. The hot concentration of his being, the dark, engulfing ache to spill his soul inside her reared in insurmountable need as he began to move, sliding and pumping, drawing and plunging into her warm moistness.

The desire, more vivid, more overwhelming than before, surged through him, sweeping him into a frenzy of dark rapture where tenderness and love were secondary to the gathering abandonment awaiting them. She twisted beneath him, caught up again in the carnal joy, her alabaster body and shimmering hair a glimpse of heaven itself. Arching her back, she offered her breasts, the perfect firm globes whose high, hard points were the sweetest he'd ever tasted. He buried his face against them, closed his teeth over each dusky, erect peak until she whimpered and clawed at his back.

Sinking against her, he caught her hand and slid it between their bodies, to those parts of them that were joined, letting the feel of the intimacy say what he could not command his tongue to admit. As her eyes opened wide and her lips parted, he kissed her, searching out the slick lining of her mouth, sucking her lower lip between his teeth until she was lifting her hips high and hard against his.

Relentlessly the assuagement gripped him, mounted until the blood thundered in his ears and that supreme ecstasy burst upon him like the singing of angels, flooding, flowing through his veins so intensely that he wept aloud to the stars overhead, "God, yes! Ah, God. God!" And he spent himself inside her, a violent repletion that left exhaustion in its wake.

For long moments they held one another. Rachel stroked the damp ends of his hair as he laid his head on her shoulder. He listened to her heartbeat, wondered at the erratic beating of his own as he gathered her to him and rolled to his side.

"You see," came her lazy, sweet voice in his ear. "It wasn't so bad."

Chapter 15

Dawn. Rachel stretched, warm and comfortable, wrapped in the heavy saddle blanket. His scent still filled her nostrils, as if it had permeated her skin. Perhaps it had. She hoped it had. She wanted it more than anything she had ever wanted in her life. She ached to be a part of him, body and soul, to fill up his life, as he had hers.

Smiling in her half-roused state, she played the events of the previous night over and over in her mind, all the intimacies, all the tender intimacies. He'd touched her like a child mesmerized by a china doll, taking such pains not to break it. Soon, she thought, the tenderness would come as naturally to him as the way he rode his horse or walked or wore his gun. But she knew, too, that there would also be that *other* side, that darker more primitive side that rose up from deep inside the human spirit, which she, herself, had experienced for the first time.

The passion, the desire that had driven her to that brink of sublime madness had found its way inside her. She liked it there, in her heart and in her groin. It was warm and arousing, like the gulf wind that whipped up the Mississippi bay on a summer day and made her pulse quicken with excitement. Even now it was churning, swirling in her nether regions and tugging like a tide, all the way to her heart.

Sleepily she opened her eyes, blinked as her thoughts focused on the reality of her surroundings. Around her the world had turned dense with fog. The sun was but a hazy globe of burning orange on the eastern horizon.

Propping up on her elbow, Rachel pushed her hair out of

her eyes very slowly, watching the antelope that had ventured close to the water's edge. Its ears up, it stared, motionless, back at her before leaping in midair and dissolving into the fog. Laughing, she rolled over to wake up Davis.

He no longer rested beside her.

Rachel sat up.

He stood at the edge of her vision, legs spread slightly, his shoulders back as he stared off into the distance. She was about to call his name, when he went for his gun. "Damn!" he swore. Replacing the Remington in its holster, he tried again. "Not good enough," he muttered. Again and again he drew the weapon, his movements a blur in the patchy fog.

There was a method to his madness, Rachel realized, and she began to concentrate on each deliberate move: his stance, the flex of his knees, the position of his shoulders. He held his hand slack, so that the butt of the pistol was between his wrist and elbow. As his hand went for the gun, he palmed the butt while his index finger slid onto the trigger guard, and his thumb locked across the hammer spur. As he pulled the gun from the holster, he locked the hammer back, turned the gun barrel up with but a pivot of his wrist, and prepared to fire. It was all flawless, or seemed to be. But Davis wasn't satisfied. He continued to draw, pushing himself to go faster and faster until he finally appeared pleased with the result.

Spinning on his heels, he caught her staring. Saying nothing, he turned and walked into camp.

He stood at the edge of the camp, watching Clyde and Pedro sleep. He told himself that he should leave them, just saddle his horse, take Rachel, and strike out for Mexico, just the two of them. But he couldn't, wouldn't. She deserved something better than a life as a fugitive. And while she might find it all acceptable now, even a little exciting, it would grow old quickly, and then where would they be? She deserved better than a pigsty for a house, dirt floors to sweep, and a life that could, at any time, demand that he leave her for months at a time. The idea agitated his insides. He was a fool to think for one minute that she'd even consider marrying him.

Smiling to himself, he watched a slow-moving, long-legged tarantula crawl onto Clyde's leg. Its bulbous behind lifting slightly in the air, the hairy black spider climbed over his knee, hesitated on his groin, then moved cautiously over his gun belt, up to his chest, and stopped.

Narrowing his eyes, Davis called out quietly, "Clyde." He kicked the sole of Clyde's boot. "Lindsey, wake up. Time to ride."

A soft gasp behind him brought his head and shoulders around. Rachel stood at the ledge of rock, her eyes like two round saucers as she stared at the spider on Clyde's chest.

Davis turned again to Clyde. "Clyde, I said, get up."

Clyde shuffled, snorted, and opened his eyes. He blinked sleepily toward the sky, then lifted his head and let out a yell that brought Pedro out of his hungover slumber. The horses, roped nearby, shied and whinnied while Clyde, in one swift leap, left the ground with a yelp and the fanciest footwork Davis had ever seen.

Trembling and cursing and gasping for air, Clyde stared down at the tarantula that was, by now, walking leisurely to the far side of the camp. Glaring at Davis, he yelled, "Ya did that on purpose, Davis! That 'bout give me a heart attack!"

Laughing, Davis walked to the spider, and to everyone's horror, bent over and picked it up. Gently placing it on his arm, he said, "Fierce-looking baby, isn't it, Miss Gregory?"

Rachel nodded, her eyes still wide and her mouth open.

Looking up from the spider that by now had crawled halfway to his shoulder, he smiled at Rachel a little sheepishly and admitted, "I exaggerated the size of its teeth."

She licked her lips. "So I see, Mr. Davis. Why are you doing that?"

Scooping the spider up in the palm of his hand, he stroked its back and, after a minute said, "Just to show you that you can't judge things on how they appear, Miss Gregory. You might have killed him, in ignorance, not knowing he is harmless, really."

She looked to his eyes. "I wouldn't have killed him," she responded.

He looked back and grinned. "No. I guess you wouldn't."

They were mounted and traveling within half an hour. By noon they had crossed the Rio Grande. Rachel noted that if Davis had any feelings at all over what had passed between them the night before, he didn't show it. Nothing in his voice or actions toward her suggested he was anything but what he appeared to be—her captor.

Now that she'd had longer to think about it all, she was more than a little chagrined over her behavior the night before. She had actually invited him to make love to her. Not once but twice. But she didn't regret it. Her feelings for Davis were growing; she couldn't deny them any longer. So what did that make her? What type of woman would willingly submit to a man with a price on his head?

By the time they crossed the Rio Grande, the fog had burned off the land, revealing a countryside no different in appearance from Texas. It stretched toward hazy blue hills in the distance and was overgrown as far as she could see with what the Mexicans called Juahia trees. There was more wildlife closer to the river. Stopping his horse, Davis pointed out to Rachel a herd of eight javelinas that, tusked snouts to the ground, grunted beneath the brush after roots or berries and prickly pears. Wild turkeys were plentiful, as were cougars, deer, and, as always, rattlesnakes. They stretched out, six feet long, over the rocks, allowing the noon sun to reflect off their backs.

They'd been traveling for some time when they arrived in San Carlos, Mexico, a small town shimmering beneath the hot August sun. The flat-roofed adobe buildings appeared vacant at first, but then Rachel, her head resting against Davis's back, watched curious faces come and go in the windows as they rode down the deserted main street.

They headed straight for the Casita Cantina. Clyde was off his horse and through the door before the others could dismount. Pedro followed as eagerly. Davis dismounted last, then lifted his arms for Rachel. As he eased her to the ground, he turned his blue eyes on her, and for the first time since breaking camp that morning, he grinned. "Would you like to sleep in a real bed tonight?"

Rubbing her sore behind, she looked skeptically at the two-story structure.

He caught her hand. Together they entered the cantina, stepping over a sleeping drunk who'd made it no further than just outside the door before collapsing. Clyde and Pedro had already taken their places at the bar, ordered up a bottle of whiskey between them, and were eyeing the dark-skinned, satin-clothed young woman who'd just entered the room and stood smiling at them from the end of the bar.

"Sit down here and wait." Davis saw Rachel settled in a chair in the darkest corner of the room before he approached the bar. She noted he said little to Clyde and Pedro. In turn, the pair eyed him suspiciously as he gathered up a bottle of whiskey and two glasses and turned back to their table.

Rachel's eyes widened as he slammed the glass on the table before her and filled it. "But I don't imbibe," she told him.

He shrugged and threw his hat onto the table. "I'm not asking you to imbibe. Just drink it."

Hiding her smile, Rachel sat back in the chair. "Oh well, in that case . . ." She took a small sip, then another. The liquor burned all the way to her stomach.

He poured another glass of the amber liquid for himself. "I don't like to drink alone," he said aloud, but Rachel sensed he was talking more to himself than to her. "Nothing's worse than drinking alone—except sleeping alone." He stared into his glass.

Something was wrong. She could see it in his downcast face, in the tenseness of his shoulders, and in the way he nursed his liquor. He drank glass after glass, not speaking, not meeting her eyes, ignoring her completely. When, growing worried, she reached out and touched the back of his hand, she might have struck him, so startled was his response.

Leaning toward him a fraction, she whispered, "You

should be relieved, Davis. We've crossed the border. Sam won't—"

"He'll be here," he interrupted, and only then did he lift his eyes to hers. "That old man's never let the Mexican border stop him." He tossed back the remainder of the whiskey, pinched his eyes closed a moment, then looked at her directly. "This is where we say goodbye, sweetheart."

"Goodbye?" She swallowed back her panic as he refilled his glass. "I don't think I understand."

"This is as far as you go." Up went the glass again to his mouth. He polished it off in one deep draw.

Watching his hand go out for the bottle again, Rachel gripped the edge of the table. "What about me?"

His mouth curled in a smile.

"I thought . . ."

"*What* did you think, Rachel?" He tapped the table impatiently with his glass, looking down at her fingers, knotted white and frail against the scarred and water-ringed tabletop. Then he said without inflection, "You simply tell them that I raped you. They'll forgive you for that. Martin Stillwell may turn up his nose at first but—"

"But you didn't." She watched as he reached for the bottle again, noted that he took two swipes at it before he finally managed to wrap his fingers around it. A sudden sense of fear gripped her as he stared at Clyde's and Pedro's backs. She struggled to remain calm. "You didn't rape me, and besides, I don't care what Martin thinks. I don't love *him*." She bit her lip. As he reached for the bottle again, she made a desperate grab for his wrist, closed her fingers about it, and said, "I thought after last night—"

"You thought what?" His blue eyes bright and fierce in his dark face, Davis leaned toward her and laughed. "Don't you think I know why you responded to me, sweet cheeks? It was only another way to redeem my soul from the pits of hell. Well, you should have saved it for someone else, someone who might have benefited from it. I'm certain my soul is too far gone to be saved by the likes of you."

Her face stung as if he'd slapped her. In a kind of waking

dream, Rachel sank back in her chair, watching the man she thought she'd come to know begin to unravel before her eyes. "What do you intend to do with me?" The words were tight in her throat.

"Do with you?" Slouching in his chair and stretching his long, denim-clad legs, white with dust, out before him, Davis shrugged. "I'll rent you a room here. You'll be safe enough for a few days. I'm certain the good captain will be along soon enough. He'll see you get to your uncle's."

"But I don't wish to go to my uncle's!"

"Where, then?"

"Rancho de Bejar." She saw his shoulders tense. It was a moment before he responded.

"Well." He turned up his glass.

"Angelique assured me her door would always be open."

"And Ramon?"

Rachel frowned, confused. "Ramon?"

"Does Ramon have anything to do with your wanting to return to San Antonio?"

"Certainly not. I told you before—"

"I know what you *told* me." He drank again. "Well then, go the hell to Rancho de Bejar."

Rachel set her jaw, waiting in silence as he looked toward the bar, to his glass, then out the window near his back. "I won't go without you," she finally announced. The words seemed to ring throughout the quiet room; Clyde and Pedro looked back over their shoulders.

Lowering her voice, Rachel took a deep breath, fixed her eyes on Davis's stony face, and said, "We don't have to go back to San Antonio if you don't want. It doesn't matter to me. We could go anywhere—South America, England, France. Sam would never follow you there, and you wouldn't have to worry about your past. No one would know. You could start over . . ."

His whiskered face was incredulous. "What the hell are you saying?"

Burying her fists into her skirt between her knees, she focused on his mouth and confessed, "I don't want to go anywhere without you."

He looked away again, but not before she witnessed the sobering confusion that crossed his features. "I see," came his quiet voice. He refilled his glass, then drained it quickly; his fingers were beginning to shake. "That's understandable," he said a bit hoarsely. "I took your virginity and you're afraid no one else will have you. I'm sorry, but there isn't any way I can make up—"

"You could marry me."

Whiskey spurted out his mouth and nose as he heaved upright in his chair. Pedro and Clyde turned fully around. The bartender peered over their shoulders, and the red-dressed harlot leaned back on her elbows against the bar, watching.

Davis turned red then purple as he gasped for a breath. Her own face burned hot as fire. Pouting just a little, she leaned toward him and said in an injured voice, "I didn't realize marriage to me would seem so offensive to you, Mr. Davis."

He threw her an amused glance as he clumsily wiped the whiskey off his chin and nose with the back of his hand. He was laughing now, disbelieving. "Lady," he said, shaking his head, "you're crazy."

That hurt. Lowering her eyes, she picked at the peeling skin on her palms while the silence dragged on interminably between them.

"Besides," came his voice, which had begun to slur, "you'd prob'ly fin' yourself a widow before the ink dried on the license. Ah! That's the catcher, huh? Bein' a widow might save your reputation. Is that it, sweet cheeks?" Leaning slightly across the table, he tipped her chin up so she had little choice but to meet his eyes.

"No," she answered in a soft voice.

Frowning, he dropped slowly back into his chair. Swiping the whiskey bottle up again, he turned it over his glass, draining it completely before snorting derisively to himself. "Stop lookin' at me like that," he said after a long silence. He turned the glass round and round in his fingers. "If you think for one minute I believe you'd marry me for any other reason . . ." He shifted his eyes to hers again and waited.

"What are you afraid of?" she asked him outright.

"Afraid!" Shifting in his chair, Davis propped his elbows on the table and thrust his fingers through his hair. "Hell, I ain't afraid of nothin'."

"Yes, you are. You're afraid of me, though I can't imagine why."

"The hell you say." Grinning a little ruefully, he said, "When I get married, it'll be to a woman who loves me. And you don't love me. You pity me."

"I don't, Mr. Davis. You do that enough for the both of us."

His fist cracked against the table.

Rachel jumped.

Coming out of his chair, Davis leaned across the table, his dark head suspended above her face as he drawled, "You're bluffing, Miss Gregory. I don't believe for one minute that you'd marry me."

"Ask me, Mr. Davis, and see."

"All right. All right . . . all right . . ."

Rachel lifted one blond brow as his hot, whiskey-sweet breath beat at her face. She wet her lips. Nervousness raised her voice an octave as she said, "Well?" When he hesitated again, she shrugged and taunted so smugly that his face turned hard as rock, "You see?"

He shook.

She waited with strained patience, knowing she was pushing him beyond his control.

He narrowed his eyes. "All right, Miss Greg'ry. All right, damn you . . . marry me." There. He'd said it.

"*Will* you marry me."

His jaw clenched. He repeated, "*Will* you marry me?"

"See. That wasn't so bad."

His face darkened further. She felt panic rise inside her, tightening her lungs, her throat, her heart. "A gentleman would go to his knee," she said a little breathlessly.

"I'm no gentleman."

"Well . . ." She plucked at an imaginary piece of fluff on her skirt. "I think this entire ordeal would be far less trying if we went about it in the proper manner. A woman gets proposed to so few times in her life. Perhaps if you shaved . . ."

His eyebrows went up.

"And bathed . . ." Her face lit up as she exclaimed, "Perhaps I could get cleaned up as well. Oh, Mr. Davis, doesn't this sound wonderfully romantic?"

He blinked.

"We could meet back here in an hour. Perhaps we could order some food and you could propose to me over our meal." Leaping from her chair, she kissed him fully on the mouth.

That unsettled him. She knew it would. The kiss, combined with the liquor and her gentle but persuasive directives, led him to put down one of Martin Stillwell's dollars for a room upstairs. He ordered a bath to be sent up to her room, as well as food to be delivered to their table in an hour. All paid out of Martin's satchel. Then he saw her to her door: Room 13.

He gripped the doorframe with both hands before saying, "You close this door and lock it."

"I will." A knot of excitement had set up a beating in her stomach like butterflies. She stood just inside the threshold, feeling small and as breakable as glass. He stood in the doorway looking like summer thunderclouds. Dark and shifting and uncertain. And powerful, too.

Davis watched her silently for a moment, then touched her cheek with one finger. "You're so damn pretty, Miss Greg'ry." More softly he added, "I like your hair."

"Even though it's not brunette?" She searched his eyes. "You *did* tell Audra you were partial to brunettes."

A slow smile stretched his mouth. It was sarcastic and drunken, and Rachel longed with all her soul to plant her lips against it. But she didn't. She just stood there before him and watched the light through the window catch fire in his eyes while he asssessed her.

"Thought you were probably eavesdropping," he told her. "Being as nosy as you are."

Her cheeks colored. "Y'all flirted with Audra outrageously. Said she had pretty hands."

He touched her face again, this time letting his fingers linger along the side of her throat. "They're not nearly so pretty as yours, sweetheart."

Rachel closed her eyes, exalting in the caress of his hand, so strong and brown and perfect. He always knew the right thing to say. "Yours are not so bad either, Mr. Davis."

"We'll make a pair, won't we? The lady and the outlaw . . ." A grin touched the corners of his mouth.

They stood in companionable silence there in the dingy, close confines to the Casita Cantina and Hotel.

He thought again of saying *I love you.*

She thought of saying *I love you.*

They both looked into one another's eyes and thought, *I love you,* but neither of them said it.

She felt conspicuous suddenly, and a little shy. She was grateful when a boy came up the hallway hauling a washtub on rollers. Water sloshed back and forth within its galvanized tin sides as he shoved it through the door. Turning his dark face up to Davis's he said, "Your bath, *señor.*"

Davis fished in his pocket as the boy held one light-palmed hand out for a reward. Closing his fingers around the coin, the young man smiled at Rachel and said, "Concepción will bring up clean linens soon." He spun on his bare heels and scampered off down the hall.

They stood again in silence while the steam from the bath condensed between them like a fog.

Smiling only slightly, Davis asked, "Need any help with those buttons?"

She shook her head.

"Guess I'll go then." He turned unsteadily toward the door. "I saw a church at the end of the street. S'pose there's a priest there who knows how to marry people?"

Her heart tripped over itself. Covering her smile with the tips of her fingers, she said, "I suppose."

He didn't stop again, just closed the door behind him. Rachel remained frozen in place, staring at the doorknob.

Finally she sat on the edge of the bed, kicked off one shoe, then the other, letting herself daydream about marriage to Davis—Tomas. It would be difficult thinking of him as anything but Davis. No doubt there would be a great deal of traveling. She looked about the squalid quarters. A cockroach at least two inches long perched on the edge of the marble-topped washstand beneath the mirror on the wall and wiggled its long antennae at her.

"Shoo!" Wrinkling her nose, she fluttered her fingers at it and ordered, "Go away!" It didn't budge. Picking up her shoe, she crept at it, waving the kid slipper before her like a shield. Still it didn't move, so she left it alone and went back to the bed.

She decided then and there that she'd simply have to convince Davis to go back to Rancho de Bejar. She could tolerate a great number of things, but sharing her living quarters with roaches the size of small rats was out of the question.

Thinking again of Rancho de Bejar, Rachel smiled. She tried to imagine Angelique's and Alejandro's face when she brought their son home. After twenty some years . . . it was going to be just grand! Everyone would weep and laugh and hug everyone else, and then Sam would show up with a badge in one hand and a gun in the other, and announce he was there to take Davis to El Paso to hang.

Her heart wrenched at the thought, and suddenly the suffocating heat in the tiny room was too much.

Jumping from the bed, Rachel ran to the window and attempted to raise it, but couldn't. Across the street she saw Davis entering a building, and the need to call out to him almost choked her. As soon as he returned, as soon as they were married, she'd convince him to forget his plans with Clyde—whatever they might be—and come away with her, before Sam could find him and kill him. Before the people who would never understand him found him and sentenced him to death.

*   *   *

Davis found a barber with little trouble. The dark-skinned, mustachioed man offered him a generous smile as he dropped into the chair and announced to the ceiling, "I wanna shave."

"*Sí, señor*." The barber's head bobbed in compliance as he wielded the single-edged razor back and forth on the leather strop.

As the man lathered over the heavy growth of stubble on his jaw, Davis grinned and announced, "I'm getting married."

The barber smiled and his head bobbed again.

The words echoed in his head. *I'm getting married.*

God, he thought, *I'm drunk*.

Closing his eyes, his head swimming dizzily, he tried to think straight. He was about to get married. How could he have let this happen? *When* had it happened? He'd been upset since morning, for certain. Waking up beside Rachel, her arms wrapped around him, had been enough almost to dissuade him from continuing this ordeal. But he had made his decision before breaking camp. He'd waded into deep water with Clyde, and there was no backing down. Now, of all times, he had to be at the peak of his performance. Everything hinged on his getting to A.J. Duncan.

The razor scraped noisily across his cheek.

The sobering image of Rachel blinking those wide violet eyes up into his and saying, "You could marry me," came like a jolt out of the blue.

"*Por favor, señor*." The barber smiled again and shrugged apologetically as Davis shifted in his chair. He was growing more agitated by the minute the more sober he became.

How the hell did she do it? She'd taken *her* suggestion that he marry her and twisted it all around so it appeared *he* was the one wanting to get married. For a minute there, he'd almost believed . . . Was she going to agree to marry him or not?

Why the hell should he care?

Good God, he *couldn't* get married now!

The barber took one last swipe at his chin before Davis left the chair. Looking in the mirror, he noted the man had done a respectable enough job to warrant the exorbitant price he demanded. He flipped the man a coin before turning for the door.

The hot sun turned his stomach. Grabbing the hitching post outside the shop, he waited on outstretched arms for the nausea to pass. One minute, then two. The ground swirled at his feet; he closed his eyes.

What the devil had happened to him? He'd lost himself in a bottle for the first time in years. He'd lost himself in a woman as well. He'd let his heart have its way this one time, and *this* is what had happened.

He'd known it would come to this, dammit. But the thought of leaving her here for Sam, and possibly never seeing her again . . . Jesus, he'd laughed a hundred times at men who'd let their feelings for a woman get in the way of business. He cursed himself and rammed the post with the butt of his hand.

He threw one look toward the tiny white adobe church with the bell tower in the distance, hesitated, then headed for the hotel.

The darkness of the cantina alleviated his sickened state somewhat. Leaning against the doorframe, he drank in the cooler air until his head stopped spinning. He glanced toward their table—his and Rachel's—to the empty whiskey bottle, the two glasses, his drained and hers half full. His hat still lay on the table where he'd thrown it. He walked unsteadily to it.

What would be so wrong with marrying Rachel? It might solve her problem about returning to her family and friends. And if he did get himself killed, there was the money he'd saved up through the years. And there was, after all, the possibility that she could be with child. All the more reason why he should marry her. No son or daughter of his would be born a bastard. And if he didn't get himself killed . . .

How bad could it be?

He'd be married to the woman he loved. He could start his

life over with the woman he loved. She could learn to love him. She *cared* for him already; that was a start. . . .

"*Señor?*"

He looked absently into the young woman's face. How long had she been there, tugging on his sleeve?

She pointed toward the bar.

Seconds passed as he searched the room. Except for the barrel-chested bartender wiping out a glass, the room was empty. And then it hit him. Panic seized him. The same mind-blinding fear that had frozen him the day before when he found Pete forcing his attentions on Rachel.

Shoving the woman aside, he started for the stairs, fractured thoughts spinning through his mind. The stairwell was empty and musty; dirt lay thick on the worn and splintered wooden planks at his feet. He hadn't noticed the filth before, when he'd drunkenly escorted Rachel to her room. This was no place for a lady like Rachel. She deserved something better than this sour-smelling hovel. Yes. He'd take her away from here. Far away. He'd tell her the truth. Forget about his obligations. He was sick up to his throat with his obligations. If the powers-that-be didn't like his decision, they could take it and shove it up—

For God's sake, which room was hers? Think, dammit, think!

The tarnished bronze number 13 glittered dully in a shaft of light spilling through the open window at the far end of the hallway—the only illumination in the suffocating tunnel. He moved swiftly down the corridor, his eyes trained on the door, his ears attuned to any sound of distress. Then he saw it, the water running into the hallway from beneath the door. His pace slowed. What the hell . . .

"Quickly, *amigo*, before Davis returns."

Pedro?

Davis's heart slammed in his chest.

"Well, now yore slippery as a fish ain't ya?"

Clyde!

Rachel screamed. "You filthy animal, Davis will kill you for this!"

"Relax, sweetheart, just like ya do fer him."

Lunging, Davis hit the door. Locked! He went for his gun, aimed the weapon at the lock, and pulled the trigger. The fire from the barrel bloomed red and white in the half-lit corridor. The explosion shook the walls. Stepping back, Davis kicked open the barrier and threw himself over the threshold.

It should have been instinct. Reflex. The space of time since he hit the door had been no more than seconds. But the world slowed, each fraction of a second clipping by like an eternity as he went through the movements. Perhaps it was the flashes of blond hair spilling over the bed, the glimpses of Clyde on his knees with his breeches down around his buttocks that upended those instincts.

Pedro spun, his gun in his hands.

Davis was already falling, going down on one knee. Cursing under his breath, he did his best to shift sideways as he watched the barrel of Pedro's gun swing his way. Somehow he managed to lift his own gun and squeeze the trigger. An explosion rocked the room, then another. Glass shattered, and behind it all Rachel was screaming. Figures, blurred with movement, flashed in and out of his peripheral vision.

Clyde. Clyde. You son-of-a—

He tried to break his fall; his knee hit the floor. A thousand thoughts assailed him. When had he last loaded his gun? No time now. No time now. His shoulder hit the floor and he rolled, attempted to scramble back to his knee while swiveling the gun up toward the figure spinning off the bed. *The gun, the gun!* his mind screamed. How had Clyde gotten his gun so quickly . . .

"You bastard!" he yelled.

A crack like thunder rent the melee.

He pulled the trigger. Too late. Too late, he thought, as Clyde's bullet slammed into his body, lifting him off the floor and driving him back against the wall. He pulled the trigger again, or thought he did, heard the explosion over and over as he began the long, spiraling free-fall toward the floor. He hit it hard. So hard, it seemed that his entire body had become dismembered. His blood swirled in the soapy warm water of the overturned bath. He tried to lift his face from the water, from the blood. But the blackness dragged him down . . . and the numbness. On the near fringes of his rational mind, he knew he was dying. "Christ," he cried out, succumbing to the blackness, "they've killed me."

Chapter 16

"Help me! Please, someone help me!" Stumbling out the door, Rachel fell to her knees. The man and woman she'd seen earlier tending bar appeared at the end of the corridor. "He's dying!" She wept and held her bloody hands out to them. "Oh God, he's dying! Someone help him!"

The man ran to the door.

The woman stooped beside Rachel, closing her arms around her heaving shoulders while attempting to help her stand. Pushing her away, Rachel crawled on her hands and knees back into the room.

"Please help him. He's bleeding! Oh please, make it stop bleeding! Don't let him die! Do something. For God's sake, someone do something to help him!"

Lifting Davis's head and shoulders into her lap, Rachel looked back toward the door at the stunned couple gaping at the blood-spattered quarters. "Someone get a doctor!" she screamed. "Dammit, can't you understand? A doctor!"

The woman made the sign of the cross over her breast before responding, "*Señorita*, there is no doctor in San Carlos."

Panic gripping her again, Rachel pressed her fingers over the gaping hole in Davis's chest. Then pressing his face against her breast, she looked back at the woman again and argued, "You cannot just stand there and let him die. There must be someone!"

Without turning to the woman at his side, the man directed, "Javier, Concepción, *pronto!*"

Whirling, Concepción disappeared down the hall.

Smiling kindly, the man approached Rachel, his hands extended. *"Venga, señorita! Venga de aquí! Venga usted de sa esa lugar tan terrible!"*

She shook her head, unable to understand. But as his hands gently closed over her shoulders in an attempt to move her away from the grisly scene, she pushed him away. "No! How can you think that I would leave him!"

He shook his head sadly and tugged on her arm.

"He isn't dead, I tell you! Leave me alone!" Cradling Davis in her arms, she rocked back and forth in her grief.

The numbness began, the shock. It dulled her senses to the bloodied battleground around her. She no longer saw Clyde's crumpled form sprawled, face up, over the bed. She took no notice of Pedro lying half in and half out of the shattered window. There was only Davis, his limp body cradled in her arms, his face bloodless and cold. So cold.

He looked like a child in deep, peaceful sleep. His dark hair was tousled and in his face. With her fingertips she brushed it aside.

She touched his face, a smile coming faintly to her mouth. "Oh," she whispered. "You *did* shave." Her palm cradled his smooth cheek. So long she'd ached to touch him in such a way that the act brought a painful tightness to her throat. "Don't be afraid," she told him. "Don't be afraid."

"Señorita? Señorita!"

Rachel looked up. The woman was back. Behind her a short man with a mustache entered the room.

Concepción, stepping carefully over Davis's legs, took Rachel's hand and smiled encouragingly. "Javier will help you," she said. "Come, *señorita*, let us get your man to another room."

Rachel shook her head. "No. No, we can't move him, he might die. Go away. Just leave him alone. Just leave him in peace. He's suffered so long . . ."

"Javier will help you."

"No!" Rachel hugged him to her breast.

More forcefully, Concepción grabbed Rachel's shoulders. *"Señorita*, please! If you do not allow Javier to move your man, he will die! He will die!"

The men stepped in as Concepción managed to move Rachel away from Davis. Gently the bartender lifted his shoulders while Javier grabbed his legs. They moved swiftly into the hall, then into the next room where they placed him carefully on the bed. The movement roused Davis. He began to groan.

Hope flared in Rachel's breast at the sound. "Can you hear me?" she asked. "Javier is going to help you, darling. I'm here as well. I won't leave you . . . *ever!* Fight. Just fight. You have enough fight left in you to beat this. I know it!"

His eyelids flickered. His chest rose and fell sharply, his breath coming suddenly in short, sporadic gasps.

Javier moved her aside. With a single-edged razor, he began cutting the shirt away from Davis's chest. As the wound was revealed, Rachel closed her eyes, fear and nausea colliding in her stomach with enough impact to cause her to sway. *Dear God, dear God.*

Concepción touched her shoulder, and Rachel opened her eyes. Davis watched her. Or so it seemed. How lifeless were his eyes. But for the shallow rise and fall of his chest, he might have been dead.

Moving up beside her, Concepción whispered, "Javier will need help. It would have been better had your man remained unconscious, but since he didn't we will have to hold him down while Javier removes the bullet. Can you help?"

Rachel nodded, unable to speak, unable to take her eyes from his face for even a moment. He'd turned whiter, if that were possible. His lips were blue. He'd begun to sweat.

"You must hold his left arm, *senorita*. Miguel will hold his legs." Concepción spoke calmly as she wrapped cloth strips around Davis's right wrist, tying his arm to the bed at his side. "You must prepare yourself, *señorita*. There will be a great deal of pain." She swung toward the table by his bedside and took up several cloths, one of which she handed to Javier. The small man, his temples damp with sweat, nodded his thanks.

Rachel lay gently across Davis's left shoulder. "Forgive us," she whispered into his ear.

Javier touched the wet towel tenderly to the wound in an attempt to clean away as much blood as possible. Davis's body flinched in response. His head thrashed back and forth, and his eyes, no longer so dazed, rolled back in their sockets.

"Is there nothing we can give him for the pain?" Rachel asked the young woman.

"No. With God's grace he will lose consciousness again. Perhaps you would care to wait downstairs?"

"No! I won't leave him!" Looking back into his face, she said, "He knows I'm here. I won't leave him, no matter what."

His body twisted as Javier swiped again at the wound, and for the first time, he spoke. "Ah, God! Rachel!"

"I'm here!"

The words appeared to soothe him; his body relaxed. Struggling, he focused on her face, or tried to, as one corner of his mouth curled up.

Her heart twisted at the sight. "Hello," she said. "I thought . . ." He'd slipped away again. Taking his large brown hand in hers, she pressed his knuckles to her lips. "Please don't die," she pleaded. "Please don't die."

Chancing a quick look at his chest, Rachel noted that, once cleaned, the wound didn't appear as bad as she'd first believed. Just below and to the right of his collarbone the injury bled still, but not so profusely as before.

Javier approached again, a knife in his hand. His face red with heat, he motioned toward Davis and directed Rachel, *"Señorita, por favor."*

Rachel turned her face away and pressed her body against his. Davis convulsed as the man began probing for the bullet. His body arching off the bed, his head back and his face contorted in pain, he screamed and wept her name, over and over until his voice became raw and hoarse in his throat. He fought them with superhuman strength until, suddenly, his body went limp. Sitting upright, Rachel searched his face, frightened by his terrible pallor. Javier dropped the bloody bullet onto the floor.

"Will he live?" she demanded of the Mexican.

He looked toward Concepción. The girl translated.

Shrugging his shoulders, Javier continued to clean the wound and sew it closed. Concepción responded. "He is no doctor . . . only a barber, so he has no way of knowing. Javier has done what he can. Only God can help your man now." More quietly, Concepción stated, "There is a priest in San Carlos. Should you need him—"

"We won't. He's not going to die, I tell you. I won't let him."

He is not going to die, she told herself over and over again. However, as afternoon dragged into night, her hopes began to sag. For the first time since the ordeal began, Rachel moved stiffly from her perch beside his bed to the washstand against the far wall, and the mirror above it. Staring in disbelief at her image, she swallowed. Her hair hung in limp, damp strands about her face. Her face was dark with dirt and blood. It appeared everywhere on her person: dark dry smears over her cheeks, down the front of her blouse, and over the better part of her skirt.

Lightly she touched her lip where Clyde had hit her. Thank God he'd managed no more than that before Davis arrived. As she eyed the purple bruise, it occurred to her that all this was *her* fault. Her presence had caused friction between the men since the onset of their escape. Davis had done his best to protect her from Clyde, and from Pete the day before. He'd ordered her to keep that door locked. She just hadn't thought to ask when the knock came. She'd been expecting Concepción to return with clean linens. She'd opened the door to Clyde without thinking.

The heat in the tiny quarters became suffocating. Moving to the window, Rachel did her best to raise it. Impossible. It hadn't been moved in years. Sitting on the window ledge, she rested her head tiredly against the dirty pane of glass and stared down the street. At the far end of town a hinged sign swung back and forth in the wind, and tumbleweeds blew along the street where they gathered in clumps against an adobe wall.

She sat there for an hour, or maybe two, listening to each

breath that Davis took rattle in his lungs. Just before dusk Concepción, in a dress of lavender satin with frilly black lace trim, came through the door, her hands burdened with a tray of food and a bottle of whiskey. Rachel smiled her thanks without taking her eyes from the man on the bed.

Dusk was sienna red, like the dust on the streets, the dust that infiltrated every nook and cranny in this godforsaken town. As orange lights began burning in the windows up and down the street, Rachel grabbed up the whiskey bottle, measured herself a glass, and took her place back at Davis's bedside.

"I've heard this helps," she said. Then turning the glass up to her mouth, she drank deeply, coughing as the fiery liquid hit her stomach.

Throughout the night Concepción or Miguel, the bartender, checked on Davis's condition. Twice they changed the bandages while Rachel bathed his face and shoulders and chest with cool water. He never roused. Just before dawn, Rachel leaned over in her chair, laid her head next to his on the bed, and drifted into a fitful sleep.

Concepción awakened her. "Señorita Rachel! Rachel!"

Her eyes opening with a start, Rachel blinked and tried sluggishly to lift her head. Bright light through the window bewildered and frightened her. How long had she slept? Disoriented, she grabbed Davis's arm. His skin was on fire.

His wet hair clung to his brow. His bloodred face shone with sweat, as did his chest and stomach. Rolling his head back and forth, he mumbled incoherently.

Throwing back the blanket she had earlier spread over his legs, Rachel began unfastening his breeches. "His fever is raging. Get me cool water, Concepción. *Pronto!*"

She hurried to the end of the bed and removed his boots, then as gently as possible, began tugging off his pants. By the time she dropped them to the floor the girl had returned with the water, and both began sponging his entire body with cool cloths. It did nothing to quell his fever, and Rachel's panic mounted. She'd seen it all before. While working as a volunteer at the Holy Mary Hospital during the siege of New

Orleans, she'd watched dozens of men brought in, their bodies riddled by bullets. And while the wounds may not have killed them outright, fever or infection had.

As Davis's fever soared, so did his delirium. He wandered in and out of consciousness. His body thrashed so that Rachel was forced to tie his arms and legs to the bed. Twisting savagely, he screamed, "Get away from me! Don't touch me! I want my mother! You killed my mother, you bastard! I'll kill you! No, no, please don't hurt me again. I'm hungry. So hungry. I'll be good if you don't hurt me anymore!"

His face contorted in agony. "I'm not one of them. Look at me. I'm not one of them. Not an animal. Don't call me that! I won't hurt you if you'll just stop fighting . . ."

Rachel held a cloth to his lips, allowing water to dribble into his mouth. His eyes opened. He stared at her hard for a moment. Straining then, half off the bed, he yelled, "Jesus, he's got a knife! Stop him!"

Doing her best to press him back down, Rachel said, "Hush. No one has a knife now. It's only me, darling; I won't hurt you."

Recognition flickered in his eyes. "Rachel." His head fell back on the pillow and he cursed in a thready voice, "That bastard, Clyde."

"Clyde's dead, remember? You killed him."

"They've killed me."

"No!" Blotting the sweat from his face, Rachel did her best to encourage him. "You're going to be fine."

"A priest. I—I want a priest."

"Why?"

"Get me a priest, dammit! I have to confess. Don't want to go to hell . . ."

"You're not going to die!" Her voice rose hysterically as she took his burning face in her palms. "You mustn't give up! You can't! Fight, damn you. I beg you, don't give up!"

His eyes rolled shut. His breathing became ragged. "Rachel," came his weak whisper. "Rachel, would you love me if I were a Bastitas?"

Burying her face by his head, Rachel broke for the first

time since the horrible ordeal began. "I would love you even if you weren't." She wept.

His condition worsened near the end of the second day. Rachel sent for the priest. His black robes sweeping the floor, he bent slightly over Davis and spoke softly. "I am here, my son."

His thrashing quieted.

The priest repeated, "I am here, my son."

"Father . . . help me. I'm dying."

Easing gently onto the bed, the priest released Davis's bound hand and took it in his own. "How may I help you, my son?"

"I have to confess."

Rachel, her back against the wall, covered her mouth with her hands as the priest looked her way. "I must have privacy," he said.

"I won't leave."

The priest turned back to the bed, bent close to Davis's ear, and said, "Begin."

The confession came, slurred with pain, and weak, meant only for the priest's ears. Rachel heard little, only bits and pieces as his voice rose and fell. She watched the small, dark man in the robe cross himself several times during the painful oration. In turn, he mumbled his response into Davis's ear. Moving along the wall, she tried to see Davis's face, but the priest's shoulder obscured it. Davis wept quietly, in his feverish semiconscious state. She saw his hand come up and cover his eyes.

All too soon the priest moved away. Rachel held her breath, afraid to look, afraid he would be gone already.

"In the name of the Father, and of the Son . . ."

Closing her eyes, Rachel sank to the floor.

She came awake slowly, an unfamiliar light in her eyes. She stared at the dancing yellow candle flame for a long moment before blinking. Then the ache began, deep in her chest, spreading outward to her stomach and up to her throat.

Concepción entered the room. Touching Rachel's tear-streaked face, she said, "*Señorita*, he has been asking for you."

Uncomprehending, Rachel tried to sit up.

"Your man." The girl smiled. "He has been asking for you. Come quickly while he's still awake."

Allowing herself to be led from the room, Rachel moved in a daze down the hall. The door stood open. Stopping at the threshold, she stared at Davis's still form. Concepción leaned over him and said loudly, "*Señor*, she is here." Turning her light brown face toward the door, she motioned Rachel in.

Surely this was a cruel dream. She would awaken at any moment and learn he was truly dead. But no. The misery she felt was far too vivid to be a dream. The sound of his heavy breathing was too distinct, the acrid smell of sweat and infection too pungent to be anything but real. She moved to the bed swiftly. Her heart turned over as he opened his eyes.

Bending closer, she touched his face. "Can you hear me?" He blinked slowly.

"You've had a rough time of it. Would you like water?" His lips parted.

With a spoon she trickled water into his mouth. Turning to Concepción, she said, "I knew he could do it. He's not going to die, Concepción. He's too damn stubborn to die."

The girl smiled in response.

Smoothing the hair out of his eyes, Rachel asked, "Have you a Bible, Concepción?"

"I can get one from the church." She hurried from the room.

Within a few minutes Concepción was back, handing the book eagerly to Rachel. Smiling her thanks, Rachel sat in the chair next to the bed, opened the Bible, and began to read:

"Chapter One. Genesis. In the beginning God created the heaven and the earth . . ."

*   *   *

He listened to the words as they played over and over in his dreams. *In the beginning . . . In the beginning . . .*

In the beginning.

He saw the woman again, his grandmother Carlota, laughing, tossing her glossy black hair over her shoulders, and opening her arms. She looked so tall and beautiful. "Come here!" she called to him.

He tried to move. Why couldn't he move? He slowly looked around, the images blurring so he couldn't focus. His mother was running down a long gray tunnel toward him, her red-gold hair like fire in the March sun. "Run!" she screamed.

Dear God, why couldn't he move?

He struggled to open his eyes. "No. No. Not again." He wept.

His mother stumbled backward, fell backward to the ground. Her face, her beautiful face . . . the blood. So much blood. "Pa! Pa, help me!"

"Hush," came the voice. "It's all right. You're going to be all right. Now, tell me your name."

"Tomas. My name is Tomas de Bastitas. Will you help me?"

"I'm going to help you. I'm going to love you. Tomas . . ."

Rachel smiled as she leaned her patient forward and fluffed the pillow behind his back. Twelve days had passed since the awful incident, and he was stronger. His color had returned, and though he was terribly stiff and sore, his spirits were good.

Rarely leaving his side, Rachel told him about her childhood, expounded on her days spent frolicking in the warm gulf sunshine while her father, never far away, went about his duties as a cotton planter. She explained the cotton business in detail.

"One hour before daylight the overseer would ring a big brass bell in the yard. By dawn all the help would be in the fields, tending the cotton. It was so marvelously exciting when harvest rolled around. The bolls would burst open, so fat and full. And at those times, the ground for miles and miles from New Orleans to Baton Rouge would look as if it were covered with snow."

"I'd like to raise cattle," he responded, joining in on the game. "Maybe someday I'd drive them up to Kansas myself."

Propping her chin up on her fist, she taunted, "Raising cotton's more fun than cows, and smells a whole lot better, too."

Slanting her a weak smile, he argued, "Isn't."

"Is."

"Isn't."

He rested his head back on the pillow, closed his eyes, and laughed.

"Tell me about your home," he said then.

Sitting back in her chair and propping her bare feet up on the bed beside him, she laced her fingers together over her stomach and stared at the ceiling. Her eyes became misty, but she smiled.

"Belle Hélène was located exactly six miles out of New Orleans, though we always considered ourselves in the city since we could climb aboard a steamboat just out our front door and sail down the Mississippi anytime we wanted. That's how we traveled, you see. By boat. We climbed aboard a river schooner like y'all hitch up your buggies. My favorite pastime was standing on the upper balcony of Hélène and watching the boats go by. Sometimes they tooted at me. Of course, they all knew me."

Davis smiled, imagining.

"Hélène was ninety feet square and surrounded by twenty-eight columns that were three feet square and twenty-eight feet high. The first and second floor galleries extended a whole fifteen feet out on all four sides.

"The first floor consisted of a double parlor, a sitting room—just in case the gentlemen smoked cigars after dinner—the library, and the dining room with the butler's pantry, of course."

"Of course," Davis said.

She cocked him a glance and grinned. "Y'all asked for it, Mr. Davis."

"Y'all continue, Miss Gregory."

"There was a hall down the center of the house with doors at each end. It allowed marvelous breezes to whip through the house, but we had a devil of a time keeping the hounds out."

"Hounds? How many hounds are we talking here?"

Lifting her head, she frowned and stressed, "Mr. Davis, no self-respecting farm is ever without at least a half dozen hounds."

"Of course. I should have known that. Go on."

"Hélène had one of the most beautiful curving staircases in the area. It curved in a spiral all the way up to the attic. The steps were of cypress and the balustrades of mahogany. The second floor consisted of four massive bedrooms, a nursery where I spent my younger years, my nanny's room, and, of course, the long center hallway. The windows in the rooms went all the way to the floor so we could throw open the shutters at any time and waltz right out onto the balcony!"

Dropping her feet to the floor, she propped her elbows on her knees, pinned Davis with her eyes, and said, "Did you know there were oak trees around Hélène that were two hundred years old? Y'all'd just have to see it to believe it!"

Rolling his head, he touched her face with his hand and stated, "You must miss it very much."

"I did once," she admitted. Then nestling her cheek into his palm, she said, "I haven't thought about it now for a long time."

She shaved and bathed him. She tended his wound with the proficiency of a doctor. She fed him broth, gently lifting his dark head in the crook of her arm while lightly resting a spoon against his lips. But all the while a nagging worry continued to haunt her. Somewhere between San Carlos and San Antonio, Sam Wells was tracking Davis.

She began spending more and more time perched on the windowsill, staring down both ends of the long street. Every time a rider approached, she held her breath, watching closely for a glimpse of gray braids and that kind but weathered brown face. She began jumping each time footsteps rang down the corridor. She kept the door locked. She rarely slept. She had come so close to losing him . . . how could she lose him again?

He awoke one morning, two weeks after the ordeal, to find Rachel asleep in the window, her pale forehead pressed against the glass, her even whiter hair spilling over her shoulders in a snowy cascade. For the first time in days he was not racked with pain. His mind was clear, no longer drugged with fever, and he realized for the first time what his ordeal had cost her. His heart twisted at the sight of her.

"Rachel."

The curling brush of wheat gold lashes against her cheeks fluttered as she awakened. He watched the dark purple-velvet pools of her eyes focus on his face. "Is something wrong?" she asked.

"Come here."

She stumbled from the windowsill, rubbing her sleepy eyes, and sat down beside him. "God," he said, "look at you." With the pad of his thumb, he brushed the dark circles beneath her eyes, traced the lines of fatigue etching the skin over her forehead and around her lips. "You've lost too much weight," he told her. "What's bothering you?"

"Sam." Her thin shoulders rose and fell as she took a breath. "The way I see it, we have two choices. We can continue to run, perhaps further into Mexico. Or we can go back to San Antonio . . . to your parents." Slowly she brought her eyes back to his. "You admitted it during your fever. Your identity, I mean. You're Tomas de Bastitas."

He narrowed his eyes.

"And even if you hadn't," she went on, "the evidence is in there." Rachel pointed to his saddle bags, thrown into the corner. "Your grandmother's scalp is in there. You still carry it with you. Angelique told me her mother was scalped by the same Indian who nabbed you from her arms. She told me how the Comanche would force captives to wear the hair of a loved one on their person. If you would only go back—"

"No."

Her small fists clenched in her lap. "Then we'll simply continue running. As far and as fast as we can."

"We." It wasn't a question.

"Oh yes." Meeting his intense blue eyes with her own, she stated, "I'm going with you."

He laughed to himself. "Rachel, I'm no longer holding you captive. I'll see you get back—"

"No." She shook her head. "I'm not going back. Not without you." Glancing around at the mirror on the wall, then back at him, she asked, "Are you strong enough to sit up? Shall we give it a try?" Smiling at his nod, she reached for his shoulders, slid an arm beneath him, and hefted him up while he clumsily slid his legs off the bed.

Grabbing the blanket, he tugged it across his naked loins. Then he looked in the mirror, slightly startled by the stranger's image reflected there.

"Do you like it?" she asked in a voice grown high with anticipation. "It changes your looks, I think. It might help to . . . well . . . Do you like it?"

With his fingertips he touched the thick black mustache. It covered his upper lip and curled in a sweep around the outer corners of his mouth. He looked back at Rachel. "Do you?"

"I don't know yet. I suppose—"

He caught her face, silencing her nervous chatter. Dragging her head down to his, he gently brushed her lips with his, back and forth, rubbing the facial hair lightly against her mouth until she giggled. Opening his mouth over hers, he gently nudged her lips with his tongue until they parted. He felt her tremble, felt the hot, sweet velvet of her tongue pulse against his in response. Then she was against him, the coolness of her skin pressed against the still slightly feverish warmth of his. Her nipples hardened against his chest. Her breathing quickened.

Pulling away just a little, he grinned and teased, "You've

missed me." Then, remembering the ugly scene he'd witnessed with Clyde, he lightly touched her face and, searching her eyes for the truth, asked, "Clyde? Did he—"

"No."

"Don't lie to me, Rachel."

"I swear it."

Relief and weariness washed over him. With her help he
sank back on the bed. As easily as possible, she lay down
beside him. On her side, she ran her fingers lightly through
the black hair on his chest and down his stomach.

"We have to talk," he told her.

Her hand ran lower.

Lifting one eyebrow, he laughed weakly. "Rachel, love,
we have to talk."

"So talk."

"There are some . . . things I have to confess."

"You confessed to the priest. Remember? When you
thought you were dying."

His head came up, and he frowned. "What the devil did I
say?"

Sliding her leg over his thigh, she scattered kisses over his
chest before replying. "I don't know. I couldn't hear. But it
doesn't matter. None of that matters. It's all behind you. God
has forgiven you and you can start over with a clean slate.
I'm going to help you start over. As soon as we're
married—"

"Married!"

"Yes, married." Tipping her face to his, her lips brushing
his cheek, she whispered, "You were going to marry me."
Her hand slid lower. "Weren't you?"

Davis's eyes narrowed the tiniest fraction. "I'll . . . think
about it."

"Think about it," she repeated. Her fingers closing around
him, she laid her head on his chest, watching as he grew
hard in her palm. "It's beautiful," he heard her say.

Laughing toward the ceiling, Davis closed his eyes and
admitted, "You're the damnedest woman."

"Oh?" came the muffled response.

"A few weeks ago you were some prim little goody two-shoes, and now look at you. Madam, have a heart. How can I perform when I'm half dead?"

"You won't, of course. I will." She looked up at him with smoldering eyes. Then, very slowly, she lifted her skirts to the tops of her thighs and slid atop him, careful of his shoulder, suspending her weight above him on her outstretched arms.

He closed his eyes, his senses focusing not on the sharp pain the movement brought to his wound, but on the liquid hot sheath that slid onto his body like a tight, tight glove. He groaned.

"If I'm hurting you . . ." She rotated her hips.

"No. Don't stop."

"I know you're weak." Sitting upright, Rachel threw back her head so her hair coiled in fine curls over his hard thighs, and she said huskily, "I fantasized this. I made a vow. If you lived I would show you in every way imaginable how much I love you."

His eyes came open slowly.

With a lift of one pale brow, she asked, "Is this how it's done?"

He groaned again and, lifting his good arm, took one of her breasts in his hand. "Take it off," he commanded, meaning her blouse.

She stripped it away. The shimmering strands of her hair spilled over her shoulders, partly shielding the full, high-pointed breasts from his sight. Only the pink of her turgid nipples peeked from beneath the silken silver-white skein. He took one between his thumb and forefinger, pulled until it gorged with blood, quivering for more. Running his finger down the middle of her stomach, he nudged up the folds of her skirt and slid his hand, palm up, between their pressing bodies.

Rachel gasped at the touch. It magnified the pressure of him inside her, reminded her of how intimately they were joined. Moistening her lips with her tongue, she looked down on his dark face with its intense blue eyes, and she thought she would die with the pleasure-pain of it all. To think she'd almost lost him. She rotated her hips again, recalling the movement he'd used on her.

He rolled his head so his cheek was buried in his pillow. His skin glowed in a moist flush of fever and desire, and he gritted his teeth. She watched his jaw work as his hands balled into fists and pressed into the bed. "Is there pain?" she asked him.

"God yes."

"Would you like me to stop?" She prayed that he wouldn't.

"Go on," he pleaded. "Do it." He swiveled his hips.

So she did. Just as she had in her dreams, her fantasies, in all the promises she'd made to herself *and* him while he struggled with death. She smoothed her hands over the hot, damp flesh of his chest and stomach while she rode up and down, up and down, feeling him grow harder and fuller and hotter, if that were possible, inside her. Soon his back was arching and his hips were grinding up against hers, each possession coming faster and harder until her breathing and his came in fast, painful little pants that sounded abnormally loud in the stifling hot room.

She lost herself to the rapture of the total communion, allowed her body to fly, to free itself of modesty and the chains of stale propriety. She writhed against him, lifted and sank until her body and his were one, so tightly and resolutely joined in spirit and soul that the pleasure, when it came, was an ecstasy so sublime, so limitless, that they each wept aloud as the fiery solace exploded between them.

They drifted back to a reality swirled with heat. Sweat tickled her scalp and trickled between her breasts, dripping onto the slick skin of his bare chest, which rose and fell with apparent pain. Throwing her hair back over her shoulders, Rachel said, "I've hurt you."

He gave a weak but pleased smile and said, "No."

Reluctant to leave, enjoying still the feel of him inside her, she sat back on his loins and smiled. "Did I do good?" she asked him.

He laughed quietly in his chest as his tongue came out and touched the end of his mustache. "Y'all did good."

Running her hands over the defined muscles of his chest, then gently up to the bandaged shoulder, Rachel eased from atop him, rolling slowly onto the bed, onto her side. Looking up into his face, she grinned sheepishly at his one lifted brow.

"Why?" he asked then.

Rachel frowned.

"Why do you love me?"

"Must there be a reason?"

"When a woman like you falls in love with a man like me, there must be a reason."

Placing her head on his good shoulder, Rachel shrugged. She'd asked herself that very question time and again these many days. Why, when before the occupation half the men in New Orleans had attempted to woo her? Why, when a man like Martin Stillwell had offered her a chance at the home she'd always dreamed of sharing? Why had her heart remained her own until Davis?

"Because you need me," she confessed, "as much as I need you."

"Do I?" The query was soft, almost sleepy with contentment.

Lifting her head, she blinked slowly, feeling the corners of her mouth curl up in a knowing smile. "Let's just say I'm a very good judge of character, Mr. Davis. Shall I continue calling you Davis? I'd much prefer Tomas." When he didn't respond, she went on, "I saw the man you really are, or could be if you allowed yourself."

A murmur of voices below their room brought Rachel's shoulders up. Propped on one outstretched arm, she listened to the low buzz of activity from the cantina. There had been something so familiar . . . It was gone now; the silence hummed with expectation.

Looking back at Davis, she said, "Do you think you'll be able to travel soon? We'll have to leave here as soon as possible. I thought, if we had the money, perhaps we could go to the gulf. Perhaps we could catch a ship, maybe to South America?"

He shook his head no. The pain was back, drumming through his shoulder and chest. "There isn't any need to run, Rachel. I should have explained to you sooner—"

A knock at the door interrupted. Concepción called, "*Señorita!* Come quickly!"

Pulling on her clothes and closing the bedroom door behind her, Rachel met the Mexican woman in the hall.

Her dark face creased with worry, Concepción looked nervously back down the hall before explaining, "There were several men here looking for you and Davis."

Rachel's heart stopped. "Was a Texas Ranger among them?"

"*Sí, señorita.* A short man with gray hair. He had a badge here." She thumbed her breast. "The other was tall and dark—"

"Where are they now?"

"I told them we had not seen any such people. When they requested a room for the night, I told them none were available."

Smiling her gratitude, Rachel reentered the room. Davis opened his eyes as she rushed to collect his saddlebags from the floor. "We have to leave," she told him. The leather bags clutched to her stomach, she turned her frightened eyes on him and said, "Sam has arrived."

"He took his good sweet time." He laid his head back on the bed.

She stared at Davis in disbelief, shocked by his apparent complacency. "Perhaps you didn't hear me correctly. Sam is here. He's come to take you to El Paso!"

His heavy browed eyes, their startling blue containing a definite degree of warmth and unmistakable humor, trained on her. "Rachel, love, if you'll let me—"

"I've been thinking." Fear scattered through her senses, Rachel began gathering up his clothes, throwing his breeches onto the bed while eyeing the bullet-riddled shirt she'd washed but forgotten to mend. "I've been thinking," she repeated, sensing he was about to argue with her. "If you turned yourself in to Sam and *did* go to El Paso, they might reconsider hanging you, but there is always prison. They could put you there for years.

"Rachel."

"I've planned it all out, you see. While you were unconscious. We can't do *anything* without money. Oh, there is Martin's money you stole, but I'm certain you will want to return that. Of course you do. You don't want that on your conscience now that you've set everything right with God. And I couldn't spend one dollar of it knowing . . . well . . . Anyway, I thought of Audra. And my uncle. He's very wealthy, you see, and perhaps Audra would loan us the money. She might, you know. She was so anxious to marry me off and get rid of me for good. And if I assured her we were going someplace far away—"

"You're rambling again, Rachel." Davis laughed.

How could he lie there and look for all the world as if nothing were wrong? Moistening her lips, she carried on. "My uncle is very wealthy. I'm certain Audra could convince him. He has the largest ranch outside of San Antonio. Perhaps you've heard of it? Las Moras Ranch outside San Felipe Springs? Certainly you've heard of A.J. Duncan?"

Davis didn't blink. "Duncan."

"A.J. Duncan. You've heard the name?"

Closing his eyes, Davis covered his face with his hands and thought, *My God. Oh my God.*

Chapter 17

A.J. Duncan. Of all the damn bad luck.

Leaning against the wall for support, Davis looked back through the shadows at the brightly lit cantina across the street. He could see Sam leaning against the bar, his bowed legs looking like wishbones and his head covered with the straw sombrero. Sam turned and spoke to someone beside him. Davis couldn't tell who. The stranger's back was to him.

Pushing from the wall, Davis moved further into the night-black alley. The pain shot crucifyingly through his shoulders and chest, and for the third time since he and Rachel had sneaked down the back stairs and away from the hotel above the cantina, he stumbled.

Going down on one knee, he stared at the ground and damned the fate that had forced him to make a choice between his love for Rachel and the obligations that had continually come back to haunt him throughout this ordeal. He should never have agreed to return to Texas. He'd been pushing his luck too far and, by the looks of things, his luck had just about run out. What made it worse was Rachel's involvement. He'd taken an innocent, well-bred young lady and turned her into a little hellion who was willing to give up everything for a man whom the rest of the world saw only as a savage, a reprobate—an outlaw. He'd hurt her in the most despicable ways and now, because her uncle was A.J. Duncan, he would hurt her again. God help him, but he would hurt her again, and this time she just might not forgive him.

Rachel dropped the reins of the horses and ran to his side.

Going down on her knees, she slid her arms gently around his shoulders. "You're too weak. Please, forget what I said about going to see Audra. The idea was irrational. I'm certain you would have a fair trial—"

"No." Shoving her away, he managed to stand. Still, she walked with him to their horses and helped him to mount. Unable to sit straight, he bowed over the saddle horn, his face in the animal's mane as Rachel mounted and rode up beside him.

"What do I do now?" came her small voice in the darkness. There was no denying the fear he heard, the confusion.

"Head east." That's all he could say.

They did, traveling throughout the night.

Near dawn Rachel moved their animals into a copse of mesquite trees. The lair was hot, but it would offer them respite from the sun and enough shade so they might be allowed to sleep. She watched silently as Davis went to the ground with a groan of relief. Turning his back to her, he fell immediately into an exhausted sleep.

Something was wrong. Terribly wrong. And it had happened the moment she'd mentioned Duncan's name. Davis had changed. The man who, only moments before, had been worshipping her with his eyes had turned back into the man who could ravage her heart with a slice of his tongue. He'd turned back into the cold, bitter renegade he'd been before Clyde's bullet had taken him virtually to death's door, before his confession to the priest had brought him solace from his inner turmoil.

Lying down beside him, she stared up at the twisted, tangled tree limbs overhead, watched as the cool morning breeze trembled the tiny leaves and beanpod seed husks so they rattled. What had become of Rachel Gregory? The girl who blushed at the mere suggestion of sex or the occasional risqué jest? Looking over at Davis, she lightly touched his arm. *You're what happened,* she thought. For better or worse she'd fallen in love with Davis the moment he'd informed her that Africa was just east of Atlanta. And he loved her, too.

She was certain of it. Somehow this would all work out. It had to.

They slept several hours before beginning their journey again. Rachel did her best to concentrate on the countryside and not on her dread of facing Audra. Her only hope was that her stepmother's desire to be rid of her would outweigh her hate. Still, as they crossed the Rio Grande and reentered Texas her nervousness grew. How she regretted ever having mentioned such a scheme to Davis! And why, she wondered, was he so obsessed with the idea of seeing her uncle?

Rachel and Davis reached Las Moras Ranch just after noon the next day. They were greeted by armed watchmen who questioned them thoroughly before obtaining permission from Duncan to allow them to enter the ranch's boundaries. As they approached the hacienda, Rachel noticed the guards standing attentively at every corner of the house. She was reminded of Rancho de Bejar, but even Bejar had not been so heavily guarded.

They were escorted into the house, into a library, and left alone together. For another hour they waited in silence. Rachel didn't bother trying to talk with Davis. He sat in his chair, stony and uncommunicative. She told herself it was the pain in his shoulder that made his face look so dark and dangerous. Perhaps his pride was wounded because he was being forced to ask for financial help.

When Audra and her brother entered the room, Rachel, in a flood of regret, decided she would rather face starvation than ask her stepmother for help. But she'd come this far . . .

Audra Gregory perched on the arm of her brother's chair, her teal skirts spilling toward the floor in layers of silk and lace and crinoline. Turning her eyes once across the room, she looked back at Rachel and Davis and smirked. "So here you are, Rachel. Again. I suspected you were probably dead by now."

Rachel clutched her soiled skirt in her fists and swallowed. She cast a glance at Duncan before responding. "I am not dead, as you can see. Are you too disappointed, Audra?"

"Nonsense. I'm quite relieved actually. We both are. Aren't we, A.J.?"

Rachel's eyes shifted back to Duncan again. His wavy brown hair was brushed straight back from his face. His complexion was pale, his features almost delicate. His long-lashed brown eyes moved over her, from the top of her braided hair to the toes of her scuffed kid slippers. He looked at her the way Davis had looked at her a time or two. But Davis's perusal hadn't made her skin crawl.

"Immensely," he finally responded. Smiling at Davis, he added, "Will you excuse us, ladies? I'd like to speak to Mr. Davis alone."

Rachel looked down at Davis. Slumped slightly in the chair, his face emotionless, he returned Duncan's appraisal. His remoteness troubled her again, but she couldn't dwell on it now. Turning, she swept from the room.

"It seems Mr. Davis has brought you down a notch or two," came Audra's voice behind her. "You look like a scurvy little street urchin, Rachel."

Whirling, Rachel met her stepmother's amused eyes, her own flashing in defiance. "I didn't come here to spar with you, Audra. I came to ask for your help."

"My help? Well, well, well, I never thought I'd see the day you would lower yourself to ask for that. What do you want, pray tell, from me?"

"Money."

Audra's thin brows shot up, and she laughed. "Money? From me?" Throwing her head back, she laughed again, sounding so vulgarly brassy that Rachel longed to slap her. "So," Audra continued, "the belle of New Orleans has been lowered to begging for money. And from me, of all people. The beautiful and wealthy daughter of James Gregory has gotten her comeuppance. God, how I love it!"

Rachel searched her stepmother's face, as she had so many times before, wanting to understand the reasons why the woman disliked her. "Why, Audra? Why have you always hated me? You have hated me since the very moment my father brought you home as his wife."

"Spoiled little rich girl," Audra responded. Her red lips pulled back in an ugly sneer, she slinked at Rachel so stealthily that Rachel was forced, out of fear for her safety, to back slowly toward the foyer. "You made me sick with your frilly little bonnets and prim white cotton gloves. Nothing was too good for Rachel Gregory. Now you come crawling to me for handouts when, if the shoe was on the other foot, you would spit in my face and leave me to starve in some New Orleans back alley."

"But that's not true. I—I always *wanted* to like you. I just never understood—you wouldn't let me."

The tears came, burning her wind- and sun-blistered cheeks. God, where was her pride? How could she ever have believed that Audra could be convinced to help them? Well, she wouldn't go through with it. She wouldn't submit to Audra's innuendos and insults any longer. They would make it without her, without her brother's money or help. They'd made it this far.

Rachel ran back toward the room where she'd left Davis. She'd convince him to come away with her now, before she bartered his pride as well. He had so little pride left as it was . . .

She stopped at the door. Davis rolled a cigar between his lips as A.J. Duncan, his ruby cufflinks winking in the sunlight through the window, closed the floor safe, walked to the desk, and began counting out currency onto it.

"One thousand dollars, Mr. Davis. I assume that's adequate reward for returning my stepniece to us unharmed?"

Reward. Rachel stared in disbelief and horror at the money fluttering onto the desktop. The sudden realization of Davis's plan ripped like a dull-edged knife through her heart. She staggered from the impact. She couldn't swallow or breathe. She could only stare at the man she'd been foolish enough to love—despite everything he'd put her through—and yearn for the first time in her life to commit murder.

Sitting stiffly in his chair, Davis shifted his eyes up to hers, blew a long stream of smoke into the air, and said, "That'll do me just fine, Mr. Duncan. Just fine."

Davis rose from his chair as Rachel came at him. He caught her wrists as she screamed, "Bastard! How dare you! How could you! Money is all you wanted from me, isn't it! Lying, thieving, murdering . . . animal!" Satisfaction sliced through her breast as hot temper flashed in his eyes. "I hope Sam Wells finds you, Davis, and hangs you from the nearest tree!"

"Temper, temper, Miss Gregory, is that any way for a *lady* to talk?"

She would have slapped his face, but he held on to her uplifted wrists and twisted so she fell against him. His dark head lowering over hers, he said very quietly, almost casually, "You were worth every penny of it, sweetheart."

Wrenching her arm free, she backed away. "I—I will never forgive you for this." A flash of some emotion came and went in his azure eyes. Was it regret? Certainly not. Not even love. *Silly simpering little fool, Rachel. Certainly not love.*

Spinning, dodging Duncan's arms as he attempted to grab her, she ran from the room. Behind her Duncan barked out orders in Spanish and men appeared from behind closed doors up and down the corridor and at the top of the stairs. Reaching the foyer, Rachel flung open the front door and ran for her horse.

A horrifying, unreasoning terror seized her as she mounted. She would never escape! But before Duncan's guards could foil her attempt completely, she dug her heels into the animal. Her soiled and ragged skirt flapping against the horse's sweating, heaving sides, she bent over the animal's neck as it flew into the wind. One thought burned through her mind. This had been his plan all along. He had allowed Clyde to take her hostage knowing someone would be willing to ransom her. It just so happened that her uncle was one of the wealthiest men in Texas; how could Davis pass up the opportunity to get his hands on that much money? Dear God, how could she have forgotten what sort of man Kid Davis was?

She rode with a blinding, desperate fury back the way she and Davis had traveled the last two days, unaware, until the steely arm wrapped around her waist, that a man had ridden up beside her. Lifted from her horse, she was smacked down across the man's thighs, the saddle horn digging painfully into her ribs so she could hardly breathe.

Her hair tumbling nearly to the ground, Rachel screamed, "Let me go! You have no right to treat me like this! You cannot keep me here against my will!"

The stranger laughed and turned his horse back to the ranch.

Davis stood by the window, looking out over the landscape outside the ranch gardens. Sheep moved in herds about the bushes, many balancing on their back legs to better reach the woody stalks of the mesquite trees. He heard the front door open, heard Rachel's fighting and cursing and Duncan's directives:

"Take her to her room, Richard, and see she stays there until I tell you otherwise." Then Duncan entered the room behind him. "Audra was right. The young woman *is* a bit difficult to handle. I'm certain, once she comes to her senses, however, she'll realize Las Moras Ranch is the most suitable place for her. Please, Mr. Davis, sit down and relax. Your injury must be grieving you terribly. Would you like a drink?"

"Thank you." Turning back to the chair, he dropped slowly and carefully into it. It wasn't the wound in his shoulder that was grieving him at that moment . . .

He heard Rachel cry out again. He looked toward the door.

"The help will give her something to calm her down. Women can be so hysterical at times." After pouring them each a whiskey, Duncan relaxed back in his chair, tapped his ruby-ringed fingers on the desk, and smiled. "So, Mr. Davis, Pete tells me you are quite extraordinary with a gun."

"Did he?" He stared at the coal of his cigar. "I'm surprised to hear he managed to crawl his way home to you, Mr. Duncan."

"He'll never use that arm again, at least not for gunning."

Davis's lashes lowered. "What a shame."

The drumming of Duncan's fingers stopped. Blunt and white and soft, they spread slightly on the desk. "What happened to Clyde and Pedro?"

"Dead."

"Both of them?"

He looked up again, staring through the curl of blue-gray smoke rising toward the ceiling. "Both of them."

"How?"

"I killed them. A bullet between Clyde's eyes and one through Pedro's throat. If you'd like further proof—"

"Not necessary." Propping his elbows on his chair arms, A.J. said pointedly, "You killed one of the best, Davis. Clyde was a damn good gunman."

"Not good enough, Mr. Duncan." He stretched his long legs out and crossed them at the ankles.

"I could use a man like you around here, Davis. What did Clyde tell you about my operation?"

Accepting another glass of Duncan's whiskey, Davis responded, "Not much. Mentioned something about your stealing cows for Juan Cortinas and driving them across the border." Crossing his ankle over his other knee, he said, "I don't care much for rustling cows, Mr. Duncan."

"No, you don't look like the kind of man who would, Mr. Davis. There are other positions in my organization, however. You seem to have a good head on your shoulders; a man like you could go places—in time. *After* I've come to know you better, to *trust* your logic and judgment."

Duncan left his chair. The stiff ruffles down the front of his shirt and around his cuffs making him look like a French popinjay, he strode with shoulders back about the room, stopping at the ornately carved rosewood piano before the farthest window.

"Do you like my home, Mr. Davis?" A weak smile curling his full lips, Duncan smoothed back an errant lock of hair from off his brow as he waited for Davis's response.

It was a moment in coming. He felt tired suddenly. The cigar was making him slightly queasy and the ache through his shoulder and chest was becoming more unbearable by the minute. The dressings needed changing. Somehow, the night before, the tender wound had broken open and begun to bleed.

Crushing the cigar into a red porcelain ashtray on the desk, he admitted, "It's different."

"Different? How do you mean different?"

The man's voice had risen an octave. Looking around, Davis grinned. "Sorry if I offended you. I'm just not used to so much . . ." He searched his mind for a word.

"*Objets d'art?*"

"Is that anything like *stuff*?"

Duncan lifted his square chin and, with a flourish, swept both hands about the room. "Mr. Davis, there isn't an article of 'stuff' in this entire mansion. It has been purchased from the finest shops in New York, London, and Paris. Take this print, for instance." He pointed to the long, narrow painting adorning the wall between two windows. "This is an original Japanese painting in watercolor by Hokusai Katsushika."

Davis looked at the painting of two Chinese, one astride a horse and another dressed in something that looked like goat hair, their conical hats covered in snow. "I'm impressed," he said flatly.

"They are worth thousands since Katsushika is now deceased."

"Hm."

"My agent found it in a very elite little shop in Paris."

"Lucky for you, I guess."

A knock came at the door. A stranger entered the room, a rangy fellow with shifty eyes, Davis noted. He also noted the gun on the man's hip, slung almost as low as his own.

"Richard, have you seen our young lady upstairs?" Duncan asked.

"I did, boss. She's a hellcat, for sure. Near bit off my thumb." Crossing his beefy arms over his chest, his eyes never leaving Davis, Richard added, "She's sure changed since New Orleans. The girl I used to see sashaying up and down the Vieux Carré would've fainted dead away at the mere thought of sitting astride a horse."

Taking up his whiskey, Davis asked, "You knew the lady in New Orleans?"

Duncan stepped forward before Richard could respond. "Mr. Davis, this is Richard Delaney. My personal body-guard."

Davis turned the glass up to his mouth. He didn't stand.

Delaney's eyes narrowed. "Ain't we met, Davis?"

He shook his head. "Never been to New Orleans."

"I ain't thinking it's New Orleans. Someplace else maybe?"

Closing his eyes, Davis trained his mind on the silence outside the room. What, he wondered, had they done with her?

Slapping Richard on the back, A.J. laughed. "Richard is always the careful one when it comes to my safety. But then, I pay him handsomely for his loyalty. I pay all my followers handsomely, Mr. Davis, as you will learn if you decide to join our organization. In turn my people are faithful to me. Peons who live along the river, as well as those who live here in my home, have come to revere me for my generosity."

Looking about the cluttered interior of the room, Davis ventured, "Seems rustling cows has paid off handsomely for you, Mr. Duncan."

"Rustling cattle is only a pastime, Davis. My fortune, of course, was made elsewhere."

"And that was . . ."

Duncan and Richard exchanged glances before A.J. responded. "It is that aspect of my operation that I would like to discuss with you in great depth. But later. Now you must rest. I have a doctor on the premises. He'll see to your injury, of course. We can't have that arm going stiff on us, can we?" His eyes shifted appreciatively to the gun on Davis's hip.

Davis tossed back his drink and got up.

"Richard will see you to your quarters. I trust you'll find them comfortable."

Davis glanced toward the floor safe one last time before walking with Richard down the corridor. He noted each closed door, niche, and corner along the way. There was a window at the end of the hallway.

Pausing at the foot of the steep staircase, he looked up at the landing and asked, "What's going to happen to the girl?"

Delaney ignored his question. "You sure we ain't met, Davis? You look awful familiar."

Davis followed Richard out the door, shifting his hat lower over his eyes. The sun beat white-hot on his shoulders as they moved toward the line of barracks in the distance.

Richard unlocked one of the many similar doors running the length of the building and shoved it open. "You'll have your own quarters; Duncan believes a man needs his privacy." Smirking a little, he said, "There's women on the premises, if you get my meaning. I suspect you'll be wanting your rest first, though."

Davis closed the door in his face.

Leaning against the door, he waited, listening to Delaney's footsteps as he returned to the hacienda. Then, taking off his hat, he flung it to the far side of the room. He dropped onto the bed, cradling his right arm with his left, and stared at the ceiling. He felt sick, and it had nothing to do with the Havana cigar or the whiskey or the heat or the fever.

He saw her eyes again, wide and wounded, more wounded than angry. He heard the words, *I will never forgive you for this,* over and over until he gripped his head between the heels of his palms and swore aloud in the sparsely furnished cubicle of a room. He cupped his hands over his ears in hopes he could somehow blot out the sound, but it drummed still, over and over through his head, *I'll never forgive you!*

He deserved no less. He'd made his choice. Reparation before love. Before *her* it had never seemed important. Before *her* he'd never felt it, the love. But he knew it now, and the loss of it hurt worse than the throbbing wound in his shoulder. It ran deeper, and would never leave him.

What, he thought, would he do without her?

"I won't!" Rachel shouted. "I won't appear at dinner in that dress or any dress for that matter! You may tell my stepmother and her brother that they can both go to hell!" She flung the bundle of gold silk at the *doncella*'s feet before shouting, "Get out!"

The girl fled the room.

Just then Audra rounded the door with a man on her arm—the same man who had plucked Rachel from her horse the day before.

"Really, Rachel, you're showing the entire household what a little termagant you can be. Do hold down your voice."

"I have been locked in this room for over twenty-four hours, Audra. I want out."

"Of course you do, but first I'd like you to meet a friend of mine. Perhaps you'll recall the name? Richard Delaney?"

Rachel stiffened at the introduction.

Audra explained while smiling sensually at Delaney. "When that dreadful war broke out in New Orleans, I suggested that Richard come here. My brother had just settled at San Felipe Springs and needed all the help he could get. I knew, in time, we would be together again."

Rachel backed away and turned to the window.

Davis was walking toward the house.

The pain of seeing him again washed over her in a flood of soul-shattering misery. Struggling against the need to press her face against the glass and weep his name, she heard Audra go on behind her:

"You will join us for dinner tonight, Rachel. A.J. wishes to get to know you better. Mr. Davis will be joining us as well."

In that moment Davis looked up. Their eyes met. Seeing the almost cruel slant of his mouth as he smiled, Rachel narrowed her eyes and responded, "I'll be there. I wouldn't miss it for the world, dear stepmama."

Their eyes clashed as Rachel accepted her third glass of wine. She noted Davis had not touched his.

"Mr. Davis has accepted my offer of employment," A.J. announced.

Cutting her narrowed eyes to Duncan's, she lifted the glass

in salute and offered silkily, "I'm not the least surprised. I would not, however, sit with my back to any windows, Mr. Duncan."

His full mouth parting in a smile, A.J. opened both hands and pointed out, "It would behoove you both to put your differences behind you. You will be living and working in close proximity, you know. I realize what went on between you was unfortunate, to say the least, but it is best forgotten. *Completely* forgotten."

Rachel placed her wineglass aside and said, "You're absolutely right. We live and learn from our mistakes. I've lived to learn that I am *not* a very good judge of character."

She looked down as A.J. covered her hand with his. It was as cold and clammy as a fish and looked repulsive against her own.

Glancing at Davis from under her lashes, she noted his eyes were on Duncan's hand as well. A tic played noticeably at his jaw.

That acknowledgment confused her. Unsettled her. She hated him for what he'd done, so why did that slight hint of jealousy thrill her so? Steeling herself against her own emotions, she feigned her most attractive and flirtatious smile for Duncan and pretended not to notice that Davis's face had gone dark.

At Audra's side, Richard spoke to Davis then, breaking the tension. "I can't shake this feeling we've met, Kid."

"We haven't," he responded. His eyes still on Duncan's hand, he shifted in his chair. Rachel noted that he kept his right arm tucked closely against his side. He appeared detached from the conversation. He ate little, drank nothing, and between the second and third courses, excused himself from the table and left the house completely.

She longed to go after him, to curse him for betraying her love. But most of all she longed to—

"I ain't so sure he's to be trusted, boss." Richard, a knife in one hand, a fork in the other, glowered at A.J. across the table. "I'm telling you, I've seen that man before. I keep thinking Pennsylvania in sixty-one."

Rachel looked over the rim of her wineglass at Delaney. Pennsylvania?

"Darling, you never mentioned having been to Pennsylvania." Audra smiled before lifting the glass of bloodred wine to her mouth.

"It was after Lincoln's election as President. I happened to be passin' through Harrisburg in February as he was traveling by train to Washington to be inaugurated. He'd been making stops to speak to the people along the way, but there was some problem in Harrisburg. An assassination plot was uncovered. There were security men swarming all over the train depot, and Mr. Lincoln, too. The train pulled out of Harrisburg and didn't stop again until it reached Washington."

Rachel placed her glass carefully onto the table. "Are you saying, Mr. Delaney, that an attempt was made on Mr. Lincoln's life at that time?"

"No attempt. The plot was foiled before anything could happen. I understand there were a few men commended for heroism." Popping a slice of mutton into his mouth, he stared into his plate in deep concentration before mumbling, "I figure I've got that old newspaper somewhere in my trunks. The entire North was buzzing with the news about the plot. Damn, but I can't shake the feeling that's where I saw Davis."

Duncan appeared thoughtful. "Perhaps I'll have Quint ride into Brackettville and do a little investigating at the sheriff's office. I'd like to know just what Davis is wanted for. There's bound to be posters. The sheriff himself should know something about him. When will Pete be back?"

Rachel's head snapped around.

"When he's up to it. You told him to take whatever time he needed to mend."

Focusing his brown eyes on Rachel's face, Duncan pursed his lips slightly before saying, "You have cost me a great deal in manpower, my dear. Clyde and Pedro are dead and Pete will be without the use of his arm indefinitely. I fear I'll be forced to use Mr. Davis's services before I feel comfortable in doing so."

Standing unsteadily, Rachel focused her attentions on Audra and asked, "Must I obtain permission to leave the table like a child, or am I free to go when I so desire?"

A.J. responded. "You are free to move about as you wish, my dear. But don't, at any time, leave the ranch without my escort. It could be . . . *dangerous* for you to do so."

As calmly as possible Rachel left the room. Lifting her skirts, she fled to her room.

She lay on her bed until late, when the lights in the distant bunkhouses were doused. Staring at the ceiling, she allowed her mind to play over the last day's events. Clyde and Pete had somehow been involved with A.J. Duncan. What could that mean? It could mean only one thing, she reasoned.

Rolling from the bed, she grabbed up her wrapper.

The halls were dark and cool and quiet. Rachel moved soundlessly down the corridor, descending the stairs as she listened intently for any hint that she might be discovered. Even in darkness the house appeared garish and gaudy, each corner piled high with statues and vases and trinkets from different parts of the world. The house reminded Rachel of an import shop she'd visited several times on Decatur Street in New Orleans. Oriental jade figurines lined intricately carved French sideboards. Delicate English bone china was stacked among Indian pottery.

Even the house itself was a hodgepodge of styles. The exterior was adobe, not unlike the Bastitases' Rancho de Bejar. The insides, however, were a mixture of Italian, English, and Spanish. Thinking of Duncan and his personal appearance—he'd worn a royal-blue velvet jacket with a purple satin waistcoat to dinner—she wasn't surprised that the house was such a mess.

The quiet murmur of voices stopped Rachel as she reached the bottom of the stairs. At the far end of the corridor, in the room where she'd witnessed Davis accepting money for her return, a light shone under the door. After assuring herself that she was alone, she moved down the hall.

Audra dropped into a chair, lifted a glass of champagne in

the air, and declared, "Here is to wealth and power, Albert. May it last forever!"

"Shut up," he snapped. "I have told you repeatedly not to call me Albert. The name is A.J. and don't forget it."

"You may be A.J. Duncan to this bunch of peons, darling, but you're Albert Durham to me. Albert Benjamin Durham III, son of Frances and Albert Durham of Brooklyn, New York. Wouldn't our father be thrilled if he saw you now? We really must see about moving him down here."

"He won't come." Dropping onto the claw-footed piano seat, he plunked at a key before sighing. His shoulders drooped. "I have written him repeatedly. He's ignored my letters."

"Like father like son." Leaving her chair, Audra swept toward the champagne bottle atop the desk. "I'm still angry with you, Albert—"

"A.J., dammit!" He thunked his fist against the piano keys.

She waved his irritation away with a flick of her hand. "I didn't appreciate being stranded in Galveston and San Antonio. Being forced into joining that horrible wagon train was a nightmare."

"It serves you right. What was I to think when I received your letter? You tell me you want me to marry some child so you can get your hands on her inheritance, and assume I am simply going to say, 'Oh, but of course, I have nothing better to do with my life'? After all, you have not been overly complimentary about the young lady in your letters. You made her sound like some insipid little mouse with the charm of a tarantula."

Rachel backed away from the door.

Tipping her glass to her lips, Audra laughed before asking, "What do you think of her now?"

"She's beautiful. A little waspish in her manner, but given time and the proper encouragement, she might come around." Stretching his fingers over the keys, he added more softly, "She *will* come around."

"Then you'll do it? You'll marry her?" Sweeping across the carpeted floor, she leaned over her brother's shoulder and said, "Just think about it. You'll have yourself a luscious little china doll wife, to do with what you will. And when she turns twenty-one, her entire inheritance will go to you, her husband. But you don't need it, so you can give it to me, since I do." Throwing back her dark head, she laughed toward the ceiling and with fists clenched exclaimed, "Damn you, James Gregory, you will rue the day you ever wrote me out of your will."

Rachel whirled and came face to face with Richard. His hands circled her in the darkness, clamping about her arms with crushing force.

"Well now, look who we got snooping around in the dark," he announced aloud to the others. He kicked the door open further so the light from the room poured over Rachel's stunned and frightened features.

She fought him. "Let go of me!"

Audra was the first out of the room. Her eyes wide and her mouth slack from too much champagne, she grabbed a handful of Rachel's hair. "You little sneak! How long have you been standing here?"

"Long enough." She struggled again.

Turning again toward the door, Audra ordered, "Bring her inside, Richard. Perhaps it's time we filled Rachel in on our plans."

Forced into the room, Rachel fixed her eyes on Audra's brother and began squirming against Richard's hold. A.J. swiveled on the piano seat. His white, smooth chest was partially bared by his open satin dressing gown. He let his eyes roam from her head to her feet so lasciviously that her repulsion made her weak-kneed and barely able to stand.

Richard shoved her into a chair and closed the door.

Looking at Audra directly, Rachel assured her, "I'm not interested in your plans. I have no intention of marrying him!" She indicated Duncan, who grinned in response. "And there is nothing you can do to change my mind."

"Certainly there is. I am your legal guardian, after all. All I need do is agree to the betrothal."

"I'll fight you."

"But it would be so much less painful for you if you didn't."
The threat hung in the air.

Rachel sank back in the chair as Audra bent toward her. "Do you think I enjoyed being married to your father? Do you think I married him for love? When I arrived in New Orleans from New York, I had nothing but the clothes on my back. I knew only one way to make money — on my back. But I hated that, all those slobbering old men pawing me. So I vowed upon arriving in New Orleans that things would be different. I'd start with a clean slate, where no one knew me for what I had been."

"So you lied to my father. You told him you were a widow and all the time you were nothing but some cheap —"

Audra slapped her face.

Falling against the back of the chair, Rachel cupped her palm against her cheek. The room swam crazily before she could focus again on Audra's features.

"I was willing enough to spend the rest of my life shackled to your father. Had you not mucked up my life, our marriage might have been tolerable. But, God, how sick I got of you and your fine manners —"

"I'm surprised you even knew I was alive. You were too busy running across town to visit him." Rachel pointed toward Delaney.

A soft knock sounded at the door. Delaney opened it a fraction, and Rachel went rigid at the sound of Davis's voice.

"I was asked here to see Mr. Duncan," he said.

"Let him in," Duncan replied.

Stepping back, Richard swung open the door.

Davis stood in the doorway, filling it, dressed in black, towering over everyone else in the room, an arrested demon power in the form of a man.

Rachel longed to throw herself against him and beat his chest, to scream out her hate, and damn him again for this treason to her heart. But the sight of him in the doorway had come like a blow, winding her and sending her heart into a frantic race with her reason. No matter how she struggled to hate him, those feelings were continually replaced by images of him wrapping his steely arms about her in an embrace, of his fingers twisting into her hair and dragging her head back so he could cover her mouth with his.

He stared at her hard for a moment, his eyes piercing her through. What would happen if she pleaded to him for help? Her stomach heaved at the thought, and she looked away, unable to face him a second longer than necessary. After his deceptions it would be a cold day in hell before she ever *spoke* to Kid Davis again, much less gave him the satisfaction of knowing what kind of position he'd forced her into. Still . . .

"How's the shoulder?" Duncan asked him.

"Sore." He moved slowly into the room, the keen instincts Rachel had grown to know so well these last weeks evident in the way he shifted his eyes about and turned his back from Delaney to the wall. A familiar half smile lifting one corner of his mouth, he added dryly, "I'd be hard pressed to use my gun in any haste. I trust you won't give me a reason to."

Rachel's head came up.

"I have a job for you, Davis." Leaving his bench, A.J. strode casually up behind Rachel's chair. Catching a silver-white tendril of her hair, he rubbed it back and forth between his thumb and forefinger as he contemplated his next words. "Cortinas is expecting a delivery of cattle in four days. A number of my men have been on the job since two evenings ago. I'd like you to join them, if you're capable."

"When?"

"The week's end." Moving around, he eased down onto the chair arm, slid his hand up Rachel's back, to her neck beneath her hair, and gripped her nape so cruelly her head snapped back. Duncan added, "Normally I might join you, but I've wedding plans to take care of. You see"—he looked at Davis and smiled—"Rachel and I are going to be married."

Davis didn't move. He didn't speak. Rachel fixed her eyes on the toes of his dusty boots and wondered why he continued to stand there as immovable as one of Duncan's jade figurines. He should laugh, sneer, drawl out some sarcasm to wound her and underscore the humiliation he had already caused her. But he didn't. He just pinned her with those damnable blue eyes and didn't even blink.

Duncan stood, forcing Rachel to stand as well. "Now, if you will excuse us, my fiancée and I are going upstairs. There are matters that need . . . discussing."

Rachel moved woodenly at his side. She yearned to throw herself from Duncan's bruising grip, but her pride forbade it. Not in front of Davis. She closed her eyes.

Never before Davis!

Chapter 18

Rachel fled to the farthest corner of her room as Duncan closed her bedroom door behind him. She searched frantically for some weapon to use against him. Grabbing a brass candleholder from a table, she raised it above her head.

"Put it down," he said.

She didn't, but struggled to hold back the sick fear that rose up in a suffocating hold around her throat. If he wanted her, a hundred candlesticks wouldn't hold him back.

"Put it down," he repeated.

She slowly opened her fingers, one at a time, until the brass piece thudded on the pine floor.

"Relax," he told her. "I have no intention of forcing myself on you, my dear. At least, not yet. I realize this has all been a great shock. You need time to adjust."

With a quick shake of her head, she countered, "I will never adjust to *that* with *you*."

"It seems you adjusted quite nicely to Davis." His lids heavy, he watched and waited for her response. When she said nothing, he persisted, "He's boasted about you. How he took you inside that *hackal* at Fort Clark."

She turned her head as he stopped before her and drew one pale finger across her face, tracing the blistered imprint of Audra's hand on her cheek. "Such a shame to mar something so breathtakingly beautiful. Should you willingly marry me, I'll see that she doesn't harm you again in any way."

"Never." She shook her head.

"She warned me you would be stubborn. I like that. De-

fiance in a woman makes life so much more interesting."
Closing his fingers onto her chin, he forced her face around
to his. "But I must warn you, my dear, I am a man who eventually takes what he wants. Not unlike Davis. Everything I
own here I have because I took it, in one way or another.
Think of it this way. Everything I have, all of my treasures
from throughout the world, will be partly yours."

"It's all disgustingly vulgar. Just like you. You wouldn't
know a true piece of art if it hit you over the head."

She gasped as his hand dropped to her throat. Closing her
eyes, anticipating that he would crush her windpipe in the
next moment, Rachel attempted to swallow. It wasn't possible. For a moment the world turned dark and tipped crazily
underfoot.

He lifted her to her tiptoes and answered, "I will kill you
if you ever say anything like that again. Remember, *I* do not
need the pittance of an inheritance your father left you. I
have more money than your father would have made in ten
lifetimes on ten of those stinking, mosquito-infested plantations. And I didn't have to break my back to get it."

Rachel gasped for breath as he eased his grip. Pressing up
against the wall, she bit back her response as he slid his hand
inside her wrapper and flexed his fingers over her breast.

He continued, repeating, "I don't need your money. I'm
doing this for my sister, but if I should, at any time, grow
tired of you after we're married you're just as good to us dead
as you are alive. I'd remember that, if I were you." He bent
his head over hers until his tobacco-sour breath filled her
nostrils. "Now, a kiss good-night for your fiancé, Miss
Gregory?"

His thumbs digging into the tender underside of her jaw,
he pressed her face up to his. As he opened his mouth over
hers, Rachel closed her eyes and forced her mind to think of
other things. Still, repulsion shuddered through her body as
coldly as if a sudden blast of winter wind had found its way
into the room.

Indeed, she felt that cold, that numb and dead as he turned
and left the room. She listened to the key grate inside the

lock. As his heavy footfall grew fainter in the distance, she slid down the wall to the floor. Pulling her legs up to her chest, she rested her forehead on her knee and thought of her father. He had once privately mentioned investments that he'd made up north. But when the Yanks had stormed the South, including Belle Hélène, she'd supposed everything had been lost.

Still, he should have anticipated what Audra's reaction would be to his disinheriting his wife. Then again, in more normal circumstances, Rachel realized, she would have already been married and safe from Audra's revenge. Thanks to that damnable war she'd been robbed of husband and father and home. Now there was every possibility that she would be robbed of her life. She didn't trust her stepmother *or* her brother, no matter what Duncan insinuated. As soon as she turned twenty-one, they would kill her. They wouldn't take the chance that she might confide to someone about their plans to rob her of her money.

What, dear God, was she going to do?

She would escape.

But how?

Springing to her feet, she flew to the window. Nailed shut. Damnation! She couldn't break the glass; the racket would bring everyone within hearing distance at a run. Somehow she would have to convince Audra and her brother to release her. But the only chance of that was to convince them that she would willingly go along with their plan. It wouldn't be easy. She'd have to come up with a lie so believable . . .

Staring out the window, at the barracks glowing ghostly white in the moonlight, she vowed to herself that she would find a way.

Davis grabbed for his gun. His hand slid numbly over the butt of the weapon, refusing to respond to his mind's directives. His body was drenched with sweat as he strove to blot out the searing discomfort in his chest and shoulder; he tried again and again until the pain grew too intense to be ignored. Slumping against the fence at his side, he clutched his arm to his chest and damned the recklessness that had made him burst into that room in San Carlos. And he damned the verbal contract he'd made that had brought him back to Texas in the first place. Then he'd never have discovered that his parents *hadn't* been killed in that Indian raid twenty-five years ago. He would never have experienced the joy of seeing them again, or the bittersweet realization that their lives had gone on without him. Alejandro de Bastitas had *other* sons to fill his footsteps, all well-bred and educated. What did the great *patron* need with a son who couldn't read his own name?

And there was Rachel. Tomorrow at noon she would marry Duncan. What was he supposed to do about that?

Rubbing his shoulder, he squinted the sun from his eyes and looked back toward the house. Rachel stood at Duncan's side, the sun spilling over her head and shoulders like a white mantle. She looked abnormally pale in the harsh light, and he wondered, not for the first time, just how agreeable she was to the idea of wedding Duncan. They were both in one big hurry, and the thought occurred to him that there might be a reason for it. At first he'd told himself it was that desire of hers to marry and make a home that prompted her to agree to wed a total stranger; she had, after all, decided to marry Martin Stillwell. But on second consideration he'd remembered that her only reason for doing that was to escape Audra.

Then he'd decided that giving in to Duncan was a case of her cutting off her pretty little nose to spite her face. She wanted to get back at him for what appeared to be cold and calculated treason on his part. Regardless, he'd run out of time. He was to leave tonight to meet Cortinas. But he didn't yet have what he needed from Duncan. The namby-pamby bastard wasn't about to talk, yet. No doubt about it, he was going to have to find some way to get into that house, into that room where Duncan kept his money. Then there was Rachel . . .

He thought of going to her and asking for her help, perhaps explaining to her at last exactly what he was doing, and why. But then he'd be putting her life in danger again, and he told himself again, as he had over these last grueling days, that the less she knew the better. Her fear and distrust of him had to be genuine if he was to see this ruse successfully to the end.

As he walked up the path to the patio, he saw her head turn. The blue-violet eyes grew wide as they met his. Her chin went up, her shoulders squared. Turning her back to him again, she reached for Duncan's arm. But her fingers were shaking. And Davis noted that the back of her neck had begun tinting the same beautiful shade of pink as the *rosas de San Juan* that grew near the path.

His pace slowed as Duncan's arm came up around her waist. When the man turned to face him, he stopped completely.

"Ah, Mr. Davis. I'm glad you're here. Are you up to the journey tonight?"

Rachel turned more slowly.

"I'm ready," he responded.

"Rachel and I were just discussing the plans for our wedding. It will be held here, in the garden. I thought the pink and orchid *rosas* would add festivity to the occasion. A shame you won't be here."

Richard rounded the corner of the house and headed their way. Duncan stepped away only for a moment, but it was long enough for Davis to touch her, just a brush of his fingers over the crisp white linen blouse that made her appear even more fragile than she was.

She shied at the closeness. Her face grew whiter, if that were possible, and her small pink mouth opened in a silent way that, like her eyes, showed her confusion. Never had he been so struck by her beauty. The realization of how close he was to losing her shook him suddenly to his boots.

He thought of a thousand words he longed to say in that instant: *Forgive me; this will all work out; trust me . . . I love you.* He realized, in that moment, that he'd never told her that—*I love you.* So he said it with his eyes. He begged her not to marry Duncan and he beseeched her to forgive him. And, as her eyes grew misty and her cheeks burned like torches, he smiled.

He looked away, as did she, when Duncan turned back to face them. He must have noted she appeared upset. "Is something wrong?" Duncan asked her.

"I'd like to go in," she replied, her voice so small that Davis knew, in that instant, that she wasn't herself.

"Nonsense, darling, we have plans to discuss." Looking up at Davis, Duncan confessed, "She's somewhat nervous. Premarriage jitters, I think. But Audra and I thought that after everything that has happened, it would behoove us to marry as soon as possible."

Davis centered his eyes on a distant herd of ewes and repeated, "Everything that has happened?"

"Certainly. Between the two of you."

Out of the corner of his eye, he saw Rachel tense. Studying the ground between his boots, he then looked back into Duncan's smug face and demanded in so quiet a voice that Rachel backed away, "I don't think I understand."

"Rachel herself has pointed out that there is every possibility that she is with child."

His mouth went dry. Hands on his hips, he asked her, "Are you pregnant, Rachel?"

She didn't respond.

Closing his fingers about Rachel's arm, Duncan smiled at them both. "You will excuse us, Mr. Davis? Oh." Pausing in his turn back toward the house, he looked around and offered, "Before leaving on your journey this evening, stop by the house. I have written you a letter of introduction to Señor Cortinas. He will see you safely hidden and employed in Mexico until the Rangers have grown weary of their search."

Duncan turned and, with Rachel, walked back to the house.

Her knees were shaking. Taking those steps back to the house was one of the hardest things she had ever had to do. She'd had to keep walking and not turn back to look once more into the one face that continued to haunt her dreams.

The one face that, no matter what Davis had done, she longed to touch again. That was a bitter realization. And with a smug sense of satisfaction she knew that the hint of her possible pregnancy had distressed him. He might not give a damn about her, but a baby . . .

Her pace slowed as mentally she again ticked off the days since her last flow. Her heart did a queer little dance as she realized that she was indeed late. That excuse had been the first one that had popped into her head when she'd floundered for a good enough reason that would convince Audra and Duncan that she had totally changed her mind about marrying A.J. Audra, of course, had believed her. Why, a lady would rather die than be shamed into birthing a babe out of wedlock.

As they rounded the corner of the house, she chanced a glance back at Davis. His eyes were on her. Intense. Penetrating. He hadn't moved at all.

Richard met them again, just inside the house. Rachel jumped as Duncan slammed the door behind them and demanded, "What is it now?"

"Quint is back from Brackettville."

Rachel looked down at Duncan's fingers as they bit into her skin. Her arm felt numb. Squeezing her eyes closed, she tried to force Davis's visage from her mind.

"He checked in with the sheriff. There ain't no wanted posters on Davis. The sheriff never even heard the name. And something else. The sheriff's good friends with Marshal Bettinger up in El Paso. He remembers that cantina brawl that killed them folk. But it took place over a year ago."

Audra entered the foyer then. Draped in yards and yards of red china silk, she appeared to have just rolled out of bed.

"Over a year ago," Duncan repeated.

"Yep."

"You're certain of that?"

Delaney nodded. "The sheriff dug out a pile of old posters and found the man who was wanted by Marshal Bettinger for that shooting. His name was Jim Hines. And he was shot by some Ranger just outside Waco two months later."

Slowly the words ebbed into Rachel's own consciousness. Lifting her face, she looked up into Duncan's features. His black eyes were glittering and vicious. "Perhaps the two of us should talk," he said.

"A-about what?" Closing her hand over his fingers, she did her best to pry them from her. The blood in her arm had begun a slow throb beneath his grip.

"Don't play the want-wit with me, my dear." He propelled her down the hall, past the Chinese porcelains of dragons and a stuffed armadillo. She stumbled on her hem as they entered the study, then went down into a chair while Duncan slammed the door closed behind them. She rubbed her arm.

Duncan paced the room before stopping beside her. "Talk," he commanded.

"About what?" She inwardly winced and glanced at his fists.

"About Davis, you lovely little fool. Who else? What do you know about him?"

Those hands were swinging like a pendulum before her face, back and forth. Opening and closing. She measured her words very carefully. "He was being transported to El Paso to stand trial."

"Try again."

"I only know what he told me."

The fist came at her before she could move. She'd been kicked in the chin by a pony once, but even that had not ricocheted through her head with such blinding, excruciating force. She shook her head to clear it of the double images that rounded clockwise before her eyes. Shock turned into pain as blood filled her mouth; she was forced to swallow it.

She flinched and covered her face as he doubled up his hand again. "He must have told you something, my dear. You were going to marry him, after all."

She shook her head.

Going down on one knee before her, he closed the fingers

of both hands on the chair arms and raised both eyebrows in mockery. "There are other ways I can make you talk."

"But I have nothing to say." She pressed her palm against her mouth, feeling blood trickle between her fingers. Closing her eyes, she prayed the nausea would not overcome her. Her head came up then, and her eyes opened as he ran one hand slowly up her leg, under her skirt.

"I've been patient," he threatened. He stared a long moment, then finished, "Very well. We'll simply do it my usual way. As I always say, give a guilty man enough rope and he'll eventually hang himself. Richard!"

The door swung open behind him.

Without turning, without taking his eyes from Rachel, he said, "Do you still distrust Davis?"

"Yep. More'n ever."

"Then have Quint keep a man on him at all times, and when they cross the border . . . kill him."

Realization took root in her subconscious as she slept: the words, the pictures, rolling over and over. He'd not committed that crime. It was someone else a long time ago. A case of mistaken identity. The true culprit had been shot by a Ranger in Waco. Sam. Oh God, Sam, did you know?

Rolling her face into her pillow, she curled her fingers into her palms and beat the bed. "I don't understand. I just don't understand!"

She lifted her face toward the clock on the dresser. How long had she slept? It was six o'clock. They'd given her something. She could taste it now, bitter on the back of her tongue. She glanced at her tea. The powdery white substance, now that the brew had gone cold, covered the tea like a skin.

A knock sounded on the door. The *doncella*'s small voice called out, "*Señorita,* Señor Duncan wishes you to join him in the library."

Hurrying to the door, she listened as the girl's footsteps grew fainter down the hall.

The piano's melodious tune echoed throughout the house

as Rachel moved to the stairs and descended, heading for the rear door of the hacienda. She kept her ears trained on the music. She needed enough time to get to Davis. To warn him not to leave with Quint to meet with Cortinas.

Dear God, he was helpless against them. His arm was still useless—she'd witnessed his attempts to draw that morning—and without his gun . . . She needed time to make her plans. She knew the exact location of the stables because she'd badgered Duncan to show her about his ranch; she had even acquainted herself with a mare by slipping the animal lumps of sugar. No, there would be little problem where the horse was concerned. After dark she would slip out of the house, onto the horse, and—

"Why, look who's here."

Halfway to the stables Rachel stopped dead in her tracks. She turned, stiff and with a pounding heart, to face Delaney. She listened for the music. It was there, still.

"What's the hurry?" he asked her.

Her reasons, excuses, tumbled over themselves in her mind. Shoving her hand into her pocket, she pulled out a fistful of sugar. She met his gaze, unblinking, and lied, "I was going to see the mare."

"The mare, huh?" Thumping his hat back on his head, he grinned. "Thought maybe you were gonna see Davis."

"Davis!" She managed a look of indignation. "Mr. Davis can go to hell."

Delaney threw back his head and laughed. Sauntering a bit closer, he said, "Pete told us you and Davis had turned pretty thick. Like this." He held up two fingers twisted together. "Pete said the night at Fort Clark him and the boys kept waitin' to hear you tussle. Says you musta been pretty willin'."

"Pete said that? I thought Davis—"

"Davis don't say nothin'."

"Well." She took a breath and looked toward the stables, then beyond to the bunkhouse. *I have to get to him*, she thought. *Warn him. Give him one last chance to explain.*

The thought burned her mind, her body, her face. Lifting

one hand, she pressed her palm against her cheek. It felt ice-cold. Ice-cold and wet.

"Rachel."

She spun, tripping backward. Duncan, his bright purple cravat tucked into a rose-pink silk shirt, regarded her coldly.

"What are you doing here?" His brown eyes flicked to her hand.

"I—I have sugar for the mare." She looked down at her palm as the sun glinted off the sugar crystals as if they were snow.

He watched her, waiting for any signs that she might be lying. Smiling then, he said, "Come along and listen to me play."

"But the sugar—"

"Forget it, my dear. Davis has gone."

Davis sat with his back against a rock, watching the light from the campfire play over the men's faces. Quint Jones looked up from behind his coffee cup and said:

"Been admiring that gun on your hip, Davis. Nickel-plated and pearl-handled. Must have put you back a few dollars. Mind me asking where you found it?"

"I don't mind you asking," he responded.

Quint laughed and tossed the cold coffee in the bottom of his cup across the ground. "You're a man of few words, Davis."

"Habit."

The man squatting beside Quint stood up and walked over to the horses. Davis followed him with his eyes before looking back at Quint. "So where's Cortinas?"

"He'll be here. Probably at dawn." Quint stretched his legs, then shifted his gun on his hip.

Davis lifted one brow, noting that the man's eyes flicked toward his gun. He looked at Jones in a way that asked, *Did you expect me to go for it?*

Quint backed away, then giving his bedroll a nudge with his foot he said, "Heard you were pretty good with that gun. You killed a friend of mine . . . Clyde Lindsey."

"There's no accounting for taste, I guess."

Quint's head came around. He didn't respond to the gibe, but dropped down onto the bedroll. "Guess I'll get some shuteye. Cortinas'll expect us to drive them cows as far as Villaldama before we sleep again." Laying his head back on his saddle, he adjusted his sombrero low over his eyes and took a deep breath before, by all appearances, drifting off into a deep sleep.

The night closed in, black and starless.

Davis didn't move, but fixed his eyes on the watchman in the shadows, only occasionally letting them drift back to the sleeping man on the blankets. The longhorn, driven into the canyon just below them, shifted about the rocky enclosure, agitated by the smell of water from the nearby river. A coyote yapped, and somewhere a cougar let out a yowl that brought a bawling response from the cattle.

Rolling to his side, Davis pulled his saddle blanket up to his chin, covered his face with his hat, and closed his eyes.

He didn't expect the move to come so quickly. The watchman walked quietly from the shadows, kicked Quint in the side, and both went for their guns. Before they cleared leather, Davis rolled, pivoted the gun from beneath the blanket, and fired two shots so quickly the explosion melded to one as it tumbled over the canyon. He caught Quint in the shoulder, driving him backward across the saddle. Stepping over the other man's body, he looked down into Quint's pain-crazed eyes and grinned.

"I'm a little disappointed in you, Quint," he said. "I thought Duncan didn't hire amateurs."

He clutched his shoulder. "Go to hell, Davis."

"Now, is that any way to talk to a man who's holding a gun to your head?" He cocked the hammer back, poised his gun against Quint's temple, and asked, "Still like my gun, Jones?"

Weakly, he looked at Davis and asked, "Who are you?"

Standing, Davis released the hammer on his gun and slid the weapon back in his holster. "Wouldn't you like to know," he responded.

* * *

"Really, my dear, you could try to look a little happier. This is your wedding day, after all." Rachel stared straight ahead as Audra walked around her. "I'll have to admit the gown is not very traditional. But there is little about my brother that *is* traditional. His tastes have a tendency to run toward the exotic." Pausing by the bed, Audra touched a cold finger to Rachel's white cheek. "I'll bet you're still pining away for that outlaw. Really, my dear, you're wasting your time, considering he turned you over for money. Oh well, he's dead by now anyway. It's a shame really, a man like that. I could see real promise there."

"Is *seeing* all you did with Davis, Audra?"

Audra looked around. "Are you asking me if I seduced him? Why, my little soiled dove, I do believe you're blushing. Well, take heart, I never quite managed it. There! Consider that your wedding present. I didn't fornicate with your boyfriend. Does that make you feel better? Yes? Then smile, darling, you have a groom waiting!" Audra turned and, with a flourish, left the room.

Rachel stared at the floor, at the folds of red silk around her feet, and searched inwardly for the strength to make the march to the patio. The heavy Oriental robes burdened her shoulders and made her sweat. Her head ached.

The burning inside her had numbed near dawn. She'd gone through the motions of eating breakfast, bathing and dressing for the wedding. The fight was gone because Davis was dead. Escape from Audra and her brother just didn't matter any longer. She turned for the door.

Davis peered carefully through the open window before hefting himself onto the windowsill and swinging his feet inside the house. He made his way to the library, closed the door quietly behind him, then moved swiftly to the safe against the wall. He went to his knees and began inching the tumbler right and left. Click, click, click. How easy. How damnably easy. If all safes were this easy to unlock, he wouldn't be in such a quandary now.

The safe door swung open. He stared at the currency before reaching for it. The bill shook in his fingers as he withdrew a piece of paper from the pocket inside his shirt. Quickly unfolding it, he glanced toward the door, listening to the low conversations of the people on the patio. Dammit, he was running out of time!

He scanned the numbers, matching them to those on the currency. Nothing. Nothing! Then . . . He grinned. Shoving the money back into the safe, he grabbed up the notes to one side, opened them up and thought, *Fool! Duncan, you're a fool to keep this kind of evidence around!*

Throwing the notes back into the safe, he quietly closed it, gave the tumbler a twist, then moved to the door, into the hallway, and down the corridor.

Standing to one side of the foyer, he stared up the staircase at the form that sat on one stair, draped in yards and yards of red silk, her head on her knees so her moonlight-pale hair cascaded over her legs to her feet. Her shoulders were shaking. One hand, as delicate and white as china, lay palm up on the step beside her.

He moved slowly, forgetting caution—his only concern, Rachel. He would end it now. Or try to. Explain it all and let her make her choice. He wouldn't pressure her or make excuses. He'd done what he had to do.

"Rachel."

Her head came up slowly. She stared at him, disbelieving, her eyes wide and full of tears. "Oh." Her lips formed a circle. "Oh."

Before he could manage another word, she was up and off the step and against him, her arms thrown open wide, then wrapped around his neck. He stumbled back two stairs before catching the banister with his left hand. Burying her face in his throat, so he felt the hot spill of her tears down his neck, she cried:

"You're not dead! You're not dead at all!!" Her head fell back as a smile crossed his features. "They told me—"

"Forget what they told you, *querida,* unless you wish to continue this conversation here on these steps. In that case I can almost guarantee that the news of my death will not be so highly exaggerated next time."

Rachel pulled away. Her fingers touched his face, the black wave of hair over his ear, his injured shoulder, detecting the bandage beneath his shirt. Real, all real. He was alive and everything they'd told her had been only lies meant to confuse her, to dispirit and hurt her.

"You're going to come with me now," he told her. "I have two horses out front." Catching her face in his fingers, he forced her to look at him directly and added, "You're going to get on one of those horses and ride. You will not, for any reason, stop or turn back—"

"No!" Rachel closed her eyes, swallowed back the fear that made her voice grow urgent and hoarse. "I won't leave without you—"

He shook her. "Dammit, girl, we've been through this before—"

"And we'll go through it a thousand times more! I'm not going anywhere without you. I know you love me or you wouldn't have come back for me. Why do you continue to deny it?"

"I haven't denied it." His fingers closed into her arms, dug into her skin as he lifted Rachel, almost to her toes, and said, "I never denied that I loved you."

"Then tell me. I won't go until you tell me."

He touched her face, spread his fingers over her cheek while his mouth hovered against her lips. "I love you," he whispered.

"Well, well, now ain't this cozy."

Davis stiffened. Before Rachel could move he pushed her away, lifted his hands from his gun while slowly turning to face Delaney.

Delaney threw a look at the man beside him and said, "Go git Duncan. Tell 'im to git to the library *pronto!*" Looking back at Davis, he motioned with his gun and ordered, "After you, Mr. Davis."

Rachel's arm was caught by Davis. He moved her down the stairs, offering her support, keeping his own body between hers and Delaney's at all times. Delaney carefully reached for Davis's gun and trained it as well on their backs as they made the long walk down the corridor to the library. Several times she chanced a look up at Davis. His face was expressionless, but his eyes—they were burning. Not with fear or desperation, but with anger.

They'd just reached the library when Duncan entered behind them. He stopped in the doorway, his eyes pinning first Davis, then Rachel.

"Found 'em on the stairs together," Delaney said. "Made a real sweet scene, they did."

Squaring his shoulders, Duncan met Davis's blue eyes and demanded, "What have you done with my men this time, Mr. Davis?"

"What do you think?" he responded, his voice caustic. "The next time you send the hired help out to do an assassin's job, make certain they're up to it. Putting them down was too pitifully easy, even with this arm."

"What in damnation do you want from me, Davis, and who are you?" Duncan's hands clenched in frustration.

Delaney stepped forward then, his eyes narrowed and his gun pointed at Davis's heart. "I can tell you exactly who he is, boss. It come to me the minute I seen him standin' there on them steps. It all come back to me as clear as a bell, where I seen him before."

Silence filled the room. Rachel stared at Delaney, wondering how he had learned that Kid Davis was actually Tomas de Bastitas, and why the fact would fill Audra's brother with such obvious dread, and Delaney with such anger.

A smirk pulling at one corner of Delaney's mouth, he shot his employer a knowing look before pulling the hammer back on the gun and leveling it between Davis's ice-blue eyes.

"No!" Rachel threw herself at Delaney, made a desperate grab for his gun, afraid he would fire it. He knocked her aside with little effort, catching her jaw with his elbow, sending her spinning to the floor in a puddle of crimson silk.

Davis moved, and the gun came up again. "Don't," Delaney ordered. Looking down at Rachel, he laughed. "If I's you, sweetheart, I wouldn't be so eager to get myself killed over a man who's used you to get at Duncan. That's all he wanted, you see, was to get in the house and get what evidence he needed to hang you, boss."

"Hang me?"

"That's right." Delaney looked again at A.J. "I remembered where it was I seen him. He was standing at the rail edge of a caboose in Pennsylvania. Right alongside of the President himself. He's a lawman, Mr. Duncan. A Pinkerton detective."

Long, silent moments passed. Rachel stared at Davis, her lips parted, her heart pounding so fiercely she could barely hear anything but the rush of blood in her ears. The realization tumbled in on her, winded her while he stood motionless, his eyes on Duncan, and then on her. And she knew in that moment that it was true. He didn't try to deny it. Just lifted one corner of his mouth in a way she knew only too well.

His face white, his hands shaking, A.J. leaned slightly against his desk. "My God. How did you find me?"

"I didn't." Davis met Duncan's eyes and didn't blink. "John Hopper found you. They've known you were here for some time, but they couldn't get close enough because of all the watchdogs you've placed about the ranch. They decided the only way to get to you, and to the evidence that will eventually hang you, was to get a man into the organization. That's me."

"But how, dammit!"

"Patience, Mr. Duncan. John Hopper has been living in Brackettville, watching your every move for a year, waiting for some weakness in the chain. That weakness turned out to be Clyde Lindsey. When he and Pedro shot that deputy, he offered us the opportunity we'd been waiting for. We hadn't expected it to be so easy." Thumbing toward the safe, he said, "You might've at least burned the bank notes and kept the currency. That's what most people do when they rob banks." Davis grinned and added, "Guess you wanted to keep them around and add them to your collection of . . . *stuff*."

His face sweating and red, Duncan stepped behind his desk and sneered. "Kill him, Richard."

Rachel lunged, catching Richard in the bend of his knees with her shoulder. The air exploded with the gunshot as he tumbled backward; his weight landed atop her as they both fell to the floor in a heap. Rachel sensed but could not see the sudden burst of activity around her. Her efforts were concentrated on the gun in Richard's hand. She clawed at his arm, her only thought to give Davis enough time to react.

"Don't move! Don't move!" It was Duncan. His voice shrill with fear, he yelled, "I'll kill you if you move, Davis!"

Rachel looked up from beneath Richard's elbow at Davis. Frozen in place, his hands inches from his own gun on the floor, he looked down the barrel of Duncan's derringer. She dared not breathe for fear that Audra's brother, his hands shaking, would pull the trigger of the gun—if not on purpose, then by accident.

A.J. looked at her and snarled, "Stupid little bitch. You'll regret your foolish, love-addled loyalty, I assure you." Turning his anger on Richard, he snapped, "Get up, you bungling idiot, before the chit makes a fool of you again!"

Richard rolled to his knees, then stood. Before Rachel could move he grabbed a handful of hair and hauled her to her feet. The pressure on her scalp bringing tears to her eyes, she looked at Duncan and beseeched him, "Don't kill him. Please, don't kill him. I'll give you anything. Anything! I'll give you my money, if that's what you want. I'll sign it over to you now—"

"Shut up!"

Davis backed away slowly as Duncan came out from behind his desk. Torn between his need to help Rachel and the need to force Duncan's hand, he could only wait and watch and damn the same idiotic weakness that had allowed him to get into the mess in the first place. Grinding his teeth in frustration, he looked toward the door, the window.

"Waiting for help to arrive?" Duncan asked. Holding the

small gun with both hands, he laughed. "Others should be along momentarily, so you've no hope of escaping, much less surviving. But before I kill you both, I'm going to make you regret the day you ever thought to thwart me." He nodded toward Richard.

Richard moved with surprising agility, catching Davis unprepared. Driving into his jaw, Richard's fist lifted Davis from his feet and knocked him back against the wall. Before he could recover from the blinding white shock and pain, he was hit again. The air driven from his lungs in a single, savage thrust, he twisted and went down, doubling in two as he fought for a breath—anything that would enable him to think rationally for a moment. When, finally, that first breath of air filled his lungs, he choked like a drowning man before turning his head toward Rachel.

Duncan hauled her to her feet. "As I recall, this was to be our honeymoon, my dear. I was rather looking forward to it, as well. What do you think, Richard? I see no reason why I shouldn't enjoy what should have rightly been mine had Davis not intruded."

Richard's lips pulled back in a smirk. "I agree, boss."

Spitting blood through his teeth, Davis fixed Duncan with a stare and growled, "You bastard, I'll kill you if you—"

"You will?" Throwing his head back, Duncan laughed. Looking then into Rachel's defiant, hating eyes, he shook his head. "I can understand now why Pete got into trouble. You have a very jealous boyfriend, my dear. Come now, surely you have enough of those lovely, alluring charms to go around."

"I'd rather fornicate with a tarantula!" she responded, fighting against his grip on her arm. She spat in his face.

He thrust his hand into her hair and yanked her head back so hard that suddenly she stumbled against him. He then rent her robe from her shoulders and tossed it at Davis's feet. With one swift sweep of his arm, he sent the objects on his desk shattering to the floor.

"Now." He smiled at her, closed his hand over her white breast, ran it leisurely, tauntingly, down the indentation of her waist and around to her buttocks. "I'm not certain I have ever seen anything so lovely. I'm going to enjoy you, my dear Rachel. Immensely."

Richard laughed, his eyes straying too long toward Rachel.

Davis sprang, the sight of Duncan's hands on Rachel's naked skin driving him beyond care. He hit Richard broadside, made a grab for the gun, and twisted it toward the ceiling. He drove him backward, Richard's body shielding him as A.J. drew the derringer again from his coat and attempted to aim at Davis. And all the while Richard struggled, planted his feet finally, and drove his elbow into Davis's shoulder.

Like white lightning the pain tore through his chest, his brain. He was suddenly falling, going down and down, reliving that first instant Clyde's bullet had buried itself in his shoulder. But he fought it, knowing if he failed now . . . "Rachel, run!" He hit the floor.

She reacted with blind desperation. Lifting her hands, she sank her nails into Duncan's face until, with a howl of pain, he stumbled away, burying his face in the crook of his elbow, smearing blood into his eyes. She turned for Davis then, saw him sprawl onto the floor while Delaney staggered for his footing, then lifted his gun to fire.

The seconds clicked by, an eternity that flashed before her as Davis raised his blue eyes to hers. She ran, mindless, and his hand came up and his mouth yelled, "No! Don't, love, no!"

She threw herself atop him, shielding him from Delaney's gun with her own body as the world suddenly exploded around them. She felt his hands in her hair, heard Davis's cry of "God, oh God!" as he rolled her to the floor beneath him.

Silence filled the room. Davis lay against Rachel, pressing her small body to the floor. His face buried in her hair, he struggled with the overwhelming fear of what he would find if he opened his eyes. He listened to the quiet, wondering why Delaney didn't finish him off, praying that he would. If Rachel was dead . . .

She moved beneath him. But only slightly. Cautiously he lifted his head, blinked, and stared down into her pale face.

Her eyes were closed, her head resting against a cloud of white, curling hair. Her eyelids were slightly blue, her mouth nearly colorless. Slowly, very slowly, she opened her eyes and smiled.

He smiled back.

Looking back over his shoulder, he noted Duncan slumped against the desk, his eyes staring lifelessly toward the floor. Delaney lay dead on his back, his gun still gripped in his hand. Then Davis looked toward the door.

Alejandro de Bastitas stepped further into the room, a gun in his hand. Their blue gazes touched.

Swallowing, Davis grinned and asked, "What the hell took you so long, Pa?"

Chapter 19

John Hopper, having propped the body of Albert Durham, alias A.J. Duncan, up on a board outside the house, ducked beneath the black velvet cape of his camera to snap a picture. "Mr. Pinkerton will be so pleased," came his muffled voice. "And I'll be so damn glad to get back to New York." Digging out from beneath the drape, he looked at Davis and added, "We'll talk in a moment. You won't go far?"

"Don't count on it, Hopper." Grinning, he turned and walked into the house.

Sam stood in the foyer, his hat in one hand, a cigar in the other. Alex stood beside him. Lifting one brow, the old Ranger scratched his chin, looked from Alex to Davis, and said, "Welp, guess I'd best go round up my men. I promised 'em a bottle of whiskey each if we pulled this off without yore buyin' a bullet, boy." Slapping his hat on his head, he sauntered out the front door.

Alex stood on one side of the foyer.

Davis stood on the other.

"So," Alejandro said.

Davis shoved his hands in his pockets.

Crossing his arms over his chest, his father asked, "Why didn't you come home?"

"I thought you were dead."

"And?"

Davis looked toward the stairs. "Where is Rachel?"

"Upstairs, resting. I searched for you for years. Your mother is frantic to see you."

"She knows already?"

Alex nodded. "When Sam came back to the ranch for Hopper, he admitted he believed you were our son. He told us about your reaction when you first heard our name mentioned. That's all I needed to hear. After our meeting that morning before you left the ranch, I felt in my heart that you were Tomas." Smiling, he added, "A parent knows these things."

Hopper reentered the house then, all business, his gray suit impeccable despite the heat and the miles he'd traveled to reach Las Moras Ranch. "There you are Da— Ah . . . *what* do I call you now?"

"Bastitas," Alex responded. "Of course."

Hopper waited.

"I—I don't know," Davis finally said. It was an admission of confusion that vibrated in the air around them.

His father's eyes turned hot. "What the devil does that mean? You are a Bastitas. You were born a Bastitas and—"

"But I wasn't raised as one."

"What has that got to do with anything! You were born Tomas de Bastitas, and by God you will die a Bastitas. You are my flesh and blood and I resent the hell out of your denying it for no better reason than that you're a coward!"

Hopper cleared his throat. "Ah, Davis, I suppose you'll be wanting this?"

Davis stared at his father.

Hopper lifted the paper. "Mr. Pinkerton thought—" He stepped away as Davis looked around and focused on his face. "Mr. Pinkerton thanks you for your cooperation throughout these last years. And recognizing that you have fulfilled your obligations satisfactorily, he hereby releases you of any further obligations to his agency." He opened the papers. "As you can see, a letter signed by Mr. Pinkerton himself."

Davis stared at the paper, feeling his skin go hot.

"Well?" Hopper smiled. "Are you pleased?"

He took the papers. His hands were shaking. He stared again, his eyes roaming over the page, feeling sweat begin to gather in every crease of his skin and clothes.

"Well?" Hopper prompted.

Closing his eyes, he said, "I cannot read, Mr. Hopper."

"Oh, well, then allow me." Hopper took the papers again while Davis continued staring at the floor, feeling his stomach ball up like a fist.

With a flourish, John Hopper began:

Mr. Davis:

I, Allan Pinkerton, do hereby release you of all obligations due to this agency. You have fulfilled them beyond my expectations. Your dedication to the cause of law and order has been exemplary throughout these last eight years, your efforts at times extending above and beyond the call of duty. I commend you, sir, on your endeavors to walk the straight and narrow. You have come far from the hostile young outlaw I apprehended attempting to rob the Chicago Bank. You have strengthened my belief that men can turn around, if offered the opportunity and the incentive. Good luck, Mr. Davis, in all future endeavors.

Gratefully, Allan Pinkerton.

"Well, Davis, what do you have to say?"

He couldn't *say* anything, it seemed. He felt, suddenly, as if a weight had tumbled off his shoulders and he was free at last.

"I don't understand," came his father's voice.

Raising his blue eyes to Alex's, he shrugged. "It's simple. Eight years ago I attempted to rob the Chicago Bank. It was my first job and I bungled it. I was arrested by Allan Pinkerton. I don't know what he saw in me, but he saw enough to believe I could turn around. He gave me two choices. I could go to prison or come to work for him. He assured me if I decided to cross over again or attempted to filch on the deal, he would find me and bury me."

Two men carried Delaney's body out the front door. Then Hopper excused himself, leaving Davis and Alejandro alone.

"Seems to me you made the right choice," Alex said.

"Did I?" He laughed. "Sometimes that wasn't so clear. I was forced to face down a lot of men."

Alex ventured closer. "That's all over now. He's released you of further obligations; you can come home—"

"Don't!" He stepped away. "I have been forced my entire life into a life that was not of my own choosing."

"What is there to choose? We are your family and have been through hell—"

"Do you think *I* haven't! I've seen things that would turn your stomach. I've done things with these hands that would make you want to think twice about acknowledging me as your own flesh and blood."

"It doesn't matter."

"It matters to me!" He beat his chest. "What do you need me for, anyway? You've raised your Harvard lawyers—"

"They aren't you."

He barked a laugh at the ceiling. "Thank God for small favors. What makes *me* so special?"

Alex moved up against him, and took his face in his hands. "If you haven't looked in the mirror, then let me tell you, you stubborn son-of-a-bitch. You're a Bastitas—the image of me and my brother and my father and his father before him. A Bastitas! And if that doesn't mean anything to you, then let me tell you. We came to this land and fought and died to keep it. The Bastitas name means something around here, or has, and there are pitifully few of my offspring who seem to want to remember that." Alex gritted his teeth. "I—I need you. Your mother needs you. She has suffered over your loss. Forget your damnable pride long enough to think of her . . . and Rachel."

Rachel. The very sound of her name sapped his strength, drained the very fight from him. He knew in that moment that it would be his love for Rachel that would defeat him, as it had nearly killed him during the last trying weeks.

Turning away, he tried to think. "I have to see her. I have to explain. God, how will I ever make her understand?"

"If you do not know how to handle a woman by now, you are no son of mine," came his father's amused response.

Taking a breath, Davis headed for the stairs.

Rachel stood dumbly in the door, watching Audra's shoulders shake with grief. "I—I'm terribly sorry for you," she said. "If I can help in any way—"

Lifting her face from her hands, Audra screamed, "Get out! Just get out! I never want to see you again as long as I live!"

Running from the room into the hallway, Rachel clasped her hands together to stop their shaking.

"Rachel."

She spun.

Davis stood in the shadows, taking up the corridor with his shoulders, causing the world suddenly to spin underfoot. She tottered.

Beside her in an instant, he grabbed her shoulders. "Steady, love."

Shaking her head, she shoved him away. "Don't 'steady, love' me, Bastitas." She hurried toward her room, her panic rising as she realized he was in hot pursuit. "Don't bother to explain!" she said over her shoulder. "Even if you *were* telling the truth, even if you told the truth for the rest of your life without one tiny white lie, I wouldn't believe you. If you told me it was dark outside and I knew it was midnight, I wouldn't believe you."

"I'd like to explain."

"Oh, don't bother. Sam has explained it all. I'm not talking to him either!"

She tried slamming the door in his face. He caught it and kicked it back open with his foot.

"Rachel. I'm sorry. Forgive me."

She froze. He watched her shoulders go stiff, her hands clench. She rounded on him, spitting mad.

"How dare you?! You goat! You snake! You—you—"

"Moron?"

"Don't you dare make light of me, Tomas de Bastitas or Kid Davis or whatever your name is! How many more lies did you tell me? No, don't bother to tell me because *that* would be a lie as well."

"Are you finished?"

She pierced him with a malevolent look. "*We* are finished, Señor de Bastitas."

She regretted the words the moment she said them. She regretted even thinking them, because she didn't mean them, and the last thing she wanted was for him to walk out the door and out of her life. Her heart stopped as, lifting one dark brow, he turned back toward the door. "Stop!"

The fight left her, the anger. Only the fear remained, the awful realization of how close she'd come to losing him again. She began to shake.

Turning away from the door, he looked down into her face, recognizing the turmoil, the confusion, the fear and . . . the love. How he regretted having been the cause of it. He caught the door with the tips of his fingers and slowly closed it.

"What are we going to do?" she asked him.

"We're going to talk about it."

His voice was quiet and deep. Rachel backed away, the sight of his hair and eyes and the mustache over his lip serving to further distress her. She simply couldn't think when he was so damnably near and handsome. Her eyelids slid closed and trembled.

He caught her hands, tugged her over to the bed where he finally sat, and pulled her up between his thighs. Looking her square in the eyes, he said, "My name is Tomas de Bastitas. I was taken by the Comanches twenty-five years ago. For the next ten years I lived as a Comanche. I stole everything I could get my hands on, participated in raids. During one such raid I was wounded badly. A knife in the back. I was left for dead. That's when Barney Davis found me. He took me back to Fort Bliss, where I spent the next year recuperating and becoming civilized again. When he was killed three years later, I left the fort and traveled, living on my instincts and my talent with a gun. I ended up in Chicago."

She touched his lips, silencing his painful oration. Sliding her hands onto his face, she smiled into his eyes and said, "Kiss me."

She leaned against him, waited a heartbeat before his head tipped, his eyelids closed.

He brushed her mouth, feather-light, with his. Once. Twice. Then hungry for more, he came back again, opening warmly over her mouth until hers parted. He delved into its warmth and wetness with his seeking, pleasuring tongue, making her moan and grow weak with desire. Slowly, slowly he lay back on the bed.

He rolled her into the middle of the feather mattress, nuzzling her neck with his face, burning her skin as he scattered moist, breathy kisses from her chin to her shoulder. Finally. Finally he was hers. No more secrets or lies or guilt. They were free to love and profess their love to the world.

Her fingers twisted into his black hair as he opened her gown and nestled his face between her breasts. He shifted again and she felt his hand on her breast. His thumb gently brushed her nipple until it strutted in wanton arousal. Then he took it in his mouth.

She made a low sound in her throat as his hands, warm and hard, slid over her. Nothing mattered now. Not their pasts. Not who or what they were. They were one and as one they could, they *would*, face whatever obstacles awaited them. She wanted to tell him that, but his mouth was too warm and his hands too deliciously sensual in their exploration of her body. The hot flick of his tongue as he moved his mouth over the sensitive skin of her breasts and stomach made speech impossible.

When he rolled away, she opened her eyes, searched his dark face and blue eyes, confused as he left the bed. But as his hands came up to slowly unbutton his shirt, she smiled.

"Do you realize this will be the first time we've ever made love with all our clothes off?" he asked, grinning.

"Will it?" she managed, moistening her lips as the shirt fell to the floor.

His long, dark fingers moved expertly down the buttons on his breeches. "You're gonna like it, lady."

Sitting up, she allowed the dressing gown to slide off her shoulders. She threw it to the floor with his breeches and boots and shirt. Lying back on the bed and opening her arms, she said, "This is the way it will be forever, won't it? When we're old and in love and raising our children in San Antonio . . ."

His eyes met hers, then looked away.

Closing her arms around his shoulders, Rachel clutched him against her. "Won't it?" she repeated, staring at the ceiling.

His hands moved over her, not so gently now. His skin became hot against hers, his breath more rapid. She opened her legs willingly, closing her eyes and letting her body begin the slow climb to its sweet gratification of love long denied, no longer forbidden.

He moved over her, fitting his body against hers. Her heart set up a wild race with her blood as she arched up against him in invitation, in need, in desperate desire and fear.

Her fingers clenched into the flexing muscles of his outstretched arms as he poised and thrust. His head fell back, his eyes closed.

He sank into her again and again, and she met each hard thrust with her own, as if the violent union of their bodies would relieve the ache of heartbreak inside her, as if giving her all in this desperate act of love would somehow change his mind, would make him realize the folly of this decision he was bound to make. He drove into her with shuddering impact, throbbed, stretched, pounded, his hips grinding, wrenching from her soul the magic that was his and always would be his alone.

She opened her eyes and watched him, filled her mind and senses with his presence. Her god. Her mountain cat, sleek and dark and wild. A power above her gleaming with lantern light and perspiration. But he'd nonetheless learned to temper that awful, mesmerizing strength so as not to hurt her. And yet he would hurt her. She knew it now. No bruises to show it, but inside, where love's fire burned as intensely as ever, where heartache never healed.

Too quickly the surcease found them. Too quickly it winged in on the glorious explosion of breathtaking, soul-shattering bliss and engulfed them. The end. "No." She wept. "Oh no."

He collapsed against her, his body wet and slippery and heavy, pressing her into the mattress with his weight. She clung to him, twisted her white fingers into his black, black hair, and cradled his head on her shoulder. Tears ran down her temples as she said, "I nearly lost you again today. I—I don't think I can bear that—the fear of never knowing each time we make love if it will be the last time. And the threat will always be there as long as you wear that gun. As long as you go out and damn and defy the world for treating you so unjustly."

She tried to swallow. "I am going back to San Antonio with your father." She felt his heart pounding against her stomach. "You will have to decide what is more important to you. Me or the opinions of small-minded strangers who would have done the same as you given the same circumstances. Me or your ideas of what is really important in a man."

Closing her eyes, she waited. He didn't move.

Finally, he said, "I love you. God, I love you."

But all she heard was goodbye.

The still silence awoke her. Dawn's light poured through the window, across the burned-out wick of the lantern on the table below the window. She didn't need to look to know he was gone.

Grabbing up her wrapper, she slipped it on and left the room, walking, then running down the corridor to the stairs and descending. Alejandro de Bastitas stood at the door, clutching the doorframe with his hands as he looked out over the countryside.

"He's gone," she said.

Alex turned. His face haggard, his shoulders slumped, he responded, "I don't know what I'm going to tell his mother."

He opened his arms then, and she ran into them.

Epilogue

San Antonio, Texas
October, 1866

She sat atop the hill, as she did every day at noon, and looked down the valley toward the river in the distance. It snaked from the northwest like a great silver ribbon reflecting the blue sky overhead. Sighing, she turned her face to the sun, letting it drench her in light and warmth, hoping it would seep into her heart and force away the dull pain, but suspecting it wouldn't. It never did.

The wind came, barreling up the incline, pressing the last of summer's grass low against the earth. A light touch of autumn briskness had dabbed color on the trees lining the river. Red and orange leaves glittered for a moment like tongues of fire against the sky. The sight made Rachel grow dizzy for a moment. That was happening frequently of late.

Touching her stomach lightly with her fingertips, she closed her eyes, letting the moment pass.

Hearing the low nicker of the horse behind her, she turned, very slowly. Somehow she knew he would be there. She'd imagined it, fantasized it a thousand times during the last month. But always the image had vanished like a mist, leaving only the hole in her soul that yawned more widely every day that came and went with still no word from Davis. She blinked, expecting this visage to disappear as well.

It didn't.

"Hello," he said.

She tried to respond, but couldn't. She couldn't blink, and

she couldn't move. She didn't want to think because she might find that she was imagining it all again, after all. And it was just too wonderful to be an illusion.

He pulled at the starched collar of his stiff white shirt as the wind blew his hair into his eyes. The hair was still a little too long, but she supposed she could live with that. He could wear it to his knees, she decided, and she could live with that, too . . . if he were only real.

He was without his gun. His hips looked so much more slender without it. His breeches were clean and his boots were new and highly polished. He had a slender black tie knotted at his throat. The ends of it danced against his shirt in the breeze.

"I missed you," he said.

Her hands came up, twisted together at her breast, and she thought, *God, oh God, it's really him.*

She smiled. "You look so different."

"You don't like it?"

"Oh yes. I like it very much. But . . ."

"But?" He tugged again at his collar.

Cautiously she approached him until he stood tall above her, this blue-eyed proper stranger with courtship on his mind. Tears stung her eyes as she said, "But it's not you." Lifting her trembling fingers, she pulled the tie from around his neck, letting it fly in the wind so it caught on the branch of a nearby ceniza bush.

"You've seen your mother?" she asked. She flipped open the collar of his shirt.

He took a breath, and nodded.

"I suppose it was all very emotional . . ."

He looked away, toward the river behind her. "I missed you," he said again. And this time when his eyes came back to hers they were shining blue fire that burned her with love and desire and all the words he longed to say but couldn't. Yet. But he was trying, she realized, as he touched her face with his fingers and said:

"I had a choice to make and I made it. I tried—God knows I tried—but I couldn't continue without you." Suddenly he pulled her to him, his face tight with emotion as he lowered his dark head over hers. "Oh, Jesus," he said softly. "I do love you. I want you. I want to spend the rest of my life with you, and if it is to be here, then so be it. If you wanted to live in the very pit of hell, I'd live there, too." Closing his fingers into her arms, he shook her. "But I won't ever live without you again, lady. Those were four of the worst weeks I've ever spent in my life. I cannot promise you I'll be the best husband, that I won't ever reach for a gun again or that I'll be the perfect gentleman. I've shut off my emotions too long. So don't expect me to change overnight. But don't leave me. Don't ever leave me."

She touched his face, her hand like sunlight on shadow. Her heart brimming with the same love that was reflected in his eyes, Rachel smiled, knowing that he spoke the truth, knowing it would not be an easy path for either of them. There would be hardship and challenge, but they would face them together, as they had in the past.

Laughing in happiness, she turned and ran down the path toward the ranch. "Are you coming?" she called, lifting her hand with beckoning promise to the man who stood solitary against the azure sky: her life, her love, her happiness.

Tomorrow, she thought, as he began that slow, graceful walk toward her. *Tomorrow I will tell him my secret.*

KATHERINE SUTCLIFFE

A native Texan, KATHERINE SUTCLIFFE decided at the tender age of twelve that she wanted: 1) to write novels, and, 2) to marry an Englishman. From a very early age, she developed the love of reading. She began writing her first book—a romance—at age thirteen. (Never having read one, it was anything but formula!) Five years and four thousand handwritten pages later, she closed the cover on it and went on to other things, though the desire to write never left her. After high school, she attended business college, then moved to Dallas to work as a secretary. In 1977, she was reading Kathleen E. Woodiwiss's *Shanna*, when in through the lobby door walked a tall, dark, and handsome Englishman. She closed the cover on the book and went on to "other" things. They now have three children and a basset hound and live in Plano, Texas.